Beautiful
noise

For
my Mother and my Father
Thank You

For my Mum: an artist, who read to me when I was little,
guided my attention to nature, taught me how to draw an apple,
scrape a carrot, gave me the world
and has never stopped helping me find my way in it

And my Dad: a deep thinker, who liked to write.
'Apply yourself' he used to say. 'You need to learn
how to apply yourself.'
And that, I have discovered, is what writers do

I am grateful, very grateful, for my parents

Beautiful
noise

HELEN SEYMOUR

PENCIL

First published in 2013
By Pencil Publishing Ltd.
20 Woodside, Windgate Road, Howth, Co. Dublin.
www.pencilpublishing.ie

Typeset by Ashfield Press
30 Linden Grove, Blackrock, Co. Dublin

Cover Design: Tim Mudie
www.timmudie.com

Cover photograph of Julie Madden outside Freebird Records, Grafton Street, Dublin
by Matt Kavanagh courtesy of the Irish Times.
First appeared on Page 1 of the Irish Times Saturday 17th September 1983.

Printed by ScandBook AB, Falun Sweden 2013

ISBN
978-0-9573590-1-7

ACKNOWLEDGEMENTS

'... Interrupting all programmes ... This is Radio Clash from pirate satellite, orbiting your living room, cashing in the bill of rights, Cuban army surplus or refusing all third lights, this is Radio Clash on pirate satellite ...'

The Clash
This is Radio Clash 1981

Pirate Radio stations are still bursting out like acne all over the adolescent airwaves

Irish Times, 19 April 1983

1982 was a bad year for Elliott, and two years later he still blamed the same four people. His mother, his father, his brother Max and Steven Spielberg. Though not necessarily in that order.

In fact the first hint that he should pull the duvet over his head and try to sleep the year out came when Spielberg released E.T, and he had to endure cretins in school, furry parka hoods zipped up or pulled down over their faces, helium styled alien voices emerging from the blackness within

'Elle-eee-yott .... Elle-eee-yott' curved index fingers reaching forward to touch his face, no matter how many times he'd slap them away. It went on for weeks. Ten of the fourth years lined up outside the maths block one day, dressed in zipped up parkas; a row of faceless furry hoods pushed up against the windows with index fingers stuck to the glass.

'What are they *doing*?' Professor Cunningham said, confused as the rest of the class muffled snorts and chokes. Elliott never watched the film. He didn't need to. His parents were about to re-enact the basic plot, but Spielberg's family would look like The Waltons by the time Anthony and Margaret were finished with each other. And Max? Well, Max did a runner, didn't he? Left, because freshly qualified with an apartment in town, he could. Left Elliott in that empty house with Anthony. Yes, he blamed Max, he blamed his father, he blamed Spielberg, but most of all he blamed his mother. Not for leaving, that he understood, but for not taking him with her.

That was two years ago, however, and tonight he was too cold to think about anything. Where was the bus? He was freezing. He'd been standing at the stop outside his house for twenty minutes, clapping hands, stamping feet, futile attempts to keep warm. Icy breath in the black night air. Cold bones. Numb feet. He looked up at the night sky, silver stars, twinkling diamonds studding a clear black sky, Dublin Bay lights like fireflies flickering in the distance. It was definitely going to snow tomorrow.

'Right, I think we're done' Squirrel walked into the main office, his 6ft 4in boney frame poured into tight black biker leathers; the daily uniform for this twenty-three-year old owner slash operator of Dublin's fastest growing courier empire.

'Fraid not' Sharon had been manning the phones all day 'last one' she waved a yellow docket 'just came in.'

'Who is it?'

'Barrington.'

'Fuck' Squirrel scowled, walking across to her. 'Not Howth?' a leather arm stretching out.

'Sorry' Sharon handed him the docket. 'Pick up at his office and drop to Howth.'

'Jaysus' Squirrel ran a hand though spiky streaked blonde hair, blue eyes rolling to heaven.

'He's our biggest customer Squirr; ya can't …'

'I know' Squirrel took the docket. 'Freezin' out there' he looked at the blackness beyond the small office window. 'Drivin' ta Howth is the last thing I need' grabbing his helmet, he zipped up his jacket and pulled on thickly padded black gloves.

'Fitzwilliam Square' said Sharon 'and then straight to Howth. He won't be there but his son …'

'Yeah, yeah, his son or the housekeeper'll take it in. Gotcha'

Squirrel pushed the door open. 'You go home. I'll see ya tomorrow.'

'Be careful' Sharon called after him. 'They're givin' warnins about black ice on the radio.'

'This was going to be a waste of time' Iris thought getting on the 31B at Clontarf. They never hired girls; it was always blokes, but anything was worth a try at this stage. And Howth was on the bus-line if she got the job. But this was a disco, a fucking disco.

'Don't worry' the manager had said on the phone. 'We have the music; we just need you to play it.' Great. She'd be playing music she didn't like to a crowd she'd probably hate. Why were there no punk clubs in Dublin? Why didn't Dublin have a Roxy, like London? Fuck it. She needed to build her profile. She'd called into all the stations but no-one was hiring.

'Punk's over' the last station had said to her. 'Pop's back where it belongs.' 'This is the Eighties' said another. 'People don't want that kind of music anymore.'

The bus was late. Elliott was thinking about turning back when he heard it in the distance; the sound of an old double decker engine straining and groaning as it pulled itself up and around Howth's steep hill. He heard it getting closer, then closer again until finally it rounded the corner, white headlights, florescent lights blinding him as brakes ground and hissed to a stop. Diesel fumes, a thick layer of dirt, muck and grime, the 31B sign barely visible above the driver's window. He paid his fare, went upstairs, and there she was. On her own. The girl with the Mohican. Head down, spikes up, examining something he couldn't see. He sat on the opposite side, a few seats up. Good choice. He could see her reflection in the windows. She looked up and stared ahead. Bold. Detached. Beautiful. His cheeks burned. *Don't look. Why? She can't see you. She might. She won't. She never does.*

Squirrel cut along the coast road, heading for Howth. Traffic had been light enough. Roads were slippy, but he'd made good time.

He suddenly remembered the match. Gunners and the Magpies at seven o'clock. If he got this dropped in the next ten minutes he could be in the Donaghmede Inn on time to watch it with a few of the lads. He picked up a gear and the bike sliced along the last stretch of the Howth Road, Dublin Bay shimmering to his right under the spotlight of a ripe harvest moon. The traffic lights at Sutton Cross were green, he dropped a gear, cleared them, picked up again and sped on towards Howth. At this rate he might even have time to stop for fish & chips. Deadly.

'They're wrong about the music' Iris thought, pulling her jacket tight around her. She didn't want to work with any of those happy clappy fuckers anyway, with their phoney nails on a blackboard make my ears bleed American accents, pathetic handles and their yak-yak-yak; just shut up and play the music, shut up and play the fucking music, even if what you're playing is as pathetic as you are, at least it's better than listening to you.

God it was cold. She pulled her sleeves down over her hands, cupped them and blew warm breath through. The bus stopped. She curled her knuckles and examined her nails. Footsteps. She looked up. The back of a head and two ears coming up the stairs. Bright red ears. He turned around. That guy. Where had she seen him before? He looked familiar. Well dressed, sallow skin, inky black eyes. French, maybe. Jewish perhaps. He was bundled up in a long winter coat and a multi-coloured thick woollen scarf. He glanced at her briefly, then sat down a few seats up on the other side.

The bike skidded as Squirrel drove past Howth Harbour. Shyte. Black ice. Lethal. Good thing he was goin' up the hill. What goes up must come down. Yeah, well, it could come down nice an' steady around the back of the hill, not the steep incline he was facing into now. He slowed and took the right hand turn that brought him up into the heart of the village.

Ask her for a light. I can't. You can. Just stand up, turn around and ask her for a light. You're getting off in two stops. Just ask her for a light. I can't. You can. Just do it. Elliott stood up. *Shit. I can't.* He sat back down again.

The guy was getting off. No, he'd sat back down again. Iris checked her watch. Plenty of time. She felt the bus lean forward as it began the steep descent down into the village.

Squirrel dropped a gear and accelerated hard as he began climbing the hill to the left of the church. In the distance, up at the top, on the opposite side of the road he saw the bus rounding the corner.

You're useless. Elliott stood up as the bus rounded the corner. *Pathetic. Why didn't you just ask her for a light? What's wrong with you?* eyes down, he reached for the pole, rang the bell and began his descent.

Everything happened very quickly and very slowly at the same time. The bus hit black ice and shot forward. The driver turned the wheel in panic and the bus nose dived into a cart-wheel, bouncing and tumbling over once, twice, three times, glass shattering, the metal frame buckling, crunching, barely holding. Elliott shot forward, the stairs beneath him as he smashed his face against a Cross Your Heart By Playtex poster. As the bus tumbled he was spun around the stairwell like a cartoon cat in a spin dryer. He looked up to see the girl flying overhead, catching a brief look at the startled expression on her face.

Squirrel didn't see it coming. It happened so fast. One minute the bus was way back up the road at the top of the hill, the next it was coming right at him. Frozen, he watched it cart-wheel towards him, a fluorescent hurdy gurdy ripped free from the fun-fair. A screaming shattering, metal on glass mass, exploding his way. Then just as quickly as it had tumbled the bus landed on its side, skidded down the last stretch, swung around, and whacked the bike. Hard. Like an ice hockey stick to its puck, it neatly flicked Squirrel and the bike over the wall of the church, catapulting him straight into the Last Supper stained glass window, smashing him head first through Peter and Luke. Suspended mid air, he rocked for a second or two, a headless leatherman gate-crashing the party. Then gravity sucked and he slid down the wall of the church, crumpling quietly on the grass below.

. . . .

Pandemonium in the O'Rourke household. Eric and Orla playing Twister with three of the kids from across the road, the dog barking furiously as they screamed and laughed, arms and legs tangling on the mat. Darren, trying to watch the news on TV, the volume up high so he could hear over the Twister noise. Belinda and Katie having a full scale argument upstairs on what she could and couldn't wear to John McGrath's debs next week, Katie's ghetto-blaster loud in the background, her hairdryer on as she dried her hair and fought with her Mother. The baby sat in the high chair covered in stew. A grubby happy smile as he watched the chaos. None of them heard the phone the first time, and it rang out. It rang out a second time. Upstairs, fight was getting louder. Darren turned up the TV. Up went the ghetto-blaster. Belinda's voice drowned by music and the hairdryer. Katie arguing.

'Jaysus!!' Darren thundered 'keep it down! Let her wear what she wants. I'm tryin' ta watch the news!!' he turned the TV up again. Suddenly there was an almighty bang, and the house was plunged into darkness. TV, ghetto-blaster, hairdryer; everything went off. The Twister tournament silenced. Only the sound of the phone ringing through the blackness. 'Now yis have really gone an' done it' Darren groping his way down the hall. 'Blowin' every fuse in the house, never mind me own. Hello!' he picked up the phone. 'Yes it is. I do. Oh sweet Jesus! Okay … okay … thank you, thank you. We'll be right in. Belinda! Belinda!!'

. . . .

'You're listening to Beaumont Hospital Radio, Dave K with you all the way through the night. Playing this for the nurses

on the late shift in St. Brigid's Ward as we mellow down for the night ahead. This is Toto - Africa ...'

Death lurks in hospitals. It hangs in the shiny clean corridors, where patients shuffle in dressing gowns and slippers; where families sit and wait for hours, where cleaners use chemicals to soften its scent. But Death pushes through, blending with the bleach, waiting patiently in line. Which is fair enough. Death, like the doctors, the nurses, has a job to do. Death is on call. Death does its rounds, checking up; taking notes, taking lives. But only when the time is right. And the Intensive Care Ward is where the time will often be right.

'Elliott?' A woman's face high above him. She looked a bit like his mother. 'Elliott' said the woman. 'Can you hear me?' There was a tube in his mouth. His throat hurt. He swallowed and realised the tube was in his throat. 'Can you hear me?' said the nurse. He nodded and closed his eyes.

'We're under attack' Iris heard her mother say. 'Mercury is in retrograde and Gemini and Aquarius are particularly vulnerable. I warned you something like this would happen Arthur, didn't I?' Iris could see her father sitting on the other side of the bed examining the drip bag, which was draining into her right arm. Her head hurt. 'I'm telling you' her mother, talking again from the other side of the bed. 'First my ankle, now this. We're going to have to be very careful for the next six months until Saturn has completely moved through.' Iris closed her eyes.

'Son? Can ya hear me? It's Mam' Belinda whispered as she stroked Squirrel's face. 'Wake up, please wake up.' She bit her lip to stop the tears. Darren, sitting on the opposite side of the bed, squeezed her hand and looked at his son's face on the pillow.

'C'mon Squirr' he said. 'Open those eyes and give yer Ma a smile.' Squirrel's eyes stayed closed.

'Hey' said a voice. Elliott opened his eyes. It was the girl from the bus. Floating in the darkness above him. 'Are you awake?' she said. Elliott looked at her.

Ask her for a light. Ask her ... what's wrong with me?

'You shouldn't be out of bed' a nurse appeared.

Shit, don't take her away. I want ... I need ... I need to tell her something.

Squirrel, free-floating in blackness. Watery echoes through a dark ocean. No sense of time or space, just him. Somewhere way above him in the distance a white light shone and he realised he was at the bottom. Blackness again. Where was the top? Near that light. But the light was gone. A nagging pain. Then black.

The telephone ringing beside Elliott's bed. He sat up slowly, eyes watering as he squinted at the sun streaming in through the windows which ran the length of the ward. His ribs felt sore, like someone had punched him hard. He looked down. His right arm was in plaster. The telephone ringing. He picked it up.

'Hello?' his head felt muzzy.

'Elliott?' the compressed sound of a long distance call. 'Sweetheart is that you?' a woman's voice. 'Elliott?' A warm, rich, familiar voice. 'It's Mum. I just heard about your accident. Max arrived for Christmas. Elliott? Can you hear me?'

Anger; dull and thick. A red rage, rising up. Elliott leant across placed the phone back on the receiver. A wave of shame as he rolled back into the pillows.

Why should I feel guilty? I'm not the one that fucked off to France. Why's she ringing, and fuck Max by the way; how can he sit in the same room with that prick Laurent ... smack! A grape hit him hard on the side of his face. Smack! Another one.

'Oi!' said a voice. Elliott blinked, squinting in the direction the grapes were being fired from. 'Get up' said the voice. 'Bored out of my mind here. Are you awake?' the voice, persistent, demanding. 'Well?' It was the girl. The girl from the bus. Sitting two beds up from him in a Sex Pistols T-shirt, sunshine bursting around her. Elliott stared across at her. 'Are you Irish?' she said. Elliott nodded. 'And what? Can you not speak?'

'No ... I ...' Elliott felt his cheeks redden. 'I ... I can speak.'

'Good' her eyes darted to the nurses' station. 'Do you smoke?'

eyes on the nurse, she had lowered her voice. Elliott stared at her. 'Do you?' she said, impatient now. Elliott nodded silently. 'Have you got any cigarettes?'

'Em' Elliott glanced at his bedside locker 'I don't think so.'

'Fuck' she looked disappointed. 'What's your name?' she picked up the remains of a bunch of grapes lying on her bed, head down, spikes up, hands moving quickly, pulling, plucking. 'I said' she grinned as she began firing more grapes in quick succession 'what's your name?'

'Elliott' he ducked and dodged the small green bullets. 'What's yours?' The last few grapes landed and rolled down into the bedcovers. She hadn't answered him. 'What's your name?' he said. Brown eyes smiled from across the bed.

'Iris' she said. 'My name's Iris.'

Iris. He'd thought she was about nineteen or twenty that first Saturday she'd got on the 31B and sat across from him. Tall, thin, she wore skin tight black bondage jeans, a Killing Joke T-shirt and a torn, bleached denim jacket. Carefully worked into each arm were rows of tiny silver safety pins, miniature train tracks travelling from the shoulders down to her hands, which were elegant, an assortment of different rings hanging loosely, safeguarded by big boney knuckles. A spiky black Mohican, cheekbones so high and sharp he'd swear she'd slashed the jacket with them.

'Fare please' the bus conductor sounded anything but.

'50p' she held up a fifty pence piece.

'Not for you love; 50p is for under sixteens.'

'I am under sixteen' an angry look flashed across her face.

'Yeah? An' I'm Donny Osmond' said the bus conductor. 'Seventy-five.'

'I'm not paying seventy-five!' angry flashing eyes. 'I'm sixteen!'

'Pay the fare or get off the bus.'

'Here's my money' she pushed the 50p into his hand.

'That's not enough' he pushed it back. 'Pay the fare or get off.'

'I'm sixteen!!' she shouted at him. 'Six! Teen!!'

'Off' the conductor snarled. 'Off now!!'

'Why don't you' the girl stood up, gathering equal measures of height and volume 'why don't you' she poked him '*fuck* off.' The driver, hearing the commotion, pulled in and opened the doors. She stepped out, and the driver, sensing a break, shut the doors and pulled away.

'Ya stupid tart!' the conductor shouted and she gave him the finger. A big mannish let's be-very-clear-about-what-you-can-do-with-yourself-because-nobody-else-would-be-remotely-interested finger.

'Disgrace' said an old lady as the bus drove off.

'Absolute disgrace' another echoed. 'Carryin' on like that.'

'The language' said a third.

Elliott saw her face all the way into town. Angry, confident, beautiful. He privately dedicated the first song on his show that night to her; Tin Soldiers by Stiff Little Fingers, his last memory of her an angry tin soldier giving the bus conductor a stiff finger as she marched away.

'Iris' he smiled. 'Nice to meet you Iris.'

'Nice to meet *you*' mischief dancing in her eyes. God she was fucking gorgeous.

'How's your leg?' Elliott nodded at her plaster cast.

'Broken' she stared down at it. 'Still' she glanced at the bed between them, 'could be worse. Could be him.' Elliott leant over to get a better look at the guy in the bed in the middle. Streaked blonde hair, freckles, a funny kind of protruding upper lip.

'I know him from somewhere' Elliott frowned.

'He looks nice' Iris studied the sleeping figure.

A sting of jealousy shot through Elliott, then he felt ashamed. How could he be jealous of someone in coma? A nurse came over.

'How are you feeling?' she said to Elliott.

'Sore' said Elliott. 'My ribs hurt.'

'Your lung collapsed' said the nurse. 'We had you on a ventilator for the first few days, but you're well on the mend now. Would you like a cup of tea?'

'I'd love a cup of tea ' said Elliott.

'And biscuits' said Iris.

'It's Intensive Care, not the Westbury' the nurse chastised 'and who asked you?' but she was smiling. 'Tell you what. I'll do you a deal. Chat to that fella' she nodded at Squirrel 'and I'll get you both some tea.'

'He's in a coma' said Iris.

'I know' said the nurse, 'but they hear things. Just chat away to yourselves, like you're already doing. His parents were in this morning and they'll be back later, but the more stimulus he gets the better, so even if you're just chatting to yourselves, it's still voices and sounds around him.'

'Okay' Iris grabbed the crutches beside her bed. 'Sounds like a fair deal.' She swung her leg around and eased herself onto the chair beside Squirrel's bed. She was wearing stripey pyjama bottoms, cut to let the plaster through. She pulled a chunky knit, well worn cardigan around the Sex Pistols T-shirt. There was a few days growth either side of the Mohican. Suddenly she didn't look so imposing, and the walls Elliott realised he had built around her dropped away. He smiled at her.

'Are you rich?' she said. Elliott shook his head.

'You look rich.'

'I'm not.'

'I don't believe you. Where do you live?' Elliott hesitated. 'You live in Howth' she said. 'I saw you get on the bus. You have to be rich to live in Howth' those brown eyes laughing again, teasing him. 'What does your Dad do? Bet your Dad's loaded.' Elliott smiled.

'My father's a barrister. Does that make me rich?'

'Filthy. Got a pool?'

'No' Elliott laughed.

'A Merc?'

'No.'

'A Jag?' she persisted. Elliott ducked his head, but he couldn't hide the grin.

'I knew it' she looked delighted. 'You've probably got two. What does your mother drive?' Something sharp stung at his face. The narrow pot-holed driveway that led to the summerhouse in France flashed before him. A rusty yellow car parked outside.

'A Citroen' he said. 'I think it's a Citroen.'

The nurse arrived and put the tea and biscuits on a table top which she wheeled around and angled at the base of Squirrel's bed.

'What's his name?' said Iris to the nurse.

'Squirrel' said the nurse.

'Squirrel?' said Iris. 'What sort of a name is Squirrel?'

Squirrel. He was born with his testicles stuck firmly up inside him, unusually large testicles which took a week to drop down.

'How's me little Squirrel?' Darren, his Da, would say to the tiny infant when he visited him each day in the hospital. 'Where are ya hidin' those nuts? Come on the little Squirrel, we know they're in there somewhere.' The doctors were concerned at first, and considering an operation, when Belinda, his Mam, woke up on the last day of her stay to find not only had they dropped but they appeared to be unusually large and strangely out of proportion with the rest of his body. 'Jays, would ya look at size ah them' Darren was fascinated. 'They're bigger than me own.'

'Don't worry' Belinda stroked the infant's face. 'They'll even out.' And she was right, they did, but only when he was six foot four and twenty years of age, and they still looked pretty big at that. Girls always said it ('Yev massif balls, ya know that? Big as fuckin' oranges.')

'Squirrel' Iris stared down at the sleeping figure. 'Right Squirrel' she pulled herself closer to the bed 'I hope you like Monopoly.'

'Squirrel' – watery echoes floating up through the dark, 'Squirrel' – womb like sounds as he drifted through black. 'Squirrel' - the roar of a wave crashing overhead. 'Squirrel' – a hand reaching down. 'Squirrel' – he was drifting off the sea bed, moving up through black. The sea swelled and sucked. Down again. Back to black.

'Grab the board' said Iris to Elliott. 'See it there, under the telly. We can set it up on his chest' she nodded at Squirrel. Sit either side' she instructed, pulling her chair closer to the bed. Elliott opened the Monopoly box and flattened the board across the sleeping Squirrel.

'What do you want?' he held out a palmful of silver figurines.

'The iron' Iris leant across the bed and rooted amongst the pile of figurines in his outstretched hand. Her fingers rubbed his palm. Firm, confident, iron–seeking fingers. He remembered the first time he saw her, the fight with the bus conductor.

'The iron' playful eyes from across the bed, a miniature silver figurine pinched between her thumb and index. 'Because I'm going to flatten you' she said. Then she shook the dice and rolled.

A rolling clatter from somewhere on high. Echoing clatters down through the ocean. TAP-TAP-TAP. The sea bed jilted. TAP-TAP-TAP. Up-Up-Up. Surging, swelling. In the distance, far away, Squirrel could hear someone laughing.

'Twelve' Iris laughed. 'Told you I was good' she tapped the iron twelve hard paces down to Marylebone Park, the Monopoly board bouncing on Squirrel's chest as she went. Elliott glanced at the sleeping head. 'Never mind him' said Iris. 'Roll!'

Elliott rolled. Six. Go directly to jail. Do not pass go. They played for the next hour until Iris had five hotels, a collection of houses and Elliott was broke in jail.

'I think I might have to admit defeat' he said. 'What else have they got?'

'Buckaroo, Kerplunk and Operation' said Iris. 'Let's do them all.' She pushed the Monopoly board up against Squirrel's chin, the money, houses, hotels, cards and figurines still on it. Elliott looked at it, balanced beneath the sleeping figure's nose. 'Why do you keep looking at him?' said Iris. 'He's hardly going to run off with all our money, is he?' she flipped open the Operation box. 'Come on' she threw the bag of plastic bones at him.

'BUZZ. FUCK!! BUZZ. BUZZ. FUCK!! BUZZ. SHIT!! BUZZ. BUZZ. FUCK!! BUZZ. BUZZ. FUCK!! BUZZ. STUPID FUCKING GAME!!'

A buzzing in the ocean, a persistent doorbell in the darkness. Someone shouting. The green lightened and the sea swelled forward again, pushing him up. Up. He was definitely starting to move up. Up where?

Elliott won. Iris had shaky hands.

'Nicotine withdrawal' she pulled her cardigan tight around her. 'I really need a cigarette' long nails scratching Mohican stubble.

'What do you smoke?' said Elliott.

'Major' brown eyes looking straight across at him.

'That's kinda hardcore' he wanted to lean across and kiss her.

'Why? What do you smoke?'

'Rothmans.'

'Rothmans are for girls. Here' she pushed the game to one side 'forget Buckaroo. My hands are too shaky. Tell you what; best of three; whoever wins Kerplunk wins the lot.'

Lighter now. Green gave way to yellow, soft at first, then it splayed around him. A bright golden buttercup. Yellow free-fall, tumbling and bumbling in a golden dew.

'What do you do?' said Elliott as they began poking red and yellow needles through the plastic Kerplunk tower.

'DJ' head down, spikes up Iris was busy pushing a series of needles through the thickening mesh. Elliott felt the skin on his arms tingle.

'You're a DJ?'

'Well' she frowned at the tower 'an out of work DJ. Come on you fucker' she stabbed a stubborn needle.

'You're a DJ?'

'Is there something wrong with your hearing?' her eyes flicked up.

'No' Elliott swallowed 'no, it's just … I DJ myself' he tipped the bag of marbles down the tower and they rattled as they hit the plastic and piled up inside.

Rattling. Machine gun rattling. Orange fireworks shooting through. Voices again. Some bloke called DJ. There was a hurler called DJ wasn't there? He didn't know any hurlers though. I'm not a hurler he thought. I'm … what am I?

'You?' she said, and he didn't like the way she said it. '*You're* a DJ?

'Well …' Elliott felt embarrassed 'only from home. I've a station at home; just me in my room, you know … nothing serious.'

'Yeah? What's it called?' sharp eyes from across the bed. Elliott hesitated. 'Go on' she pushed. 'What's it called?'

'Hill Sixteen' Elliott cursed himself for not coming up with a better name.

'Hill Sixteen?' she said. 'Hill Sixteen?'

Hill Sixteen. This DJ bloke was a hurler alright. He never went hurling. Football was his game. He liked football. He loved football. But he wasn't a footballer himself. He was … what was he? Orange sucked, morphed to purple and pushed him forward. Up again. Up through purple. The voices again.

'It's a stupid name' Elliott pulled a red needle from the bottom of the mesh to start the game.

'It is' there was an amused smile on her face. 'It's a very stupid name' she studied the needles. 'How long are you on-air?' she tested then extracted a yellow.

'About two years' Elliott pulled out a red.

'Was it hard to set up?'

'No' Elliott shook his head. 'Not at all; in fact, if you like' he could feel the colour seep into his cheeks 'if you like I could set one up for you. Might help build your profile; help you get a gig' he cleared his throat. Iris didn't reply. She studied the tower again for a minute or two.

'Maybe' she said. 'Yeah. Maybe.'

The hurler was going to help the girl. Help her set something up. Get her a gig. What kinda gig? Tinglin. Somethin' tinglin. Ahh! Fuck!! Mad tinglin. Everywhere. His whole body. Pins and needles. Aches and pains. Purple changing. Blue. The voices again.

'Your move' Iris nodded at the tower. Elliott slid out a red. Iris a yellow. Red followed yellow, plastic needles piling up on the bed between them as the game progressed. 'You getting any other work?' she stared at the tower.

'Not really' Elliott watched her test a yellow 'just the show at home, and I kind of have a job with RTE.'

'RTE?' her head shot up. 'How did you get a job in there?'

'Em …' Elliott didn't want to tell her his Mother had got it for him 'it's not a proper job' he struggled 'it's just work experience. I make teas, coffees, do research for shows; that kind of thing. I … I've never actually broadcast.'

'Do they know you're a Pirate?' she grinned.

'No' Elliott laughed. 'Shit no. And I won't be telling them either. Pirate's a dirty word in RTE.'

Pirates. Somethin' about RTE. The tinglin' again. Tinglin' everywhere. His arms, legs, face. Blue. Bright blue pushing through. Eyes. He could feel his eyelids. Heavy. He tried to lift them. Can't open me eyes. Open. Come on. Open. The voices again.

'How long are you in there?' Iris slid the yellow needle she'd been testing out of the Kerplunk tower. A rattling as marbles rolled and dropped.

'Two years' Elliott pulled a red and watched them shift again.

'That's good experience' Iris tested a yellow. 'You could get a gig on one of the Pirates with that kind of experience' the marbles lurched, then settled in vulnerable balance around the remaining needles. 'You could' she said, then when Elliott didn't reply 'why don't you try?'

'Dunno' Elliott lied. Silence. He could feel her looking at him. 'Hardly what you'd call a proper career' he mumbled.

'Says who?' her voice went cold and too late he remembered it was in fact her choice of career.

'I don't know' he muttered. 'My Father for one.'

'What's he got to do with it?'

'Nothing' Elliott wavered 'doesn't matter … look' he blurted 'I'm a Law Student. I'm studying Law.'

'So?'

'So … you know' Elliott struggled for the right words 'radio is great, but Law' he faltered 'well it's probably where I'm going to end up.'

'End up?' she stared at him. 'Why would you want to *end up* somewhere?' incredulous eyes from across the bed. 'Why would you want to end up *anywhere*? Fuck that' she was angry now. 'Fuck that' she turned back to the Kerplunk tower.

Yer woman was havin' a right old gush whoever she was. Fuck this, fuck that. Tinglin' again. Pins and needles attacking, raining down in angry stabs. Bright lights. White pushing through blue, then back to blue again. Blue, white, blue, white. What's wrong with me eyes? Why won't they open? Come on. Open ya bastards.

Elliott looked at the remaining needles in the Kerplunk tower. The mesh had thinned. A bit like the conversation.

'Sorry' she said.

'It's okay.'

'It's not. If you want to study Law that's your business.'

'I don't' he slid a red needle back and forth and watched a

marble roll with it. First time he'd admitted that. To himself never mind anyone else.

'Then why are you?' she frowned.

'No choice.'

'What do you mean you've no ...'

'Long story' he cut her off. He was tired. He couldn't do this conversation right now. 'I think I might win' he nodded at the tower, hoping to distract her.

'Do you now?' the competitiveness was back in her voice. She looked at the tower for a second or two then reached in and slowly pulled a yellow needle back.

RAT-TAT   two marbles dropped
RAT-TAT   the spiky head jerked

Did he move?' said Elliott.

'No' said Iris.

'Are you sure?' said Elliott. Iris glanced at the sleeping figure.

'Positive. And he'd better not by the way. Not when I'm about to win. Your move.' Elliott looked at the Kerplunk tower. Not many options left. He pulled a red needle out.

RAT-TAT   two marbles dropped
RAT-TAT   Mam! Mam!

'He moved' said Elliott. 'I'm telling you. He moved. I think we should call the nurse' he looked around.

'I think' said Iris 'you should stop trying to distract from the fact that you're about to lose.' She pulled out a yellow needle and handful of marbles clattered to the tray below:

RAT-A-TAT-TAT TAT-TAT-TAT-TAT-TAT-TAT ....
Mother ah ... MAM! MA!! Crashing, flashing, blinding lights. MA!! MA!! Hurt me leg. It's only a scrape, sure you're a big boy now. Drowning in the sea on the beach at Howth. Darren for God's sake grab him, he's goin' under. Salt water down his throat, up his nose, great big mouthfuls of salt. Blue sky. Green sea. Choking. Up for air, sucked

back under. Rushing bubbles, a sucking sea. Da's arms reaching down. Air again. Sea. 'Doesn't look good' said the hurler.

'Doesn't look good' said Elliott. He pulled a needle back slowly and watched the marbles lurch. He pushed it back.

'Come on' said Iris. 'Just pull the needle.'

RAT TAT-TAT TAT-TAT TAT-TAT
The marbles came crashing down

RAT TAT-TAT TAT-TAT TAT-TAT
Squirrel came surging up

shot through blue, speeding through white on white, a bright white light, as the ocean that had held him down now spewed him up, a pressure cooker released, a glorious geyser from Donaghmede rushing up, crashing through. A gasp, then two bright aquamarine eyes opened, blinked several times, and as the spiky blonde head came up, they squinted, trying to focus as they looked down at the pile of Monopoly money.

'I Win! I Win!!' Iris' shouting drowned out Squirrel's initial gasp, as Elliott sat there looking at her. 'I Win' she said. 'You owe me a pack of smokes.'

'We never bet' said Elliott softly.

'Doesn't matter. I'll settle for twenty Major.'

From the top of the bed, a low disorientated groan. 'I'll settle for knowin' what's goin' on.' Monopoly houses sliding, the bedclothes shifting, moving. Elliott and Iris jerked and stared. Spikey blond hair rising up. 'Who are ya?' bleary eyes, blue and struggling. Iris and Elliott stared in shock. 'One ah yous needs ta start talkin' Squirrel coughed, then cleared his throat. 'Where am I? Who are you? An' what the fuck is this?' he scowled at the Monopoly remains.

'You're in hospital' Elliott moved the board away.

'Shyte' Squirrel rubbed his eyes.' His head felt heavy.

'There was a bus accident' said Iris. The screaming cart wheeling double decker flashed before Squirrel, rolling, crunching, crashing. He blinked.

'How long am I here?'

'Thirty years' said Iris.

'Fuck off.'

'It's 2015.'

'Whaddaya mean twenty fifteen?'

'It's two thousand and fifteen.'

'Ya what?'

'You're Ireland's longest living coma person.'

'I'm what?'

'The Times did a piece on you last week.'

'They who … they … are you serious? Two thousand an' fifteen? I'm in the future? I'm in the fuckin future!!' Squirrel sat up straight, blue eyes wide awake. Iris bit her lip, cheekbones pressing forward as she curtailed a smile. 'Yer messin' Squirrel's face broke into a smile of relief. 'You're messin' he threw himself back against the pillows and laughed. 'Fuck's sakes; scarin' the shyte outta me.'

A high pitched scream from the door of the ward. A slim good looking woman with the same aquamarine eyes and a tumble of long black curls moaned then burst into tears as she clattered in high black heels towards the bed. Elliott stepped back as she threw herself on Squirrel, sobbing loudly.

'My son, my son, my little son' she planted kisses on his face, cheeks, eyes.

'Ah Ma' he laughed, clearly happy to see her. 'Relax will ya' he hugged her as she clung to him sobbing. 'Jays Ma, come on. Yer embarassin' me here.' He looked at the two of them over the shaking shoulders 'Mothers whah?' he laughed, his manner conciliatory. Iris gave him a small half smile, and from the other side of the bed Elliott bent down to pick up the Monopoly pieces that had fallen on the floor.

. . . .

'... You're tuned to Rocket Radio, Monday fifth of January, a brand new year an' I'll tell ya what, it's not off to a good start for RTE. Latest JNLR figures confirm they're bottom of the ratings, while yours truly, Rocket Radio are Number One. Michael St. John, with you all the way til ten, get out those skippin' ropes, it's Malcolm McLaren, the Double Dutch, go on ya good thing, Rocket Radio, Dublin's Number One Station ...'

'Christ' from behind his desk, Roger Ingram, RTE's Director of Radio Programming reached across and turned off the small transistor sitting on the filing cabinet beside him. Listenership down, advertising down, and the Minister down. On Roger. Like a ton of bricks. He bit off a small piece of skin from the corner of his middle finger. JNLR figures weren't his only problem. He glanced at the Lansdowne Market Research Report sitting on the desk. According to Lansdowne, a new breed of Pirate had emerged. The Super-Pirates. Sophisticated, with experienced UK radio people behind them, they'd taken large chunks of RTE's audience and from what this research suggested they practically owned the youth market. In the seventies the Pirates sounded like Pirates; amateurs working from their homes with weak signals, bad sound and patchy reach, but things had really turned around in the last five years. The Pirates had become smarter, sharper. They'd built powerful transmitters, the Jocks were personalities in their own right and the Government raids to shut them down were having no effect at all. Thankfully the Minister was at a radio conference in Japan, so at least he didn't have to deal with his reaction to the JNLRs for the moment.

Roger swivelled his chair around to face the window. Putting his feet up he lit a cigarette, and looked out at the TV and Radio aerial masts, standing strong in the front of the RTE grounds. Shaped like miniature Eiffel Towers they were symbolic of the Station's strength. There were aerials exactly like it all over the country bouncing signal to signal. The irony of the situation was that the Pirate's aerials were actually feeding off these signals. Harnessing RTE's horse power to work against them.

Feet still up, Roger flicked ash into the bin beside him and pulled hard on his cigarette again as he looked out at the aerials. He hadn't reckoned on radio being this difficult. Radio for Roger had always been a short term step in a long term strategy. Long term Roger intended to be the next Director General. Director General was the most senior executive post in RTE. Director Generals controlled television and radio and represented RTE at International events. Sheila, Roger's wife, was particularly excited about the International Events. But to be truly worthy of the position, a Director General needed to have spent several years in radio and television, proving their ability to helm both ships. Roger had been hoping for a relatively quick move into TV but the Pirates were starting to seriously damage his credibility and jeopardize his future. The intercom on his desk buzzed.

'Roger' it was Breda. 'The Minister is in reception.'

'The Minister?' Roger's feet hit the ground. 'He can't be! He's in Japan.'

'He *was* in Japan' a flat familiar voice drawled, as the door to his office opened and Richard Horn, Ireland's Minister for Communications walked into the room holding a neatly clipped Bonsai tree in his hands. His shirt and suit were slightly crumpled, there was an inch of stubble on his chin, and fine lines around his eyes.

Christ thought Roger. *He's come straight from the plane.*

'Good morning Roger' the Minister carefully placed the Bonsai on the desk in front of him. 'Or as they say in Japan 'Ohayou Gozaimasu.'

'Minister' Roger forced a smile. 'How was your trip?'

'How do you think it was?' the Minister sat down. 'A week of smiling and nodding and trying to keep up with translators. Radio market's interesting enough. We definitely picked up a few ideas. Food's revolting' he watched as Breda left the room. 'Right' he sighed, rubbing his eyes. Roger tensed, and braced himself, but the Minister didn't speak. He was looking at the Bonsai. 'Remarkable isn't it?' he said.

'Beautiful' said Roger, not really caring.

'You know Roger, Japanese folklore has a theory that a tree left growing in its natural state is a crude thing.'

'Really?' Roger wished he'd get on with it, but the Minister didn't appear to be in any sort of hurry. He leant forward and examined a small fresh green shoot that had pushed it's way up through the soil at the base of the Bonsai.

'They hold the view' the Minister lightly brushed the top of the shoot with his fingertip 'that it's only when humans intervene; when they modify or cultivate the tree in accordance with a human ideal, that *only then* can the tree's *natural beauty* become *true beauty.*'

'I see' said Roger, not seeing at all.

The Minister cleared his throat. 'Let's talk for a moment Roger about these dreadful, and I mean truly appalling, latest set of figures. Now I could tell you that I bought this tree all the way from Japan to make a point. I *could say* that this tree' he framed the Bonsai with his hands 'represents a perfectly structured, regulated radio market, and that Pirate Radio' reaching in, he pinched the base of the the small green shoot growing up through the soil 'is the raggedy, runty, *fuck weed*' he tugged on the shoot 'that threatens to choke and strangle the very foundations on which this perfect beauty resides.' The shoot emerged, and he held it up to the light.

'I could say that' he examined the tiny transparent roots 'but I'd be lying. The truth in fact' the Minister stood up, and walked across to the waste-paper bin 'is that I bought the plant as a present for my wife, my *dear* wife, who informed me this morning that she doesn't want it.' Rubbing his fingertips he discarded the shoot into the bin, then drawing breath he stretched the stretch of a man who had spent thirteen hours on a long haul flight. 'These Pirates Roger' he yawned. 'These people, who hijack our masts to broadcast their tripe, who take our listeners and our revenue faster than it takes to change the channel. It's time to weed them out. To *wipe* them out. He eyed the Bonsai. This is not about modification or cultivation. There's nothing beautiful about Pirate Radio. It's noise Roger. And we need to find a way to silence that noise before it puts us all out of business. This is no longer about containment. This is seek and destroy.' Roger looked at him.

'Seek and destroy?'

'Kill the noise.'

'You can't kill noise' Roger snapped. I'm not Captain Kirk. There's no magic button I can press. You don't just point a laser and ...' he stopped. 'Christ' he turned to look at the RTE radio masts standing tall in the grounds outside. 'Jesus. Christ. Breda' he pressed the intercom on his desk.

'Yes Roger?' Breda's voice, compacted through the small metal box.

'Get Bobby. I need him up here now.'

'He's away until Thursday Roger. Transmitter checks in Cork and Limerick.'

'Right' Roger frowned 'well leave word in studio and diary it for Thursday; I want him up here as soon as he returns.' Releasing the buzzer he sat back in his chair and smiled at the Minister. 'I think I might have the answer' he said. He looked out the window at the radio masts. 'I think maybe the answer's been staring us in the face all along.'

'Excellent.' The Minister stood up. 'I'll leave it with you' he began walking to the door 'but I expect results this time Roger. We need them, and we need them fast. Keep me posted.' Roger watched him pull the office door open.

'Why didn't she want it?' he said. The Minister turned in the doorway.

'Who?'

'Your wife. Why didn't she want the Bonsai?' Suppressing a smile, the Minister rubbed his eyes, then he yawned again before looking at Roger, a weary, somewhat bemused expression on his face.

'My wife holds the opinion that the Japanese suppress their women. She says they bind their feet to keep them small. She opened the front door this morning, took one look at the Bonsai and said *and now they're suppressing their trees as well.* Refused to let me in the house with it. Which is why I came here. I'll tell you what; she could learn a thing or two from the Japanese.'

. . . .

'Elliott?'

'Max?'

'Why did you hang up on Mum when she rang you in hospital?'

'She hung up on me' Elliott, standing in the kitchen at home, felt his throat tighten.

'That's not what she said' Max sounded annoyed. 'She said *you* ...'

'She hung up on me two years ago' said Elliott. 'Don't you remember? I think she hung up on you around about the same time. And Dad.'

'Christ' he could hear the impatience in Max's voice 'you don't even fucking get on with Dad. Grow up Elliott. Have you ever stopped to consider it from her point of view? You know how difficult Dad is.'

'She left me Max, she *left* me. She left us.'

'You didn't say us. You said me. You need to stop feeling sorry for yourself Elliott, because this wounded martyr routine, this self pitying, sanctimonious ...'

'You know what Max?' Elliott cut him off 'I'm just out of hospital. I have a broken arm, a recently re-inflated lung and I'm not up to this shit, so why don't you fuck off with your opinions and your psycho-analysis bullshit. Happy New Year to you too by the way. Hope you had a great Christmas; hope you had a bonne fucking Noelle over there with her and that prick Laurent' he slammed down the phone as the sound of a motor-bike machine-gunning to a halt crunched and skidded on the gravel outside. Fuming, Elliott grabbed his jacket from the chair, a small twinge of re-inflated lung guilt as he stuffed his cigarettes inside. Crossing the hall, he knelt down by the stairs and pulled out a plastic bag he'd stashed there earlier in the week.

'Ya ready?' Squirrel's tall leather frame filling the doorway as he pulled it open.

'Yeah. Shit, is that your bike?' Elliott stared at the powerful looking silver blue chrome polished machine parked the drive. Squirrel grinned.

'Nearly worth smashin' through that church window ta get this' he swung a long leather leg over the saddle. Then he stood up and jumped down, kick-starting the bike in one fluid natural movement, signalling to Elliott to climb on as the revs got louder.

They sliced down the back of Howth Hill, Elliott's shoulder inches from the road as Squirrel bent and leant the bike around corners. Engulfed in a hot cold swirling vacuum, the engine was like angry bees as the road swarmed up, curled down, bent in and around them in one loud beautiful fluid motion. It was music, dancing, drinking, drugs; it was running, jumping, falling, flying. It was freedom bottled. They cut along the Coast Road, the wind whipping, ripping, competing for earspace above the noise of the engine, Elliott's good arm wrapped tight around Squirrel, the broken one tucked in by his side, legs barnacled to the bike's frame. The distinct possibility of imminent and immediate death made him feel strangely alive. The bike growled to a slow as they arrived in a small cul-de-sac.

'Number twenty-six' Elliott pulled out the address Iris had given him the day they'd all left hospital. 'That's it I think' he pointed to the house in front of them.

'Must be renovatin' said Squirrel. A rusty scaffolding tower straddled the doorway of number twenty-six. It ran just beyond each side of the front porch and climbed the full height of the house. Wooden planks at intersections provided various points of ascent. There clearly had been a series of bad extensions to the house already; a poorly constructed two storey wing to the right and to the left a strange looking round tower sitting directly on top of the garage, topped with a Disney style turret.

'One of these kids is doing their own thing' said Elliott as he glanced at the rest of the tidy kept houses circling the small estate.

'Bit like Iris' Squirrel ran his hands through his hair. 'C'mon.' They walked in underneath the first layer of scaffolding, Squirrel bending his head to avoid a plank. The doorbell was missing. In its place, two wires, sticking out; a red one and a green one. 'State ah this' said Squirrel. He put his helmet between his knees, picked up the wires and pressed them together, the doorbell sounding loudly down the hall as he did so. A dog barking furiously. A woman's voice getting closer.

'Jimmy, stop it, Jimmy, oh for goodness sakes' the door fell back, a grey mongrel shot out and a woman Elliott recognised from the hospital as Iris' mother stood there in a turquoise kaftan, a yellow and orange headscarf tied over flame red hair. Close up she was very beautiful. 'Hello!!' she shouted, joyous as she threw her arms out and enveloped a surprised Elliott in a tight hug. 'Come in, come in!!!' she beckoned, leading them down a long narrow hallway, a wall of plastic sheeting hanging to her left. 'Perfect timing' she flashed a bright smile at them. 'Gemini has been stuck' she weaved her way in and around stacks of cement blocks positioned at different points along the hall 'practically imprisoned' she continued 'in this terrible cycle of obscurity but Jupiter *finally* crossed the sun ... Iris, your friends are here!!' her voice rose in a joyful trill as Elliott and Squirrel followed her into a large sun filled room where a scowling Iris sat in an over-sized armchair with a marmalade cat asleep on her lap, a second dark grey one stretched out in front of the fire beside her.

'What were you talking about Mum?' she looked concerned.

'I was just telling your friends' Jackie began, 'about how Jupiter ...' the doorbell rang. 'Client' she muttered. 'Help yourselves' she gestured at the kitchen, a trail of floating turquoise narrowly escaping the door as she closed it behind her.

'Sit down' Iris looked embarrassed. She was wearing another pair of men's pyjamas, slashed like the previous ones to let her plastered leg through. Her head was freshly shaven, Mohican black, shining, sharply spiked, and Elliott noticed she had a small silver snake in her nose. Something else however was commanding his complete and immediate attention. Directly behind Iris, running left to right, floor to ceiling, was a wall of wooden shelving filled with albums, neatly filed. The shelves were split into large square shaped pigeon holes. He scanned them. Five across, five down, at least a hundred albums per pigeon hole. He did a quick calculation. There were roughly two and a half thousand albums sitting on those shelves. Shit, she was a DJ. A DJ with a serious collection. Bigger than his own. In front of the shelves and along the sides of the room were more albums, stacked in piles of different heights, and to the right, along the wall, a line of them snaking half way down the room, leaning back like dominoes mid fall. A thousand. There were at least another thousand albums on the ground.

'Is this all yours?' he pointed at the shelving.

'Yep' Iris smiled, running long nails across the marmalade's back, who purred in response, squeezing but not opening its eyes.

'Can I have a look?'

'Sure' she seemed pleased he'd asked. Uncertain where to start Elliott stood up, picked a mid section and began flicking through, respect jostling envy as he slid out cover after cover. David Byrne and Brian Eno *My Life in the Bush of Ghosts*, Kraftwerk *Trans Euro Express*, Pere Ubo *The Modern Dance*, Virgin Prunes *If I die, I Die*, Bowie's *Low*, Richard Hell and the Voidoids *Blank Generation*, Grace Jones *Nightclubbing*, Siouxsie and The Banshees *The Scream*, Public Image *The Metal Box* in its original metal box sleeve.

'I have this' he smiled. Something caught his eye. He pinched and pulled a sleeve. Mortal Coil's *Song to a Siren;* it was the 12 inch, she had the twelve inch.

'Are you gonna look at those all day?' said Squirrel from the chair behind him.

'Sorry' Elliott forced himself to stop. He pushed Birthday Party's *Junkyard* back into the shelf. 'Here' he handed Iris the plastic bag he'd taken from underneath the stairs at home 'bought you a present.'

'What is it?' Iris pulled the bag open. 'Elliott' she squealed 'it's a transmitter!!'

'I know' Elliott grinned, pleased at her reaction. 'I'll set it up if you like.' He reached for the transmitter and tore off the packaging. 'Is in here okay? Would you prefer it in your bedroom?'

'No' Iris shook her head. 'This is perfect. All my music's here, and it's kind of my room anyway.'

'You an only child?' said Squirrel. A pause. Startled eyes.

'There's just the three of us' she said.

'No brothers or sisters?' said Squirrel. Her eyes flicked.

'Go on' she said to Elliott. 'Set it up.'

'Is this all ya do?' Squirrel was fascinated as he watched Elliott kneel down by the stereo. 'Just hook up that yolk and off ya go? Ya've a station in yer gaff?'

'Well, this is small stuff' said Elliott as he turned the stereo around and started working wires 'we're only going to get a limited reach.'

'Whaddaya mean reach?'

'The signal we get with this' Elliott held up the transmitter 'will only reach so far. Radio is all about sound and reach. It's obviously about music and what you put on air, but if you have a poor sound people won't want to listen to you or if you have a weak signal or reach then only a few people will get to hear you anyway.'

'So how much money d'ya make?' said Squirrel to Elliott as he worked.

'How do you mean?' said Elliott.

'Off yer station. How much money d'ya make from the ads?'

'I don't make money. I just do it because I enjoy it.'

'I enjoy ridin' bikes, but I'll tell ya what I enjoy even more; gettin' paid for ridin' bikes. How much do RTE make?'

'In advertising?'

'No, rice crispy buns.'

'I think it's about two million a year' Elliott smiled.

'Two million? What about the Pirates?'

'Not sure' said Elliott 'though RTE are down about half a million this year because of them.'

'So you're tellin' me there's five hunded grand floatin' around out there?'

'I guess' Elliott shrugged.

'An' the Pirates are moppin' it up?'

'Only the top ones. The top five.'

'Five ah them?' Squirrel stared at Elliott. 'That's a hundred grand each. Would you not go after a piece ah that?'

'Not that easy.'

'Mightn't be as hard as ya think. C'mere' Squirrel turned to Iris 'mate ah mine, Mick; he's settin' up a club. Looking for jocks if you're interested.'

'What kind of club?' said Iris.

'Dunno' Squirrel leant back in the chair. 'Callin' it Berlin.'

'Berlin?'

'DJ box is gonna be a wall.'

'What kind of music?'

'Not sure' Squirrel shrugged. 'Mick's got a rake ah clubs. Ya any good?'

'No. I'm shyte.'

'I'd say you're shyte alright' Squirrel grinned, staring at the wall of shelving. 'Any Randy Crawford in there?' he nodded at the albums.

'What do *you* think?' she grinned.

'This is ready' Elliott turned the stereo around. 'Do you want to test it?'

'Not now' said Iris. I'll play around with it tonight, but maybe you'll come back if I get stuck.' Something inside Elliott lifted. Hope. He looked at her. Nothing in her eyes other than what she'd just said. A flicker maybe.

'Sure' he said. 'No problem.'

'Right' Squirrel stood up 'better hit the road. Got a date' he winked.

'Yeah?' said Iris. Who?'

'Young one I met in Saints' Squirrel zipped up his jacket. 'Gorgeous so she is. Takin' her ta the Oval. 'C'mon' he said to Elliott 'I'll give ya a lift inta RTE.'

'I can get the bus' Elliott was thinking he'd like to spend some more time with Iris.

'Nah, you're alright; I'll drop ya in' said Squirrel. 'I'll get Mick ta give ya a shout' he said to Iris 'see can we get ya inta Berlin.'

. . . .

'You want to what?' Bobby, RTE's head sound engineer was standing in Roger's office. If it's strange that a disc jockey enjoys nothing more than spending two to three hours alone in a small room listening to the sound of their own voice, then it's stranger still that someone else would want to spend their entire time obsessing about the level, pitch and tone of that voice and all the other voices the station broadcasts. This however is precisely what sound engineers do and they're central to the success of any station. Obsessive, introverted and intensely serious about sound, if Bobby wasn't listening to the station at home he was listening to it in the car, and if you couldn't find him in either of those places chances were he was tinkering deep in the bowels of the station, down in the engine room making the slightest of adjustments here and there to get the sound just right.

'Jam them' said Roger.

'You mean block their signal? Are you serious?'

'Serious times, serious measures' Roger examined his nails. He did hope Bobby wasn't going to be difficult on this, because union or no union he'd over-ride him and make it happen. 'What I'm asking you' said Roger 'is if it's technically possible to broadcast one signal on top of another signal?'

'Yeah, technically, it's possible' said Bobby. 'We'd have to build a transmitter specifically for that, but technically yes, it can be done.'

'And we'd kill the Pirate signal?'

'We won't kill the signal, but we would destroy the sound. If we broadcast white noise directly on top of their signal, all their listeners will be able to hear is a hissing sound.' Roger sat back in his chair and looked pleased.

'Hissing. Well nobody's going to want to listen to hissing for very long are they?' Bobby was quiet. 'What's wrong?' said Roger.

'I don't like it' said Bobby. 'There's no integrity to something like that. It's not the answer.'

'I see' said Roger. 'And what do you think the answer is? Roll out the barrels and throw them a *congratulations on your ratings* party? Maybe we should invite the advertisers while we're at it. Let them all get cosy over some warm wine and cheese sticks. Perhaps you think we should just give the Pirates the keys to the building? Come on in boys, pick a studio, steal a frequency. Fuck it, why don't I just give them the pin to my Pass Card?'

'We need to focus on our programming' said Bobby.

'Our programming?' Roger's voice was dangerously soft. 'Christ, why didn't I think of that?'

'It needs a radical overhaul.'

'A radical overhaul. Fantastic, excellent suggestion. Tell me Bobby, what does the sign on my door say?' Bobby shifted. His eyes flicked to the window.

'Director of Programming' he said quietly.

'Director of Programming. Very good. You're not here sixteen years for nothing. Now, you telling me that our programming needs a radical overhaul is a bit like me telling you which one of the hundred tiny knobs on a sound desk to twist just a nano-fraction to the right so listeners in Limerick don't get middle ear pain. Do you see what I'm saying? Do you see the very subtle point I'm trying to make? Now fuck off and build me a transmitter that will take these bastards down one by one, and come back with the remote control when it's ready.' Bobby turned in silence and began making for the door. 'Actually, hold on' said Roger. 'I need to talk to you about Studio One.'

'Studio One?'

'The upgrade' Roger reached for his cigarettes.

'Studio One doesn't need an upgrade.'

'I'll decide what our studios do or do not need' an irritated snap, flick as Roger lit his cigarette. 'The Minister's approved the budget, the equipment has been ordered; all I need you to do is look at the layout. I want a smooth transition, a quick changeover and I want it done by the end of March.'

'March?' said Bobby. 'When's the equipment arriving?'

'It should be here the last week in February' said Roger. 'I need to think about colour schemes, furnishings; I'll do that with Breda; you just be ready to jump when I need you. I'm going to launch the Summer Schedule from the new studio; bring the press in. I want this new studio to make a statement. I want people talking.'

'It's our programming we want them talking about' said Bobby 'not the equipment or the colour of the walls.'

'Tell you what Bobby' a dull red colour had set in across Roger's cheeks. Why don't you just focus on the technical side and leave the rest to me? Oh, and Bobby?' he said as Bobby made for the door.

'Yeah?' Bobby turned around.

'Just with regard to what you said earlier. If you ever question my integrity again, I'll fire you. I'll make your life incredibly miserable, and then I'll fire you.'

. . . .

Squirrel dropped Elliott to RTE.

'I'll give ya a call' he said. 'C'mere, we should have a pint if we get a chance. Talk the station idea through a bit more.'

'What station idea?'

'Our station' Squirrel grinned.

'What are you talking about?'

'You don't believe we could do it, do ya?'

'No' Elliott smiled 'I don't. It's a nice fantasy, but that's all it is.'

'It's not a fantasy' Squirrel kick started the bike. 'It's not a fantasy' he shouted over the revs 'it's a hundred grand reality!!'

. . . .

Elliott found Tom, the Station Manager, finishing up a meeting with the Breakfast Show Producer.

'Elliott' he smiled. 'Welcome back. Jim, you go on; I'll catch up with you later. Now ...' he began running through a list of stuff he wanted Elliott to help him with, most of which was legwork for different shows; phoning, faxing, bits of research '... and there's a production meeting for Monday's Breakfast Show in an hour' he finished. 'Can you sit in on that? They need an extra pair of hands this week.'

'Sure' said Elliott. 'Anything else?'

'Don't worry, that'll be more than enough' said Tom. Elliott had an hour to kill so he grabbed a coffee, slung his record bag over his shoulder and went downstairs to the studios. He loved it down here. Dark corridors, pockets of light, soft carpets, thick glass. A door pushed open and light fell into the corridor as two girls in their twenties emerged laughing, followed by a long haired man in his mid thirties. Broadcast Assistants and the Producer for the Morning Show.

'Hey Elliott' the girls called as they went past.

'All done?' said Elliott.

'Yep. Going for a coffee. We need one after that.' Elliott watched them disappear up the stairs. He looked in the window of the studio they'd just left. Studio One. It was empty. He glanced at his watch. Twelve o'clock. The News would go out from Studio Two, and the afternoon show would be Studio Three. He pulled the heavy door open and went inside. Studio One was RTE's lead studio. Soft lighting, a comfortable working area, leather sofas, plants, low coffee tables. He walked over to the production team desks. Through the glass in front of them he could see the top of the mixing desk and the DJ mic. Quick glance at the corridor outside. No-one around. Most of them would be either at lunch or in studio on a show. He pulled the outer door to the presenter booth open. There were two doors leading into the booth, both insulated with thick carpet that ran across the top of the door, down the side and underneath along the bottom. Between them they completely insulated the booth from any outside sounds. He let the second door close tight behind him, dumped his bag on the mix desk and slid into the presenter chair. He checked the room outside, and beyond that to the corridor again. All clear. He pulled his bag over and took out the albums. Quick equipment scan to make sure nothing was running or recording. No. Everything off. Flicking the sound to studio, he sat up in the chair, pulled on the headphones and leant close into the mic.

'Good afternoon Dublin, we're live from Studio One; everything's pretty much the same. No jobs, no money, but we do have The Clash.' He slid up *Clampdown* then leant back, scanning the sleeve lyrics before lining up the rest of his set. He followed *Clampdown* with R.E.M's *Radio Free Europe*, The Flying Lizards *Money*, Stiff Little Fingers *Alternative Ulster*, The Pop Group *We are all Prostitutes* and Gang of Four were half way through a spectacularly loud *Damaged Goods* when the studio door pushed open and Bobby walked in.

'Elliott!' he shouted over the music 'what the hell are you doing!!'

'Shit' Elliott pulled off the phones and brought the sound down.

'Christ, are you on-air?' Bobby leant across and scanned the desk.

'No! No!' Elliott ducked around him. 'Honestly, I swear, look, the sound's switched to Studio … I was just playing it in here, seriously Bobby, I swear.' Bobby stopped scanning and visibly relaxed but he still looked annoyed.

'Jesus Elliott. You shouldn't be in here. You don't know what you're doing.'

'I do' Elliott cheeks reddened.

'Yeah?' said Bobby. 'How? Who trained you?'

'No-one' Elliott looked at the ground. Probably not the best time to confess he had his own station. 'I just … I watch the jocks, you know. Honestly Bobby, check the equipment, it's fine. I really do know how to use it.' Bobby looked at him in silence for a minute or two, then he picked up the R.E.M. album.

'So what's this about?' he fanned it. Elliott shrugged. 'Look' Bobby's voice softened 'if you want to jock, talk to Tom. Maybe there's a late night slot you could sit in on, but you need to stay out of studio unless it's cleared. You're looking at thousands of pounds worth of equipment here' he gestured at the desk. 'I don't doubt you can use it, but things break, even with the professionals they break, and if you damaged something in here there'd be war. You're not even an official employee. If Roger had come in just now, there would have been killings, you know there would.' He fell silent, small dark eyes running furtively across the mix desk, up the cart machine.

'Honestly I haven't broken anything' said Elliott.

'It's alright' said Bobby. 'I'm not looking at that. I actually came down here to try to work out how to get this equipment out. Studio's being upgraded.'

'Upgraded? Why?'

'Good question. Waste of perfectly good equipment.' The phone on the mix desk rang. Bobby picked it up. 'Hello? Yeah, just about to start. Sure' his voice tightened 'on my way.' He put the phone down. 'Roger' a look of annoyance. 'Wants me down here, wants me up there. We'll keep today to ourselves Elliott but for your own sake stay out of the studios; you're only asking for trouble.'

. . . .

'No … no … Nick, you're not listening to me' Anthony was on the phone, pacing the kitchen when Elliott got in the door later that evening. Dressed in a navy pinstripe suit, he had a glass of red wine in one hand, the kitchen portable pressed to his ear in the other. 'Nick' he sounded impatient 'I don't want to *skipper* the boat, I want to crew. Yes–yes, Nick? I *know* it's my boat; I'm not a fucking moron. What I'm saying is I'll appoint you skipper. Why? Because you've chartered the Arctic; you know these waters.' Silence. Insect sounds from inside the phone. Anthony stopped pacing. 'I'm not a control freak. Christ Almighty anyone who shows any kind of fucking initiative these days is a control freak. In case it escaped your notice I'm relinquishing control. I'm appointing *you* skipper. Look, bottom line Nick; I've never sailed the Arctic, you have. Many times. It's a simple logic. You skipper. I crew. Case closed. Now what do you say?'

Elliott pulled the fridge door open and surveyed the shelves. He flipped open the freezer box and took out a frozen lasagne. 'Where are you now?' Anthony was swirling the last of the wine in the glass. Elliott took the lasagne out of the box, put it on a plate and opened the microwave. He stared at the small frozen square.

Ask him. There's never going to be a right time. Ask him now.

'Why don't I meet you in the yacht club?' tilting his head Anthony drained the last of the wine. 'Why? Because we need to start charting a course.'

Tell him. Just say it.

'Franz-Joseph?' Anthony placed the empty glass down on the kitchen counter.

'Franz Joseph will be a fucking nite-mare. Freeze our bollox off, and we won't get a visa; Russians won't let us in ... what?' Anthony picked up his car keys from the table, then he laughed, a deep booming sound that filled the room. 'I think you'll find the Russians have pretty good radars; listen I'm on my way' he shouted into the phone 'I'll see you in the club' hooking the portable back onto the wall unit he caught sight of Elliott. 'Ah! There you are. How was college? Good day?'

'Mmm' Elliott mumbled. From the corner of his eye he could see the lasagne, circling inside the microwave. *Ask him. Just do it.*

'Excellent' Anthony patted the doorway. 'I'll see you later.'

'Dad' Elliott felt the blood rush to his cheeks.

'Yep' Anthony's head jerked around.

'I was thinking ... I was thinking about maybe changing courses' Elliott kept his eyes on the microwave. Silence. The sound of the lasagne turning, then from behind him, Anthony's keys chinked, clinked.

'Why would you do that?'

'Well' Elliott swallowed, 'I just ... it's just ...'

'It's just what?'

'I was thinking about Communications' Elliott kept his voice light, casual. Silence. The microwave grinding as the lasagne turned. 'It's just' Elliott struggled 'I always wanted ... it's a good degree ... you know ... it's a good degree.'

'It's a wankers degree' Anthony dug a thumbnail at something lodged between one of his teeth. 'You can forget that' he examined the offending article, 'you can absolutely forget any idea of that, and frankly I'm disappointed you're even suggesting it.' Elliott chewed his cheek as he felt the heat rise up through his face.

'Maybe I don't want to do Law' he muttered.

'What's that?' Anthony's head snaked forward.

'Nothing' Elliott swallowed. He watched the lasagne circle.

'Maybe. You.Don't.Want' Anthony tapped the weight of each word out against the doorframe, keys jingling as he did so. 'I see. Right. Well maybe Elliott, *I don't want*, to waste my money on an excuse of a degree that isn't worth the paper it's written on.' Elliott watched the digits on the microwave tick down as the lasagne turned. 'You can forget Communications' Anthony's eyes were dark, glittering. 'Your Mother might have indulged that kind of horse-play but I won't. You'll do Law, you'll get your degree and that's the end of it.' Elliott said nothing. 'Have I made myself clear?' A loud high pitched 'beeeeep' as the microwave stopped. 'Have I?' Anthony barked. Elliott nodded. 'Because just in case I haven't, let me be clear; let me be very specific. I will not entertain' Anthony paused 'I will not *fund* that kind of bollox. You can find somewhere else to live, and someone else to feed and clothe you if you choose to pursue that route. Right?' a final clink, chink of keys, then from the hallway, the front door slammed.

. . . .

'**Good morning Dublin! Radio Andy, Andy here, 11am on the last day of February, the wettest February the Met Office has ever recorded. Word on the street says David Lee Roth is about ta leave Van Halen. Why? What's goin' on? Marvin Gaye said that and he's dead. Probably said it just before his father shot him.**

'**What's goin' on Da?**'

'**You're a drug addict son. Trust me, it's for the best.**'

'**Bang. Lights out. But back to Van Halen. Does David Lee Roth know somethin' we don't? Is Van Halen a sinkin' ship? Because if it is Dave …. if Van Halen really is a sinkin' ship … well, ya might as well jump …**'

Elliott swore as the opening beats of *Jump* came up on the tiny transistor behind the café counter.

'What?' Squirrel squatted down on the torn leather stool opposite him, placing two steaming mugs of tea on the table. Elliott jerked his head in the direction of the radio. 'Andy?' Squirrel grinned. Elliott lit a cigarette and threw the matches on the table.

'Does my head in. I know you think he's funny but he's not. He's just a shit DJ.'

'Well, ya know the answer' Squirrel lifted his mug and blew on the hot tea.

Elliott smiled, squinting as the sun sliced gold fingers through two months of thick winter muck and grime on the cafe window. He was meant to be at a lecture. He was meant to have been at lots of lectures over the last month but he'd skipped most of them to meet Squirrel, Iris or both of them depending on how the day shaped up. It had taken nearly all of January to get Iris' station up and running properly; it hadn't been as easy as he'd thought.

'Yis are wastin' yer time' Squirrel had sat like a broken record on the couch as he'd watched them fiddling with wires and testing frequencies. 'Pissin' around in yer gaffs when ya could be settin' up a proper station and makin' a bit ah cash.' In fact lately Elliott seemed to be missing lectures just so Squirrel could give him that same one over and over. Still anything was better than Civil Procedure, Advocacy or Property Law. College was getting worse and while on one level he felt guilty about skipping lectures, the only time he genuinely felt right about himself was when he was working in RTE, DJ'ing at home or helping Iris with her show.

She was up and running. Squirrel had come good on his promise. His friend Mick visited, took one look at her, clocked the collection and hired her on the spot. Elliott was friends with her now. Proper friends. Not just two people who'd met in hospital. She still had no idea how he really felt about her but that was fine. In fact it was better. Friends for the moment was much safer than the threat of losing her. She had however completely inhabited him. A permanent fixture, a constant presence. He day-dreamed about her in lectures, had imaginary album debates with her at the racks in Freebird, and at night when he closed his eyes he saw her face, heard her voice. She was the first and last thing he thought about every day.

Squirrel in a very different way had become an equally important part of his life. He was the most clear-cut, clear thinking, determined person Elliott had ever met. Big hopes, big dreams and an absolute certainty he would achieve them. Squirrel had hope, vision, conviction. But that wasn't all. Squirrel had something else. Squirrel had a ten year plan.

'... an' after that I want a Hiace, and in the next five years a whole fleet ah vans an' by 1995, which I know seems a long time away, but by 1995 Lightening Couriers will be Lightening Transport with trucks, artics, and that's what long term plannin' is all about. D'ya think yer man Branson sat around in his bedroom playin' records? Vision. Ya gotta have vision. Are you listenin' ta me?'

'Sorry' said Elliott. 'I wasn't. What did you say?'

'Not just my future I'm talkin' about' Squirrel looked annoyed 'yours an' all.'

'Really?' Elliott picked up his tea and warmed his hands on the mug. 'Where exactly do I fit into Lightening Transport then?'

'Capital' said Squirrel. 'I need capital. T'expand the business.'

'And you think I have it?'

'No, but I think you can make it. Correction. I think we can make it.'

'How's that then?'

'Fucks sakes. Sometimes I think I'm havin' this conversation with meself. The station Elliott, the radio station!' A truck thundered past and the café windows shook. Elliott blew on his tea, then took a sip.

'Look Squirrel, that's not going to happen. It's a nice idea, a fantasy, but that's all it is.'

'You're wrong' Squirrel shook his head. 'There's no reason why we can't be clearin' a hundred grand a year like every other Pirate.'

'Top five. Top five, and it's not that easy.'

'It is. Look how easy ya just set up Iris' station. What did it take? A month?

'All you're talkin' about is doin' that on a bigger scale.'

'I can see how it looks that way' said Elliott 'but you're actually talking about something much bigger. Bigger and not without cost.'

'It didn't cost anything ta set up the station in Iris' gaff.'

'You're right' said Elliott. 'It doesn't cost a thing for me, Iris or ten thousand other amateurs to sit in our bedrooms or garden sheds broadcasting music we like, but put us together and that's where the costs rack up. A serious station needs proper premises, decent equipment; it needs light, heat, people to answer the phones, to sell the ads that make the money, people to run the station. The Super Pirates, the ones you're talking about, the ones who are clearing a hundred grand a year, they have all those and they have enough DJs to do a twenty four hour shift, but all these things Squirrel; they cost money. A lot of money.' Squirrel who had silently been sipping his tea took a hot swallow and put his mug down on the table.

'Oh really? Is that what a business needs? Jeez, I'd never ah thought ah that. This is an opportunity Elliott, a real one. I can feel it. Feel it in me balls. An' my balls never lie.'

'Thanks for sharing that with me' said Elliott. 'If I'm ever in any doubt over something I'll be sure to give your bollox a call.'

'Could do worse' said Squirrel. He shifted on the stool. 'Look. Way I see it there's you, there's me, an' there's Iris' he popped up three fingers to represent each of them. 'You' he pointed at Elliott 'know all about how ta run a station.'

'I hardly think work experience in RTE constitutes the ability to run a station.'

'Don't give me that shyte. You might not believe in yourself but I do. I listen ta ya Elliott. I've been listenin' ta ya for nearly two months now, and when you're talkin' about radio, which is most of the time by the way, ya really know yer shit; even what ya rattled off just now about what the Pirates have, an' all the stuff we'd need. Ya know it. Better than ya think.' Elliott stayed silent. 'Iris' Squirrel pointed in a direction Elliott could only presume was Clontarf 'accordin' ta yerself *and* Mick is one of the best DJs Dublin has ta offer, an undiscovered talent Mick says, an' I my friend' he patted his chest as though he were pushing the final piece into an easy jigsaw puzzle 'have the commercial wherewithal.'

'The where with fuck all you mean' Elliott ground his cigarette out in the black plastic John Players ashtray. 'I hate to bring you back to money Squirrel but I have to. You're talking about doing this to raise money to expand the courier business but you'd need serious money just to get it up and running.'

'How much?

'How much what?'

'You know for a fella going ta college yer very slow. Don't think I'd want you representin' me in court. I'm askin' ya how much it'd cost ta set up a radio station.'

'I can't just give you a figure off the top of my head.'

'Just gimme me a ballpark.'

'I can't.'

'Try.'

'I can't. There's too many things involved.'

'What kinda things?'

'Christ! What? Do you want me to write you a list?' said Elliott. Squirrel gave him a sharp look, then shot off his stool and for a minute Elliott thought he was walking out but he stopped and leant over the counter.

'Decco! Fire us over a few ah those napkins. What? No, I didn't spill anything, just give me a couple ah poxy napkins. None ah yer business what for, just shut up and gimme the napkins, will ya?' He came back over and squatted down on the stool. 'Fucks sakes, Spanish Inquisition. Here' he pushed a napkin in front of Elliott.

'What's that for?' said Elliott.

'The list. D'ya need a pen?'

'I'm not following you.'

'The list' Squirrel tapped the napkin. 'List ah the costs.'

'Of setting up a radio station?'

'No, of messages for me Ma.'

'Are you serious?'

'Do I look I'm jokin?'

'It's pointless.'

'An' sittin' here with me when ya should be at one ah yer lectures isn't? Come on' Squirrel patted the napkin. 'You're not in your lecture; ya've nothin' ta do; not goin' ta cost anything ta write a list; here, you start an' I'll get us another cup ah tea.' He stood up again and walked over to the counter. Elliott stared at the white napkin on the table. Shaking his head he slipped his hand inside his coat.

'Futile' he muttered to himself 'utterly futile.' He took out a pen, then holding the napkin steady, wrote the words 'RADIO STATION' at the top and underlined them. Twice. He looked at the words for a minute. 'RADIO STATION'. They looked back.

'Good man' Squirrel had come back and was peering over his shoulder.

'Don't look so happy' said Elliott. 'It's just a list. In fact when you read this you're going to be decidedly unhappy because you'll realise that this is not achievable. Not. Achievable.'

'D'ya want a bun?' said Squirrel.

'No thanks.'

'They look nice. Cream and jam.'

'Alright' Elliott stared at the blank napkin.

'Might have ta come off yer wages.'

'Well if we make a hundred grand I'm sure we'll be able to afford a cream bun here and there won't we?' Elliott murmured staring at the white sheet. He thought for a minute, then wrote

1 Premises

'I wouldn't be able to give up college' he said to the napkin, then wrote:

2 Equipment

'I mean I'd have to stay in college' the napkin staring up at him. 'Not that this is going anywhere' he said. Squirrel came back and put the teas down.

'Just concentrate on the list' he said. 'Don't think too far ahead. All we're doin' here is speculatin. Havin' the craic. An' don't worry about college' he turned back to the counter 'ya'll fit that in. Don't forget Iris'd be helpin.'

3 DJs

'She might not have time' said Elliott as Squirrel put the bun down beside him. 'Not with her new career in plastics.'

Iris was working in a sex shop. She got the job a week after she started in Berlin. Jackie and Arthur thought she was working in insurance; it was easier that way. They'd been surprised an insurance company would employ her.

'Telesales' said Iris at the dinner table. 'No-one sees you.'

'Well, I guess that's the Eighties' said Arthur to the air just in front of his face.

'Wouldn't have happened in the Sixties' said Jackie. 'I think the real fuss about punk was in the seventies. It's more widely accepted now. A bit like Gandhi' she beamed as though Gandhi were listening, sitting at the table with them, smiling as he finished his chicken kiev.

Iris' look was in fact perfect for 'Slave' which sold an extensive range of sex toys and clothing but specialized in fetish and bondage.

'Y'wor that wee dog collar every dye?' Eddie, the 5ft 4, balding Northern Irish guy who owned the place, eyed the thin leather silver spiked strip on Iris's neck.

'Most days' she'd replied.

'Fontostic. Wor it hor. All the tayme. Job's yors. Vinnie thor does socoradee' he nodded at the pockmarked 6ft built like a brick shithouse 'thing' that was standing at the door. 'Costumes look a wee bit scorey but most of these porvorts are big business mon; politicians, liars an' the lake. Gentle as lombs. Porvorted wee lombs mayndue, but we like porvorts when they spend thor money hor' he gave her a greasy grin. 'Ya con start n'Mundi. I'll pay ya cosh. Sondra thor' he pointed at a fat girl in a pink plastic skirt with ripped fishnets and a woolly black jumper 'wee Sondra'll give ya a trainin' curse on how ta fit the robber suits. I'll see you in a month for your rav-yuy.'

'Right, here you go' Elliott pushed the napkin across the table. Squirrel picked it up and scanned it, streaked blonde spikes swaying as the head beneath moved furiously, an oil blackened finger moving along each line, muttering as he read:

1. Premises – somewhere central, secure, discreet
2. Equipment – transmitter/aerial/desk/mixer/headphones /sound-proofing
3. DJS (enough to cover a 24 hour shift)
4. Broadcast Assistants
5. Sound technician/engineer
6. Music – a lot – separate list for this
7. Music programmer (could be me or Iris or both of us)
8. Sales/marketing/advertising person (could be you)
9. Administration person to back that person up
10. Phone-lines + receptionist to manage them

'See what I mean?' said Elliott. 'With the exception of the limited amount of free time the three of us have everything else on that list costs money.'

'Lot there alright' Squirrel frowned, re-reading the list.

'It's just not possible' said Elliott.

'Mmm' Squirrel was studying it hard.

'It's a nice thought, but you can see what kind of money would be involved.'

Squirrel looked up.

'I'm not scared by this' he shook the napkin.

'Squirrel' said Elliott 'there's at least twenty-five grand sitting on that napkin.'

'Don't tell Decco' Squirrel glanced at the counter. 'Hard enough ta get it off him in the first place.' He folded the napkin. 'You under-estimate me. And yourself.' He zipped up his leather jacket and looked at the cream bun. 'Y'gonna eat that?' he said. Elliott shook his head. Squirrel pushed the finger shaped bun deep in his mouth, biting at the centre point, then rolling it around like a cement mixer he spoke intermittently between chews and rolls. 'Leave this' he shook the napkin 'with me. You go and talk ta Iris; get her warmed up. I'm off for a few' he widened his eyes, looked at Elliott with a big creamy grin 'exploratory conversations.' Shoving the remaining half of the bun down his throat, he grabbed his helmet, stood up like a leather lamp-post and lopped out the door.

. . . .

'Warmed up!' Iris uncrossed skinny legs in tight red tartan trousers. She was wearing a furry black mohair jumper and shiny doc martins with bright yellow laces. 'What does he think I am? A new bike?' She stood up and began flicking through albums, loose sleeves falling back as she reached and stretched for the top shelf. They were in her living room, a soft fire glowing against the grey nothingness of the day outside. He'd called in to see her after meeting Squirrel. She had Mondays off on account of having to work Saturdays. There was no point going into college at this stage; he'd missed the morning lectures and there was only one in the afternoon. Fuck it. Any excuse. Before she'd got her cast off, when she was stuck at home, he'd taken to calling round at least twice during the week, and again at the weekend. Now she was working in Slave he either called in there or to the house on her day off. One way or the other he was seeing her about three or four times a week. Things he knew about her now. Music was her life. She listened to albums every day, all day on her days off. She went to gigs at least twice a week. She read Rolling Stone and NME. She had an encyclopedic knowledge of bands. She loved the Pistols, Clash and Joy Division. Stiff Little Fingers were the first punk band she had listened to and she found Suspect Device relaxing. That had really freaked Squirrel out.

'How the fuck could she find that shit relaxin? Rah merchants screamin' about bombs.'

'They're not Rah merchants. It's a great track.'

'You just want ta ride her. If she liked the music for the Magic Roundabout you'd say it was a great track.'

'She does.'

'What?'

'She does like the music for the Magic Roundabout, though if it came to a toss up I think she'd prefer the theme tune for Roobarb & Custard.'

'Jaysus! Is that the kinda *shyte* you talk about when you're together!'

That was exactly the kind of shyte they talked about and he loved it. Other things he knew as a result of the shyte. The Sound of Music was the first film she'd ever seen. Her DJ handle was Julie Andrews. She lived on Findus pancakes, cheese-burgers, cherry yoghurts and Tunnocks tea cakes. She was a shop-lifter. A good one. She drank bottles of Beck's with whisky chasers. Her left ear was pierced four times, the right one five. She loved animals nearly as much as she did music. She had two cats (Ian Curtis and Leonard Cohen), one dog (Jimmi Hendrix), a budgie (Michael Stipe) and an over-weight hamster (Alexei Sayle). She had small high breasts. She had a perfect bum. She had a brother who died. She didn't talk about it, but there were photos of a seven year old boy throughout the house, and every now and then, Jackie would make reference to Frank.

'What was on the list anyway?' Iris had her back to him as she reached and stretched for an album.

'What list?' Elliott stared at the tiny tartan bum.

'The list you made for Squirrel' she was on her tippy toes, fingernails scratching at plastic on a shelf above her.

'Em ... premises and equipment were the first two' he watched fingers prise then extract the album. Patti Smith. Horses.

'What else?' she knelt by the turntable, and ran a soft cloth over the vinyl.

'I think DJs were next' Elliott watched her put the needle down 'but there's no point looking for DJs unless you've somewhere to put them and something for them to play on.' Iris nodded, as Patti slipped into the room.

'And he really said he wasn't scared by it?'

'Yeah, but come on, he's living in a dreamworld. Squirrel's smart, he's resourceful, but; okay, premises, where's he going to find the money for premises?' Iris didn't answer. She poked the fire and threw another log on.

'What about his office?' she watched the flames take hold.

'Too small, I've been in it' Elliott replied 'and even if it was big enough the equipment would still cost a fortune. I know he has contacts but no matter how good they are he'd still need money.' Iris stood up, Mohican spikes punctuating a furry tartan silhouette as she leant against the sliding doors and stared out at the garden. The rain had set in, fat splodges collapsing in long tears down the glass. Outside, grey gave way to black, making the softly lit room feel all the warmer. Cosy. Safe. Except it was a false reality. Something, Elliott wasn't sure what, pricked his conscience. He really should start attending lectures soon. Anthony would be down on him like a ton of bricks if he failed his first year exams. He pushed the thought away and looked at Iris. Eyes glazed she was deep in thought. The door creaked and Ian Curtis padded his way across the room and sat by the fire.

'Would you do it?' she said. 'If Squirrel could get it together?'

'Dunno' said Elliott. 'Hadn't really thought about it. Why? Would you?'

'Yeah' she said, 'I would.' Elliott didn't know what to say. He hadn't thought she would even consider it.

'I thought you were going to try for a gig on one of the Pirates' he said 'you know, once you'd established yourself at the club. Isn't that what you wanted?' He felt her sit down on the sofa beside him.

'It was' she said 'but I like the idea of having our own station.' She leant forward and picked up her cigarettes off the coffee table in front of them. 'You know' boney knuckles jutting out as she cupped a small orange lighter 'all those Pirates' she lit, pulled, exhaled 'all those stations I called into looking for work last year; I didn't like them Elliott. I didn't like the people who ran them, I didn't like their jocks, I didn't like the music they played' she leant back against the couch and burnt a stray thread off the tartan trousers with her cigarette. 'Having a station of our own would mean we could do it on our own terms. But I'd only do it if you did' she glanced at him. 'Squirrel's great, but he knows nothing about music. Or radio. You on the other hand' she stopped and burnt off another stray thread. 'Well, you know enough' he could see a small curve, a hint of a smile beginning as she picked at the seams for another thread. Something warm glowed deep in his stomach. He felt like the Readybrek kid. *You know enough.* Ian Curtis purred in front of the fire. *You know enough.* That was a compliment. That was a definite compliment. A stupid grin slid across his face which he knew he should wipe off, but couldn't. The fire crackled and spat. Ian Curtis purred like a madman. 'So would you?' she gave him a sideways glance. 'If he managed to get the money together, would you do it?'

You can't. Not with college. She was looking right at him now, brown eyes scanning, searching, seeking. His chest felt tight. Could hearts swell? Did they actually physically swell?

'Well?' she smiled. Such light in her eyes. Such incredible light.

No. You have to say no. He could feel his heart, big and full, in the background Ian Curtis and the fire, purring and crackling in symphony. *No. The answer is no.* 'I … I guess I'd find it hard to say no' he heard himself say. Which was the truth. Sort of.

Funny he thought as the 31B rattled along the coast road, *Squirrel sends me to warm her up and I end up sitting by the fire agreeing we should do it.* He wondered if Squirrel had called her. Didn't matter. Agreeing it would be nice didn't mean it would happen. The odds of it happening were extremely low. He'd said that to her before he left. 'It's highly unlikely Squirrel's going to get that kind of cash together' were his exact words. And she'd given him this look.

'I know' she'd said. 'Be nice though, wouldn't it?'

'Be brilliant' he'd replied. Which was the closest he'd gotten to telling her just how much he liked her.

· · · ·

Eamo was in the kitchen when Squirrel got home to Donaghmede, which was a surprise and a concern. A surprise because his visits were rare, and a concern because they always created tension with Belinda. Eamo was the eldest of the three O'Rourke brothers, Tommy the middle child and Darren, Squirrel's Da, the baby. Eamo was in carpets, Tommy had an electronics shop, and Darren had the roller blinds business, which he'd set up after he married Belinda; the year Squirrel was born.

Old Ma O'Rourke made sure her three boys all went into trade early, pulling them out of school around fifteen or sixteen, though Eamo started earliest at the age of fourteen, as a carpet shop delivery assistant, followed by an apprentice as a fitter before quickly making it as a salesman which is where he really came into his own. Eamo had what it took. Eamo could sell sand to the Arabs. Eamo could sell his Granny. Eamo would sell his Granny.

He saw early on that the only way to really make money was to set up his own carpet shop. So with a wink here, a nod there and a whole lot of cash swept under a private carpet of his own, he siphoned off ten grand in backhanders, cash deals and, his personal favourite, magic carpets, where he took and fulfilled carpet orders, but didn't put them through the books, taking the stock, fitting the carpets and pocketing the cash which after two years gave him the deposit he needed to set up his own business.

'I don't want him near the kids' Belinda would say to Darren. 'Crooked as a fifty pence piece that fella. He's not welcome in this house.'

'Alright Eamo' Squirrel's leathers creaked as he sat down at the kitchen table opposite him. Belinda an' the rest were in the living room with the fire; no point disturbing them.

'Squirr' Eamo responded, moving his own long legs to accommodate Squirrels' at the small table.

'Make us a cup ah tea Da' said Squirrel to Darren who was leaning against the sink.

'Make it yerself' said Darren. The kitchen was tiny. Not much bigger than the center unit in Elliott's; he could drive the bike around Elliott's kitchen if he wanted to. Squirrel lit a cigarette. 'Outside with that' said Darren.

'Ah Da, it's freezin.'

'Outside I said. Me'n Eamo have things ta discuss. G'wan.'

'Fair enough' Squirrel went outside and sat on the back step, pulling the napkin from his pocket as he did so. A snort, a spit, then with the list in his right hand he lit a cigarette with his left, and began to read the list again, the cigarette tip burning a bright orange glow in the cold night air as he scanned Elliott's specifications. *Twenty five grand. An' the rest. Maybe we could start small. Test it here. Elliott and Iris are broadcastin' from their gaffs.* He stood up, went to the phone and called Elliott.

Elliott was lying on the couch not watching M★A★S★H. 'What kinda premises do we need?' said Squirrel.

'How do you mean?' Elliott muted the sound.

'For the station. What size? Where would they have to be?' Elliott yawned and sank deeper into the couch. It was late now and he was tired.

'Well' he rubbed his eyes 'somewhere soundproof for starters. You need to absorb sound for radio; you need to insulate the entire area. And you'd need security. BBR had their aerial hacked down last week.'

'By who?'

'Everyone in RTE reckons it was Rocket.'

'Sure Rocket are Number One.'

'Exactly' said Elliott. 'BBR threatened their listenership so they dealt with it. The Government send the Gardaí; the Pirates deal with it their own way.' Squirrel was silent for a moment.

"How big does the space hafta be?"

'Big enough to get the basic equipment in' said Elliott. 'Transmitter, sound desk, mics, headphones, space for records, ideally a place a broadcast assistant can sit and take calls or handle requests. Then of course we'll need a Green Room.'

'A what?'

'A Green Room' Elliott's smile was well hidden at the other end of the receiver. You know, the place we bring our celebrity guests and give them champagne and canapés before they go on-air.'

'Ya can fuck off witcher Green Room. D'ya talk ta Iris?'

'I did.'

'And?'

'And I think you'd already had a word with her.'

'Whatcha mean?'

'Because she actually likes the idea.'

'Deadly. That means you're in.'

'It does *not* mean …'

'Listen. She has you by the short and curlies. If Iris said *let's all jump off Liberty Hall for the craic* you'd be first up.' Elliott laughed.

'Well be that as it may, it's a long list, a lot of money and I know I sound like a broken record but it's highly unlikely ….'

'Elliott!!' Anthony's voice bellowed as the hall door opened.

'Shit' Elliott lowered his voice 'I have to go' he hung up.

'Elliott! Where are you?' his father's voice, closer now.

'In here' Elliott called, muting the TV. Flipping open a book he picked up a pre-filled notepad, which he hoped Anthony wouldn't look at because if he did he'd see that he'd been cataloguing his albums. He looked at the table. Too neat. He ripped a few pages off the back of the notepad, crumpled and scattered them, then pushed another book onto the carpet. Sticking a pen in his mouth he sat back and waited for the evening inspection.

Squirrel put down the phone and looked up to see Eamo leaning in the kitchen doorway watching him.

'Alright Squirr' a knowing smile curled around a tanned leathery face, blue eyes twinkling out under an oil slick of black teddy boy hair. 'Whatcha upta?' he gave him a conciliatory grin.

'Doin' a bit ah wheelin' and dealin? G'wan, ya can tell yer Uncle Eamo' he winked. Squirrel looked at him. It had been a while since he'd seen Eamo but he hadn't changed. At 6ft 4 he was exactly the same height as Squirrel, the kitchen doorway barely accommodating his boney frame as he leant across it. Funny that the shiftiest member of the family was the only one who could look him in the eye. Metaphorically speakin' ah course. 'Well?' Eamo was waiting.

'Sure if I told ya that, I'd hafta kill ya' Squirrel eyed up Eamo's shiny polyester suit, which like all the suits he owned, struggled with his height, the sleeves falling several inches short of gold covered hairy wrists, trouser legs swinging half mast above white cotton sports socks pushed into fake leather loafers.

'D'ya like it?' Eamo, a telegraph pole of grey fleck turning in the doorway so Squirrel could admire the tailoring. 'Smart Brothers. Fifty lids. Gotta dress the part Squirr. When ya gettin' outta those yokes?' he nodded at Squirrel's leathers.

'When I stop ridin' a bike' said Squirrel.

'Stopped ridin' bikes when I started ridin' young ones' Eamo looked wistful. 'Thought I was Evil Kenevil up until then' he lit a cigarette.

'You had a bike?'

'Had a few' said Eamo 'but on a winter's night, when ya can't go ta your house an ya can't go ta hers, a nice little carpet van comes in very handy, a fact you may hafta face shortly, if ya haven't already. Jays, where's yer Da?' he looked at his watch. Told him I was under pressure. I'll hafta go. Nice talkin' ta ya Squirr' he loped down the hall.

'Yeah, you too Eamo' Squirrel eyed his Uncle's bony frame.

'Tell yer Da he can drop the cash inta the shop whenever he has it. Ah would ya look who it is!' Eamo cried as the living room door opened and Belinda emerged with a tray in her hand. 'Me favourite sistr'n law.'

'Eamo' Belinda's voice was tight, barely acknowledging his presence as she pushed past him, not making eye contact.

. . . .

'Ah! There you are' Anthony stuck his head around the door then pushed it open, scanning the room, clocking Elliott's books and the notepad. 'Hard at it I see.' He was dressed in a charcoal suit, with a white wing tipped shirt, the kind he wore to court but usually changed out of in his office. It must have been a busy day.

'Tests next week' Elliott mumbled, sucking the pen.

'Mmm' Anthony rumbled, pushing his hands deep in his pockets. Elliott stared at the notebook, waiting for him to leave. 'Mmm' Anthony rumbled again, rocking back and forth on his feet as he watched the muted News, silent images flashing up on the TV screen.

What's he doing? Why is he standing there? Anthony sat down. Shit. Not good. Elliott could feel his father looking at him but he kept his eyes on the book. Silence for a minute or two. Glancing out of the corner of his eye Elliott saw Anthony press his hands together and make a small steeple with his fingers.

'You need to start thinking about summer' he said.

'Summer?'

'Summer' Anthony peered into the steeple as though a miniature congregation were waiting inside to find out what might happen in Summer. 'It's only a few months away and you need to decide where you want to practice.'

'Practice?' Elliott was confused. 'But I'm only in first year. I don't have to start practicing until I leave, until I qualify?'

'Have to … no you don't *have* to' Anthony's hands collapsed together then splayed apart 'but why on earth wouldn't you? What else would you do?' Elliott tried to collect his thoughts. 'Travel? That it? Some sort of, trip?' Anthony twisted the signet ring on his little finger, a sign Elliott knew meant he was getting impatient.

'No' Elliott looked at the TV screen. 'I just thought I'd spend the summer in RTE.'

'RTE?' Anthony laughed out loud 'what on *earth* would you do that for?' He shook his head and ran a hand across his face, stretching the skin, pushing his fingers against the stubble of the day. 'Dear oh dear. You know sometimes Elliott I don't understand you …'

Sometimes?

'… I really don't. You're bright, brighter than Max; I shouldn't say that and I don't recommend you do, but for someone with such a high intelligence you don't seem to grasp the natural flow of events' Anthony shook his head again and sighed, pinching the furrow of his brow. 'You know it disappoints me greatly that it appears necessary for me to map it out. RTE was a diversion Elliott; something to dig you out of the hole you were about to fall down after your mother left.' He flicked his wrist and checked the time. 'I suppose you could say in hindsight it was an introduction to a semi-professional environment of some sort, but this is where your career begins Elliott; today, not when you graduate.' He stood up, walked to the sideboard and picked up the whisky decanter. 'I don't think you realise just how privileged you are' the clink of glass as he poured. 'There are hundreds of Law students who would kill for the kind of doors I can open for you.' Elliott stared at the carpet. 'Now, I made a list today …'

Funny that, so did I.

'… and I think you'll be very interested to have a look at it.'

Why? Is yours for a radio station as well?

'Here' his father handed him a white folded piece of paper. Elliott flipped it open and saw three names, neatly typed. 'That Elliott is a list of the top three Legal Practices.

So?

'None of them take interns …'

Fuck.

'… but they'll do it for me. I'd
it's your choice.'

My choice? Don't make me lau

'And don't worry about R
heading for the door.

'Roger?' Elliott scramble

'Ingram. I'll let him kn

'No! No!' Elliott strug

'Right' Anthony frov
the end of March as a c

Squirrel walk
parked the bike o
dry off there for a wh
of ha

'March?' Elliott couldn't hide his dismay 'but that's less than a month ...'

'Elliott!!' Anthony slammed his hand against the living room door. 'Your exams are coming up. If I were you I'd have left already. March, and I want a name off that list by the end of the week. Christ Almighty. How much hand holding do I have to do? You should be down on your knees thanking me for my help, not fretting about your last month in the playground.' He shook his head. 'I don't understand you Elliott. What is *wrong* with you? For such an intelligent person you can be so incredibly stupid. You have huge potential, more ability than anyone I know but you fail to grasp the simplest ... Friday' Anthony knocked back the last of his whisky. 'I'm going to the Club. I'll see you tomorrow.'

Nothing for a while. Everything kind of stopped. Elliott wasn't sure how long he sat there but when he looked up Dallas was on TV. JR and Cliff in a bar. He turned up the sound.

'You're a loser Barnes' said JR, swilling the ice in his bourbon 'just like your Daddy.'

. . . .

Capel Street, Dublin. A landing strip for traders, bargain hunters, publicans, perverts, stray journalists, drunk poets and street children. Fast dealing, slow moving, a steady line of big trucks and small vans squeezing between the cars parked either side of the street. A built up corridor that the sun, when it shone, ran through early in the morning and late in the afternoon, warming the wall to wall red bricked terraced buildings, blinding the distant view of the Liffey. About half way down sandwiched in between a second hand guitar shop and an army supplies store was The Persian Prince, Eamo's castle, where after twenty years of graft, he was most definitely the King.

ed in to the shop and shook off the rain. He'd the path outside under the canopy; it could

'Lookin' for Eamo' he said to the blonde girl behind the desk. She was very pretty. Big blue eyes and a nice smile.

'He's widda custamahhh' she said, her voice deeper than a family grave. 'D'ya wanna way-forrim?'

'Eh …' Squirrel started but was interrupted by a loud

'Squirr!!' and there like Showaddywaddy's Manager in a black tipped powder blue suit was Eamo, arms open, smile wide, charging up the centre aisle. 'What's this?' he grabbed Squirrel's hand 'twice in one week? D'yer Da send ya in?'

'Nah' Squirrel's eyes travelled down at the long brightly lit room with rows of carpet rolls, rugs and stacks of swatch books. 'Desperate day, whah?' he nodded at the traffic backed up in the rainy street outside.

'Lousy' said Eamo. 'Dead so it is. Midaswell shut up shop an' go home. Ta Lorraine' he took a package from the gravedigger and tore it open. 'Fucks sakes' he frowned, peering in at the contents. 'Here. Lorraine' he passed the package back across 'tell him ta fuck off; come back when he's serious. Whatcha say Squirr? Yer Da sent ya did he?'

'Nah' Squirrel was still staring at the long brightly lit aisles. 'Just in the neighbourhood Eamo. Just cruisin' ya know.'

'Cruisin' Eamo's eyes flicked to the traffic and the rain outside.

'Lotta carpet' Squirrel nodded at the showroom.

'Lot more outside said Eamo.

'Yeah?'

'C'mere' Eamo turned on his heel and walked towards a metal door at the end of the shop. 'Mind' he pointed to a raised step built into the door frame as he pulled it open. Both men bent their heads and lifted their feet, long frames scrunching like accordions to fit through the small space.

Straightening up as they stepped inside Squirrel's eyes widened. They were standing in a huge warehouse, about sixty thousand square feet, which had hundreds of long industrial sized carpet rolls, stacked high and wide. The building climbed at least fifty feet, an old structure with white stone walls, exposed metal girders, and right at the top, directly over the mountain of carpets, enormous skylights cutting large squares of light across the center of the building. 'This is where it all happens Squirr' Eamo shouted as a forklift drove past. 'Stuff in the front is just for show' he explained as and they walked around the giant mountain of carpet rolls. 'Once they pick what they want, the order gets sorted at this end.' As they rounded the corner Squirrel saw two huge double doors pulled back with three big Persian Prince transit vans reversed in to fill the space. 'Load on and take off here' said Eamo 'an' that' he pointed to a small hut in the corner 'is where the shops get sorted.' Men scurried about, moving carpets, loading vans, whistling, shouting to each other, directing forklifts. Squirrel stared at the hive of activity.

'You own this?'

'Lock stock' Eamo saluted a rough heavyset man dressed in black standing at the load-in entrance. 'Reggie' he said to Squirrel. 'Security.' They walked around the carpet mountain, brown woven undersides tightly rolled in huge drums covered in shiny clear plastic.

'They're inside out' Squirrel stared at the identical brown rolls.

'Protects the carpet' said Eamo.

'How can ya tell one from another?'

'How does a Shepherd know his sheep? Like me children Squirr' Eamo patted a drum. 'I know every yard, every inch, every thread ah carpet in this place. An' they know that' he pointed to the men working. 'Which is why none ah them'll ever think about robbin' from me.' There were a series of long narrow aisles in between where one stack of rolls ended and the next began. They walked down between them, Squirrel looking up at the skylights above the towering rolls of carpet either side. The deeper they went into the carpet stack, the more quiet it became, then the warehouse noise faded and all they could hear was the sound of their own footsteps against the concrete floor. They took a left turn, then a right, tunnelling their way through, the thick heavy smell of freshly glued new wool permeating the air. Eamo took a deep breath. 'Smell that?' he said to Squirrel. 'Smell ah money that is.'

'Could be' Squirrel looked up at the carpet drums either side of them.

'No could about it.'

'Very quiet' Squirrel nodded up at the drums.

'That's the carpet' said Eamo. 'See that shop outside? That can be full ah people an' ya'll hardly hear them. Carpet just soaks up the sound.

'Insulation' said Squirrel.

'Whatcha mean insulation?' said Eamo

'They carpet the doors in RTE' said Squirrel.

'What they do that for?'

'Same reason you might' Squirrel stared up at the drums.

'The fuck would I be doin' carpetin' doors?'

'Eamo' Squirrel grinned, planting a hand each side of his Uncle's shiny blue suited shoulders. 'Eamo me aul' son, how would you like ta have your very own radio station?'

The merits of locating the station in a carpet shop were debated back and forth a few times, but they all agreed it was a good option. First off, no-one would think of looking for a radio station there. The warehouse was completely secure and even if the police arrived it would be difficult to raid without a series of conversations which would allow time to get the transmitter out. Furthermore, Eamo would give them the space for free. Not only that, he would help build the studio and soundproof it. Naturally, there were terms. Eamo wanted a share in the station, and a percentage of the advertising. He also, and this was the bit Squirrel felt the other two would resist most, wanted his own show.

'What kind of show?' said Iris. 'What sort of music?'

'Dunno' said Squirrel. 'We'll hafta ask him.'

'We'll have to tell him' said Iris. 'We decide what gets played. I'm not doing this if we end up playing old man music.'

'We'll give him a Sunday show' said Elliott.

'Graveyard slot'd be better' said Iris. 'Four am when no-one's listening.'

'Cross that bridge when we come to it' said Squirrel. 'I'm

more worried about what percentage he wants. An' you two need ta meet him. I'll set it up.'

Iris thought about it on the bus going home after work that night. If the station was a success and they made money she'd be able to afford to move out and get a flat of her own. Somewhere the walls didn't move, where carpets weren't pulled up or the heating system taken out. Turning the key in the hall door she noticed a sign stuck to the glass, written in Arthur's neat hand-writing. 'Careful – hall floorboards are up.' Irritated, she pushed the door open and surveyed the hall from the step. The floorboards had been ripped out; only the supporting beams remained, four of them, like long thin rulers on their sides, lying even spaced over the darkness below. A light beamed up from the foundations.

'That you?' Arthur called. 'Mind how you go. I'm re-wiring.'

Iris didn't reply. She made her way down the beams, concentrating as she went, balancing one dock martin carefully in front of the other. Reaching the kitchen door she stepped inside.

'Fucks sakes' she muttered as she walked to the counter. Michael Stipe twittered and chirped. She put her face down to the cage. 'You wouldn't like it if someone took out your floorboards would you Stipey?' she opened the door and extended her finger to make a little step for him. 'No, you wouldn't' she said as Michael Stipe hopped on, small claws scratching her skin, curling tight around her finger. He chirped, blue green feathers on his neck ruffling as he twisted his head to look at her. She stared at him for several moments as he shifted his small weight up and down her finger, the feel of his tiny claws calming her. She let him back on his perch and shut the door. Opening the fridge she took out some brown bread, cheddar cheese and a tomato and began preparing the basis of a toasted sandwich. She started thinking about the station and a name for her show. Julie Andrews. Just stick with the handle she already had. Julie Andrews and The Sound of Music. Perfect name for a Punk show. Buttering the bread she turned to the cooker to put her sandwich under the grill, then stopped. There was an empty space where the cooker used to be; in its place a grey patch of wall with a wire sticking out of the centre, covered in dust and cobwebs. She stood there with the sandwich in her hand for a moment or two, staring in confusion at the empty grey space; then her eyes flicked as the penny dropped. She pulled opened the kitchen door.

'Where's the cooker?' No answer. 'Where' she repeated to the foundations below 'is the cooker?' A small scuffle from beneath the beams.

'Ahh, slight problem there' Arthur shone the flash-light up onto her face. 'It's in the living room. I took it out to have a look at it. I'm going to see can I fit a microwave into the top section. Would you like me to …'

Iris slammed the kitchen door, threw her sandwich in the bin and kicked a kitchen press several times in an angry rage, frightening Michael Stipe who twittered and chirped as he flew around the cage. Fuming, she pulled on her jacket, made her way back across the beams and stormed out the drive-way. She tore up the road, not really knowing where she was going when she bumped smack into Elliott.

'Hey' he said. 'I was just coming to … what's wrong?' She didn't answer him; just looked out over his shoulder, anger burning in her eyes.

'Stupid house' she muttered to the air, eyes shining.

'Come on' Elliott said. 'Let's go to the pub. Have you eaten?' She shook her head. 'We'll get fish and chips ' he said.

One hour, two singles of fish and chips later, they were on their third drink in Connelly's and although Iris wasn't angry any more she seemed to have sunk into some kind of depression.

'It's a disease you know' Elliott tried to lift her out of it.

'What?' Iris was picking at the label on her bottle of Beck's.

'DIY' Elliott watched her nails curl in, flick, then tear a strip away. 'It's like an addiction. People think they can control it. A spliff here, a pint there, what's the harm? Before you know it they're banging up. Bet the DIY started nice and simple didn't it?' Iris nodded but didn't speak. A sharp tearing sound as the rest of the label came away. 'A few loose plugs here, a new shelf there' Elliott rambled as she turned the bottle and scratched at the label on the back 'next thing he's ripping up floor-boards, tearing down walls and trying to install a microwave in a cooker. He can't help it' Elliott watched thin shards of paper float down as sections of the back label joined its brothers from the front on the table below. 'It's an addiction Iris. Why else would somebody rip the shit out of their house twenty-four-seven?'

. . . .

Arthur. He started the first extension the week after Frank's funeral. Jackie had agreed it was a good idea. They didn't really need the extra space, not now, but it would take his mind off things. She went away the weekend he began digging the foundations, to attend a beginners course in astrology.

'New foundations for us both' she said with as bright a smile as she could manage. Iris who was four at the time sat on the back step with Ermintrude and watched her father working. Standing with his back to her he swung a pick axe at the ground, heavy breaths of exertion escaping each time he drove it down onto the cold grey concrete. At first he only managed to make white scratches along the grey, then a small crack appeared, short and thin at first, but it grew with each new blow, snaking ahead, forking behind, splintering to the sides.

'Daddy, look!' Iris cried, pointing as small cracks ran deep, little cracks held hands, and big cracks streaked ahead. Arthur swung harder, faster, omitting heavy hollow rasps as each blow struck. 'Daddy!' a long crack had spidered to the step where she was sitting. Pulling her knees to her chest she held Ermintrude tight. This new crack looked like a skeleton's hand. It might reach up and pull her down inside the ground. The ground was for dead people. That's where Frank went. 'We're not dead' she said to the crack. Standing up she pressed herself against the door. Daddy wouldn't see if the crack pulled her and Ermintrude in because he had his back to her. The pick rose again and Arthur made a sound like an animal in pain, a soft low moan as he swung down with all his might, driving shards of concrete up from the point he'd struck. He moaned again and the pick went high. Was Daddy crying? A sound in the wind as the pick swung again. She couldn't see Daddy's face. He kept his back turned as he swung harder, faster, soft sobs escaping each time he struck. 'Daddy?' Up went the pick. Down went the pick. Out ran the cracks. 'Daddy?' Keeping her eye on the crack by the step she backed through the door and went inside to watch the Magic Roundabout.

· · · ·

'... Crack – A narrow opening between two parts of something which has been split open or broken. A sharp blow. An attempt to do something. Give way under pressure or strain. Hit hard. Suffer an emotional breakdown under pressure. Also craic – chiefly Irish – enjoyable entertainment; a good time! You're tuned to BBR, that was the Breakfast Show's word for the day, and this, is China Crisis ...'

'I think we should have a crack at it' Eamo turned the sound down on the radio in his office. They'd just toured the warehouse and he'd shown them where the Station could be. At the very back, hidden by the towering stack of carpet rolls, was an old wooden portacabin. Raised high on a platform, it overlooked the floorspace below. 'Boss man used ta work up here' Eamo was out of breath as he tried to kick the stiff door open. 'Come on ya bastard' he kicked again. 'Before I owned it, the warehouse was a fruit factory' he grunted as he pushed. 'Boss fella sat up here and kept his eye on what was goin' on down below' putting his shoulder to the door he threw the weight of his body at it and it burst open. Dust tickled their throats and a stale musty smell hung in the air as they stepped inside.

'It's a good size' said Elliott as they walked from the outer office into the room next door. Both rooms were of a similar shape though the far one was slightly bigger. Large windows ran the length of each.

'See this?' Eamo tapped the dividing wall between the two rooms. Elliott nodded. 'Cut a window in this' he tapped the wall again 'thick glass, double glazin, professional like. Then we'll get yer Uncle Tommy ta mic it up' he said to Squirrel 'so yis can talk ta each other through the glass.'

'What about sound-proofing?' Elliott glanced at the portacabin's thin walls. Eamo walked over to the portacabin window.

'See the fifth one in?' he pointed down at the top row of identical brown drums. 'Lambswool. High end. Best ya can buy.' His eyes glazed for a moment, and a muscle flickered on his face as he stared down at the drum.

'What's wrong with it?' said Squirrel.

'Nothin' wrong with the wool' Eamo lit a cigarette and turned away from the window. 'Wool's perfect. Colour's the problem.'

'What colour is it?' asked Iris.

'Purple' said Eamo.

'Purple's alright' said Squirrel.

'Yeah, well this purple has orange whirley-gigs swirlin' all over it' said Eamo. 'Person who designed it musta been on LSD. Thought it'd be good in a niteclub. Tried every club in Dublin. Couldn't shift it for love nor money.' He turned and walked into the centre of the room. 'So here's what I reckon. I'm gonna take that roll' he pointed at the window 'I'm gonna take that, an' fit it' he gestured around the portacabin 'top ta bottom, floor ta ceilin. Inside and out.'

'Why outside?' said Squirrel.

'No point sealin' it up once it's open' said Eamo. 'Not gonna ta shift it inanyways.'

'How long will it take?' said Squirrel

'Two weeks for the carpet an' the glass partition' said Eamo. 'Lads'll lash it up.'

'Can you trust them?' said Elliott. 'This needs to be kept quiet.'

'That lot?' Eamo nodded at the warehouse. 'They won't give

a fuck. Pocket the overtime an' fuck off ta the pub, that's what they'll do.' He ran a hand down the wall. 'Do a nice double underlay; tell ya what it'll be better than any ah those other stations by the time we're finished.'

This could happen said a voice in Elliott's head as they made their way back down the wooden stairs in single file, Eamo leading the way. *This could actually happen.*

Something warm glowed inside again, like it had that day in Iris' house. *You haven't got the equipment. Squirrel'll get it. What about college? What about work experience? You have to pick a name from the list.*

'Elliott!!' someone was shouting his name. He blinked. Iris, Eamo and Squirrel were at the bottom of the stairs looking up at him.

'What are you doing?' Iris shouted.

'Just looking at the warehouse' he shouted back 'just getting a bit of an overview' he hurried down to join them.

'Fifty percent' said Eamo. They were in his office, a dark messy space to the left of the showroom, privacy provided via cheap and badly dented red venetian blinds, which Eamo had pulled a hole in earlier to bang on the window and shout at Lorraine for four coffees, a request aided by his curling his index and thumb into a 'C' and holding up four fingers.

'Twenty' said Squirrel. Eamo laughed.

'Squirr, I know you're family, but I'm the one puttin' up the dough. I'm the one with the exposure.'

'What exposure? Carpet ya can't shift an' a portacabin ya don't use?'

'I'll have ta pay the lads ta fit it out. That's two week's overtime.'

'Still not worth fifty percent' said Squirrel. 'We're the ones who'd be across it day ta day. You'll just be shovin' a bit of cash in upfront, then sittin' back and collectin' the cheques.'

'Forty' said Eamo.

'Twenty' said Squirrel. Eamo leant across the desk.

'You're gonna hafta learn how ta negotiate sunshine. What's ta stop me settin' up me own station?'

'Nothing' Elliott was surprised to hear himself interject 'but it'd be a disaster. You don't know anything about radio Eamo. You know as much about radio as we do about carpets. You don't know how it works, what music people want to hear or how to make programming that will appeal to advertisers without alienating listeners, and without those Eamo there is no station and most importantly from your point of view there's no money.' There was a small silence, then Iris spoke.

'We know our music' she said. 'We know what people want to listen to, what they'll pay to listen to, what they'll lock their dial to and won't switch off.'

'See that?' Squirrel pointed at the two of them like a proud parent at sports day. 'Ya can't put a price on that Eamo!' Eamo didn't answer. He stared over the filing cabinets at the street outside.

'Thirty. An' fifty percent of the advertisin.'

'Twenty-five an' twenty-five' said Squirrel 'an' let's not forget The Persian Prince ads are free, which brings the value up.' Eamo laughed.

'Tell ya what Squirr. Ya didn't lick it off a stone. Right' he stuck out his hand. 'Twenty five and twenty five.' Elliott nodded. Iris smiled. Squirrel grabbed the outstretched hand.

'Looks like we've got ourselves a station' said Eamo.

'We've got an agreement' said Elliott. 'What about the equipment?'

'Get Tommy' said Eamo. 'He runs an electronics shop for Jaysus sake.

Tommy'll sort that no problem.'

'An aerial?' Tommy had been summoned from his shop down the road and was reading Elliott's napkin, which was starting to look grubby by now. 'What kinda aerial?'

'Something big enough to broadcast across the city' said Elliott.

'Hafta build that' said Tommy. 'Wouldn't be easy.'

'Ya'll lash it up' said Eamo.

'Have you ever built a fuckin' aerial?'

'What about the transmitter?' said Elliott. 'Can you build that?' Tommy sighed and ran a hand over his balding head.

'Yeah I can do that, but it'd take time an' ideally I'd need some kinda technical spec.'

'I'm in RTE tomorrow' said Elliott. 'I'll see if I can find something in there.'

'What about the rest of it?' said Eamo.

'Sound desk, the mixer, the mics, all that stuff I can get' said Tommy 'but yer lookin' at the guts ah ten grand, an' that's a trade price; there'd be no margin on that for me.'

'Ya've got ta be Jaysus kiddin' me' said Eamo. 'Ten grand' he grabbed the napkin and looked at it again.

'Professional sound desks aren't cheap' said Tommy. 'For proper gear that's what yer lookin' at.'

'Could ya not stroke some?'

'Steal?'

'Liberate.'

'Steal. Ya want me ta steal gear. Do I look like a fuckin' eejit?'

'Ah come on Tommy. Where's the Pirate in ya?'

'I'm no Pirate' said Tommy. 'I might do you a favour and try ta build ya an aerial or a transmitter, but don't ask me ta steal gear. I won't do it.' Four sets of eyes turned towards Eamo.

'I don't know what yis are lookin' at me for' he said. 'I've done me bit; gev yis a bleedin' premises. Point one on the list, Oh-ficially ticked by A-mondo. I'm not a bleedin' cash register. Here' he threw the napkin back across the desk. 'Yis are gonna hafta sort the rest yerselves. I've a rake ah deliveries and stock splits in the next hour, an' the lads'll be tryin' ta skive off at lunchtime ta watch the qualifier, so if yis don't mind pissin' off now, that'd be great. Call me when ya get the gear.'

'Fuck!' Squirrel looked despondent as the three of them stood on the path outside. He leant against the wall and lit a cigarette.

'Fuck it anyway!' an angry look flashed across his face and it was the first time Elliott had seen him genuinely frustrated.

'What'll we do?' said Iris.

'Dunno' Squirrel stared down Capel Street as though the answer might happen to be strolling up the road. 'Bankin' on Tommy for the gear' he scowled. 'Gear was the one thing I wasn't worried about; shop's full ah shyte he doesn't use. I thought it might be a couple ah hundred, but ten grand?' he kicked a piece of gum stuck to the pavement. 'Ten grand' a series of hard kicks as he worked the gum free 'where the fuck' a final kick sent the gum flying 'are we gonna get ten grand?'

'Maybe we can find someone else who can get us the equipment' said Elliott.

'No-one can get gear cheaper than Tommy' said Squirrel. 'No-one.'

'So we're fucked?' said Iris.

'Looks like it' Squirrel sucked down hard on his cigarette, then he flicked it with a force, swung a leg over his bike and stuck in the keys.

'Where are you going?' Elliott suddenly felt panicked. This station was his last shot at staying in radio once his time in RTE ended.

'Head's wrecked.'

'But you're not giving up?'

'No, but we need ta start thinkin' fast about how we're goin' ta get the guts ah ten grand together because trust me, that sort of equipment isn't gonna just land in our laps like a big present from Santy.'

'I believe you're leaving us' Tom popped his head over the partition.

'How did you …' Elliott started.

'Your father rang Roger. I'm sorry to hear that Elliott; I thought we might have persuaded you to stay.'

'I was going to tell you myself' Elliott felt his cheeks redden.

'Don't worry about it' said Tom 'though we'll be sorry

to see you go, and so soon as well; Roger said you're off tomorrow.'

'Tomorrow?'

'That's what he said' Tom looked concerned. 'You did know about this?'

'Sure' Elliott lied 'sure … I … I just hadn't realised tomorrow was Friday.'

Fuck. We agreed the end of the month. Why did he have to call Roger?

'The thing is' Tom was saying 'I had you slotted for pre-production on the Breakfast Show, but now that you're leaving, there's not much point.'

'No.' *That's the end of it then.*

'So I was wondering if you'd give Bobby a hand in Studio One?'

'Sure' Elliott pulled himself together. 'What does he need?'

'Well' Tom looked embarrassed 'it's kind of shitty work, but both his tech guys are out sick and he's gutting Studio One.'

'Oh yeah' said Elliott 'there's a whole new Studio going in, isn't there?'

'Mmm' said Tom. 'Don't know why; won't make a blind bit of difference to the programming. Anyway, we need to get it shifted, and I'm sorry, I know it's not really what you …'

'It's fine' said Elliott. 'I'll go straight down to him.'

High pitched drilling and loud banging interrupted the usually quiet corridors as Elliott made his way downstairs. Turning the corner he followed a trail of wires, boxes and furniture leading the way to Studio One; leather sofas stacked on top of each other, plants, tape racks, chairs, decks, cart machines and, looking strangely out of place on the ground, the Sound Desk and Mixer. Elliott stared at them for a few minutes, then his eyes widened as he stepped in through the open door. Studio One was gone. Everything had been ripped out; only the carpets and walls remained, wires and light sockets hanging down from the ceiling as workmen on ladders drilled and banged. Bobby stood in the centre, directing chaos.

'Okay Frank, you can start on that wall now, and you, yeah you, take all the lights out; we'll re-grid once the new layout's in place … Elliott … just the man' stepping over cables and around boxes Bobby crossed the room. 'I hope you're here to help.' Elliott smiled.

'Tom sent me. What do you need?'

'See this?' Bobby pushed Elliott back out through the doorway. 'I need all this' he gestured at the equipment filling the corridor 'round the back to the storage units by the TV Building. The new equipment and furniture is arriving at three o'clock.' Elliott eyed the equipment filling the corridor.

'Okay …'

'Is there anyone upstairs who can give you a hand?' said Bobby. 'You're not going to lift the desk and the sofas on your own, and I need to keep going. Typical Roger, you know? Sits on this for two months while he decides what colour scheme he wants, then he expects me to do it all in half a day.'

'Bobby!' a shout from the far end of the corridor.

'Here we go' Bobby muttered as Roger strode towards them.

'When's this crap being moved out of here?' Roger came to a halt.

'Elliott' said Bobby 'is just going to sort that now.'

'Right' said Roger. 'Well see it's done fast.' He looked at Elliott. 'Have you anyone who can help you?'

'Everyone upstairs is busy' Elliott thought on his feet 'but I have a friend who has a van. If he's not busy I could get him to help me carry it up to Reception and then we could drive it round to storage.'

'Good thinking' said Roger. 'I suppose he'll want money for that?'

'He might do it as a favour if he's not busy.'

'Right. Well be discreet' said Roger 'the last thing I need is hassle from the Union about official employees, even though every official employee appears to be sick today. Remarkable how sick days coincide with World Cup qualifiers. Get it done as quick as you can. I'll be back when the equipment arrives' he called to Bobby as he strode back down the corridor.

A small door opened in the back of Elliott's mind as he made his way up the stairs to ring Squirrel and a thought looked in. He pushed the thought away and shut the door. It opened again. He closed it. It opened. The thought walked into the centre of his mind and sat on a chair. *No. Forget it.* The thought sat there. *I couldn't.* The thought said nothing. It just sat there. *No. Absolutely not.* He made his way into the main office area, moving quickly, searching, seeking, collecting his thoughts above the sound of loud chatter, phones ringing, music playing, girls laughing, finally, an empty office. He shut the door and lit a cigarette. His heart started to hammer. *I can't do this.*

'Sharon? Is Squirrel there?'

'He's on a call Elliott.'

Bobby said it's a waste of perfectly good equipment.

'Would you mind interrupting him and telling him it's urgent?'

It's just going to lie in storage forever.

'Putting you through now Elliott.'

It's stealing. You can't do this.

What's so bleedin' urgent?' said Squirrel.

Two hours later they loaded the last of it into the van. Squirrel hadn't been able to stop smiling as they worked.

'Daylight bleedin' robbery' he'd kept chuckling in delight.

'Stop talking, please stop talking' Elliott's heart was pounding, pulsing. They'd taken everything. Even the DJ chair. And Bobby had thanked them.

'We need people like you' he'd said 'not afraid to roll up their sleeves. It's a real shame you're leaving.' Wham! Wham! Wham! Elliott's heart slamming hard.

I'm going to have a heart attack, I am; I can't breathe, oh Christ.

'Elliott!' someone shouted and he saw Roger emerge from the Radio Centre.

'Shit! Shit! It's Roger!!' Elliott dropped to his knees behind the van.

'Jaysus!' Squirrel hissed. 'Get up! Get fuckin' up!' he yanked

Elliott by the collar. 'We're not out ah the premises; far as he's concerned we're only gettin' ready ta go round the back. Relax will ya!'

'Is this your friend Elliott?' Roger panted as he reached the van.

'Yes' Elliott's cheeks were burning 'we're just going round the back now.'

'I can see that' Roger snapped. 'Tell me' he nodded at the Lightening Transport signage on Squirrel's van 'do you think you can get rid of those for me' he nodded at the two leather sofas which were sitting on the grass. Take them to the dump?'

'Cost ya' said Squirrel.

'How much?' said Roger.

'Fifty quid.'

'Done' Roger took out his wallet, peeled off a bill and handed it to Squirrel. 'Good work lads' he patted the side of the van and headed back into the Radio Building.

'I can't believe you charged him' Elliott was in shock.

'Be pretty fuckin' suspicious if I didn't' said Squirrel. 'You need ta calm down. He picked up the radio. 'Squirrel ta base; over.'

'Base; over' Sharon came back.

'Shar, I need a van; call Ronnie, his is the biggest. Tell him I need him out ta RTE quick as he can. There's two sofas on the grass outside the radio building. Tell him ta load them up and get them down ta Eamo's place.

'Roger that' said Sharon. Squirrel looked at Elliott.

'Roger that is right' he grinned. 'C'mon' he threw the fifty quid at him. 'Reckon we've earned ourselves a drink.'

The guilt stayed with Elliott for days. A constant companion, it sat on his shoulder, tugged at his conscience, gnawed on his mind. He couldn't eat, couldn't sleep; he even forgot about Iris for a while. He started behaving strangely; went to lectures, studied for a test and half way through the week he telephoned Max.

'Max?'

'Elliott?'

'Max what do you think about the Commandments?'

'What Commandments?'

'The Ten Commandments.'

'Is this about Mum? Because if it is …'

'Max, it's not about Mum!'

'So you're not going to start going on about adultery?'

'No. I just want to know what you think about the Commandments.'

'What do you mean what do I think about them?'

'Would you break one? Have you ever broken a Commandment Max?'

'Jesus Elliott, I don't know. I don't think so.'

'Okay, well if you *were* going to break one, what would be the worst?'

'I don't know' Max considered. 'Thou shalt not kill I suppose. Can't get much worse than that.' A wave of relief. Of course. Killing was so much worse than stealing. Stealing wasn't that bad. He knew he'd been right to ring Max.

'And I'd never steal.'

'What? Sorry Max, what did you say?'

'I said I'd never kill and I'd never steal.'

'Is stealing bad?'

'Stealing is awful' said Max. 'I mean I'm not perfect; in fact now that you've got me thinking about it I've probably broken a lot of them; I definitely covet, I covet all the time; girls mainly. I take the Lord's name in vain on a regular basis …'

'But you wouldn't kill or steal?'

'No.'

'Right. Thanks Max.'

'Why are you asking me all this?'

'Oh nothing. Just something for college. Thanks Max.'

With guilt came fear. He lived on his nerves, couldn't eat, couldn't sleep and silence was loud again. Loud like the week his mother left. Loud where there's nothing to be said because the silence says it all. A week of guilt and fear, and fear and guilt, and nothing Squirrel or Iris could say would pull him out of it. Then gradually it began to subside. He started to walk easier in his skin, the nagging ceased, and despite himself he began to feel excited about the prospect of building a studio, creating their own station. A new sound. A new voice. His mind became rich, fertile; programming ideas pushed up like young shoots, he forgot about college and one day he woke up thinking about point three on the list. DJs.

'Hot Press' said Iris. They'd called in to see her at work. She was unpacking a new range of rubber suits.

'These are like those yokes divin' fellas wear' Squirrel pulled one of the shiny black moulds out of the cardboard box on the ground.

'Wetsuits' Iris was two tone today, dressed in black and white leopardskin jeans and a tight long sleeved black top that grazed her knuckles.

'Yeah, wetsuits. Who the fuck buys these?' Squirrel held the suit against himself. 'Can't be easy ta get inta.'

'They're not' Iris removed another suit from its plastic cover 'I have to zip them in.'

'C'mere, what are these yokes for?' Squirrel had pulled on a black rubber mask down over his face.

'Those' Iris grinned, as she reached behind and zipped the mask tight on his head 'are big sellers.'

'Jaysus' Squirrel's voice was muffled behind it. 'Could rob banks wearin' these.'

'Not all of them' said Iris. 'Some of them cover the whole face; eyes, nose, the lot.'

'How do they breathe?' said Elliott.

'Dunno' Iris shrugged. 'Beats me.'

The door opened and a tiny man walked in to the shop. Expensively dressed in a full length black winter coat, he had a clean, pink, almost scrubbed looking face, circular silver rimmed glasses and short white hair, neatly trimmed. He paused briefly to look up at Squirrel in the mask before giving Iris a polite nod.

'Good afternoon Irith' he had a high pitched girlish lisp.

'Hi' Iris gave him a warm smile. 'Go on in' she nodded at the changing rooms. 'I'll be with you in a minute.'

'Thuper' the man disappeared into a changing room.

'Who'th yer man?' Squirrel's voice was still muffled behind the mask.

'Sshh' Iris whispered. 'He's here for the new stock. 'Go' she whispered, unzipping Squirrel's mask. 'He hates people in the shop. I'm on lunch after this. I'll meet you in the pub.'

'I think she actually likes working there' Elliott reflected to Squirrel as they sipped their pints in the pub across the road. *'Good afternoon Irith'* he imitated the customer's high girlish lisp. 'Ow!' his ear stung as someone gave it a sharp flick.

'That my drink?' Iris sat down. Elliott nodded, rubbing his ear.

'Cheers' she picked up the bottle, long nails immediately flicking at the front label.

'Who's that aul' fella?' said Squirrel.

'Thuperman?' Iris tore off the label in two short, swift strips. 'Hygiene freak' she turned the bottle round. 'Buys a new suit every week' her nails curled around the back label; 'Won't touch anything in the shop' a ripping sound as she tore it off.

'Very well spoken' said Elliott.

'Refined' Iris dug her thumb nail into the silver foil around the base of the neck.

'Exactly' said Elliott. 'Doesn't look like the kind of person you'd see in a sex shop.'

'Why?' said Iris. 'What should our customers look like? Dirty old men in macs?' she ran her nail the length of the foil, forcing it off.

'Suppose it is a bit of a cliché' Elliott lit a cigarette. 'He's just not the sort of person I'd expect to find in there.'

'Tell ya where ya won't find him' said Squirrel. 'DJ'in' on our station.'

'I told you already. Put an ad in Hot Press' said Iris. 'Ask for demo tapes.'

'Where'll we get them ta send them?' said Squirrel, signalling to Eamo who had arrived and was making his way across the bar.

'Brendan!' Eamo shouted to the barman as he reached where they were sitting. 'Pint ah plain an' a doorstop; hang on' he pointed at the three of them 'd'yis want a sandwich?'

'Yeah, if you're buyin' said Squirrel.

'Make it four!' Eamo shouted. 'Four doorstops! What's the story?' he rubbed his hands together. 'How's our station? Tommy's up on the roof cursin' yis from a height. That's one big fucker of an aerial he's buildin; we're going ta hafta hold it with a moxy load ah cable an' hope ta fuck no-one sees it.'

'They won't' said Squirrel. 'C'mere Eamo, where can we get DJs ta send demo tapes? We need a place they can send their tapes an' do interviews.'

'Do it in here' said Eamo. 'Brendan won't mind.'

'Can't be a pub' said Elliott. 'We might have DJs who are under eighteen. We need a café or some sort of public place in the centre of town but away from here. We don't want people anywhere near the station until they're definitely on-board and we know we can trust them. It's too risky in terms of raids or other Pirates.' Eamo picked up a beer mat. He tapped it against the small table for a moment or two.

'Tony might do it' he said as Brendan placed a pint of Guinness and the first of the Doorstop sandwiches on the table.

'Who's Tony?' said Squirrel.

'Mate ah mine' Eamo bit into the sandwich. 'Owns a kebab shop down the bottom of O'Connell Street. Near the Ambassador.'

'What's it called?' said Elliott.

'The Big Kebabby' said Eamo around a mouthful of sandwich.

'The Big Kebabby?' said Elliott.

'Think his missus came up with the name' Eamo picked up his pint. 'Probably 'cause Tony is a big fuckin' kebabby' he sank his nose down into the pint and emerged with a creamy moustache. 'Anyways' he wiped his lip 'Tony'll do me a favour. Might hafta give him a few ads.'

'That wouldn't be a problem' said Elliott.

'D'ya want me ta set it up ?' said Eamo.

'Yeah' said Squirrel. 'Any other ways we could pull people in?' he looked at Elliott and Iris. 'Just in case Hot Press isn't enough?'

'We could print leaflets' said Iris. 'Drop them in the clubs, hand them out at gigs.'

'Nice one' said Squirrel. 'I'll get them done. One ah me clients is a printer. Shyte' he glanced at his watch. 'Hafta go' he stood up. 'Gettin' me streaks done at two.' Elliott and Iris exchanged a smile. Squirrel caught them and grinned. 'C'mere' he said to Iris. 'What d'ya think about blokes with perms?'

'I think they look like fucking eejits' she said.

'Young one in Peter Mark is always on at me ta get one.'

'Trust me' said Iris. 'The streaks are enough.'

'She's gorgeous but' Squirrel looked out the window. 'Takin' her ta The Apartments tonight.'

'The Apartments is a kip' said Iris.

'Kip full ah gorgeous young ones' said Squirrel.

'Good man Squirr' grinned Eamo. 'Maybe I'll come with ya.'

'You? Yer too old' said Squirrel.

'What are ya talkin' about?' Eamo looked hurt. 'I'm only just gone forty.'

'Too old for The Apartments' said Squirrel. 'Ya wouldn't get in' he picked up his helmet. 'Catch yis later. Gimme the wordin' an' I'll get the leaflets done up.'

. . . .

'Don't start that talking, I could talk all night, My mind goes sleepwalking, While I'm putting the world to right, Called careers information, Have you got yourself an occupation? Oliver's army is here to stay, Oliver's army are on their way, And I would rather be anywhere else, But here today ...'

89

Elliott pulled off his phones and let the single play as he stared at his notes on Contracts and Torts for the hundreth time. He'd gone to college on Monday and got quite a shock. Not only was he was seriously behind; he'd failed every single mid term test. Granted he hadn't shown up for one of them, but when had they covered all that stuff? It was March now; his exams were in May. It'd be alright. *It won't. You can't set up a radio station and get your exams.* He leant into the mic.

'**Elvis Costello, Oliver's Army ...**' he started, then a sound caught his ear. *Shit.* The slightest movement outside the door. Tilting back his chair, he flicked the curtain and glanced down. Anthony's Jag was sitting in the driveway. Fuck. Elliott sat very still. It took a few minutes but then he heard it again. On the other side of the door. The sound of someone trying to hear without being heard. *Wanker. Can't leave me alone. Right.* Slipping his shoes off, he centred his weight, and let his feet fall softly as he made for the door.

Anthony pressed his ear against the door. Damn. Quiet again. He pinched one eye in as he strained to hear. Suddenly the door pulled open and he jumped in guilty fright.

'What are you doing?' Elliott's accusation was polite, direct.

'I ... what ... what are *you* doing?' Anthony shot back.

'I'm going downstairs to get a glass of water' Elliott lied. 'Why are you standing outside my room?'

'I stopped to think about something' Anthony looked away.

'About what?'

'About ... something I might have left in the car.'

'Well, you'd better get it then, hadn't you?' Elliott stepped past him and walked down the landing. *Fucker; go on, have a good look, you won't find anything.*

Anthony darted his head into the room. Nothing unusual. Desk light on, study books open, a record playing on the turntable. He stood there for a minute then went downstairs. Pouring a whisky he went into the study and sat behind his desk, the low lamp spotlighting a small space in the dark room. He reached for his rolodex then pushed it away. He pulled it back. Thumbing through, it took him a few minutes to locate the card he was looking for. Frowning, he held the card back at a distance, squinted, grunted, then flicked on his glasses. Bushy eyebrows beetling together, he stood up and pushed the study door shut as he dialled the number.

Elliott decided the remainder of the broadcast would have to be a mixed tape. That was the third time his father had been outside the bedroom door like that in the last few weeks. What was his problem? When he'd first started broadcasting he'd worried that his father might hear him from his bedroom next door, but he'd never said anything, and Anthony wasn't backwards about coming forwards. *He should just be happy I'm studying. He should be pleased I've signed with Hydes for this work experience.* Elliott had picked Anthony's preferred choice of firm; might as well stay in his good books. Why had he been standing outside the door? Elliott couldn't work it out. A bit like Contracts and Torts. Just couldn't work it out. He flipped the notes he'd been trying to study back open, then closed them. Fuck it. He'd pick it up tomorrow. He moved over to his bed and lay there listening to the tape as it played. Great mix. He closed his eyes. He'd make a copy for Iris in the morning.

Anthony sat at his study desk, and waited for the number to click through, and as the phone began to ring, he reached for his whisky.

'Hello?' a soft voice through the receiver. Anthony swallowed.

'It's me' his fingers tightened around the glass. Silence. Anthony sipped the whisky, cleared his throat. 'I need to speak to you about Elliott. He ...' Anthony cleared his throat, and when he spoke his voice was thick, reluctant. 'He's been talking to himself.'

Professional DJs wanted
For new radio station
Send your demo tape to:
The Big Kebabby
O'Connell Street
Dublin 1

Successful candidates will be contacted for an interview

The response to the ad was slow. And the leaflets didn't seem to make much of a difference, despite Squirrel and Iris posting them everywhere. Nothing for two weeks. Then Tony called Eamo to say a tape had come in. He called a day later to say three more had arrived. Then he called to say there was a pile of tapes behind the counter and could they please come and get them. Squirrel sent a bike and they met at Elliott's house to go through them.

'No, no, yes' Iris threw tapes into three different piles in the centre of the living room. 'Thanks' she took the cup of tea Elliott was offering.

'What's in that pile?' Squirrel pointed at the largest of the three.

'Rejects' said Iris.

'Why are you rejecting this?' Elliott had picked up a tape covered in hearts and stickers, with the word 'Candy' written on it in bright pink marker.

'Pop' said Iris.

'Kids love Pop' said Squirrel.

'Yeah, exactly' Iris stuck a cigarette in her mouth. 'Kids' she cupped and flicked her lighter. 'We're not going' she puffed and pulled 'to be a station for kids.'

'No' said Elliott 'but we'll need a Pop slot somewhere in the mix.'

'Why the fuck would we want Pop in the mix?' Iris scowled. 'I'm not DJ'ing on some stupid Pop farce.'

'It won't be a Pop farce' said Elliott 'but any station worth its salt will have a mix of programmes. We're trying to appeal to different groups of people. Plus by the way we've a big schedule to fill.'

'What are the other two piles?' Squirrel nodded at the smaller groups of tapes.

'Daytime and Nite-time' Elliott ignored the look Iris shot him as he threw Candy's tape into the Day-time pile.

'This looks good' Iris had opened another envelope and was holding a tape in one hand. 'Neal O'Neill' she was reading the letter that had accompanied it. 'Synth, and he has access to live gig recordings.'

'Neal O'Neill?' said Squirrel. 'Parents havin' an off day there, weren't they?'

'It's his handle' Iris was studying the letter. 'He has a college radio show.'

'Live recordings would be great if the sound quality is good' said Elliott. 'We'll need to tune into his show to see what he's like. What else have we got?' They opened up a mix of different sized and shaped envelopes, all of which went in the reject pile. There was a man who wanted to do a gardening show, a priest who wanted to create a Sunday show and a girl called Donna Larkin who wanted to do a teenage talk show called 'The Mad Donna Show.'

'Ridiculous' Iris fired the tape onto the reject pile.

'Bit thin on the ground' Squirrel eyed the tapes they'd approved.

'These look good' Elliott held up two letters. 'Someone called Declan; that's clearly Reggae' he threw the brightly coloured tape into the Nite-time pile 'and this one' he held up the second tape 'from Benny in Killester, is Ska.'

'What about this?' Squirrel pulled out a glossy black and white photo of a good-looking blonde girl. 'Carly. She's a yank. Says she's worked as a DJ in New York and California.'

'What's she doing here?' said Iris.

'Dunno' Squirrel stared at the photo. 'Nice-lookin' bird. I'm puttin' her in the Daytime pile.' Iris and Elliott looked at each other. 'What?' said Squirrel. 'Yous two have picked loads. What? She's a nice lookin' bird.'

'Yeah' said Iris 'I'm sure our *listeners* will agree.'

'We've got a problem' Elliott was staring at the two piles on the floor.

'What?' said Squirrel.

'We've nothing for Daytime' said Elliott. 'Well sorry, the Pop show you don't want' he said to Iris 'and a good-looking girl no-one can see.'

'She'll be good' Squirrel protested. 'Yanks are deadly at radio.'

'We need a Breakfast Show' said Elliott. 'Radio peaks in the morning. We're not going anywhere unless we have a Breakfast Show.'

'What kinda person do we need for that?' said Squirrel.

'Someone who doesn't mind getting up early' said Elliott. 'Someone with energy.' He looked at the Daytime pile. 'Someone with a bit of a gob on them.'

Squirrel dropped Iris home and headed across to Donaghmede. He was hungry. Spiceburger would go down well. He walked into the chipper. The usual late night suspects. A group of pissed teenagers. An elderly couple. And Wayne Conroy.

'Squirr' Wayne glanced at him briefly as he studied something on the notice board.

'Wayne' Squirrel nodded back.

'Cheese-burger! Cheese-burger! Cheese-burger! Chips!' the girl behind the counter shouted and the queue lurched forward. Squirrel glanced at the notice board to see what Wayne was reading, then did a double take. It was one of their leaflets. He'd forgotten he'd stuck one up in here. He moved a bit closer.

'Whaddaya reckon?' he nodded at the leaflet. Wayne shrugged.

'If it didn't interfere with me day-job I'd nearly have a go. DJ'd all through me teens. Only gev it up when I got the milk round.' Squirrel leant against the wall.

'Will ya send in a tape?'

'Nah' said Wayne. 'Too much hassle. 'Sides, probably be just the same as all the other poxy stations.'

'How d'ya mean?' said Squirrel.

'Dublin radio's a joke' said Wayne. 'Gob-shytes an' arse-holes, talkin' shyte, playin' shyte. Someone needs ta take it by the scruff of its neck and sort it out.'

'Yeah? What would you do?' said Squirrel.

'Take all that American crap off for starters' said Wayne. 'All those phoney fuckers talkin' like they're from L.A when they grew up in Darndale or Raheny, an' ya know what's worse? If it's not some Irish arse-hole pretendin' ta be American, it's an American arse-hole pretendin' ta be happy. Rick Dees!! The fuck is that all about? And Casey Kasem? Don't get me started. Ya know what Casey Kasem is? He's an album, a fuckin' album!! He's not even in the studio; just an album that comes in from America an' they stick on every week. Fuckin' yanks. Countin the charts down backwards. Hard enough ta go forwards these days without listenin' ta some Yank goin' backwards.'

'Smoked cod an' a single ah chips!' the girl behind the counter shouted.

Wayne pushed a fiver across the counter.

'Don't mind me Squirr. I'm a bit of a radio freak. Bob Gallico, there's another one; ya know what?' he shook his head 'I'd better just shut up' he unwrapped the chips releasing a hot salt and vinegar steam.

'Spiceburger' said Squirrel to the girl. 'Wayne?' he lowered his voice.

'Yeah?' Wayne was poking around the hot chips.

'What if I could get ya an audition for that new station?' Squirrel nodded at the leaflet on the notice board. 'Would ya be interested?'

'Might be' Wayne blew on a chip. 'Why? D'ya know who's doin' it?'

'I am' Squirrel kept his voice low. 'Me an' a few mates.'

'Thought you had a courier business.'

'I'm expandin. Give us your number an' I'll set up an audition for ya.'

'An audition? Jays I don't know about that' Wayne broke off a piece of cod.

'Go on. It'd be easy' said Squirrel. 'Sure what have ya got ta lose?'

'Nothin' I suppose' Wayne shoved the cod into his mouth.

'Good man' said Squirrel. 'This is gonna to be big. Bigger than RTE.'

'Bigger than RTE? What planet are you on?'

'Spiceburger' the girl shouted.

'Wait n'see' said Squirrel. 'Here' he handed the girl two quid. 'What time d'ya get up for yer milk round?' he pocketed his change as they walked outside.

'Four' said Wayne.

'Four in the mornin!'

'Not that bad. Ya get used to it.'

'What time are ya finished?'

'Seven.'

'What about a Breakfast Show? Come straight in from your round, work through till nine or nine-thirty.'

'I'll think about it' Wayne shook the chip bag.

'Do that' said Squirrel 'an' while yer at it, think about the fact that this time next year you could be the Breakfast Show presenter on the biggest station in the country. Birds'd be all over ya. Ya'd be fightin' them off.'

'You're a spacer Squirr' Wayne laughed. 'Alright, let me know where the auditions are an' I'll be there.'

'Good man' said Squirrel.

'I'll see ya' said Wayne.

'See ya' Squirrel unwrapped the spiceburger and took a bite. He straddled the bike and watched Wayne walk away. Down the road, past the shopping center, across the empty car park, a small figure beneath the soft glow of the orange street lamps. He looked at him one more time before he disappeared around the corner. Iris was right. Blokes with perms looked like fuckin' eejits.

RTE LAUNCHES NEW SPRING SUMMER SCHEDULE

RTE unveiled their new Spring Summer schedule yesterday morning with Minister Horn and celebrity guest Miss Ireland in attendance. The station, which has been struggling to compete with Super Pirates BBR and Rocket, is hoping the new schedule will claw back heavy audience figures lost to competitors in the last JNLR rating. Speaking at the launch RTE's Director of Radio Programming Roger Ingram said *'we're very excited about the new schedule which is packed with the kind of professional programming the Pirate stations simply can't provide'* and went on to say that *'he was confident the next set of JNLR figures would reflect this.'* Industry critics are cynical however, labelling the new schedule a cosmetic exercise which can at best temporarily disguise the lack of energy and innovation in RTE's staid programming and tired, wooden presenting. Radio critic Jean-Anne Quigly commented 'it's only a matter of time before radical changes will have to be made if RTE is to hold its own in a fast changing market driven by youth audiences who at this point in time are listening almost exclusively to the Pirates.' Roger Ingram was not available for response to the criticism.

'Stupid bitch!' Roger balled the paper and hurled it in the bin. 'Breda!' he shouted at the intercom. 'Get me Bobby!' A knock at the door. 'Come!' Roger snapped. The door opened and Tom walked in. Roger felt a small surge of anger. Tom irritated him. Had done from day one. Always trying to put forward new ideas for programmes which anyone with half a brain could see wouldn't work in a Semi-State. 'Tom' he gave him a cursory glance.

'Hi Roger" Tom approached the desk. 'Have you got a minute?'

'Not really, but you're here now. What is it?' Roger began re-organizing a group of papers on his desk. Tom hesitated, then sat down in front of him.

'The thing is ...'

'Hurry up' Roger continued rearranging. 'I haven't got all day.'

'Well, I don't know if you saw the papers this morning?'

'I did as it happens' Roger reached for his cigarettes.

'Well, it's just I think we can turn this around if we put our minds to it.'

'We are turning it around. Have you seen the new schedule?'

'I have' Tom nodded. 'Of course I have, but it's not enough.'

'Says who?' a dull red tide began rising up Roger's face. 'You?' he lit a cigarette and leant back in his chair. 'Are you telling me you think you know how to run this station better than I do?'

'No. No, of course not' Tom's cheeks flushed 'but I think Jean-Anne Quigly has a point. The Summer schedule is ... well ... it's ... it's ...'

'It's what?'

'I think it could be better. Look, here' Tom pushed a set of papers across the desk. 'I hope you don't mind, but I've so many ideas ... I drafted these last night; they're very rough, but if you like them I can polish them up quickly Roger. You know it's not that we don't have the talent. We have some really strong jocks, but their hands are tied; they just need to given the freedom to ...

'Tom, do me a favour will you?' cigarette balanced in his fingertips, Roger rested his head in his hands for a minute, a thin line of grey smoke trailing up towards the ceiling. 'In fact do yourself a favour.'

'Sure' said Tom. 'Anything.'

'Stand up' said Roger. 'Walk over to the door, open it, go through it, close it behind you, and after that Tom, just do your job; the one we pay you to do, which is to manage the programme schedule. Not *create* the programme schedule. *Manage* it. That's all I'm asking. Do you think you can do that?' Tom's face had paled. He nodded silently. 'Thank you' said Roger. A soft knock at the door, then Bobby's head appeared around it.

'Roger, you were looking for ... oh ... hiya Tom. Sorry. I'll come back.'

'No. You're alright' Tom stood up and Bobby caught a glimpse of his frustration.

'Bobby' said Roger as Tom closed the door. 'Where are we with jamming the Pirates?' Bobby's eyes flicked to the window.

'Pat and Fiachra are working on it.'

'I see. Well when will they be finished working on it?'

'Couple of weeks maybe.'

'Excellent. Remind me again how this is going to work.'

'We'll programme the transmitter we're building to broadcast a signal directly on top of whatever Pirate we target, which will put a white noise over their broadcast, so essentially all you'll be able to hear is a hissing sound.'

'Will the listener be able to hear anything at all?'

'If you strain your ears you'll just about hear whatever they're broadcasting in the background, but it'll be very faint. It'd drive you mad. No-one would bother listening to it.'

'Excellent' said Roger. 'Target BBR and Rocket first and if they move to another frequency I want that jammed as well. Let me know when you're doing it and I'll alert the PR Department in case we have to field any questions.'

'We shouldn't be doing this' said Bobby. 'We should be competing on our own merits.'

'Fire with fire' said Roger. 'The Pirates haven't played fair with us. They're only getting what's been coming to them for a long time.' Bobby shook his head.

'We need to focus on our programming.'

'There's nothing wrong with our programming' Roger snapped. 'Christ, what is it with you and Tom? The Summer schedule is the best piece of programming we've had in years. I have one hundred percent confidence in it.'

'Yeah? Then why are we doing this?' said Bobby. 'If we have such confidence in our programming why don't we just get on with it?'

'All we're doing is levelling the playing pitch.'

'By wiping out the other players?'

'You can look at it that way if you want' Roger stared out

the window at the radio aerial 'or you can simply say we're employing new tactics. One way or the other Bobby, like it or not, it will happen, and when it does, not only will it show the existing Pirates exactly who they're dealing with, but it'll make anyone in the process of setting up a station think very seriously about what they're taking on.' He smiled. 'No-body in their right minds will try to take us on after this.'

· · · ·

'Fuck me' said Squirrel.

'I thought we were trying to be discreet' said Elliott.

'It's like a space-ship' said Iris.

'Work ah art, that's what it is' said Eamo.

They were standing at the bottom of the stack of carpet rolls looking up at the portacabin, which now that the outside had been covered in the purple and orange carpet, had taken on a life of its own and seemed to be hovering beneath the skylights.

'Ya weren't jokin' said Squirrel. 'Whoever designed that carpet musta been off their head.

'Yeah well' Eamo stared up. 'People did all sorts ah liquorice in the Sixties.'

'The Sixties?' said Squirrel. 'Ya bought it in the Sixties?'

'1962' said Eamo. 'Nearly put me outta business that carpet. Walked all over town tryin' ta sell it. Went ta every niteclub in Dublin. C'mon' he started up the stairs. 'Want yis ta have a look at the studio.' They climbed the stairs, the portacabin floating like an exotic fish tank above them.

'Jaysus, beam me up Scottie' Squirrel panted. 'Wanna be fit for this.'

The smell of new carpet hit Elliott as he stepped through the door, immediately followed by a sharp rush of emotion. He could hear the others talking; Iris excited, Squirrel and Eamo wise-cracking, but all he could do was stand in silent awe as he looked around and took it in. Tommy and Eamo had done an incredible job. Studio One lay before him, not on the ground or in the back of a van, like the last time he'd seen it, but fully assembled. The portacabin had been transformed; the glass panel fitted into the dividing wall, and through it, in the far room, he could see the sound desk and mixer re-built into an L-shaped wooden console. Two DJ mics hung out over it, and sitting center stage, waiting for action, was the leather presenter chair.

'Whaddaya reckon?' said Eamo.

'It's incredible' Elliott had a lump in his throat. The purple and orange carpet had been fitted throughout, covering the floor, the walls, the doors, everything, but instead of the psychedelic glare he'd been dreading, the carpet was strangely mellow, pulling the whole thing together in a warm, rich, groovy softness. 'It's so professional' he said. 'Everything. It even *smells* professional.'

'That's the carpet' said Eamo. He closed his eyes and took a deep breath. 'Beautiful' he said. 'One ah the nicest smells in the world. Better than a woman.' Elliott caught his eye. Eamo grinned. 'Alright' he said 'maybe not *better* than a woman, but it's up there.' The outer room they were standing in still had plenty of space. There was a leather sofa against each wall and someone had built a desk directly underneath the dividing window, for an assistant to sit at and take calls. Iris walked across the carpet and pushed the door into the studio open. The soft sound of carpet brushing carpet, then through the glass they watched her slide into the presenter chair.

'Testing, testing one' her voice barely audible through the open door.

'It's not hooked up yet' Eamo shouted. Elliott walked through to join her. He ran a hand along the sound desk, the shine on the wood reflecting the new spotlights Tommy had fitted overhead.

'We've got the makings of something really special here' he said.

'What are ya sayin?' Squirrel shouted from the outer room. Elliott looked out through the glass and smiled. Squirrel was stretched out on one of the sofas, biker boots and leather legs dangling over the side.

'I said …'

'Speak up!' Squirrel shouted. 'Can't hear ya!' Elliott walked back into the room.

'I said we've got the makings of something really special. What are you doing?'

'Thinkin' about Carly. Her an' all the other gorgeous young ones we're gonna meet' Squirrel, eyes closed, was smiling.

'Any nice lookin' birds in there for me Squirr?' Eamo, dressed in four shades of brown in yet another Smart Brothers suit, had stretched out on the opposite sofa.

'Too young for you Eamo' said Squirrel to the ceiling.

'I'm only forty' said Eamo from his couch.

'Forty-four' said Squirrel from his.

'Some women like older men.'

'Yeah. Older women' said Squirrel. 'Older women like older men. DJs we're takin' on will be way outta your league.' Eamo turned his head and looked at Iris who had made her way out from the Studio.

'What age are you?' he said.

'Nineteen' she replied.

'D'you think forty-four is old?'

'Ancient' she grinned.

'Fuck you' a confident smile stretched across Eamo's face. 'Run rings around the lot ah yis, so I would.' He opened one eye and looked at her again. 'Sure ya don't feel like a father figure?'

'Positive' Iris grinned.

. . . .

'Hi Mr Henley' Elliott had come to collect Iris to go in to the Big Kebabby for the DJ interviews.

'Elliott!' Arthur looked out from under the car bonnet and gave him a warm, pleasant smile.

'Is your car alright?' Elliott enquired.

'It's better than alright' Arthur patted the roof of the car 'it's energy efficient.

Come and have a look' he walked from the front of the car

around to the boot and opened it up. Elliott peered inside. A large cylinder shaped grey tank had been bolted into the center of the boot.

'What's that?' said Elliott.

'It's a gas tank' Arthur replied.

'Right' said Elliott.

'So I can run the car on gas' Arthur shut the boot '*and* petrol' he smiled at Elliott. 'Sit in' he held the door open and Elliott sat in behind the driver wheel. 'See that switch just under the indicator?' Elliott nodded. 'That switch' said Arthur 'allows me to convert the car from petrol to gas. Switch it to the left and I'm driving on petrol. Back to the center for a few minutes, then switch to the right and I'm running on gas.'

'Why would you want both?'

'Because oil prices have gone through the roof.'

'I see. And you did this conversion yourself?'

'I did' Arthur smiled. 'Not the easiest thing but …' the door to the house opened and Iris walked towards them. Bondage jeans, bondage jacket, purple v-neck, white tee, Mohican tightly shaved. She was wrapping a red PLO scarf around her neck.

'Off anywhere nice?' Arthur enquired.

'Town' Iris fished a hoop ear-ring out over the scarf.

'Henley! I want a word with you!' an irate man appeared on the other side of the garden hedge. 'That eye-sore' he pointed at the tower over the garage 'has to go! We had a residents meeting last night and we're all agreed it's lowering the value of the estate. Now you had *no* planning permission for that …'

'Prick' Iris muttered.

'What did she say!' the neighbour squawked. 'I heard that!! How dare you!!'

'How dare *you*!' Iris shot back. 'Don't talk to my father like that! We don't give a fuck about your residents association! Why don't you take your …'

'Iris! Iris!' Arthur had taken hold of her arm. 'It's alright' he spoke softly 'go on … on you go' he patted her arm. Iris glared at the neighbour.

'See you later' she leant in and gave Arthur a small kiss on the cheek.

'Good girl' Arthur turned to face the hedge. 'Now George I'm sure we can sort this out …'

'Who was that guy?' Elliott lit two cigarettes, one for each of them, as they walked up the road.

'George Radcliffe' Iris frowned. 'Stupid prick' she muttered 'thinks we should be living in some sort of Fisher Price town … residents fucking association' eyes dead ahead she ranted to the air. Elliott thought about the way she'd defended Arthur, protected him almost.

'You get on okay with him really, don't you?' he held out the cigarette he'd lit for her. She didn't answer, just stuck it in her mouth and kept walking. Walking, smoking, smoking, walking. Quietly fuming. 'Your Dad?' he clarified. She didn't answer.

'Iris?'

'What?'

'Your Dad? The two of you get on alright?

'Of course we do' impatience flashed across her face. 'He's my father Elliott. What do *you* think? Shit! Bus!!' Zips flashing, straps, chains, belt swaying she took off down the road. He watched her for a moment, then threw his smoke on the ground and sprinted after her.

Run, Rabbit, Run, Rabbit, Run, Run, Run his mother played that record to him when he was small and he could hear it now as he ran down the road, *Bang! Bang! Bang! Bang! goes the farmer's gun* jumped on the bus, *He'll get by without his rabbit pie,* paid the fare, *So Run, Rabbit, Run, Rabbit, Run, Run, Run* … and followed her upstairs.

The Big Kebabby wasn't hard to find thanks to a giant neon sign of a smiling baby brandishing a kebab in one hand and a Pepsi Cola in the other. It hung over the entrance to the restaurant and had the words 'The Big Kebabby' flashing out from the neon baby's diaper pin. An eyesore by day, a lighthouse by night. A beacon, a guiding light for the alcohol poisoned, beer goggled zombies who staggered up O'Connell Street in search of the hot lamb and spicy garlic holy ground. Tony could have served most of his night-time customers hot rat and spicy cockroaches for all the difference they'd notice. Kebabs between 12 and 6am were a currency unto themselves; a license to print money. Daytime trade however was a sober and somewhat slower affair, which was why Tony didn't mind giving Eamo's nephew the use of a booth for his radio interviews. There were conditions of course. Condition number one: The Big Kebabby would receive a free radio advertising campaign on the new station. Condition number two: If the Gardaí arrived Tony and the Big Kebabby would deny any association or knowledge of the interviews. Condition number three: Eamo's nephew and his two friends must each buy a Big Kebabby Happy Nappy Meal Deal while they were on the premises.

'Two teas an' a Coke' said Squirrel. Tony looked at him.

'Bit early for the Kebabs' said Squirrel. 'Have them after the interviews.'

'Alright' Tony looked suspicious. 'What time yis startin?'

'Eleven' Squirrel checked his watch. It was ten to. He carried the teas over to Iris and Elliott who were sitting in the booth reading the running order he'd brought along. Sharon had called the people on their short-list and set up times for each of them. She'd allowed twenty minutes for each audition and ten minutes in between to allow for any run-overs or questions.

'What are we going to say to them?' said Iris.

'Nothing' said Elliott. 'We'll let them do the talking. 'Jocks talk, that's what they do. We're just going to sit back and listen.'

At precisely three minutes to eleven a short skinny guy with shaved blonde hair walked in the door. He was wearing a perfectly fitted, neatly pressed black trouser suit, the trousers tapered in at the ankles and shooting out from that were shiny black pointy shoes. The suit was teamed with a crisp white shirt, a skinny black tie, a black pork pie hat and a pair of black sunglasses which he removed to ask Tony where the radio interviews were taking place. Tony pointed to the back booth. Straightening up, the little guy flicked his glasses back on, pulled at his cuffs, twisted his head and walked towards them, knees bending out in a jaunty little walk.

'Looks like one ah the Blues Brothers' said Squirrel.

'Benny?' Elliott stood up.

'That's me sir' Benny took off the glasses, and offered a hand, bright blue eyes popping and shining through a hailstone of freckles. He placed his hat on the table and sat down opposite the three of them. 'Let's get down ta business' a megawatt smile lit up his small face. Benny was great. Eighteen, working in his uncle's butchers since he was fifteen, he hacked up cows by day and tore up the dance floor by night, DJ'ing at Dublin's only Ska Club. 'Ask anyone' he said 'I'm the best.'

'How come you're not on another station then?' said Squirrel.

'Cos none of the fuckers'll do a Ska show. I've written to them all' he said. They looked at each other.

'You're in' said Iris.

'What nights can you do?' asked Elliott.

'Can't do Tuesdays' said Benny. 'Club night, and I need two days off. Count me in for Mondays, Wednesdays, Thursdays and Saturdays. That gives me a Friday night with me bird and Sunday off. When do I start?'

'Couple of weeks' said Elliott. 'We'll be in touch to confirm the date.'

As Benny stood up to leave a gang of girls burst through the door. One was small and pretty in a lots of make-up sort of way, the other two tall, heavy and definitely not pretty despite lots of make-up. All three were dressed in similar attire; black lacy leggings cut off mid calf, ra-ra skirts, bustiers, denim jackets and one of the big ones carried a ghetto-blaster the length of the three of them. They wore skinny black bangles jammed half way up each arm, interspersed with silver studded wristbands. The small one and one of the big ones wore fingerless white lace gloves. All three had badly bleached back-combed hair, tied up with lacy ribbons. Mini Madonna and two wrestlers dressed as Madonna. Tony, wiping a cup, stared at them.

'S'cuze me, where's the radio interviewz takin' place?' the small one asked. Tony inclined his head towards the back booth.

'Who the fuck is this?' Iris grabbed the sheet from Squirrel as the three Madonnas squared out and made their way towards them.

'Dunno' said Squirrel. 'They're not on the list.'

'Yous-doin-de-radio-interviewz?' the small one said as they reached the booth. She talked quickly, quicker than Elliott had ever heard someone speak.

'Who are you?' said Iris.

'Donna Larkin. Who're *you*?'

'You're not on the list' Iris' voice was cold.

'D'yis noh geh er tape?' Donna directed her question at Squirrel and Elliott.

'The Mad Donna Show. I sent-ih.'

'Well, we did get that tape ...' said Elliott

'And we've no interest in your show' said Iris.

'Whah! Why noh??'

'How d'ya know the interviews were on today?' said Squirrel.

'Grape vy-en' Mad Donna sulked, blue eyes belting out like headlamps through a forest of clumpy black eyelash. Then she changed tack. A playful, childish expression crossed her face and she smiled. 'Yis havta listen t'us. Plee-aze!' she pleaded 'plee-ahze!' lacey hands clasped in prayer.

'Right' said Squirrel 'see'n as yer here. We're not gonna get rid ah them' he said to Iris who's face had blackened. 'But if we don't like ya' he eye-balled the three girls 'that's the end of it, an' yis go quietly. Deal?'

'Deal' said Mad Donna. 'Thanks. Yis won't regreddih. Ready girls?' The two big Madonnas nodded and the one on the left balanced the ghetto-blaster on the ledge of the booth.

'Reeh?' she said in a gruff voice.

'Righ' Mad Donna fluffed up her hair and licked her lips. The big Madonna hit play and the opening bars of a familiar tune began on the ghetto-blaster.

Holly-day HAY !! sang little Mad Donna – not a bad impersonation
   Selly-bray HAY !! veering off a bit
   If ya tuke a holly-day – cut the Big Madonna on the left –
deep as a shovel
   HOLLY-DAY-EH - boomed the Big Madonna on the right
Tuke some time ta selly-bray
   C'mon, let's SELLY-BRAY !! shouted Mad Donna
   Ih wou bee-HEE
   Ih wou BE so NIZE

The big Madonna nearest to the ghetto-blaster switched it off.
   'So-its-like-thah-fff-ya-know-whaddeye-mean?' the small Madonna said faster than the DART on the last stretch into Connolly 'thas-de-intro, then-me-an-Manda' she nodded at the big Madonna on the left 'starrup-the-chah.'
   'You *what-the-what*?' said Iris.
   'Starrup-the chah' said the small one 'the chah; ya know' she grabbed the salt cellar in front of her, held it like a microphone and spoke rapidly into it: 'Hiyis-hiyis-howeyis-whoefwegoh-whoefwegoh? Lion-one, lion-one, no-wandere-lion-two, no-wandere, lion-tree Charlene-whadaff-yougot-tah-say-yah?' she finished the last 'yah' like a hi-yah karate kick, clicking her fingers and pointing to Charlene, the big Madonna on the right as she did so.
   'I wanna wanna know what's hoh!' said the big one on the right.
   'An' I wanna know what's noh!' said the big one on the left.
   'D'yis geddih?' said Mad Donna. D'yis see how ih works? Play the song, blast ah chah, more songs. What d'yis reckon?'
   'Well I'm confused' Iris was dry, cutting. 'I don't really understand what you're trying to do. Why did you sing? It's not a band audition.'
   'We know thah!' Mad Donna scowled. 'We're not thick! That was just ta show yis how it'd work. Fucks sakes' she bristled, pouting.

'Donna' said Elliott. 'I remember your letter, and I can see what you're doing, singing the song; I can see that's just to show us that you'd play a track, that it'd be fun and then you go into the show, yeah?' Mad Donna nodded, still sulky. 'But once you've done that, what's the show about?'

'What's it *abouh*?' Mad Donna looked at him like he was stupid. 'It's abouh *life!*'

'Life?' Elliott waited for her to elaborate.

'Yeah. Life an' shit, ya know' she looked down and adjusted a bangle.

'Donna' Elliott leant across the table, 'I'm not being smart, but I need you to give me a bit more than *life*. If we put you on-air' he watched her eyes sharpen 'if we gave you an hour every day, how would you fill it? What aspects of life would you cover?'

'What aspects would ya like?'

'I don't know' Elliott tried to think 'teenage pregnancy, drugs, what you want to do when you leave school…'

'Yeah, well, that's what I was gonna do. I was gonna do all thah' she gave him a coy smile and Elliott couldn't help smiling back. She was a piece of work.

'Sure you were' said Iris.

'I was!! Righ!!' Donna snapped.

'Okay' Elliott stepped in again. 'Donna' he pointed at the ghetto-blaster. 'See that? Go home, get a few friends, hit record, and discuss your first topic. Get everyone in the room to contribute. If it works, great; if not' he shrugged.

'Righ' Mad Donna stood up 'c'mon girls. See yis' she flashed Squirrel and Elliott a cheeky smile, scowled at Iris, then turned on her heel and walked away, flagged by Manda and Charlene either side.

'D'ya reckon she'll be back?' said Squirrel.

'She'll be back alright' said Elliott. 'What'll be interesting is what she comes back with.'

'A hitman if you turn her down' Iris murmured lighting a cigarette. 'Who's next?'

'Declan Kelly alias Marley' said Squirrel looking at the sheet.

'He's late' Iris looked up at the clock.

'Hey' Tony shouted over from behind the counter 'are yous gonna talk to that giant pimple beside ya before he bursts? He's been waitin' over half an hour. An' he hasn't bought anythin!' They looked at the booth next to them. An acne ridden boy sat hunched in the corner. Torn jeans, army jacket, thick dirty matted hair, white pimples studding an angry rash of lumpy red and purple craters that ran across his face and down his neck. He was looking down into a record bag on his knee, flicking at the albums inside. 'Been lookin' in that bag for the last half an hour' Tony had walked over to the booth. 'Pretendin' ta be busy. Hey you!' he said. The boy put his head deeper into the bag. 'Hey! Spotty!' Tony shouted. The boy looked up. 'They're ready for ya' said Tony. Clutching the record bag to his chest, eyes glued firmly to the black and white tiled floor, the boy made his way around to them, mottled complexion deepening with each approach so that by the time he reached them his face and neck were a solid purple mass, white pimple heads blending through like tapioca pearls. He shuffled to a halt in front of the booth and raised his hand in a small, feeble wave.

'Howeya Declan!' if anyone could relax someone it was Squirrel. 'Sorry about that. Didn't realise ya were there.' Matted hair nodded furiously at the ground.

'Have a seat' Elliott indicated a chair. Declan pulled it out and sat down. He stared into his record bag and Elliott could see he was trembling. 'So, big reggae fan then?' he tried to relax him a bit.

'Yuh-yuh ...yesss!'

Shit. Was that a stutter? Elliott looked at Iris.

'We think a reggae slot would be great Declan' she pulled on her cigarette, 'have you DJ'd anywhere else?'

'Nnnn .... nnn ... no!' Declan mumbled, then buried his head further down his chest.

'*Fuck*' Iris mouthed at Elliott and Squirrel.

'Give us a look at your ... eh ... collection' Squirrel broke the silence as he reached across the table for Declan's record bag, which he released without lifting his head. They pulled out the albums and flicked through them in silence for several minutes.

'Good stuff' said Iris finally.

'Misty in Roots' Squirrel studied an album sleeve 'poor an' needy, whah?"

'Look, Declan …' Iris began.

'You-you-you … you think I cah cah–can't do it?' Declan stuttered and shook. 'I cah cah–can!' his body jerked. 'Juss–juss gimme me a chuh–chuh chance!'

'Declan' Squirrel leant across the table. 'These two' he thumbed at Elliott and Iris 'these two are the experts but even I can see this wouldn't work. You're a brave man comin' here today, I admire ya for that, I do, but you're not cut out for it. I'm sorry.' Declan stretched his arm out across the table and curled his fingers around the salt cellar. He'd obviously watched Mad Donna doing her audition the same way. He pulled the salt cellar towards him and eyes closed, his head came up as he held it like a microphone to his mouth.

'Doblanne' he drawled, and stuttering Declan was gone, replaced by what sounded like a very stoned Jamaican. 'Dis is jah manne Declanne, and I is in dee Big Kebabby. Aye wants ta play dis far dee folk in Harmenstowne,' Eyes still closed he started to sing, pitch perfect Jimmy Cliffe:

> You can get it if you really want,
> You can get it if you really want,
> You can get it if you really want,
> but you must try,
> try and try,
> try and try

Eyes still closed his face contorted and he sang again:

> Get up! STAN UP!
> Stan Up For Ya Rights-ah !
> Get Up! STAN UP!
> Don't give up the fight-ah !

He opened his eyes. 'Sss-sss … hee?'

'*Fuck* me!' said Squirrel. 'That's like listenin' ta Bob Marley! Ya sounded exactly like Bob Jaysus Marley!'

'How did you *do* that?' said Iris.

'Think I'm a juh … juh-Jamaican' Declan mumbled, then he gave them a shy half smile 'juss tra … tra-trapped in a why-why … why-man's body' he shuddered.

'Can you stay in that voice?' said Iris. 'Can do a whole show like that?'

'Me con talk like dis far de week if you wan' Declan shrugged 'far dee hole year.'

'I think you've got yourself a gig' said Iris. Declan's face broke out into a huge smile, pimples creasing, pockmarks folding, a tide of acne rippling back.

'Fffff … fffff … fffff … thanks. You–you … wowe-wowe … won't regreddih.'

'We will if you stutter' said Iris.

''Scuse us for a sec' Squirrel stood up and went over to a small guy who was standing at the counter chatting to Tony. Dressed in baggy denims and a black bomber jacket he had shoulder length tightly permed streaked hair and a moustache.

'I think that might be the Breakfast Show guy' said Iris.

'Okay' said Elliott 'just one thing Declan. Can you do any other impersonations?' Declan nodded. 'Who?' said Elliott.

'Em … hello' said Declan sounding like Latka from Taxi. 'Tenk you veddy much' he said. Elliott smiled. 'Elly-ott, Elly-ott' Declan said in a familiar alien's voice, then without skipping a beat 'Mork calling Orsen, Come in Orsen.'

'Who else?' said Iris. Declan bent his head into the collar of his jacket. 'Captain's log … Star Date March 85 …' he stopped and glanced over his shoulder at Squirrel talking to the guy at the counter. He turned back to them, suddenly speaking in Squirrel's voice. 'Howeya Declan! Sorry about that. Didn't realise you were there. *Fuck* me! That's like listenin' ta Bob Jaysus Marley!' Iris and Elliott stared at him in shock for a minute then Iris fell forward laughing. She was still laughing, choking, when Squirrel came over.

'Ready for the next fella? What are you laughin' at? Don't mind that one Declan' he put a hand on Declan's shoulder. 'Women whah?' he rolled his eyes. 'I'll grab yer man' he went back to the counter.

'Women whah?' said Declan in Squirrel's voice.

'We'd better wrap it up' Elliott grinned. 'Declan, we'll give you a call in the next few weeks to let you know when we're starting.'

'Gray-gray-great stuff' Declan stood up as Squirrel came over.

'Good man Declan!' Squirrel shook his hand. 'See ya soon' he shouted as Declan ambled out the doorway, record bag slung over his shoulder. 'Lovely fella' Squirrel slid into the booth. 'This is Wayne.'

'How's it goin?' Wayne had a very strong, confident air about him. 'Hear yis are settin' up a station' he ran a thumb and index finger around his moustache, a gold sovereign ring flashing as he smoothed the hair down. 'Whaddayis gonna call it?' The three of them looked at each other.

'We haven't decided' said Squirrel.

'When's it's kickin' off?'

'Once we get the DJs in place' Elliott realised they hadn't really discussed that yet either. 'Probably in the next month or two.'

'An' ya need someone to do a Breakfast Show?'

'Yes' Elliott nodded. 'Do you think you could do that?'

'No problem' said Wayne. 'When I was a kid we had a tape-recorder at home with a little microphone an' I used ta record meself sayin' *this is Wayne Conroy! This is Wayne Conroy!* Over an' over' he laughed. 'No idea what I was doin; I just knew I wanted ta talk into a box and hear my voice come back out again. Then when I was old enough I'd go up to the shoppin' center, meself an' the brother, we'd interview people with the tape recorder. The brother got bored but I kept doin' it for years. Askin' people all sorts ah shit; still have the tapes at home. Got a set ah decks when I was fourteen, saved up for them, DJ'd down the Community Centre, did parties an' that, but I hadta stop when I got the milk round. Always wanted ta have my own show but; a proper talk show.

'What would you call it?' said Iris.

'The Wayne Conroy Show.'

'You wouldn't have a handle?' said Elliott.

'Nah, fuck that' Wayne shook his head. 'Hate that shyte.'

'Okay' said Elliott. 'Well, we probably need to thrash it out a bit, but …'

'Ya serious?' Wayne's face broke into a smile. 'I'm in? I've got me own show?'

'You're in' said Elliott. 'We need to work out the format, but you're …'

'Excuse me' a seriously pretty girl was standing by the booth. She was tiny, a petite blonde doll with huge blue eyes, rosebud cheeks and a shy sweet smile. 'Sorry to interrupt' her voice was soft, feminine, 'but are you the people doing the radio interviews? I'm Candy.' Wayne's chair clattered to the floor as he shot to his feet.

'Wayne Conroy! Breakfast Show!' he stuck out a hand.

'Oh … hi Wayne' Candy blushed 'nice to meet you.'

'Nice ta meet *you*' Wayne patted his perm as he leant against the side of the booth 'yeah, Breakfast Show; lead presenter an' all that. What show ya doin' yerself?'

'Candy' Squirrel stood up, dwarfing Wayne. 'Thanks for comin' in' he leant across and shook her hand 'can ya give us a few minutes? We're just finishin' up a meetin' with Wayne here but we won't be long.'

'Sure' said Candy 'I'll be over there with my Dad' she pointed to a heavy-set man standing at the door. 'He wants to meet you if that's okay' she blushed.

'No problem. We'd love ta meet yer Da' Squirrel nodded across at Candy's Father. 'Wayne' Squirrel lowered his voice as Candy walked away 'see her? Stay clear. Her aul' fella hasn't come here for kebabs.'

'She's not that young' said Wayne looking over.

'Wayne, she's wearin' a school uniform.'

'Right' Wayne stood up 'give us a shout when ya get sorted.'

'The Wayne Conroy Show?' said Iris as he walked away.

'I know' said Elliott 'but I think we're just going to have to work with it. He's got a good voice, he loves to talk, and we don't really have any other options do we?'

'Right' Squirrel stood up. 'Better convince this fella we're legit' he beckoned to Candy and her father.

'Do you really think that's why he's here?' said Iris.

'Know by the look of him' said Squirrel. 'Me Da'd be the same about Katie' he muttered as Candy and her father approached. 'Hiya Mister …'

'Cronin' the man said as Squirrel put out his hand 'Dessie Cronin.' Heavy hooded eyes, a vice like grip, squeezing once, twice, three times as they each introduced themselves. 'Now' Dessie sat down, shifting his considerable bulk on the chair 'just a few questions. First off, where's this station gonna be located?'

'Well,' said Elliott 'for security reasons we're not …'

'Don't think ya heard me son. Question I asked, an' it's a very simple question …'

'Capel Street' said Squirrel. 'The Persian Prince.'

'Eamon O'Rourke's place?' Dessie sat back. 'Is he involved?'

'He's one ah the owners' said Squirrel.

'An' yous three are the rest?' said Dessie. Squirrel nodded. 'Eamo's alright' said Dessie. 'It's important me daughter's safe; d'ya understand that?' then, before they could answer 'how much are ya gonna pay her?'

'Dad !!' bright pink spots appeared on Candy's cheeks.

'Just …' Dessie patted the air beside him.

'We've no money' said Elliott. 'As soon as we start making money the DJs will be the first people to get paid but until we get it up and running it's voluntary.'

'I see' Dessie folded his hands, fat fingers interlocking. 'When's it all kickin' off?'

'In the next month or so' said Elliott 'once we get the DJs in place.'

'What are ya callin' it?'

'We haven't decided' said Elliott. Dessie muttered something to himself they didn't quite hear, and rolled his eyes at the ceiling. He sighed, a long deep sigh, then turned to Candy.

'D'ya want the job?'

'Dad!! They haven't offered it to me!' pink spots on Candy's cheeks again.

'D'ya want it or what?'

'Da-aad …' she groaned putting her head in her hands.

'Candy' Elliott reckoned it was probably safe enough to talk directly to her at this stage, 'your tape was great. Was it mixed in a studio? It didn't feel like you'd done it at home.' Candy nodded.

'I'm in a band' she said. 'I got a sound engineer to work on it with me.'

'Are yis takin' her on or what?' said Dessie.

'Dad! Stop!!' Candy rolled her eyes. 'Sorry' she winced.

'Simple question' said Dessie. 'Simple question, yes or no answer.'

'Tell you what' said Elliott 'how about we start you off on a three month trial? Saturday afternoons, your own show, Pop, stuff from the charts. Does that sound okay?'

'*Okay?*' Candy's face lit up. 'Are you *serious?* Oh my God, I can't *believe* this! Thank you!' she squealed. 'Thank you *so much!!* Dad!!' tiny arms wrapped themselves around Dessie's thick neck 'Dad! I'm going to be a DJ!' her face lit up. 'A DJ! On the radio!!'

'Course ya are' Dessie's voice was gruff. 'Just one more thing' he said to Elliott.

Shit, what now?

'I've a taxi business. Thirty six cars on the books an' another twenty three dippin' in an' out. Get yerselves some stickers an' let me know what the frequency is; I'll make sure the lads are tuned in an' we'll sticker all the cars.'

'Wow! That'd be great; thank you Mister Cronin.'

'Dessie. Now remember' the vice like grip as he shook Elliott's hand again 'look after me daughter.'

'Fuck!' Elliott exhaled deeply and ran a hand through his hair.

'That's our cards marked' said Squirrel.

'I'm starving' said Iris.

'Yeah, me an' all' said Squirrel. 'Murder a kebab now. What time is it?'

'One o'clock' said Iris looking at the list. 'Just Neal O'Neill and Carly to go.'

'This looks like it might be Neal coming in now' said Elliott. 'Ya fuckin' queer!' someone from the street shouted as a tall boy with high hair walked through the door. The hair, bleached blonde, was shaved tight from the ears down, but worn long on top, gelled high at the sides, plunging into a V-shaped fringe which covered the entire right hand side of his face. He was talking to Tony, tossing his head to the right, shaping and re-shaping the fringe as they spoke.

'Sure that's him?' said Squirrel.

'It's him alright' said Iris as Tony pointed in their direction and the guy made his way towards them. He was wearing a long herring-bone coat, black trousers and pointy black Chelsea boots.

'Sharon?' he looked at Iris.

'No' Iris smiled.

'Hi' Elliott stood up 'I'm Elliott, this is Iris …' Iris smiled again 'and Squirrel.'

'Alright Neal, how's it goin?' Squirrel shook his hand.

'Hiya' Neal sat down. Elliott watched him smile at Iris again.

'So Neal' the sharpness in his voice surprised Elliott. *Take it easy.* 'Neal, I tuned into your show' *just be professional* 'and it's great, really great.'

'Thanks' Neal smiled at Iris again.

Stop smiling at her. She's not your girlfriend. She's not yours either Elliott. No, but she will be. Yeah? When? You're never going to ask her out. I am. You're not. You're too scared she'll say no. I'm not scared. Okay I am. I just need time. I'll do it in my own good time alright? God, look at them. Look at the way she's smiling at him. What if he asks her out? Maybe we shouldn't take him on.

'Great. See you in a few weeks' Iris was shaking Neal's hand. *What? Has she just hired him? She can't have.*

'I'll give you a call' Iris was still holding Neal's hand. *Let go his hand.*

'I'll look forward to it' their eyes were locked and holding. *Let go his hand. I can't believe she's taken him on. It's meant to be a joint decision. He's good. You know he's good. Today was a formality. He had the gig before he walked in the door.*

'Elliott?'

'Elliott, Neal is saying goodbye to you' said Iris.

'Bye Neal.' *Fuck off Neal.*

'Bye Elliott' a wide even toothpaste smile. 'Really looking forward to working with you.'

'Yeah. You too.' *Prick. Prick with your live concerts. Synth's on the way out. She doesn't even like Synth.*

'He's great' Iris lit a cigarette as Neal disappeared out onto the street.

'Bit gay' said Elliott.

'What's gay about him?' said Squirrel. Elliott shrugged.

'Don't know. Let's eat. I'm starving.' *I feel sick. I couldn't eat a thing. I don't want to work with him. I don't want her to work with him. I don't want him anywhere near ...*

'Elliott!!' Iris was shaking his arm. 'What's wrong with you?' she said.

Elliott looked around. Tony was standing at the side of the booth with a notepad and the three of them were staring at him. 'What kind of kebab do you want?' she said.

'Em ...'

'Doner or Taco?'

'Taco.'

'Really?'

'No, sorry. Doner' he said to Tony.

'Whatcha wanna drink?'

'Coke.'

'It's Pepsi' said Tony.

'Sure, whatever.'

'Are you alright?' said Iris as Tony walked away.

'Yeah, fine' Elliott pushed out a smile. 'Just thinking, that's all.'

'Are you worried about your exams?'

'I should be. I should be scared shitless, but all I can think about now is you and that prick.

'Kind of' he lied.

'When are the exams?' said Squirrel.

'Two months' Elliott lit a cigarette.

'Are you guys the *radio crew*?' a surprised American voice drawled and they looked up. 'Kinda young aintcha?' the voice matched the tape but the face from the photo had aged about ten years. Still good looking though, a tumble of blonde hair, sultry eyes and shiny pink lips. 'I mean, what are you? Eigh-*teen*? *Twenny*?' generous breasts spilling over the top of a turquoise gypsy dress as she pulled out a chair, slim tanned legs crossing as suede cowboy boots flicked out. 'Omi-gaad, you're *baay-bies!*' she laughed, pulling an over-sized white leather bag onto her lap, silver bangles jingling as she rooted. 'I thought this was like, a *regular* radio station' she pulled out a packet of Marlboro 'you're just a bunch ah kids! Are you seriously setting up a station? Kawffee, black, two sugars' she dismissed Tony who had just put their kebabs on the table. 'Un-fricken-believable!!' a stop sign with one hand as she cupped a gold lighter and fired up a cigarette with the other. '*Iyre-land*' she pulled down hard, tapping long perfectly manicured pink nails on the table top. 'I mean what is this *bullshit?*' she blew out a line of smoke. 'Green hills, land of the welcomes; it's cold, it's grey, *everyone's* fucking miserable! I left L.A for *this?* Aw, whaddaya gonna do?' she dismissed her rant with a wave. 'Men! Ya fall in *love*, you're on a *plane*, where was I? Oh yeah' pink nails ground the cigarette out 'I wanna work. DJ'd all my life, New York, L.A., so just because I've fallen in love and moved to this' she looked around the Big Kebabby '*hell hole*, doesn't mean I'm not gonna jock. Anyway, business, business' she tap-tapped the table 'what's the best slot and how much are you gonna pay me?' she gave them a bright smile.

'Well, we don't actually have any money' said Elliott.

'Whaad!! You don't have any money? You don't have any *money?* How do you expect to set up a radio station without any Goddam money? Omigaad this sucks! This *whole country* sucks ...'

'Why don't you fuck off back to America then?' said Iris.

'Iris … Jesus Iris!' Elliott and Squirrel together.

'What?' she stared at the two of them 'she's allowed to sit here and slag us off and I can't speak my mind? Why did you come here today?' she glared at Carly. 'What were you expecting? Fifty grand and an expense account? We're in a kebab shop for fucks sakes' she sat back against the booth and scowled.

'Carly …' Elliott began.

'No! Shit! Sorry. Dammit. She's right' Carly looked embarrassed. 'Sorry' she said to Iris 'I did not mean to insult your country. It's just so Goddam weird being away from home' she lit another cigarette and pulled down hard. 'I shoulda dumped all that shit on a therapist; are there *any* fucking therapists in this country? I haven't met any' she sat back in her seat 'anyway the advertisement said it was a new station and I thought *maybe* with the experience I have …' she sighed. 'I am *so sorry* I insulted your country' bangles jingled as a slim tanned arm reached across the table to Iris.

'It's okay' Iris softened. 'It is a hole. Everyone's leaving. Look, we liked your tape. You've a great voice and the music; well to be honest it's not my thing, but it is good. Elliott thought you might work well for an afternoon or weekend slot.

'Alright!' a wide Californian smile. 'When do we start?'

'In a month or two' said Elliott.

'You got producers?'

'No' Elliott sighed. 'Not yet.'

'Why don't you let me produce? I produced shows in L.A, New York; look I have *nothing* to do; I am like, *super* bored. My boyfriend works all day; let me help. You guys need all the help you can get, right? Hey! Who's doing your IDs?'

'Our what?' said Squirrel.

'Station IDs' said Elliott. 'It's like a jingle that sings the station name. We haven't got that far yet' he said to Carly 'and I doubt we will; IDs cost a fortune.'

'Tell me about it honey. Hey! You know what?' her face brightened 'I think KCNB might be able help us out on that one.'

'KCN who?' said Squirrel.

'My old station in LA' said Carly. 'They do IDs all the time. They have an ID Department. It's like a whole separate business.

'We don't have any money' said Elliott.

'Sweetheart, they'll demo for free. You only pay if you use them, and if our station's a hit, the advertising will pay for it. Those guys love me. And they owe me. What's the station name? I'll get them to work something up.' Iris and Squirrel looked at Elliott.

'Well, to be honest we haven't actually got a name yet' Elliott confessed.

'*Whaad??* You haven't got a *name?* You haven't got a *name?* Oh my *Gaad!!* You guys have a *lodda* work to do! You're on-air in, like *a month* …'

'Two' said Elliott. 'Two months.'

'Okay, two months. Whad.*Ever.* You need to get your shit together, starting with the name! You *need* a name. You can't go on-air without a Goddam name.'

'She's right' said Squirrel. 'We need a name. Quick.'

14ᵗʰ April 1985
Provence

Dearest Elliott,
I hope you're well. Dad says you're working hard, getting ready for the exams. I'm writing to you sweetheart because I want - I need, to tell you how very sorry I am to have hurt you so much. I handled things badly, lots of things, but especially you. I know you don't want to see me or hear from me, I know how much I've hurt you, and I have come to realise that each time I try to make contact with you all I'm doing is reminding you of that hurt.
So I've made a decision. I'm going to stop calling. For now anyway. I don't want to; it's the last thing I want to do, but I realise that each time I try to force my way back into your life I'm

only hurting you more. So I'll stop calling, stop writing, stop trying to make any sort of contact, but you are my son Elliott, I will never stop loving you, and I hope and pray that one day, somehow, you will find it in your heart to forgive me and trust me enough to let me back in your life again.

You really are so very special and precious to me

Mum

Elliott pushed the letter back in the envelope and slid it down a gap between albums. Leaning forward he pulled back the fade and spoke into the mic. **'Safety Dance, Men Without Hats ... great track, appalling video ... Iris Henley that was for you, because for some strange reason you like it, and for stranger reasons I like you. Hill Sixteen, this is Velvet Underground ...'**

Shit. I hope she didn't hear that. She won't. She's playing Berlin tonight. She'll never hear it. Cigarette ... he shook the pack lying on the desk. Empty. He'd have to run to the pub. Maybe Anthony would give him a lift. He could hear him moving about in his bedroom next door. Probably getting dressed. Thursday night. He'd definitely be going to the Club for dinner. Elliott glanced at the clock on his desk. Bit early. Give him another while.

In the bedroom next door, Anthony had climbed up onto the bed and was kneeling on the pillows, holding on to the brass headstand, his ear pressed hard against the wall. Muffled sound. Elliott's voice, stopping, starting, stopping again. Music. Anthony pressed his ear hard against the wall again. Nothing. Silence. No. Wait. There it was. He'd started again.

'Lou Reid, Satellite of Love' Elliott pulled the music back, **'before that Roxy Music, and Elvis Costello who produced the Pogues new album – NME have given that a big thumbs up; we'll have it for you soon I hope. Dead Kennedys up next, It's a holiday in Cambodia ...'**

Right. Cigarettes. He lined up the tape. See if Anthony was

going to the Club and if he could cage a lift. Elliott opened his bedroom door and turned down the corridor.

Anthony, still kneeling on the pillows with his ear pressed to the wall, jolted as Elliott pushed the bedroom door open, then sprang backwards quickly off the bed and began a concentrated effort of smoothing of the covers. Elliott stared at him.

'What are you doing?'

'I'm … ah … examining the walls' Anthony, head down, gestured at the space behind the brass headstand whilst continuing to straighten the sheets. Elliott looked at the wall, then back at his father, still smoothing the bed covers.

'What for?'

'Cracks' Anthony kept his head down.

'Cracks?'

'Yes. Cracks' Anthony's tone was curt, dismissive. 'We may ah … we may have to sell at some point' he straightened up, crossed the room and began a focused examination of the opposite wall.

'Sell the house?'

'When you qualify Elliott' Anthony peered closely at the wall, then stepped back as if to consider a fresh perspective 'it's highly likely you'll move into town as Max did' he turned and moved to the end of the room, running his hands across, then down the back wall. 'No point me rattling around here on my own' he said over his shoulder. Elliott stared at his father's back.

'Did you find any?'

'Any what?'

'Cracks.'

'Cracks? Oh. Yes. I did. I found a few. In fact' Anthony turned and headed for the door 'I should telephone somebody about that now' he pulled the handle and made off down the corridor. Elliott stood in the centre of the empty room for a moment or two, then he walked over to the side of the bed and stared up at the wall behind it, eyes scanning left, right, travelling over smooth, perfectly finished plasterwork.

· · · ·

'Top ah the world Ma!! Top ah the world!!'

'Squirr, get *down* offa that!!'

'It's not connected!!'

'Doesn't matter, you'll fall. Come down, *please* !!'

'Don't be such a shower ah chickens … *hey Tommy !!* I can see your gaff. Come up! Come on!! Ya can see everything. It's *massive!!* Dublin! Dublin !! *Dub-liiinn !!'*

They were on the roof. Well, four of them were on the roof, and one of them, leatherman, was at the top of the newly erected aerial, shouting at the City.

'I can't look' Iris bent her head into her palm.

'It's not on' said Tommy. 'He'd be toast if it was.'

'What if he falls?'

'Squirrels don't fall' said Eamo 'they fly. Tree ta tree; come down ya fuckin' eejit will ya!!' he shouted up.

'How high is it?' said Elliott as they watched Squirrel begin to make his descent.

'Twenty feet' said Tommy looking up at the aerial, which now straddled two of the three buildings that made up The Persian Prince.

'That's a good job Tommy' Eamo tested one of several metal wires holding it in place. 'Nice an' secure' he tugged on it.

'How's the transmitter coming on?' said Elliott.

'Done' said Tommy. 'Big bastard. Two kilowatts. We can start testin' frequencies. Whatcha want ta broadcast on?'

'Not sure' said Elliott. 'Most stations are on MW but it's only a matter of time before they switch to FM.'

'What are ya talkin' about?' said Eamo. 'FM's for Pilots.'

'It's a better sound' said Elliott. 'A lot of the music coming out of the States is being engineered specifically for FM. BBR and Rocket are already broadcasting off both so they don't lose listeners. 'Can we do both?' he turned to Tommy. 'MW and FM?'

'Yeah, shouldn't be a problem' said Tommy as Squirrel hung, swung, then dropped off the bottom rung.

'If-I-were-a-rich-man' he Cossack stomped his way towards them 'Yubba Dibby Dibby Dibby … unbelievable' a big grin on wind-whipped cheeks 'ya can see everything up there' his eyes sparkled and shone. 'Deadly isn't it?' he stared out at the view. Dublin stretching as far and wide as the eye could see. Hundreds of rooftops, high then low, red brick, grey slate, spires, steeples. The Liffey, the Custom House, the dome of the Supreme Court, cars on the Quays, Liberty Hall standing tall in the distance as the mouth of the river widened out into Dublin Bay.

'That's our city' said Elliott. A Spring breeze blew up around them, light, playful, then a strong gust. It blew harder and they braced themselves against its force.

'C'mon' said Eamo. 'What did ya think of me name by the way?'

'We're not calling it Radio Persia.' They'd climbed back down inside the warehouse and were sitting in the studio, Eamo on one leather sofa, Iris and Elliott on the other, Squirrel stretched out on the psychedelic carpet, black leather splayed against the purple and acid orange swirls.

'Why not?' said Eamo.

'Because it's stupid' said Iris 'and it's too close a name to the Persian Prince. You might as well just hand the Gardaí a map for the raid.'

'C'mon Eamo' Squirrel reasoned 'it's a bit bleedin' obvious.'

'We need something different' Iris stood up and walked over to the studio door. 'The other stations are trying too hard' she pushed the door 'the name should sound like we don't give a fuck' the sound of carpet brushing as she went inside, then through the glass they watched her slide into the chair. 'Testing testing-one' her voice came over the speakers as she flicked the switches on the console. 'Okay' she looked out at them from behind the glass 'let's try a few. Give me some names.' Silence. Three sets of blank eyes looking in through the glass at her. 'Useless' she pulled on the headphones 'Julie Andrews' she leant into the mic 'live from Studio One ... testing, testing-one' her voice echoed around the outer room 'Julie Andrews, you're listening to The Sound of Music, *live* from Studio One. Levels are good' she said to Elliott through the glass 'we should get some music in here, start testing it.'

'Hang on' said Elliott. 'Say that again.'

'Say what?'

'Julie Andrews live from Studio One.' Iris looked at him for a second.

'Okaaay' she pulled the headset back on 'Julie Andrews' she made a face at him through the glass 'live from Studio One.'

'Say it again, say more' said Elliott. 'Anything with Studio One.' Iris leant into the mic again.

'Good afternoon, we're live from Studio One … *Studio One*…' she went up a beat 'that's the News at *Ten* on *One*, sport and weather are next …*Good Morning!* We're *live* from Studio One … you're *tuned* to *Studio One*… Studio One on an all request weekend … Studio Wuh-hun!' she sang. She stopped. 'Shit, that's it!' she looked out at Elliott through the glass. 'That's it! Apart from anything else it's the truth. We *are* broadcasting from Studio One. It's just not in RTE anymore.'

'Sounds a bit serious ta me' said Squirrel. 'Doesn't sound like the other Pirates.'

'Exactly' said Elliott. 'That's precisely why it works.'

'It sounds like a music studio' Iris cut in over the speaker 'like a band working in-studio, recording. It has a proper music feel to it, not just another bunch of DJs playing records; it feels like a space, a place; somewhere you'd want to hang out in.'

'What d'ya reckon Eamo?' said Squirrel.

'Think it's genius' said Eamo. 'Steal a studio offa RTE, then take it back on-air a few months later with the same name? She's right an' all' he nodded at Iris 'does sound like a proper recordin' studio.'

'Excellent' said Elliott. 'Studio One?' he looked at Iris.

'Studio One' she smiled at him through the glass.

'Studio One' Squirrel nodded, then turned to look out at the carpet mountain. 'Number one' he tapped the window. 'Number fuckin' one baby.'

. . . .

The next month was spent working the shows. Elliott introduced Wayne to Declan and the three of them worked up ideas for characters and impersonations for the Breakfast Show. Carly met Mad Donna and listened to the demo she'd done.

'Omi-gaad' she laughed. 'You guys got a radio aw-thoridy here? Because we are *gonna* get complaints. That's our shock jock. Right there' she pointed at Mad Donna as she rehearsed with the girls behind the Studio glass. 'You know she's gonna launch with a show on virginidy? Open with Madonna's *Like a Virgin* get teens to call the show and talk about losing their virginidy; she's got like ten kids lined up already.'

'Might shut us down before we start' said Elliott.

'Naw' Carly shook her head. 'Gonna put us on the map. Trust me.' They brought all the jocks in studio, gave them time on the equipment, looked at set lists and Squirrel brought his sister Katie in to work as the B.A.

'She's after gettin' fired from her job' Squirrel whispered as himself and Elliott watched her practice talking to Wayne and Declan over the mic to the Studio inside.

'I can *hear* you' Katie turned around. 'I'm not deaf ya know. An' I wasn't fired. I left. There's a difference.'

'Jays, I wouldn't tell Ma that.'

'Ma knows. That's why she's freakin' out, though I can tell ya one thing Squirr, she'll be freakin' out a whole lot more when she finds out you're workin' with Eamo.'

'Yeah, well; cross that bridge when I come to it' Squirrel leant against the wall.

'Why did you leave your job?' Elliott asked Katie. 'What were you doing?'

'Workin' in a washin' machine complaints department' Katie was a smaller female version of Squirrel, with the same streaked blonde hair and aquamarine eyes.

'You know you look exactly like him' said Elliott. 'Prettier of course' he smiled.

'That wouldn't be hard' she grinned.

'Why did you leave?'

'Boss was a bully' Katie brushed her skirt. 'Could hack the job. Job wasn't a problem, but he was. So I left, which is stupid I know when there's no jobs to be had, but I won't be bullied, not by him, not by anyone. I'll be good at this' she nodded at Wayne and Declan in studio. 'Been workin' in a washin' machine complaints department for the last six months. Aul' wans givin' out shyte ta me all day about spin cycles. I can handle a switchboard an' I can handle the public.'

'And you don't mind working for free?' Elliott looked at her.

'Nah' said Katie. 'Collect me dole, keep the head down, an' as soon as we start makin' money you can start payin' me. Squirr' says we're gonna be number one' she grinned.

'Yes. Yes, he has said that many times to me too' Elliott smiled.

'Dunno what yis are laughin' about; we *are* gonna be number one' said Squirrel. 'Told ya before, I'm not in this for the craic. I'm in it ta make money and we *are* gonna make money.'

'Whatever you say boss' said Elliott.

. . . .

Tommy tested frequencies.

'Right' he said. 'Ya can have 100 on MW and FM , which means it's the same frequency an' people wind up an' down the dial ta get to us, or we can be clever an' have 100 MW an' 86 FM which means we're at the same point on the dial all the time an people just have ta just push the MW or FM button ta hear us.'

'Go with the second' said Elliott.

'Why?' said Squirrel. 'Wouldn't it be better ta have the same number? Easier ta remember one number than two.'

'Yes, but much better not to have to be winding up and down the dial' said Elliott. 'Much better to lock onto one frequency, and then when they push the FM or the MW button either way they're still listening to us. People are lazy. Pressing a button is easier than winding a dial, and who knows what other stations they'll find as they go up and down the dial.'

'You sure about this FM thing?' said Squirrel.

'Positive' Elliott replied. 'MW's going to disappear. It's only a matter of time.'

'How's Carly gettin on with the ID yokes?' said Squirrel.

'Demo's done' said Elliott 'and it's done for FM which means it'll sound great but we can't broadcast anything until we can pay for it.'

'Better get on-air quick' said Squirrel. 'Start makin' some money.'

'When are yis kickin' off?' said Tommy.

'Soon as my exams are over' said Elliott.

'When are they startin?'

'Next week.'

'Fuck' said Squirrel. 'That came in fast.'

'Mmm' Elliott ran his hand along the console. 'Did alright.'

. . . .

He knew something was wrong as soon as he stepped under Trinity's high grey arch. A blinding day, the kind you always get for exams. The sun beat down as he walked from Tara Street up. His clothes felt hot, heavy, uncomfortable. How many lectures had he been to? Ten? Twelve? *Relax. You've covered enough in the last few weeks. Stay calm. You did this for the Leaving and you got Honours. You'll be fine.* The sun hot on his head as he turned in the main entrance. Hot bright sun, suddenly cold as he walked through the wooden doors and under the arch. Something felt wrong. His heart began to thump as he came back into the light, squinting at the glare on the wide cobblestone court. The place felt strange. He looked around. Japanese tourists taking photographs, a group of Americans. Empty. It was empty. Where were the students? Where was the bustle? He broke his stride and began to jog. *Shit, they can't be inside already.* Quicker now, across the courtyard, veering right, up to the main building, through the revolving door. *They couldn't have started. It's only 9.15. It's a 9.30 start.* He raced down the corridor to the exam hall. *Where is everyone? Where are they?* The sound of his shoes bouncing like a squash ball around the clean white corridor. He pushed through another set of double doors, and came to a halt outside the exam hall. *Okay… shit … okay.* He caught his breath, then pulled the door. It didn't open. He pulled it again. It was locked. *Shit! Come on.* He pulled the door harder, rattled it. *Come on!!*

'Can I help you?' a security guard had appeared beside him.

'Hi …' Elliott caught his breath 'it's … my exams … Law … my exams; they're starting today … it's locked … I can't get in.'

'Today? I think you might have that wrong' said the guard. 'No… look … here's my timetable' Elliott pushed his hand in his back pocket and pulled out the piece of paper he'd had for the last two months. 'See?' he stared at the paper, trying to catch his breath 'see … there it is … Monday' … *oh fuck … that can't be right … oh God.*

'Yep, there you go' a clean pink finger appeared in front of him 'Monday May 5th' the guard underlined the dates at the top of the page. 'The 5th to the 16th. Today's the 19th. Exams finished last week. They're over.' Something was falling away, something. His head felt light. 'Are you alright?' the guard was looking at him. 'You're very pale.' Elliott couldn't speak. He turned and walked slowly back down the corridor, hot head, cool wall, he trailed a hand along to steady himself. Double door one, push. Double door two. Up the steps, back into the sun. He was freezing. *Fuck.* Hot. Cold. Dizzy. He sat on the grass.

What am I going to do? Oh God what am I going to do?

He rolled onto his back. *Oh God, oh God.* Closed his eyes. Put his hands over his face. 'Fuck! Fuck!'

'Har-rowe?'

'Fuck!'

'Har-rowe? Ess-cuse pwease?'

Huh? He opened his eyes. Long shiny black hair swinging in his face.

'You take pikshah?'

'Sorry?'

'Pickshah? You take pikshah?' A Japanese girl smiling. 'Wis my fama-wee? 'Pwease?' she pushed the camera at him.

'Oh … sorry … sure …' his legs shaking as he got to his feet '… sure … okay … that's it … smy … smile.' Click.

The weight of the city, the heat of the sun, the filthy stench of summer. Buildings closing in. Westmoreland Street. Taxis, cars, a line of buses belching thick black smoke. Red faced drunks melting on the path, sliding down in pools of brown overcoat. O'Connell Bridge. Low tide. No tide. The dregs of the Liffey rotting, stinking, burning in the sun. Bootlegs for sale, button badges. He turned down Abbey Street. Hollow space. Emptiness. *Can't breathe.* He sat on the side steps to Easons and put his head in his hands. *Can't breathe.*

'Move along, ya can't sit on these steps; move along now.' People. The heat. Capel Street. Finally. Capel Street.

'Hey' he pushed open the door to Slave. Iris, sitting behind the counter in a Dead Kennedys T-shirt, looked up.

'Hi … I thought you were … what's wrong?' she said.

'I missed my exams' he bit his lip.

'What do you mean you missed them?'

'I missed them' he tried to steady the wobble in his voice.

'What?' she started to laugh. 'All of them?' she laughed harder. He leant against the wall, closed his eyes and slid to the floor.

'Hey … shit' a clean, fresh, lemony smell as she knelt beside him. The shop door jingled.

'What's the story?' said Squirrel. 'Thought ya had an exam.'

'He missed them' said Iris.

'Whaddaya mean? Which one did ya miss?' said Squirrel. Elliott flicked up the exam timetable. Squirrel studied it for a moment. 'These exams were two weeks ago.'

'I *know*' Elliott clenched. 'I fucking know that *now*.' Squirrel laughed.

'Jaysus. What's yer aul fella gonna say? How the fuck d'ya do that? Ya missed every exam on the paper.' Elliott closed his eyes and leant his head back against the wall. He felt light, dizzy.

Fuck. Shit, what am I going to do. He'll hit the fucking roof. Someone pushed something into his hand and when he opened his eyes he saw Iris had given him a glass of water.

'Drink that' she said. 'And take off your coat. You look like you're going to faint.'

'What am I going to do?' Elliott groaned. He put his head between his knees.

'Tell him' said Squirrel. 'Tell him ya don't want ta be a lawyer.'

'He'll throw me out' Elliott's voice was muffled.

'So?'

'So' Elliott brought his head back up 'so where will I live?' his eyes felt hot. 'What the fuck will I live *on?*'

'He's not gonna throw ya out' said Squirrel. 'He'll throw the head, an' then yis'll just get on with yer lives.'

'You don't know my father.'

'Alright' said Squirrel 'let's look at the options. Option number one, ya tell him.'

'That's not an option' Elliott closed his eyes again.

'It is' said Squirrel. 'Open yer eyes. Open your fuckin' eyes an' look at me. It *is* an option. You're just decidin' not ta use it. What's the second option? Come on. What's the next option?'

'I'm going to have to hide the results' Elliott's brain was starting to kick in.

'Hide them?'

'I'd have to repeat first year' Elliott tried to think it through.

'Hide them?' said Squirrel.

'Hide them, fake them' Elliott pushed a hand through his fringe. 'Fake them and pretend I'm going into second year even though I'm actually repeating first.'

'What happens when you come to second year?' said Iris.

'I do it' said Elliott,

'But yer aul fella'll think you're in third year' said Squirrel.

'Exactly' Elliott swallowed 'then when I get to what he thinks is fourth year I just pretend I failed my finals. He'd accept repeating finals easier than repeating first year.'

'Fuck that' said Squirrel. 'Are ya really gonna go through the next four years livin' a lie? I couldn't hack that. You're not your own man.' Elliott leant his head in his hands. He felt drained. Exhausted.

'I can't believe I fucked up the dates' he was suddenly annoyed at himself for being so stupid. 'I'm a moron. I'm a fucking moron!'

'You're not' said Iris. 'We've been up to our eyes with the station. I forgot to open up yesterday. One of our suppliers left a box of cock harnesses on the path and now they're being sold in Moore Street.' Elliott gave her a half smile. 'It'll be okay' she squatted down in front of him. 'So you missed your exams. Big deal. Lie if you want, tell the truth, do whatever feels right. Come on' she tugged on his hands 'I'm on a half day, Sandra's in the back making tea but I can go in the next ten minutes. Let's get some cans, go up to the Green. Hang out.'

'I've got a better idea' said Squirrel. He nodded at the window.

'That's not your bike' said Elliott.

'It is today' said Squirrel.

'Why is the mud guard so high?' said Iris.

'Trials bike' said Squirrel 'for scramblin; rallies an' that. Swapped with one ah the lads in work. Why don't we take it ta Howth? Go up the West Mountain, do the dirt tracks, fuck around. I only have it 'til eight o'clock.'

'There's three of us' said Elliott.

'So?' said Squirrel. 'Sure she's so skinny she doesn't count' he nodded at Iris. 'Stick her in the middle, you on the back with a helmet, two ah yis sit nice an' close' he winked at Elliott 'no-one'll even know she's there. C'mon' he grinned. Not like ya have an exam ta do or anything is it?'

Fresh air, all the way to Howth. Iris' shoulder blades deep in his chest. His arms. Her waist. The tightness, the tension of three wrapped as one, the pull and tug as Squirrel changed gear. The power of the bike, the wind around them, the fear, the thrill of knowing they might get caught. Everyone should break the law. Bend the rules. Disobey. Knowingly, willingly, blatantly disobey. *You're not your own man. Do you really want to spend the next four years living a lie? I can't tell him. I can't.*

'Right' Squirrel stopped at the dirt track led across the West Mountain. 'Let your legs hang' he shouted, revving the engine 'an' hold on!' Rocks, mud, great clouds of dry dirt billowing up and around them as the bike tore up the track, nose-diving in and out of pot holes, flying up and over small hills, bouncing off rocks.

'Fuck !!! … ahh !! … Squirrel!!' dirt, grit, Iris, laughing, screaming as the bike shot, dragged and flew up the track. 'Yeee-haaw !! Yeee-hawww !!!' a full three sixty skid as Squirrel turned the nose of the bike right and they rode the flatland out to the peak, bumping, jumping, holding on. 'Slow down!! We're going too fast … Squirrel! Slow down!!' four legs dangling, one man standing 'we'll go over … shit Squirrel … slow down … we're gonna go over … aaaahhhhh!! …' stones shot as the bike skidded and swung to a halt inches from the edge of the peak. Squirrel cut the engine and flicked the kick. 'Top ah the world Ma' he swung a leg over the front of the bike and walked to the edge. Elliott helped Iris off and the three of them stared out in silence. A sheer drop down to deep green valley, the dip and peak of purple mountain, yellow gorse and way beyond, yawning wide around them, a vast expanse of golden sand and pale blue sea. Silence. Nothing. A gentle breeze. Just a still silence and the majesty of the mountain.

'D'ya reckon Heaven's like this?' Squirrel stared out at the view.

'I don't believe in Heaven' said Iris.

'What d'ya think happens when ya die?'

'Think you just die' she said. 'Think you go into the ground and that's it.'

'Jays that's a bit depressin.'

'I believe in Heaven' Elliott stared at the sea.

'Are you serious?' said Iris. 'Why?' she looked disappointed.

'Don't know' said Elliott. 'Just do' he shrugged. 'Just do, the same way you don't.'

'So. What? You think there's some *man* up there waiting at the gates to meet you?'

'I don't think it's as simple as that …' Elliott began.

'Me Irish teacher told us a story once' Squirrel walked over to the bike, lifted the seat and took out a six pack they'd bought in the village. 'Said there was this man an' he died' he squatted down against a rock 'well he drowned an' he was nearly dead but they brought him back ta life an' the people who brought him back sez to him

'Did ya go ta Heaven?' And yer man sez

'Yeah I did an all', an' they sez to him,

'Did ya see God?' An' yer man sez

'Yeah I did', and they sez

'What was he like? What was God like?' An yer man looks at them for a minute or two an' then he sez

'She was black.'

'She was black!' Squirrel laughed. 'Tellin' ya' he gestured out at the sea, 'when I die, I want Heaven ta look like this an' I want God ta be a black bird.'

'Yeah, well, I don't think you have to worry about that for a while' Iris sat down on the ground in front of him.

'Takes the best ones first' said Squirrel.

'Jesus, you're so bloody competitive' Iris reached into her her jacket 'even when it comes to dying you want to be first' she pulled out a long, slightly flattened joint.

'Where'd you get that?' Elliott watched her gently squeeze it back into shape.

'Declan' she rounded the joint between her thumb and finger. 'Gave it to me on Friday when he was testing his set.'

'Fuckin' muck' said Squirrel. 'Wreckin' your brains with that shyte' he pulled out a red and gold packet of cigarettes.

'Dunhill?' said Iris. 'When did you start smoking Dunhill?'

'Nothin' wrong with Dunhill' said Squirrel.

'Sure' Iris lit the joint. 'If you're a *wanker*' she exhaled, flashing him a bold smile.

'Fuck you' Squirrel grinned. 'Dunhill' he pulled a can off the plastic ring 'are sophisticated. Birds love Dunhill. I look like James Bond smokin' these ... shyte!!' the can fizzed, spat and foamed. He covered it with his mouth, blue eyes wide as it exploded inside.

'Yeah, you look like James Bond now alright' Iris passed the joint to Elliott, 'with your gob wrapped around a Carlsberg.' Squirrel swallowed, set the can down, then opened another and sprayed her.

'Aaaahhhh, fuck off!!' she laughed, grabbing a can and spraying him back. 'Don't waste it' she squealed as he soaked her. 'Squirrel! Stop! We've only got six!! Here, give Elliott that; state of my top' she wrung out the end of her T-shirt. Elliott took the can Squirrel was offering. He closed his eyes and put the can to his lips. The beer tasted warm, semi-flat.

Top of the world Ma. The sun licking his face as he sipped again. He pulled on the joint.

'Y'alright?' said Squirrel.

'Yeah.'

'Don't think about it.'

'I'm not.'

'Well just in case ya are, I'm gonna give ya something else ta think about.'

'What's that?' Elliott pulled on the joint again. *Shit, that's strong.*

'Now that yer exams are over, why don't we launch the station this week?'

'Mmm' something warm, deep, mellow, spreading across his face. He pulled on the joint again. Squirrel's voice. Far away.

'Fuck sakes; gimme that' the joint was snatched from his hand.

'Don't throw it away' he heard Iris shout. 'I haven't had any.'

'Fuckin' muck' Squirrel passed it to her. 'Gateway ta smack that is.'

'D'you never smoke?' she asked him.

'No, an' I'm not startin' either. Look at the state ah him; he's like a fuckin' zombie.' Somewhere, from behind his eyelids, Elliott felt his face smile.

'I've had a stressful day' he laughed.

'Stress' Squirrel sounded annoyed. 'Wouldn't know stress if it jumped up an' bit ya. Come on' he shook Elliott. 'Wake up. What do we need ta do ta get this show on the road?' Elliott took a deep breath and stretched.

'A schedule' he shook his head and tried to focus. 'We need a schedule of who plays what show when' he yawned, rubbing his eyes. 'Shit' he shook his head and blinked 'that's really strong' he said to Iris.

'I know' she smiled. 'Mellow though.'

'Right, well when yis have finished comparin' *hashish* notes' Squirrel stood up and walked to the bike. 'Don't know why I bother. I'm goin' for a spin. I'll see ya in a while' he jumped on the bike, gave it a quick kick and took off down the track.

'I think we're annoying him' Elliott rubbed his eyes.

'I think you're right' Iris moved over and sat down beside him. 'C'mon, let's have a go at a schedule. Have you got any paper?'

'Just this' Elliott pulled the exam timetable out from his back pocket. 'Right' he reached for a pen inside his jacket. Leaning back against the rock, he pulled up his knees, flattened the back of the timetable against his thighs and sketched out a grid.

'What slot do you want?' he started jotting times down the left hand side of the chart.

'Nine o'clock' she leant against his arm as he wrote. 'Means I can go straight to the club afterwards' he could smell her perfume and somewhere in the distance, the lawnmower sound of Squirrel's bike as he scrambled up and down the tracks. 'Give me Tuesday, Thursday, Saturday' she pulled on the joint 'and Sunday. They're my club nights.'

'Okay' he wrote her name in 'Benny there' he murmured 'no, that's too early; okay Neal here' Squirrel's bike buzzing in the distance, fading in and out. Her body felt warm against his. Soft, comfortable. *I could kiss her now.*

'Will Carly be alright with that?' she pointed at the grid.

'Yeah, she asked me for that slot.' *Kiss her. Kiss her.* 'Means she

can produce Donna and hang around for Candy if we need her.'
Iris passed him the joint. He smoked for a minute or two then
passed it back. He felt completely relaxed. Squirrel's bike in then
out. The sky softening, flattening out in pinky hues. He put his
arm around her, and without thinking, bent down and kissed the
top of her head. Soft stubble. The oily base of Mohican. He
smiled, kissed it again. He felt her pull back then she looked up.
Brown eyes searching.

Iris. He dipped his head.

'Nearrrommm' Squirrel shot over the hill and stones sprayed
as the bike landed in a sharp skid in front of them. 'Aw man!!' he
shouted over the engine as the two of them scrambled to their
feet 'I want this bike! I fuckin' want it!! Did ya see me up by the
masts? Did ya see me?' he cut the engine. 'Unbelievable!!' The
moment was gone. As suddenly as it had been there it was gone.

'What *are* those masts?' Iris turned towards the three Eiffel
tower frames dotted along the far side of the mountain. 'They're
like bigger versions of our aerial' she stared across at them.

'They're the RTE masts' Elliott tried to sound as detached as
she did. 'In fact' he pushed a hand through his fringe 'once we're
up and running, we'll be tapping into them. Here' he handed
Squirrel the schedule.

'Lotta gaps' Squirrel frowned as he studied it. 'No-one after
Wayne, nothin' after one am, Saturday half full an' Eamo's our
only jock on Sunday. Thought you said we had ta have a twenty-
four hour programme?'

'We do' said Elliott, 'but that's all the jocks we have for the
moment. Hopefully once we kick off we'll get more people
interested and we can fill those slots.'

'When *are* we kickin' off?' said Squirrel.

'Dunno' Elliott looked at Iris. 'Thursday?'

'What time?' said Squirrel.

'Evening' said Elliott. 'We should launch with your show' he
said to Iris.

'My show?' she looked surprised.

'First show says a lot about what kind of station we're going to be' said Elliott. 'Makes a statement. As does the first song. We need to think about that. The first song is important.'

'What about Queen?' said Squirrel. 'Radio Ga-Ga.'

'Too obvious' said Iris.

'What's wrong with obvious?' said Squirrel. 'Obvious is good.'

'Obvious is *shyte*' Iris kicked a stone.

'You pick a song' said Elliott. 'Your show, your song.'

'You're makin' a mistake about Queen' Squirrel kicked the bike to life. 'Freddie Mercury's gonna be pissed off' he shouted over the engine.

'He'll get over it' Iris shouted back. 'Someone else'll give him a better gig.'

'Yeah, they will! An' then ya'll be sorry ya didn't listen ta me!' Squirrel roared over his shoulder as she climbed on and Elliott got on behind her.

Iris thought about the song all the way home. Songs, hundreds of songs running through her mind as she went into the garage to get some ice-cream out of the deep freeze. She opened the door, flicked on the light, walked past her mother's car. 'Hey Lenny' she scooped Leonard Cohen off the top of the big chest freezer, and placed him down on the ground. He hissed and walked back into the house, tail up in disgust. Iris pushed up the door and bent over the freezer, ear-rings falling forward as she rooted. She blew on her knuckles, which were reddening from the cold. Ian Curtis appeared from underneath Arthur's workbench and began drawing a furry purry figure of eight between her tightly laced docks.

'Gotcha' she tugged up the ice-cream and pulled the freezer door down.

'Miaow' Ian Curtis hopped up on the flat surface, head-butting her arm, pushing up, pawing under.

'No ice-cream for you mister. You're nearly as fat as Alexi' she rubbed the pouch of his cheek 'aren't you?' she circled her finger as he pawed the air trying to catch it. She turned to go back inside then stopped. Jackie's car was on the ground. Not whole, like a car should be, but disassembled into several parts. The frame removed, lay hollow, strangely vacant beside what appeared to be the engine, spread out in pieces on sheets of newspaper. Doors leaning against the wall. Tyres stacked on top of each other behind the engine. Front and back seats on top of a pile of scaffolding in the corner. She stood in silence for a few minutes then went inside. The steering wheel was on the kitchen table.

'Mum?' the ice-cream carton was thawing in finger spots on her hands.

'Mmm?' Jackie was making a cup of tea.

'Have you seen your car?'

'Mmm? Oh yes' Jackie looked up. 'Your father's fixing it' she smiled. 'The ignition's a bit loose.' Iris took a bowl out of the press and pulled the cutlery drawer open.

'You know he's taken the whole thing apart?' she dug a spoon into the tub.

'Yes, I saw that' Jackie murmured 'I did see that' she pulled open the fridge. 'I think we're out of milk. Did you feed Ian Curtis?'

'Aren't you worried he won't be able to put it back together?'

'Well I can always drive his' Jackie gave her a bright smile. 'Sweetheart I'm going to get some milk. I've a client due at eight. If they get here before I get back will you show them up to the tower?'

'The Tower?'

'Yes' Jackie smiled. 'It's finished. Go up and have a look. It's really beautiful up there; so peaceful. Wonderful energy. No corners. You could meditate up there. Meditation would be good for you sweetheart. You're very tense. I think that insurance company might be a bit serious for you.'

'Mmm' Iris stuck a spoon of ice-cream in her mouth and pulled it out slowly, 'maybe it is.' She stuck the spoon back in her mouth, picked up the ice-cream tub and walked through the kitchen into the record room, softly kicking the door shut behind her.

STUDIO ONE
STATION SCHEDULE

Time	Mon	Tues	Wed	Thurs	Fri	Sat	Sun
8-10am	Wayne Conroy Breakfast Show	Wayne Conroy Breakfast Show	Wayne Conroy Breakfast Show	Wayne Conroy Breakfast Show	Wayne Conroy Breakfast Show		
10-12pm							
12 –3pm	Carly West Coast Soft rock	Carly West Coast Soft rock	Carly West Coast Soft rock	Carly West Coast Soft rock	Carly West Coast Soft rock		
3-5pm	Mad Donna Teen Chat	Mad Donna Teen Chat	Mad Donna Teen Chat	Mad Donna Teen Chat	Mad Donna Teen Chat		Eamo Music TBC
5-7pm	Candy Pop/Chart	Candy Pop/Chart	Candy Pop/Chart	Candy Pop/Chart	Candy Pop/Chart		
7-9pm	Benny Ska	Neal O'Neill Synth	Benny Ska	Neal O'Neill Synth	Benny Ska	Neal O'Neill Synth	
9-11pm	Elliott Rock New Wave	Julie Andrews Sound of Music	Elliott Rock New Wave	Julie Andrews Sound of Music	Elliott Rock New Wave	Julie Andrews Sound of Music	
11-1am	Declan Reggae	Declan Reggae	Declan Reggae	Declan Reggae	Declan Reggae	Declan Reggae	
1-3am							
3-6am							
6-8am							

'Look! Look, that's me! There I am! Wayne Conroy! Top ah the chart, The Wayne Conroy Breakfast Show!! That's me! That's me!!'

'You need ta calm down honey. It's just a radio show.'

'Who'er you? You're gorgeous … are you a jock? You're fuckin' gorgeous – here, are you from America?'

'Sure am honey. Haay Donna …'

'Hiyis …'

'Haay Manda, Charlene, you guys look beautiful. I love your hair.'

'Tanks …'

'Yeah, tanks.'

'Manda n'Charlene? Here, are yous jocks?'

'Whatsit-ta-you?'

'Wayne Conroy, Breakfast Show. That's me, up on the chart.'

'Donna Larkin. That's me there.'

'Ya serious? Mad Donna!'

'*Hi everyone!! Oh my God, I can't believe we're about to launch a radio station! This is so exciting!!*'

'Haay Candy. Donna have you met Candy? Her show's right after yours.'

'Alright Candy!! Wayne Conroy! Breakfast Show. D'ya 'member me? We met at the … oh … howeya Mister eh …'

'Cronin. Dessie Cronin.'

'Right. Nice ta meet ya Mister …'

'Dessie.'

'Dessie. Right … eh … Elliott, what time are we startin?'

'Half an hour Wayne. Sorry excuse me for a sec, I just need to find, oh there she is … Iris … are you alright?'

'Fine. I just need to get this music inside.'

'Okay, let me give you a hand. Where's Squirrel?'

'Gone to the off-licence with Eamo.'

'Hey guys!!'

'Hi Neal …'

'Iris! You look gorgeous. Give me a hug!'

'Sorry Neal, Iris is in a bit of a rush. We're just going to get her set lined up.'

'Oh sure Elliott, sorry. Is there anything I can do to help?'

'No, no … you're alright.'

'Are you sure? I can sit in if you like.'

'No! No … thank you … em … Neal, have you met Benny? Benny has the same slot as you on Mondays, Wednesdays and Fridays.'

'Hiya Neal. Nice ta meet ya. When are we kickin' off Elliott?'

'In about twenty minutes. Declan, have you seen Squirrel or Eamo?'

'Wenta get sss–sss–sss … hum beer …'

'They better hurry up. We've only fifteen minutes left.'

'Alright lads!! We're back!! Wrap yer laughin' gear 'round these! Wayne!! Catch! Carly, come on over here! Is that Dessie Cronin! Where'd you come from? Hey Elliott!! What time are we kickin' off?'

'Ten minutes.'

'Where's Iris?'

'She's inside getting her set ready.'

'Did she tell ya what song she's openin' with?'

'No. She wants it to be a surprise.'

'Hey Squirr!! *We.Are.Fah.Mah.Lee !!* …'

'Jays Eamo, relax will ya?'

'*… I got all my DJs with me !!* C'mere, ya never told me Candy was Dessie Cronin's young one. I'm after havin' a close call over there … Tommy!! How we doin? Transmitter okay?'

'Yeah, sorted. Ready ta go.'

'Don't open that Champagne yet Squirr!! Wait 'til we go live. I want ta pop it the exact time the station starts. How're we doin' Elliott?'

'We're on in five. Squirrel, I'm going inside to Iris. Keep everyone else out here yeah?'

'No problem. Right lads! Settle down!! We're on in five!!'

'Shit' Elliott pushed the studio door open 'it's mad out there. Are you okay?' he looked at Iris who was sitting in against the mix desk, phones around her neck, a stack of albums laid out beside her.

'Grand.'

'Nervous?'

'A bit. I'm not going to talk much Elliott. I'm going to let the music do the work.' She looked out at the partying beyond the glass. 'They're hammered' she grinned.

'I know' Elliott watched Wayne and Squirrel dancing with

Mad Donna and Candy. 'I think Eamo bought half the off licence. Right' he glanced up at the clock. Ready?'

'Ready' she said. Elliott flicked a switch on the desk.

'Two minutes Katie.' From the other side of the glass Katie gave him the thumbs up. 'Okay' Elliott sat in beside Iris 'I'll intro, you play.'

'Go for it' she grinned. He flicked the switch back to the outer room again.

'One minute!!' he shouted. The party noise dropped and a sea of faces turned and looked in at him through the glass. 'Standby' Elliott glanced up at the clock again 'okay, that's thirty…' he smiled at Iris who was pulling on her headphones. 'Good luck' he said. Her eyes met his.

'You too' she smiled.

'Okay' he shouted to the faces beyond the glass 'here we go. And we're on in ten … nine … eight … seven … six … five … four … three … two … one …' Elliott opened the mic and leant in close: **'Good evening, broadcasting on 100 MW and 86FM you're listening to Studio One, a new sound for Dublin. More music, less chat, a station that brings you the music you want to hear, when you want to hear it. Up until now you could only hear her play Berlin, but right now, *Live from Studio One*, you're listening to Julie Andrews, and this … is the Sound of Music …'**

Iris didn't speak. She cut straight to track, a familiar eerie bassline echoing up around the studio. Elliott smiled. Of course. Through the glass he could see confusion on Squirrel's face, but it made perfect sense. It wasn't obvious but it was. It was if you knew Iris.

'Radio …' Ian Curtis, raw, stark *'… live transmission … Radio, live transmission. Listen to the silence, let it ring on. Eyes, dark grey lenses frightened of the sun …'* Through the glass Elliott watched Eamo dance and shout, pop Champagne, spraying Carly, grabbing Donna. He watched Benny, Neal and Declan rock along, Donna, Candy, Mandy and Charlene jumping up and down, *'… Dance, dance, dance, dance, dance to the radio ….*

Dance, dance, dance, dance, dance to the radio' Squirrel gave him the thumbs up through the glass. Elliott beckoned to him to come inside, and watched him make his way through the crowd. A burst of noise and cigarette smoke as he pushed the door open.

'We did it!!' Squirrel's eyes were shining. 'We fuckin' did it!!' he slapped Elliott on the back then grabbed him in a rough hug. 'Proud ah ya' he pulled Iris' phones back and kissed her cheek. 'This is just the start' he said. 'See them?' he pointed to the jocks partying behind the glass. 'See us? Right here. Dublin's number one. Number fuckin' one' he jumped up and down, singing along to the track *'... Dance, dance, dance, dance, dance to the radio .... Dance, dance, dance, dance, dance to the radio ...'*

. . . .

So they were up and running. Well, sort of. Elliott's hangover woke him early the next morning. He turned on the radio. Nothing. Over in his house Squirrel did the same. The phone rang. It was Eamo.

'Where's that fuckin' milkman? Katie's up there on her own.'

'Shyte' Squirrel shook his head awake. 'I'm on me way.'

Wayne was running down Capel Street as Squirrel pulled up.

'Where were ya?' Squirrel shouted.

'Sorry' Wayne puffed to a stop. 'I forgot' he leant on his knees as he caught his breath. 'Just went home after me round. Autamatic. Won't happen again.'

'Better not' said Squirrel. 'C'mon. Elliott's on his way, but ya don't need ta wait for him. Tommy said yer all set ta go.'

'Eh ... right' Wayne looked a bit queasy.

'Y'alright?'

'Grand. Yeah, grand.'

'Ya hungover?'

'Kinda' Wayne followed him through the showroom and they made their way up to the Studio.

'Right. Off ya go. Ya need anything?'

'Nah. I'll see ya later' Wayne mumbled. Squirrel eyed him.

'We'll be grand Squirr' Katie was pulling on her phones. Squirrel ran down the stairs and stuck his head into Eamo's office on the way out.

'Sorted' he said. 'Kickin' off now.'

'Yeah?' Eamo turned up the silence on the transistor beside him. 'When?'

'Hey' Elliott pushed past Squirrel in the doorway. 'Is he here?'

'Here alright' Eamo muttered. The radio suddenly crackled to life.

'... Eh ... Studio One ...' Wayne's voice came over, '... Studio One, eh, broadcastin' live ...'

'Jays he doesn't sound great' Squirrel stared at the speaker. 'Thought ya rehearsed this.'

'We did' Elliott frowned. 'He was fine.'

'... Live on 100MW and 86FM ...' Wayne's voice rose and fell.

'Sounds like Kermit the frog' said Eamo.

'...You're listenin' ta the Wayne, the Wayne, the Wayne ...'

'Sounds like Declan' said Squirrel. 'Stutterin' all over the shop.'

'He's nervous' said Elliott.

'Better get up there' said Squirrel. Elliott ran through the showroom, across the warehouse and took the stairs two at a time. Breathless, he pushed the studio door open.

'... an' now here's Paul Young, Love ah the ... rrrrip ... shyte ...' Wayne looked up through the glass. 'I think I broke the needle' he said, still on-air.

'Kill the broadcast' said Elliott to Katie as he crossed the room. 'Close the mic.' He pushed the door to the studio open. 'What's wrong?' he said to Wayne.

'Dunno' Wayne looked at the floor. 'I just ... me voice froze ... it was like someone was squeezin' me throat; I couldn't ... fuck!! I can do this, I've done it a thousand times. I dunno what happened. I think I broke the needle' he lifted up the arm on the deck. 'Shyte. I broke the fuckin' needle.'

'Doesn't matter' Elliott pulled open a drawer 'Tommy left us a spare. Take a break; go out to Katie, make yourself a coffee' he busied himself with the needle. Through the glass he watched Wayne kneel down by the kettle, then stand up and talk to Katie, head shaking, hands moving, perm flapping.

'Okay' said Elliott over the speaker five minutes later. 'Wayne Conroy Show, take two.' Wayne came back in, coffee in one hand, smoke in the other. His hand shook as he pulled on the cigarette, the gold sovereign ring flashing several times in quick succession as the moustache was smoothed and re-smoothed.

'Try to relax' said Elliott. 'Forget you're speaking to hundreds of people. Talk to the mic like it's one person because that's how each listener hears you. If you fuck up, ignore it and move on. Stick on a track and come back out of it like you've just gone on air for the first time. Mistakes are in the past; the listener only cares about what they're hearing now. Okay?'

'Okay' Wayne nodded. 'Okay, I'm ready.'

'Good man' Elliott went back outside and sat down on the other side of the glass. 'Okay Wayne. In your own time.' Wayne took a deep breath and leant into the mic:

'Live from Studio One! The Wayne Conroy show! 11am, this is Wham, Wake me Up, before you ... rrrriipp !! ... shyte!! ...'

'Fuck. Kill it' said Elliott to Katie. He stood up and walked back into Studio where Wayne had lifted up the arm of the needle and was looking at it in dismay.

'I'm after breakin' the spare' his face had turned bright red. 'Fuck! Shyte' he put his head in his hands. 'Suppose ya want me ta go home.'

'I'd prefer it if you went to Tommy's' Elliott lifted up the arm to examine the needle.

'Tommy's?' Wayne looked up.

'Carly's on in half an hour. She's not going to be able to play without a needle.'

'You're not firin' me?'

'No.'

'But I was shyte. I was brutal' Wayne looked depressed.

'I know' Elliott pulled the remains of the needle out of the arm 'but you'll be better next time.'

'How d'ya know?' said Wayne.

'Because I was the same the first time I broadcast, and so are lots of jocks. Your voice freezes, you feel like everyone's watching you even though you're sitting in a room on your own, and the more you think about it the worse it gets. We're a Pirate Wayne; chances are nobody's listening to us. Keep going. You've a great voice. It'll fall into place. Besides, not like I've ten other jocks vying for your slot, now is it?'

'Haay guys?' Carly cut in over the speaker from the room outside. She was dressed in a hot pink jumpsuit, a snakeskin belt with a gold butterfly clasp clinching her waist. 'How ya doin? I'm on in twenny.'

'Right. Run for those needles' said Elliott to Wayne. 'Tell Tommy you'll take whatever he has and tell him he'd better re-stock, because you won't be the only one who breaks them.'

'Grand' Wayne pulled off the phones and stood up.

'And Wayne?'

'Yeah?

'Call Declan. Pull out the stuff we pre-recorded with him and get working on more. Just fun things we can drop into the show. It'll be easier if you don't feel like the whole thing's resting on your shoulders.'

'Deadly' Wayne made for the door. 'Cheers Elliott.'

'Haay Dublin, Studio One, omigaad we finally got some good weather out there, temperatures up in the twennies, Carly with you all the way to three, from Rumours, Stevie Nicks, this is Fleetwood Mac, Don't Stop ...'

'Now *that's* what I call a professional' Eamo pointed at the radio. The four of them were having lunch in his office listening to Carly's show.

'She's great' said Iris from behind her sandwich. 'Amazing voice' she wiped coleslaw off her cheek then bit in again.

'FM's deadly' Squirrel pushed the button on the radio on top of the filing cabinet for the umpteenth time. He'd been flicking back and forth from MW to FM for the last ten minutes, fascinated by the difference in sound quality. 'Tell ya what, MW's gonna die' he pressed the button again. 'Gonna die a fuckin' death.'

'Really?' Elliott gave him a wry smile.

'Alright, I know you've been sayin' it, but it's only when ya hear it ya know what ya mean.' He pressed the FM button again.

'Jays Squirr leave that feckin' thing alone for a minute, will ya' Eamo moved the radio onto his desk. 'Doin' me Goddam head in' he muttered angling it around. 'She's gorgeous that Carly one' he nodded at the speaker. 'What's the story with her Squirr?'

'Dunno' Squirrel leant against the doorway. 'Livin' with some business fella. C'mere Eamo, what about your show on Sunday? Have ya decided on the music?'

'Better not be showbands' Iris scrunched up her sandwich paper and fired it at the bin in the corner.

'I have a little playlist comin' together' Eamo grinned.

'I'm leaving if it's showbands' said Iris. Eamo's grin got wider. 'I mean it' she looked at Elliott, then Squirrel. 'I'm not playing on a station that …'

'Relax yer cacks' Eamo picked up the Benson & Hedges lying on his desk. 'Not doin' showbands' he stuck a cigarette in his mouth. 'Decided ta go for somethin' more sophisticated' the cigarette dancing up and down as he spoke.

'Like what?' said Iris.

'I was thinkin' ya know' Eamo flicked his lighter 'what sort ah music would bring a bit a class ta the station' he pulled down hard. 'Somethin' the more discernin' listener would appreciate' he grinned. Iris eyed him. 'An' the more I thought about it' Eamo swung his legs down 'the more I realised there's only one man for the job.'

'Who's that then?' said Squirrel.

'Come fly with me, lets fly lets fly away' Eamo suddenly sang, clicking his fingers.

'Jays that's not bad Eamo!' Squirrel laughed.

'If you can use, some exotic booze, there's a bar in far Bombay ...'
Eamo stood up and swayed.

'Frank Sinatra!!' Iris looked shocked.

'Come fly with me ... yeah Frank Sinatra' Eamo cut off abruptly 'I backed off on Radio Persia, but I'm standin' me ground on this one.'

'Sinatra's too old' said Iris.

'Sinatra's legend' said Eamo. 'That man laid the foundations.'

'He's a dinosaur' said Iris. 'No-one's going to listen to that.'

'No-one *your* age' said Eamo 'but no-one your age is listenin' ta radio on Sunday are they? They all watchin' yer man Hanley on MT USA.' The three of them looked at each other.

'Well. He has a point' said Elliott.

'Frank Sinatra' Iris looked depressed. 'Christ' she lit a cigarette. 'What's your handle going to be? The Godfather?'

'The Godfather?' Eamo's eyes narrowed. 'Jays I like the sound ah that' he stood up. 'The Godfather' he walked over to the window and stood with his back to them, looking out at Capel Street through the narrow blinds.

'I was joking' said Iris.

'The Godfather, whah?' Eamo straightened his back as he stared through the blinds at the street outside. A small white haired woman passed by the window and stopped to examine her reflection in the glass. Eamo bent down to face her from behind the blinds.

'Are you talkin' ta me?' he said. The old lady fixed her hair in the window's reflection. 'Are you talkin' ta me?' said Eamo. The old lady took out a lipstick and applied it carefully. 'I don't see anyone else here' Eamo double checked behind himself. The lady smiled at her reflection, patted her hair and walked away.

'Maaaad-Donna!!! Live from Studio One!! Are you a virgin Charlene?'

'Nowe.'

'Whaddabouh you Manda?'

'Ya know I'm noh!'

'Thas-righ-I-do-know-but-the-reason-I'm-askin-is-we're-talkin-aboud-ih-today.'

'Talkin-abouh-whah?'

'Virginidy gerlz, if-ya've-lost-ih-whenya-lost-ih-how-ya-lost-ih-whoya-lost-ih-with-d'ya-geh-me?'

'Getcha.'

'Gotcha.'

'Righ! You!! Out-there-in-your-gaff-sittin-in-yer-room-listenin-ta-this-geddup-off-yer-arse-an-call-me.Mad Donna-Studio-One-8722321-the-lines-arrrr-open!! Meantime-it's June-an-June-as-we-all-know-means-one-an-one-thing only ... *Holiday, Celebrate, Holiday, Celebrate* ...'

'Great Donna!! Great delivery!!' Carly cut in to studio as the Holiday 12 inch played out. Donna was a natural. Relaxed, confident, she came alive in front of the mic, rocking on her seat as she spoke, energy coursing around her. 'She sure talks fast' Carly muttered as they watched her work. 'She's the fastest talking jock I've seen and I'm tellin' ya, New Yorkers can talk.'

'Pity no-one's listening' said Elliott.

'Doesn't matter' said Carly. 'We got six of her friends lined up with stories' she gave him a big Californian smile. 'I'm a professional honey' she winked. 'You don't produce New York and LA without putting a few tricks up your sleeve.'

'Holy Mother ah ...' Katie muttered beside her.

'What's wrong?' said Elliott.

'Lines are hoppin' Katie's hands hovered over the flashing switchboard. 'Hello, Studio One?' she flicked up a switch 'Studio One, can you hold? Studio One' she flicked up and down the switchboard 'Studio One, yes you're through to the Mad Donna Show, can you hold for a minute? Fuck' she turned to face Elliott and Carly. 'There's ten calls holdin' an' I can hear more on the line. There's people listenin' an' they're not Donna's mates.'

'Well don't just sit there honey' said Carly. 'Line 'em up. Talk to them. Get their stories. Gimme the top five calls. Hey Donna' she flicked the intercom into studio 'you're on fire sweetheart; Katie, who have we got?'

'Line two' Katie cut in. 'Siobhan. Lost her virginity backstage at Mosney with the Entertainments Officer.'

'... An' then he said he was gonna marry me, an' ya know yer man Jim Diamond's song *Shoulda Known Better* ... he said it was our song, an' he sang it ta me ...'

'So ya slept with him?'

'I did Donna. I slept with him.'

'Because he sang the Jim Diamond song an' said it was your song?'

'Yeah.'

'An' what happened then?'

'He burgled me gaff.'

'He burgled your gaff?'

'Took the telly Donna.'

'Shoulda known better Deirdre. I'm not bein' funny. That's not a Jim Diamond joke, I'm serious; ya shoulda known better. Next time ya see him, give him a different kinda box, one he won't forget in such a hurry. That's all for today, tune in tomorrow for more Mad Donna, playin' us out, this is Borderline ... *Something in your eyes is making such a fool of me ...*'

Donna pushed off the phones and gave Elliott and Carly a big smile through the glass as the track played out.

'She's a winner' said Carly. 'How many calls?'

'Thirty-two' said Katie. 'Put through eight; that's all we'd time for.'

'Borderline' Eamo sang as he pushed the studio door open 'Borderline' he crooned. That was deadly!' he clapped his hands before rubbing them vigorously together. 'We sound like a proper station; the genuine article. They're all listenin' down in the showroom. 'Great show pet; well done' he said to Mad Donna as she made her way out of Studio. 'Very professional' he winked.

'Yeah, well, I am a professional' she flirted back.

'Y'alright there love?' said Eamo to Carly, perched on white stilettos as she knelt by the kettle on the floor. 'That was a great show ya did yerself earlier on' his eyes ran over the pink jumpsuit.

'Hey guys?' Carly didn't look up. 'Are we gonna do news breaks?'

'Here love, let me get that' Eamo knelt down beside the kettle. 'Don't need ta be botherin' yourself with that. That's a lovely outfit you're wearin' by the way.'

'Why *thank you!*' Carly gave him a bright smile. 'That's so sweet of you' blue eyes smiling up as pink lips pulled down on a Marlboro.

'Tell ya what!' Eamo rubbed his hands together 'I'm gonna like workin' here; all these gorgeous women' he winked at Carly. 'She's right about the newsbreaks' he said to Elliott. 'We hafta have news.'

'We can't afford it' said Elliott. 'We'd need a team of people to put a news programme together. We're a long way from having a news programme Eamo.'

'Are we now?' said Eamo. 'What time is it?'

'Five to five' said Elliott.

'Hi everyone' Candy appeared around the Studio door. 'Sorry I'm only here now, all those nice men down in the warehouse thought I was buying carpet, and they kept talking. I had to explain to them that I'm a DJ ...'

'Shit Candy' Elliott ran a hand through his hair 'no-one's meant to know what we're doing up here.' Candy's eyes widened.

'Oh God, I told them! I'm so sorry. I forgot. I was so excited.'

'Don't worry' said Eamo 'I'll square them off.' Elliott looked at him.

'Relax' said Eamo 'they know how ta keep their mouths shut. Reggie'll sort them.'

'Oh no' Candy squeaked 'it's a minute to five! I'm on now!!'

'You're alright love' said Eamo. 'Make yerself a cup ah tea; we'll stick ya on after the news' he pulled the studio door open.

'The news?' Candy's eyes widened. 'We're having news? That's so professional!' Elliott followed Eamo into the studio.

'What are you doing?'

'Watch and learn' Eamo scanned the console. 'C'mere how do we turn on just the ordinary radio?' he said to Elliott. Elliott leant across him and flicked two switches. Eamo reached for the dial. Three sharp twists and RTE came over the speakers. 'Not on-air are we?' said Eamo to Elliott.

'No. What are you doing?'

'Watch and learn' said Eamo. 'How do I go live on-air?'

'Switch that, then that, and see that?' Elliott pointed at the desk. 'That's the fader. Slide it up, and you're live, but what are you ....'

'Watch and learn' keeping the fader down, Eamo turned up the RTE frequency. Up came the RTE news jingle. Eamo pulled it back, cleared his throat, pushed up the fade and leant into the mic:

'Live from Studio One' he pointed the Studio One mic at the RTE news, **'this is the news at five o'clock'** pulling back from the mic he pushed up the sound and broadcast RTE's news live over the Studio One frequency.

'What are you doing?' Elliott hissed. 'Eamo! What the fuck are you doing!!' Through the glass he saw the far door push open and Iris made her way in.

'Sport next ...' said the RTE presenter. Iris smiled at him through the glass.

'An' that my friends is how it's done!' a triumphant Eamo pulled back the sound as the RTE news came to an end.

'Eamo!!' said Elliott 'you just *stole* RTE's news!! You can't *do that*!! We'll be fucking arrested.'

'The news is meant ta be shared!' Eamo grinned. 'That's why it's called The News.'

'I don't think RTE will see it that way.'

'Don't worry about RTE. Think they'll be bothered tunin' in ta the likes of us? They've more important things ta be doin.' Iris pushed the door open.

'Ready for Candy?'

'Always ready for Candy' said Eamo. He looked at Elliott. 'Relax will ya? Far too serious for a young fella your age. Come on' he shook Elliott's shoulders, 'trust yer Uncle Eamo. It's all about trust' he winked. 'All about trust.'

'Trust me' Elliott heard Anthony say to someone on the phone as he slipped in the door later that night 'unfair dismissal won't stand up. Constructive dismissal, sexual harassment, failure to comply with standard trading practices, that's what we'll go after them with.' Elliott made his way up to his room as quietly as he could. He wanted to catch the end of Declan's show before he went to bed. Opening the door, he stopped. There was a Louis Copeland bag sitting on his bed.

What's ... stiff card, tissue rustling, the smell of new wool. He reached in. Soft fabric met his hands, silk sliding as he pulled a tailored jacket out of the bag. He looked at it for a second, then reached in and took out a pair of matching trousers. It was a suit. He looked into the bag again. Five packs of shirts and two ties.

'Ahh! You found it!' Anthony had appeared in the doorway dressed in his own Louis Copeland pinstripe, a stack of letters in his hand. 'How were the exams?' he leant against the door-frame as he flicked through the envelopes. 'Last day?' he didn't look up.

'Yeah' Elliott swallowed 'last day.'

'How'd they go?' Anthony ripped open the first envelope.

'Fine, yeah, they were ... grand' said Elliott.

'Hmm' Anthony's eye-brows shot together as he studied the letter. 'Cretin' he muttered and began thumbing open the second.

Come on Dad, fuck off. I need to listen to Declan's show. Anthony looked up.

'Well try it on' he nodded at the suit on the bed, then looked back down at the letter.

'What's it for?' said Elliott. Anthony smiled as he read the second letter.

'Excellent' he murmured 'about time. What's that you said?'

'What's the suit for?' said Elliott.

'Hydes' Anthony flicked to third letter. 'Monday, remember?' he dug a finger into the corner of the last envelope then looked up over his glasses. 'I got Max to bring a pair of your trousers and one of your jackets into Louis and had him make it up from those; didn't need to drag you in for fittings, what with the exams' he trailed off as he fingered then tore open the envelope. Something hard hit Elliott in the chest. Hydes. He'd completely forgotten about his work experience. 'Try it on' Anthony nodded at the bag. 'Might need some alterations, but should be ...' he broke off as he stared down at the letter in his hand. 'Do I want to' he muttered, scanning the page. 'Mmm' bushy eyebrows, a long questioning growl, then 'what would be better?' he said to Elliott 'do you think I should sponsor the chimpanzee house, the tiger cage, or a new saltwater pool for polar bears?'

'Emm ... how do you mean? Elliott was staring at the suit in his hands.

'The Zoo' Anthony held up the letter. 'It's my annual sponsorship. They've given me three options; chimpanzees, tigers or polar bears ...' from the hallway downstairs, the sound of the telephone ringing. 'Bugger' Anthony glanced around, irritated as the phone continued to ring 'left the fucking portable in the kitchen' letters in hand he turned and went downstairs.

'Fuck' Elliott whispered. Down in the hall he could hear Anthony pick up the phone. Pulling off his T-shirt he opened one of the shirts from inside the bag. *Shit.* He stepped into the trousers. *What am I going to do?* he tucked the shirt in. *Come on. Think.* He slipped on the jacket. His chest tightened and suddenly he couldn't catch a breath. *No air in this room.* He crossed to the window. *Can't breathe.* He pulled the window up and stuck his head out in the warm night air. *Oh God, I'm wasting his money. I'm wasting so much money.*

'Right! Let's have a look!' Anthony had reappeared in the doorway. Elliott stood back, looked down at the suit, then tried to smile as he looked up again.

'Not bad, not bad at all' Anthony nodded approval. 'Tie's not right; here, let me' it was the closest he'd stood to his father in a long time. 'Mmm' Anthony flipped the tie over once, twice. 'Rrr–ight!' he pushed the knot tight against Elliott's neck, then stood back. 'Well. I say. Very smart' he nodded 'very smart indeed' he admired the suit.

Do you really want to spend the next four years living a lie?

'Dad …'

'No need to thank me' said Anthony. 'This is your career. It's important. Now. I'm going to bring you in on Monday. I told David Hyde I'd breakfast with him at eight o'clock, so be ready to leave at seven fifteen sharp. Enjoy your last weekend of freedom' he slapped the doorframe on the way out 'if I know David he'll have you working around the clock. See you in the morning' his voice disappeared down the corridor. Elliott looked at his reflection in the wardrobe mirror.

You're not your own man. You're not your own man.

. . . .

'Start spreadin' the news, I'm leavin' today, I want to be a part of it, New York, New York, These vagabond shoes are longing to stray, right though the very heart of it, New York, New York, I want to wake up in a city that doesn't sleep and find I'm king of the hill, top of the heap, these little town blues …'

They were watching Eamo do his first Sunday show and to be fair to him, for a man who'd never broadcast before he was making a pretty good go of it.

'Look at him; he's fuckin' lovin' it' Squirrel laughed as Eamo high kicked his way around the studio as the track played out.

'Let's hope no-one's listening' said Iris.

'He's very comfortable with the equipment' said Elliott as they watched Eamo slide back into the presenter chair.

'That's 'cause he got Tommy ta give him a crash course' said Squirrel.

'Really?' said Elliott.

'Eamo doesn't mess around' said Squirrel. 'No use doin' it the second time; ya have ta do it the first, that's the way he thinks.

He's right an' all. No way I'd go in there' he pointed at the glass 'unless I was a hundred percent sorted on how it was gonna work. Tell ya, I'm worried about Wayne. I'm really beginnin' ta regret puttin' him forward.'

'Don't be' said Elliott. 'He's got a great voice. He just needs to relax.'

'Yeah? What if he can't? An' what are we gonna do tomorrow? He's bad enough with you beside him. What's he gonna be like without ya?' The track was coming to an end. Eamo leant into the mic:

'Studio One, three-thirty on a sunny Sunday afternoon, the Godfather with ya all the way 'til five. Ask not what your radio station can do for you but what you can do for your radio station ...'

'What is he *talking* about?' Iris scowled.

'I think it's some sort of reference to Kennedy' said Elliott.

'Yer man who was shot?' said Squirrel.

'What's a dead president got to do with his show?' said Iris.

'What's a singin' nun got ta do with yours?' said Squirrel.

'Mine is ironic' Iris replied. Squirrel looked at her.

'Ya know, you an' Eamo have more in common than ya think. Both take yerselves far too seriously for starters.' Iris snorted. 'Seriously, what are we gonna do about Wayne tomorrow?' said Squirrel. 'While you're on this work experience?'

'I don't know' said Elliott, 'Look I'll think of something. I don't know what but I'll think of something.'

He didn't though. He didn't think of anything and suddenly it was Monday morning, he was in his suit, and Anthony was doing eighty along the coast road as they headed into the city. Another hot day. The suit clung to him, cloying at his skin. He tugged on the tie and looked out the window. Blinding sun on shimmering sea. Grey buildings getting closer. Silence. Anthony never talked when he drove, just put the foot to the floor. Elliott looked at his watch. Five past seven. Wayne should be on now. He slipped on his walkman and tuned to Studio One.

' … eh, an' that was the news … kickin' us off now, this is … rrrippp ….'

Fuck. Come on Wayne. Come on.

' … this is Wham, Club Tropicana … *Let me take you to a place … rrrriiirip … Let me take you to a place … rrripp … Let me take you … rrrrriiipppp …. Let me …. Rrrrriiippp …. Rrrippp-riip-riippppp … Club Tropicana drinks are free …*'

Fuck. He's a mess. I should be in there with him. Buildings around them as they reached the city's outskirts, Busaras flashing by. They crossed the bridge, turned right on the quays, then the traffic slowed and there were cars either side. *What am I doing?* Elliott looked out at the traffic. People in suits going to work. Rows of cars with people in suits going to work. Beyond the cars people on the path walking to work. *Is this it?* an image of Iris suddenly flashed into his head; shoulders back, Mohican sharp. Tall. Free.

'Come on' Anthony was getting irritated beside him. The traffic wasn't moving. 'What is keeping them?' Anthony leant on the horn and the people in the cars either side turned to look.

I can't do this.

'What on earth' Anthony slapped the dashboard 'are they doing!!'

'Dad …'

'Should have taken the toll bridge' Anthony twisted his head around to see if he could reverse.

Tell him.

'Bugger' there was a truck behind them. 'The whole fucking road's jammed' Anthony leant to the left of the wheel, then right, trying to see what was causing the problem. Elliott swallowed.

'I didn't do my exams.'

'Right' Anthony glanced at his watch 'well, it's only seven thirty; even if we're stuck here for the next twenty minutes we should still make it for eight.'

'I didn't do them, and I don't, in fact I'm not … I'm not going to work in Hydes.'

'You know the annoying thing?' Anthony stared at the long line of cars. 'The annoying thing is David's office is just around the corner.'

'I'm going to work in radio …'

'I mean we could actually get out and *walk,* and we'd be there in five minutes.'

'Dad …'

'Tell you what' Anthony glanced at his watch 'if this doesn't clear shortly I think you should get out and go on ahead; no point in us both being late and you can let David know what's happened. We don't want to create the wrong impression on your first day.'

'You're not listening to me Dad.'

'Of course I'm listening to you' Anthony murmured, staring at the traffic.

'So you heard me say I'm not going to work in Hydes?' Elliott's stomach flipped. Anthony glanced at him, then looked back at the traffic.

'Well I know that' he said in a calm voice. Silence. Elliott blinked.

'And … you're okay with that? You don't mind?'

'Of course I don't mind' Anthony flicked on the air-con. 'I never expected you to take a permanent position' he started adjusting the temperature up. This is work *experience* Elliott; something to put on your CV. You can go somewhere else next year; doesn't matter once you rack up the experience.' Elliott's heart sank.

Tell him. He swallowed. 'I mean I'm not going to do the work experience Dad.' A pause. 'I'm not doing the work experience.'

'I'm not following you' Anthony gave him a sharp look as hot air blasted through the vents on the dashboard. 'What are you talking about?'

'I'm not doing it' electric currents shot through Elliott's chest and down his arms.

'What do you mean you're not *doing* it?' Anthony's voice

began to rise. 'Of course you're *doing* it! We're in the car, we're going to be there in next ten minutes if these fuckers' he shouted at the traffic 'get out of my fucking way!!'

'I'm sorry Dad' Elliott pulled the door handle. Anthony grabbed his arm.

'What are you doing? What on *earth* are you doing!!'

'I can't do this' Elliott's voice wobbled 'I can't. Sorry.' He pushed the car door open, and almost immediately felt Anthony pull him back.

'Where are you going?' he said.

'I've got a job in radio' Elliott couldn't look at him. 'I want to work in radio.'

'Jesus Christ! Shut the door. I said shut the *fucking door!!*' Anthony shouted. 'What are you *saying*? What the *fuck,* are you trying to say? Are you saying, are you actually … Christ Elliott!! What the fuck are you saying to me!!' his father's face had turned deep red.

'I didn't do my exams!' Elliott shouted. 'I didn't do them! And I'm not going to finish my degree!! I'm going to work in radio. Do you understand *me* Dad? Do *you* understand, what I'm saying to you?' Something funny was happening. Light. He was floating, suspended, watching the conversation as though he weren't part of it. He saw the shock register on Anthony's face, then as information sank and anger rose he saw his father's lips move, fast, furious, but he couldn't hear. He watched him red-faced, ranting in front of him but he couldn't hear him. A silent hammering in his head but he couldn't hear anything. Nothing. He looked at the clock on the dashboard. Quarter to eight. If he left now he'd still get an hour in with Wayne.

'I'm sorry' he pulled on the door handle. Anthony's hand grabbed his wrist and pulled him back.

'You can't stop me' Elliott struggled 'you can't … stop … me.'

'If you get out of this car' Anthony's voice was thick with rage. 'If you. Get out, of *this car*, if you Let.Me.Down, with David Hyde, I will wash my hands of you. Do you understand

161

me Elliott? I will wash my hands.' Elliott nodded. Silence. He looked down at his father's hand on his wrist. 'I won't support this' Anthony let go of his arm. 'Be very clear' his voice hardened. 'If you pursue this, you pursue it alone. You can find somewhere else to live and someone else to feed and clothe you.' Elliott pulled the door handle. 'Where are you going to live!!' Anthony shouted as Elliott stood up out of the car. 'Eh?? Answer me that! Where! Will you live!!' Elliott shut the door and walked around the front of the car. The window slid down. 'And you can forget about Max!!' Anthony called as Elliott began to weave his way through the traffic. 'I gave him the deposit for that apartment and I will be instructing him not to support you. He. Will not. Support you!!' Elliott didn't reply. Eyes straight ahead, he loosened the tie, lit a cigarette and headed for Capel Street.

'... And there's a new man in the Kremlin. At fifty four Mikhial Gorbachev is the youngest man to take over as General Secretary of the Soviet Communist Party. Mr Gorbachev's acceptance speech gave a hint of the changes to come. He spoke of his desire to freeze the deployment of weapons and reduce the international nuclear weapons stockpiles ...'

Wayne had the mic pointed at the RTE news when Elliott walked into the studio just after 8am. Squirrel and Eamo were sitting in the outer room.

'What's the story?' Squirrel stood up.

'Where'd ya get the threads?' Eamo eyed Elliott's suit.

'What happened?' said Squirrel.

'I told him' Elliott sat down on the couch.

'Told who?' said Squirrel.

'My Dad' Elliott lit a cigarette and pulled down hard. 'Told him about my exams. Told him I had a job in radio.'

'What'd he say?' said Squirrel.

'Said he'd wash his hands of me' a small smile. 'Said not to bother coming home.' Then it hit him. Like a sledge hammer at full whack, came the enormity of what he'd done. Panic scattered and his insides collapsed. 'Shit' he felt his voice sink down inside 'I've nowhere to live' his whole body began to shake 'I've nowhere' the door pushed open and Iris walked in.

'He' she pointed at Wayne in-studio 'is a disaster. Are any of you listening to that?' She looked at Elliott. 'What are you doing here?'

'He told his Da' said Squirrel.

'Good' Iris walked over to the desk and she flicked off the sound. 'I can't listen to that any more. What happened?' she said to Elliott.

'He needs a place ta live' said Squirrel.

'Well, I'm sure you can stay in the tower for a night or two if you want' she took out her smokes. 'My Mum' she grinned, flicking the lighter 'keeps trying to get me to sleep in there. Says there's a healing energy.' Pull. Puff. Grin. Mischievous brown eyes. Elliott gave her a half smile. 'You've done the right thing' said Iris. 'You know you have.'

'I know' Elliott put his head in his hands 'I just don't know what ... I've no job, no money. Where am I going to live? What am I going to live *on*?'

'Alright-alright, don't panic' said Squirrel. 'Sort somethin' out' he stood up and walked to the window. 'Pity ya can't drive a bike. Skello's after doin' his leg in.'

'Couldn't ride a bike wearin' that' Eamo pointed at Elliott's suit. 'Looks more like ...'

'Looks more like what?' said Squirrel. Eamo didn't reply. 'Eamo?' said Squirrel. Eamo was studying Elliott, his eyes travelling up and down the Louis Copeland suit.

'I need someone in the shop' he said. 'Someone ta cover when I'm not there. Aul wans'd love him in that get up' he nodded at the suit. Squirrel looked at Elliott.

'D'ya reckon ya could do it?'

'Dunno' said Elliott. 'I could try.'

'Be a bit ah cash' said Eamo. 'Hours'd be flexible; ya'd have plenty ah time for the station. Why can't you wear a suit like that?' he said to Squirrel.

'Because I don't want ta' said Squirrel. 'How much are ya gonna pay him?'

'What are you?' said Eamo. 'His manager?'

'He's gonna hafta find somewhere ta live Eamo. 'That's not gonna come cheap.'

'Yeah, well I might have an answer for that an' all' Eamo stood up. 'Johnny bleedin' Forty Coats. C'mon' he made for the door.

'Where are ya goin?' said Squirrel. Eamo didn't answer him. 'Where are ya goin!' Squirrel shouted as Eamo went out the door. 'Where the fuck is he goin?' he said to Elliott and Iris. The studio door pushed open again.

'Are yis comin' or what?' Eamo stuck his head back in.

'Where?' said Squirrel 'are ya goin?'

'Just folley me!' said Eamo. 'Shut up the fuck, an' folley me' he disappeared out the door again. The three of them looked at each other. Squirrel shrugged.

'Right. C'mon.'

They caught up with Eamo in his office, rooting through the top drawer in his desk.

'Where the fuck' he muttered 'Lorraine!' he shouted 'Lorraine!!' he pulled open the second drawer. 'Gotcha' he held up a bunch of keys. 'Right, c'mere' he walked out of the office. The three of followed him through the showroom and out onto the street.

'Eamo, where are ya goin?' Squirrel shouted but Eamo had stopped at a door right beside the end of the showroom windows.

'Haven't been up here in a while' he turned the key, pushed the door and they followed him up a short dark narrow stairway. The smell of damp carpet, a staleness in the air. As they reached a door at the top of the stairs the bottom one swung shut and suddenly they were in darkness. 'Shyte' said Eamo. 'Hang on' they heard him pat the wall beside them. 'Switch here somewhere' the sound of his hands, patting, pressing the wall, then click, the stairway was filled with a pinky glow.

'Smell ah death in here' said Squirrel.

'What the fuck would you know' the keys jangled again as Eamo went through them 'about the smell ah death? Smell ah damp, is what that is. Death' Eamo muttered 'right, here we go' he slotted a key into the door, then light filled the stairwell again as he pushed it open and they stepped inside. Bright sunlight filling a small room, warming the stale damp air. An old fireplace in the centre, a bed in the corner, torn sheets and a blanket strewn across it. Faded wallpaper peeling away.

'Part ah the buildin' said Eamo. 'Got it when I bought the showroom.' Elliott looked around. The room was filthy. 'There's a bathroom over there' Eamo pointed at a door in the corner. Elliott nodded. He knew what was being offered, he knew he should be grateful but it was a smelly, filthy, stinking ...

'I love it' said Iris. Elliott stared at her. 'It's perfect' she walked into the centre of the room. 'Look at these windows; look at this *light*, and you're right on Capel Street; you're a minute from the station. God, I'd give anything for a place like this. You could put a couch here' she pointed at the fireplace 'music there' she turned 'stereo here' and as Elliott looked around again he began to re-consider.

'I suppose we could paint the walls' he said.

'Poster them' said Iris. 'Gig posters, album covers. Mick has lots of stuff in the club.'

'What about the bed?' said Squirrel. 'Wouldn't fancy sleepin' on that. Rotten so it is. Probably full ah hoppers' he shivered. 'Be scratchin' after a night in that.'

'That's easy fixed' said Eamo. 'I'll get the lads in Bargaintown ta throw me a new one. I'm always doin' them favours.' Elliott looked around again. Iris was right. The light *was* nice the way it came in. He walked over to the window and looked down at the street. 'Well?' said Eamo. 'Are we doin' this or what?'

'Yes' Elliott heard himself say 'I think we are.'

'Right' Squirrel slapped his hands together. 'Better organize a van so.'

'What for?' said Elliott.

'Shift yer gear outta yer gaff before yer aul' fella gets home. Ya need your music don't ya? An' clothes?' Elliott nodded. 'Right' said Squirrel, 'c'mon.'

And so, within the space of a morning, he went from Elliott Barrington Law Student to Elliott Barrington Station Manager, from living in Howth to living in a box and from running and hiding to being his own man. And when he lay on the blow up bed in the tower in Iris' house later that night he realised that for the first time in a long time he was on the right path, that he was doing what he was meant to be doing. Then he thought about his mother. Eyes open he lay in the dark and thought about her for the longest time, until finally he drifted off and went to sleep.

. . . .

'Good morning! 9.30am on a bright sunny Tuesday, you're tuned to Rocket Radio, and this is ffffzzzzzzzzz … fffffffffffffzzzzzzzzzzzzzzzzz … ffffzzzzzzzzzzz'

'Bee Bee Rrrr!!! Cominatcha!! Nine forty-five, BBR, it's a beautiful …. ffffffff-zzzzzzzzzzz ……… ffffffff-zzzzzzzzzzzz … ffffffff-zzzzzzzzzzzzzzzzzzzz'

'Gotcha' said Roger to the radio as it hissed in the corner. 'Gotcha, gotcha, gotcha. 'Is that it? They can't reverse this?' he said to a white faced Bobby sitting across the desk from him.

'No' Bobby's voice was flat. 'It's our signal broadcasting on top of theirs. There's nothing they can do. The only option they have is to set up on another frequency.'

'Well if they're stupid enough to try that we'll just jam them again' said Roger. 'We'll jam them and we'll keep jamming them until they get the message. God I'm good' he smiled. 'I knew there was a reason I got this job; I'd just forgotten what it was. All those raids; Gardaí running around like headless chickens and all that time, all we had to do was just sit here and zap them.' He leant back in his chair. 'They'll never recover from this, because no matter what they do, we'll just press a button and wipe them out.' He reached forward and pressed the intercom on his desk. 'Breda!' he shouted.

'Yes Roger.'

'Get me a list of of every single Pirate Radio station in the country along with the frequency they're broadcasting on.' Releasing the intercom he smiled again. 'See this?' he said to Bobby. 'Tonight is just the start. We are going systematically jam every single Pirate Station in the country. We're going to bring these bastards down one by one.'

'You're going to get a lot of flak' said Bobby.

'That's what the PR Department's for' Roger patted a folder beside him. 'The press release is lined up and ready to go. That's if Rocket and BBR and the rest of them actually manage to work out what's hit them' he smiled at the hissing radio.

'This is the end Bobby. Pirate radio is coming to a grinding, shuddering halt and I for one am going to take so much pleasure in watching it die.'

. . . .

'Mork calling Orsen, come in Orsen. I've just been to Dublin where earthlings are listening to a strange device called a radio. The radios come in different shapes and sizes, but they all have stations inside them – places that transmit news, popular culture and information, but best of all Orsen – a thing called music, all types of music, enough to fill a whole galaxy, possibly the universe. It appears many stations are transmitting this music but the one that does it best is a station called Studio One.'

'Studio One Mork? How can a studio for one play enough music for an entire galaxy?'

'I don't know Orsen, but they do, and the people here can't get enough of them, including myself.'

'Stay tuned Mork. I want a daily report. Perhaps you should get a job in Studio One ...'

Elliott put Declan on the Breakfast Show with Wayne. A daily slot impersonating Mork which he'd pre-record each night after his show and leave there for Wayne to slot on in the morning.

'Can you do the weather?' Elliott had asked him.

'How-how ... how d'ya mean?' said Declan.

'I mean do the weather as Mork. Do it in Mork's voice.'

'How-how'll I nnn- know what the ffff-uckin' weather ... sss-gonna be like?'

'Doesn't matter' said Elliott. Make it up. It's Mork they want to hear, not the weather. In fact the more off the mark it is the better. Tell them pigs'll fly and to watch out for giant talking chocolate ants.'

He'd moved into the flat three weeks ago. Eamo had replaced the bed and given him a huge oriental rug to cover the carpet. Squirrel found a sofa on the back of a skip which they covered with Indian throws Iris took from home. They put his stereo by the fireplace and his music in piles everywhere.

'You need shelves for those albums' said Iris as she staple-gunned a Siouxsie and the Banshees poster to the wall.

'Needs a wardrobe more like' said Squirrel eyeing the boxes and bags Elliott had jammed his clothes into the day he left home.

'Use this' Iris held up the staple-gun 'just staple all your clothes to the wall, pull them off in the morning and then gun them back up at the end of the day. 'Here' two dull thuds as she gunned one of his T-shirts up. Elliott smiled. 'I'll get you a rail from the shop' she said. 'We've loads of them.'

As the apartment came together, so did the station. Elliott started each day by sitting in with Wayne. After the Breakfast Show he'd stick on a mixed tape to cover the mid morning slot which they still needed a jock for, then he'd go for breakfast with Wayne to work on ideas for the next day's show. Carly produced her own show, then worked with Donna; Candy ran solo from 5pm, and depending on what day it was, either Benny or Neal played the 7pm slot, followed by Elliott or Iris at 9 o'clock.

Declan played 11 to 1am, and after that it was a mixed tape until Wayne came back on at 7am the next morning.

In between shows Elliott put on his suit and sold carpets. Carpets, underlay, rugs and remnants. Cut Pile, Loop pile, Shag. And as he sold he listened. The radio in the showroom was permanently tuned to the station. He talked fibres and thought playlists. He threw rugs on the floor and ideas in the air. He watched customers finger swatchbooks and heard listeners play requests. He watched the switchboard get busy. He listened as more and more people began to call the station. Slowly, very slowly, an audience was building.

'... I know a girl who's tough but sweet, She's so fine she can't be beat, She's got everything I desire, Sets the summer sun on fire, I want Candy, I want Candy ... **Studio One, Candy with you all the way til seven, this is Murray Head, One Night in Bangkok ...** *Bangkok, Oriental City ...'*

'We need ta start sellin' ads' said Squirrel. They were watching Candy do her show.

'We're not ready' said Elliott. 'We don't have a full schedule yet.'

'Fuck that' said Squirrel. 'Could take a year ta get a full schedule. We need ta start makin' money. I keep tellin' ya; we're not doin' this for the craic. We're doin' this ta make money. How long are BBR an' Rocket off-air?'

'About a month.'

'Where's that money goin?'

'I don't know. Back to RTE I suppose.'

'It's not' said Squirrel. 'Sittin' there waitin for us ta take it. 'We need ads' his eyes flattened. 'We need ads ta get ads. If people thought other people were advertisin' with us they'd be in like a shot.'

'If we need them to get them' said Iris, 'how do we get them in the first place?'

'Same way we do the news' Squirrel glanced at Elliott 'lift them offa RTE.'

'No' said Elliott 'no way.'

'RTE won't know we lifted them' said Squirrel. 'People put the same ad on different stations all the time. They're more likely ta suss us nickin' their news than their ads.' Elliott was silent. 'D'ya think those jocks are always gonna work for free?' Squirrel pointed at Candy behind the glass. 'We're gonna hafta start payin' them at some stage, otherwise we'll lose them. 'An' *we* need ta make money. Do you wanna sell carpet for the rest of your life?' he looked at Elliott. Silence. 'Do ya?'

'No' Elliott conceded. 'Alright, I'll record some ads tonight and drop them in across the shows tomorrow. You go and see if you can drum up some business.'

'No problem' Squirrel rubbed his hands together 'no problem.'

'Hey guys!!' the door pushed open and Neal walked in, a stack of albums under his arm. 'Hi gorgeous' he smiled at Iris from beneath his fringe.

'Hey' her face broke into a wide grin and Elliott felt a sharp sting. He had, he'd realised too late, made a fundamental mistake slotting Neal and Iris back to back three nights a week, something Squirrel had been quick to point out.

'Ya know yer after handin' her ta him on a plate?' he'd said. 'Three nights a week. What were ya thinkin?'

'I wasn't thinking' said Elliott. 'I was stoned when I wrote that schedule. The only thing I was thinking about was kissing her and I was getting pretty close until you nearly landed the bike on top of us.'

'Yeah, well ya fucked up good an' proper' said Squirrel. 'Three nights a week. An' don't tell me he won't be hangin' around ta walk her ta the bus stop, 'cause he will. You're gonna hafta watch him.' So Elliott watched. Watched Neal come in week after week, hair high, smile wide. Watched him tease, flirt, present copies of bootlegs, light her cigarettes, sit close; *why* did he have to sit so close to her all the time? And as for his latest tactic.

'Where's my hug?' a sing-song voice as Neal threw his arms open wide in Iris's direction. There, right there. The hug.

'Hafta hand it to him' Squirrel had said the first week it happened. 'It's a good move. I've been huggin' girls left, right an' centre since I seen him doin' that, an' it works. Like something their Ma or Da'd do. Give us a little hug' he winked 'then we might have a little ride.'

'Shut up' Elliott didn't want that picture in his head.

'Ask her out' said Squirrel. 'Just ask her out.'

'Can't. It'll fuck up our friendship.'

'Fuck up a lot more if ya don't.

'How do you mean?'

'I mean you're just sittin' there week after week, thinkin' about her an' not doin' anything about it. Long as you're doin' that you're never gonna be able ta move forward.'

'What is it with you and moving forward?' said Elliott. 'We don't all want to move forward you know. Did it ever cross your mind some of us might be happy standing still?'

'Would you ever fuck off' said Squirrel. 'Never heard such a load ah shyte. You stand still long enough' he pointed his finger at Elliott 'an' life'll pass ya by.' Without warning, he grabbed Elliott's T-shirt with both hands, balling the material around his fists as he pulled him close. 'Time ta participate' he rocked Elliott back and forth. 'Time ta stand up. Ta say this is what I want, this is what I need, now give it ta me. Ask and ye shall receive' he released his grip on the T-shirt. 'Keep it zipped an' ya'll get fuck all.' He clicked his fingers inches from Elliott's nose. 'It's over like that' he said. 'Stop waitin' for it ta happen. Make it happen.'

Elliott watched Iris disappear into Neal's bear hug.

How does he do that? How can he just do that? Fucker. 'Fucker.'

'What did you say?' said Iris.

'Nothing.'

'You said fucker.'

'I didn't.'

'You did. I heard you.'

'I think Elliott needs a hug' Neal grinned.

'Nah' Elliott backed away 'you're alright thanks.'

'I think you do' Neal sang. 'I think Elliott needs a bit of love' he cocked his hand into an imaginary gun and aimed it in Elliott's direction.

Elliott needs you to fuck off, that's what Elliott needs. Elliott needs you to put your stupid gun away and get out of here. 'No, honestly Neal, I ... uff' Neal had grabbed him.

'We're gonna give Elliott a bit of love' he squeezed him tight. Over a herringbone shoulder Elliott watched Squirrel and Iris grinning as he extracted himself.

'Right, thanks Neal ... what ... em ...' he nodded at the albums on the sofa 'what have you got lined up for tonight then?'

'Yazoo' Neal rearranged his hair. 'BBC gig they did last week' he twisted and teased the fringe. 'You gonna stick around for my set?' he flicked an eye in Iris' direction.

'Maybe' she grinned.

'I hope you will' Neal flashed her a bright smile. 'By the way' he picked up his albums 'you guys want to see the Human League in October? A friend of mine's doing the door.' Elliott laughed.

'Thanks Neal but the Human League wouldn't really be my ...'

'I'll go' said Iris. Elliott stared at her.

'Why are you looking at me like that?' she said.

'The Human League?' said Elliott.

What's wrong with the Human League?'

'Nothing. Shit. Everything. The *Human League?*'

'I don't want to manage them' Iris snapped. 'It's just a gig Elliott. Gig's a gig' she scowled.

Gig's a gig my arse. This is Neal. This is that fucker over there with his smile and his hugs and his fucking gun.

'I think we should all go' said Squirrel. 'Important for the station.' Elliott felt his cheeks sting. He knew what Squirrel was at and he was right. There was no way he was letting Iris go to that gig on her own with Neal.

'Suppose we should know what's going on out there' he muttered.

'Four tickets then?' said Neal. Elliott nodded.

'Yeah. Thanks' he muttered in Neal's general direction.

'Deadly' Squirrel clapped his hands together. 'Don't you want me baby?' he sang to Iris, 'don't you want me, oh-oh-ohhhh' he grabbed her and Elliott felt none of the jealousy he had with Neal earlier, just relief there was a smile back on her face and everything was okay again. For the moment anyway.

. . . .

'Max?'

'Elliott! Where *are* you? What happened with Dad?'

'What did *he say* happened?'

'Well, he didn't give me specifics.'

'What *did* he say?'

'He said ... he thinks' Elliott could hear Max laughing.

'What? What Max?'

'He's convinced you're having some sort of breakdown.'

'Why? Because I don't want to be like him?'

'He asked me to persuade you to see a psychiatrist.'

'He's the one that needs a psychiatrist. Examining walls for cracks that aren't there. Lying about selling the house. I might not be studying Law anymore but I know a fucking lie when I hear it.'

'What are you talking about?'

'Nothing' Elliott's cheeks felt hot. 'Doesn't matter.' From the other end of the receiver Max sighed.

'He's worried about you Elliott. As am I. Where have you been living for the last month?'

'Never mind.'

'Oh come on Elliott' Max snapped. 'I'm not going to tell him. Don't you trust me?'

'I do' said Elliott 'of course I do. It's just easier if you don't know; it means he can't put you under any pressure. I don't want him coming in here ...'

'Coming in where?'

'Nowhere. Look I'm okay Max. I'm happy. I have a job and I'm happy. And I have somewhere safe to stay. I'll be in touch.'

'Okay, but promise me ... Elliott? Elliott?'

' ... Why must you record my phone calls? Are you planning a bootleg L.P? Said you've been threatened by gangsters, Now it's you that's threatening me ... **Studio One, Benny the Beat with you all the way 'til nine o'clock, bringing you the best Ska in Dublin ... this is The Specials ... Gangsters ...'**

Benny was a little fire cracker. An instant on-air success. Every night he turned up bang on time, dressed in the same sharp black suit and pork pie hat he'd worn to the interview. And every night he brought an entourage. Girls in two tone, boys in Ska suits. A constant party in studio. It worried Elliott at first.

'Benny we can't have people coming into the studio; it's too risky. If people know where we are it's only a matter of time before we get raided.'

'Don't worry about raids' said Benny. 'Me mate Jackie works in the P&T. He sits right beside the fella who's in charge ah the raids. He'd a deal goin' with BBR an' Rocket before they got jammed. Anytime a raid was gonna happen, he'd get on the blower ta let them know they were on their way, so the station could get the transmitter outta there. Don't worry boss' he winked. 'Jackie'll look after us. They're all listenin' ta me show in there. Half the fellas in his office were playin' requests last week. Relax. We're sorted. We'll get the nod if anything's gonna happen an' we'll have that transmitter outta here long before they land on our doorstep.'

'Studio One, you're tuned to the Wayne Conroy show, line one, it's Rachel. Rachel, are you there?'

'I am Wayne! I most certainly am!'

'Back again Rachel; that's the fourth time this week! What are you going to talk to us about today?'

'I'll tell you what I want to talk about Wayne. I want to talk about what happened with Rocket and BBR and what appears to be happening to every single other Pirate station out there. Now I know they're your competition, at least they were until RTE took them off the air, but I don't think that should stop us talking about the principle, or rather the disgraceful *lack* of principle behind what RTE have done, and the reason I *think* you need to be drawing attention to this because it's only a matter of time before it happens to you ...'

Wayne was improving. He'd stopped breaking needles, his voice didn't shake anymore and Elliott had built in a series of segments to break up the show. Declan did the weather in Mork's voice, one of Squirrel's bikers called in a daily traffic report and Robbie, one of Wayne's mates, had started coming in to do five or ten minutes of sport every day. Elliott had also introduced a debate section. Wayne would put up a topic, usually something from the papers, for listeners to call in and debate. Callers varied depending on the subject, but a housewife called Rachel had been consistently on-air from the start. Opinionated, quick witted and razor sharp, she always sparked a lively discussion, and lately if she wasn't happy with the subject Wayne put up for debate, she'd just come on-air with her own topic and off she'd go.

'She's good yer woman isn't she?' said Squirrel.

'She is' said Elliott. 'She's very good.'

'... It's a disgrace Wayne! Competition is healthy. We *need* competition. RTE are not providing the kind of programming the general public want to hear. If they were we'd be listening. It's as simple as that. The reason the Pirate stations have done so well is because they're offering something RTE aren't ...'

Elliott listened to her for another few minutes. 'Katie?'

'Yeah?' Katie glanced over her shoulder.

'Do we have a number for that woman?'

'Yeah, why?'

'I might ask her if she'd like to do a show. We still need someone for the slot right after Wayne, to fill the gap between himself and Carly.'

'She'd be great' said Katie. 'Got an answer for everything that one. There's another fella been lookin' for work. Askin' about the news. Yer man Christian. Says he's studyin' journalism in college an' could pull it together for us.'

'Christian?'

'Young fella who sounds like an aul' fella' said Katie. 'Rings in all the time.

'Christian' said Elliott, then suddenly he knew exactly who Katie was speaking about and could hear him clearly from a phone-in the week before:

'One of the things I struggle with greatly' Christian had a soft cultured voice **'is why people complain 'oh my life is so this, my life is so that' – if it's so awful, if it's so miserable, then do something about it'** calm, logical, authoritative. **'Really, the only people who have any right to complain are the sick and starving. The rest of us need to cop on to ourselves.'**

'I know him' said Elliott. 'I know exactly who you're talking about. Get a number for him. If he can do any kind of news, even a basic report, that'd be amazing. I hate the fact that we take it from RTE.'

The shows were slowly taking shape, and from what Elliott could gauge by the volume of calls, they had started to gather and build audiences. The station voice was forming; a clear and distinct Studio One sound was emerging. Then two things happened which pushed them onto a whole new level. Carly's IDs arrived from the States and Tommy upgraded the transmitter.

Richly layered and textured, the IDs were over twenty different variations of the same message:

'Studio One' – a rich American male voice

'Studio One' – a sexy sultry American female

'I listen to Studio One' – a breathy Marilyn Monroe voice

'Studio Wuh-hun!! The weekly top fordeee !!' – Californian girls singing

'**Studio One on an all request weekend**' – American male again

'**Oh-oh … Studio … Studio Wuh-Hun!!**' – Stevie Wonder impersonator

'Mental' said Squirrel. 'Never thought ya could say the same thing so many different ways.' There were Soul versions, Classic, Blues, Summer jingles, spooky Halloween voices. 'Here! There's a Santy!' said Squirrel. 'Listen ta this!'

'**Ho! Ho! Ho! Studio One!**' – Santa with jingle bell sound effects

'They're brilliant' said Iris.

'Pity we can't afford them' said Elliott

'Why don't we just use them on the sly?' said Squirrel. 'KCNB are in America. They'll never hear them.'

'I'm sick of doing things on the sly' said Elliott. 'We're not using these until we can pay for them. Besides, they're not broadcast quality, and KCNB won't release the masters until we've paid for them.'

'I'll sub ya' said Eamo. They looked at him. 'What are ya lookin' at me like that for?' he said. 'Ya'll be payin' me back. How far away are you from sellin' a few ads?' he said to Squirrel.

'Nearly there' said Squirrel. 'Lot ah agencies lookin' at us at the moment. It's gonna happen. They're gonna start landin' soon. I can feel it.'

'Grand' said Eamo. 'I'll sub ya. Get them on-air. Sooner they're on, sooner those ads'll be in.'

The same week the IDs arrived, Tommy bumped up the transmitter.

'It's not necessary' said Elliott. 'It's fine as it is.

'No' Tommy shook his head 'it's not. Just wait an' see.' And sure enough, three days later, as they sat in Eamo's office, the sound suddenly morphed and ballooned around them. Liquid gold. A rich fat juicy sound.

'Fuck me' said Eamo. 'What's after happenin' there?' The three of them looked at each other. Elliott stood up and walked over to the radio. He tuned up and down the dial, listening to the different stations.

'Get another radio' he said. 'Has Lorraine one in the showroom?' She had. Eamo brought it in and they put the two of them side by side as Elliott went up and down the dial comparing the new Studio One sound to the other stations.

'That's Premier Division' said Squirrel.

'Mmm' Elliott ran his hand through his hair, trying to push aside a nagging concern.

'What's wrong?' said Squirrel.

'RTE' said Elliott.

'What about them?' said Eamo.

'The better we get' said Elliott 'the more popular we get, the more listeners we get, the greater the chances are that RTE will jam us.' Eamo sat back in his chair and kicked his feet up on the desk.

'RTE don't scare me' he said.

'Eamo' said Elliott 'if RTE jam us there is nothing we can do to stop them. They broadcast a frequency on top of ours and we're gone. Wiped out. And each time we move they'll just do it again. Look at Rocket and BBR. They've both moved frequency three times in the last month and each time they did RTE jammed them again straight away.'

'D'you think I built all ah this' Eamo gestured at the showroom 'without runnin' into a bit ah shyte along the way? Don't worry about RTE' he lit a cigarette. 'RTE so much as look at us sideways, I'll be all over them like a rash.'

'You can't stop a jam' said Elliott. 'They broadcast a frequency on top of us; you can't physically stop it.'

'No' Eamo blew a thin line of smoke across the room 'but I can physically knock the shyte outta them. And believe me, if push comes ta shove, that's exactly what I'll do. So don't you' he pointed the cigarette at Elliott 'tell me they're a threat, because they're not. Not ta me.'

Later on, when Carly was finished her show Elliott went back down to the showroom to help get new stock in. He spent an hour with Eamo clearing space and at around four o'clock Squirrel pulled up in the transit and they began loading in the new samples.

'Get a move on' said Eamo 'we're blockin' the street. Gards'll be on my case. Here! Squirr! Catch!' he threw a sample book at him.

'Take it easy there Eamo' said Squirrel. 'Doin ya a favour here.'

'Shut up talkin' an' keep workin' said Eamo. 'Gards said they'd fine me the next time I left a van hangin' around' he scanned the street.

'Relax' said Squirrel. 'Have this outta here in no time.' They kept working, Squirrel inside the van, breaking down the pallets, Eamo off-loading and Elliott carrying into the shop. Engrossed in their work they didn't notice a tall man striding down Capel Street in the distance. They didn't see as he drew closer, a good head above everyone around him, a sense of purpose to his gait as he wove in and around people slower than him on the path. They didn't see his fleeting glance at the transit or the double take that halted him in his tracks. They didn't notice him step into a doorway and watch as they worked for the next twenty minutes.

'Elliott' said Eamo as they came to the end of it 'look after her will ya' he nodded in the direction of a woman who had just pushed a pram into the showroom. 'Me'n Squirr'll sort this' he pointed to the empty packaging on the ground.

'Sure' Elliott went inside. The man watched Eamo and Squirrel from the doorway across the road, as they tidied the packaging back into the van. He watched them for a minute or two then he crossed the road towards the shop.

'Alright yer Honour?' Eamo grinned. The man glanced at him, did not reply, then stepped inside the showroom.'

'Shyte' said Eamo. 'What does *he* want?'

'Dunno' Squirrel bolted the back of the transit. 'Tell ya what though Eamo, I don't think he's lookin' for carpet.'

'And this one is £12.99' said Elliott to the woman. 'It's more expensive but much harder wearing.'

'Everything alright yer Honour?' Eamo had caught up with the man who was now standing at the top of the showroom staring down at Elliott and the woman. 'No problem with anything is there? Not in trouble are we?' he laughed. The man didn't reply. His eyes were fixed on Elliott at the end of the showroom.

'You do need underlay' Elliott was explaining to the woman 'there's no point cutting corners; now this is one of our ...' something, he wasn't sure what; something for some reason gave him pause. He looked up and felt the blood drain from his face. 'Shit' he said.

'Sorry?' said the woman.

'Sorry' Elliott's mouth was dry 'sorry, excuse me for a second.' *Shit*. He made his way up the showroom towards the tall figure in the black robe and white wig. 'It's okay' he said to Eamo as he reached the two of them 'it's okay ... it's ... this ... I ... this is my Father.'

Anthony didn't acknowledge Eamo. His eyes were angry, glittering. 'Eh ... can you?' Elliott inclined his head towards the woman waiting at the end of the showroom.

'Oh ... yeah ... sure ... no problem' Eamo took off down the shop. Elliott felt his cheeks burn red.

'Hi' was the best he could manage.

'What's this?' Anthony gestured at the showroom, the slightest movement, the briefest glance, but in that moment, in that one gesture, he managed to belittle everything it stood for, and in the same split second, the fear that had initially gripped Elliott, turned to rage. 'Answer me' said Anthony 'what *is* this?'

'What does it look like?' said Elliott and he watched the skin on his Father's face tighten and pull back.

'It looks like your story about wanting to work in radio was fabrication' said Anthony. 'In every sense of the word. It looks like my son' he drew breath 'my son who less than three months ago had a promising legal career ahead of him, the same fellow who was so *confident* he could forge some sort of future in radio broadcasting, has in fact been reduced to working as a carpet shop salesman.'

'Well if that's what it looks like' said Elliott 'then that's what it must be.' *Fuck you. If that's what you want to believe, then that's what you can believe.* 'Get out' he said, surprised how good it felt. 'Go on' he said 'get out.' A brief shock registered on his Father's face, then dark angry eyes stared back at him.

'You're making a colossal mistake' Anthony wagged a finger 'a fundamental, monumental, misjudgement, and one day Elliott, one day, you will wake up and you will realise the *enormity* of your error. I only hope it's not too late' he turned on his heel and strode out the door, the black cloak billowing behind him. Queasiness. A slipping, sliding stomach. Elliott turned, but as he did Anthony reappeared back through the door, red faced beneath his white wig. 'I want you to know something' he blustered. 'I want you to know that I accept responsibility for my part in this; that I realise this breakdown you're having is a direct result of your mother and I ...'

'I'm not *having* a breakdown' Elliott clenched.

'Oh you are' Anthony laughed 'you most certainly are, but if or when you ever come to your senses ... well, you know where I am' he turned and left the showroom for a second time. Elliott stood staring at the empty doorway for a minute or two, then something sharp pierced his chest and he realised he'd forgotten to breathe. Then he realised he couldn't breathe. Hard fast breaths but he couldn't catch one. Choking for air, he crashed against the door to the staff toilet door.

Can't. Nausea ballooning. *Fuck. Fu-uhh* ... the violence of the first retch doubled him over. 'Shit' he coughed. Spat. A knocking on the door.

'Y'alright?' Eamo's voice.

'Fine' Elliott rasped.

'Y'alright?' Eamo knocking harder.

'I'm fine' Elliott called back. Clearing his throat, he turned the tap and splashed cold water up on his face. Straightening up he looked in the mirror. He leant on the sink and studied his reflection. Stared into his eyes. Dark pools of light.

You're making a colossal mistake.
'Fuck you' said his reflection.

. . . .

'*What a beautiful noise, Comin' up from the street, Got a beautiful sound, Got a beautiful beat, It's a beautiful noise, Goin' on everywhere, Like the clickety-clack of a train on a track, It's got rhythm to spare, well it's a beautiful noise, it's a sound that I love ....* **Studio One, that was Neil Diamond and this is Carly, with you all the way to three pm, boy is it hot out there today ...**'

Summer passed and suddenly as you tuned up and down the dial, the station coming through stronger than anyone else was Studio One. The station IDs, the new sound swelling up, a palpable feeling in the air, a tension, an excitement, the realization that something big was starting to happen. The first place to notice was the switchboard.

'We need more lines' said Katie 'an' I think we need another person. I can't handle what's comin' in.'

'Great' said Elliott. 'Someone else we have to get to work for free.'

'We may not hafta' said Squirrel.

'Why?' said Elliott.

'Because we're in business' Squirrel's face split into a wide smile. 'Three grands worth ah ads booked this mornin.'

'Three grand!' said Iris. 'Are you serious?'

'Never joke when it comes ta money' said Squirrel. 'We can pay Eamo for the IDs an' we can start payin' the jocks. Did the figures this mornin. We can put them on salary from next week. An' that's just the start of it. There's a lot more where that came from. A whole lot more. An' we' he pointed a finger at Elliott, 'are goin' after it.'

Stronger. Every day it grew stronger. More listeners, more ads, more chance they were going to pop up on RTE's radar any time soon. There came a point when Elliott realised it was futile trying to keep the station location under wraps because everyone knew where they were. People started calling into The Persian Prince who had no interest in carpets. DJs looking for work, punters with requests, fan mail for the jocks, girls dressed like Madonna and random weirdos with bizarre requests.

'No sorry, we're just not interested in that kind of thing' Elliott tried to explain to the man in front of him with the Iguana. 'We're not going to do a pet corner; we're a music station. Sorry. Yes?' he said to the two blond boys hovering behind Iguana man. They could have been Neal's cousins. High hair, shaved at the side, baggy trousers, pointy shirts, pointy shoes. Lots of jewellery and one of them, the smaller one, was heavily made up.

'Hi' said the tall one, 'I'm Barry and this is …'

'Gary' the smaller one had the softest sounding voice.

'We're the West End Boyz' said Barry. 'We DJ in Shaft. We heard you might be looking for people.' Elliott sighed. He'd tested several jocks in the last two weeks, all of whom had called in on spec, none of whom had worked out.

'I'd need to hear you play' he said.

'Come and see us in the club' said Barry. 'We're there every night.'

'I'd have to bring Julie Andrews with me' Elliott realised this was a perfect excuse to get Iris out on her own.

'Sure' said Barry. 'We'll put your names on the door.'

'The hills are alive, with the sound of … rrr-iip … with the sound of rrr-iip … rrr-iip … there's no point in, no point in … rrr-ipp … with songs that have been sung … no point in asking you'll get no reply … rrr-iiip … Live from Studio One, it's Julie Andrews … there's no point in asking you'll get no reply, just remember, don't decide, I got no reason its all too much, you'll always find us, out to lunch, oh we're so pretty oh so pretty …'

Elliott watched Iris through the glass. Inspired by Wayne's shaky starts she'd recorded an intro for her show, breaking up The Sound of Music, ripping it, and scratching in her own ID, under which she'd bring up whatever track she was opening the show with. She rarely spoke on-air.

'People want the music' she said to Elliott. 'I don't want to hear people talking over tracks so why would I think people would want to hear me do that?' Head down, spikes up, immersed in the music, Elliott watched her work.

'I like the Pistols!' Neal was standing beside him. 'You like them? You like the Pistols?'

'Mmm.' *Shut up Neal.*

'Iris is beautiful. Don't you think she's beautiful?'

Christ. I can't believe I slotted you in for the same nights as her. How could I be so fucking stupid?

'Hey gorgeous' Neal flicked the sound to studio. Iris looked up and smiled.

'Don't distract her' Elliott flicked the switch back.

'I think she likes me' said Neal.

Squirrel's right. I might as well have just handed her to him on a plate.

'Yeah. She definitely likes me.'

She likes cheese-burgers. Doesn't mean she wants to go out with one.

'She's the kind of girl you have to get to know though.'

You'll never know her.

'Spend time with her.'

'What time's your bus?' Elliott looked at his watch.

'I'll wait for Iris' Neal ran his hands through his hair. 'I can take over if you want' he gestured at the desk. 'You don't have to stay.'

'I always stay for Declan' Elliott lied.

'Hey Iris' Neal flicked the sound to studio 'you want to go for a drink after this? Elliott's staying for Declan but we could go for a pint?' Iris looked up.

'Sure. Why are you staying for Declan?' she looked at Elliott.

'Eh …' Elliott struggled.

'He always stays for Declan' said Neal.

'No you don't' said Iris. Elliott felt his cheeks burn.

'Yeah … well … you know … just helping him settle' he mumbled.

'He is settled' Iris looked confused. 'He's been settled for months. He's one of our best jocks. Why are you worried about him?' she frowned.

'I don't know' Elliott mumbled 'just want to keep an eye on him.'

'Whatever you want' she shrugged, before returning to flip through the pile of albums in front of her. Neal flicked the sound off.

'Don't worry' he winked at Elliott 'I'll look after her. Give her the ole Neal Diamond' he cocked a gun finger in Elliott's direction.

'Sorry? What?' Elliott snapped. 'What are you talking about?'

'You know' Neal grinned.

'No I don't' Elliott was getting really angry.

'Don't worry' Neal patted Elliott's arm 'I'll take good care of her. See she gets home safely' he winked. 'Hurry up babe' he flicked the sound to studio 'pub's waiting.'

' ... *Wonderful world, beautiful people, you and your girl, things could be pretty, but underneath this, there is a secret, that no-body can repeat ...* I'm talkin bout da wonnerful world ... beautiful people ... Declanne jah manne, man ah jah's pee-pal, Studio One ... Declanne ... with you all the way til one am ...'

Elliott watched Declan lean back in the chair, eyes closed, head nodding as the single played out. He looked down at the switchboard lights flashing. Declan had from the outset refused to take calls.

'Nnn-nnn not talkin' ta fff-fff fuckin eeejits; I juss wanna play the mew-music righ?' Elliott flicked the switch to studio.

'Lot of calls coming through Dec.'

'Nnn-nnn nod interested' said Declan. 'Ffff-fuckin' wankers. Sssh-sssh shuddup callin' me an' listen to the puh! puh! poxy music ... fuckin' eejits' he pulled down the fader and pressed his lips close to the mic, his voice dropping low:

'Doblanne ... dis is jah manne Declanne ... Misty In Roots, this is Poor And Needy ... an-an ... a ... nnn-nnn-nodder ting' he said to Elliott through the glass as he pushed the sound back up 'I ssh-ssh-shubby gettin' extra money.'

'For what?' said Elliott.

'Fff-fff-forda voices.'

'For Mork?' Elliott didn't like where this conversation was going.

'Fff-fff-for them all' said Declan. 'Elvis, sss-sss Tar Trek, them fuckin' all.

'Give us a chance will you?' said Elliott, 'Elvis and the other voices haven't aired yet. Mork's the only one we're using at the moment. *Christ. What happened to shy Declan?* 'We'll review what you're on in a few months time' said Elliott, 'depending on how much we're making on the ads. Is that fair?'

'Fff-fff, okay' said Declan. He took a hit off the joint resting in the ashtray in front of him. Then he leant back in his chair, interlocking his fingers into a headrest behind his neck. He pulled on the joint again, staring at Elliott through the glass, a lazy smile stretched across his face. Then he spoke. 'You-you …you-fff…. hancy Iris dontcha?'

'Who told you that?' said Elliott, annoyed. 'Sss-sss-sss …'

'Squirrel?' Elliott scowled.

'Nnn-no' said Declan 'sss-sss bleedin' obvious, that's all. Why-why-why dontcha ass-ass … hask her ouh?'

'I will' said Elliott. 'I will ask her out. *I don't believe this.* In my own time' he added.

'Neal my-might beatcha to it if yer not quicker' Declan started lining up his next track 'he's ow-ow-ouh wither now, issen he?' Declan had watched them leave for the pub earlier.

'Yeah, well' Elliott looked at the flashing switchboard, 'I'm going out with her tomorrow night.'

'Elliott?' It was Max. In person. Standing on the other side of the showroom counter, his big brother, dressed in a sharp suit; ruffled hair, laughing eyes, relaxed yet strangely out of place. 'Elliott, what' Max glanced around the showroom 'what are you *doing* here?' he whispered across the counter.

'What are *you* doing here?' Elliott felt a sudden rush of pleasure. It was good to see Max. No. Scratch that. It was great to see Max. 'How did you know where I was?' he stepped out onto the showroom floor.

'How do you think?' Max made a face.

'Oh. Right' Elliott tensed.

'So now that you're not talking to *either* of our parents' said Max 'I thought I'd better keep in touch. Just in case you needed a kidney or a lung at some stage' he gave Elliott a gentle punch.

'Don't punch me' Elliott smiled, punching him back.

'It's good to see you' Max punched him again.

'Good to see you too' Elliott couldn't stop smiling. He'd missed his brother.

'You look good' Max was studying Elliott's face. 'Older' he said.

'Yeah well, I feel older' Elliott had stayed for a few hours after Declan left, working on mix tapes for the night shift, then got up early to sit in with Wayne.

'Why?' Max glanced around the showroom 'why carpet?' he looked confused. 'I never realised you were interested in this kind of thing' he had a funny look on his face.

'Look ... Max ...' Elliott began.

'I should have been around' Max blurted. 'I shouldn't have just fucked off when Mum left; no wait' Max held up his hand as Elliott went to speak. 'I don't care where you work Elliott; if selling carpet is what you want, that's fine by me. I don't understand it, but if this is what makes you happy then it's all that matters. I just want you to be okay' there was an earnest concern etching his face. Elliott laughed.

'You think I've had a breakdown as well, don't you?'

'No' said Max. 'It's just' he stared at the rows of carpet 'I don't ...'

'C'mon' Elliott turned and walked towards the end of the showroom. 'Something to show you' he pulled open the small metal door that led to the warehouse.

'What is this?' said Max five minutes later as he watched Rachel glued to the mic behind the studio glass. 'Is this a radio station?'

'It's not *a* radio station' Katie handed him a coffee 'it's *the* radio station. This is Studio One' she smiled at him.

'Studio One?' Max stared up at the Studio One signs Iris had stuck to the walls to remind the jocks to namecheck the station each time they opened the mic. 'Hang on' he pointed at Elliott 'are you working *here* as well as the carpet shop?'

'Doin' more than that' said Katie, then when Elliott didn't speak 'he owns the place' she said.

'You *own* it?' Max's eyes widened. 'You *own* a radio station? Where did you get the backing?'

'Eh …' Elliott felt colour flood his cheeks.

'Contacts' said Katie.

'Contacts?' Max stared around the studio again 'contacts?' Elliott braced himself for an interrogation, but instead Max simply said 'well hang onto them whoever they are.' Then he laughed. 'Shit! My brother owns a radio station!' a smile split his face, and he looked at Elliott with something he hadn't seen before. Respect. 'Elliott!!' Max gave him a look of pure pride. Then his face straightened.

'This is a very different picture to the one Dad painted' he said. Elliott's eyes dropped. 'You should tell him' said Max. 'And Mum. She'd get such a kick out of this.' Elliott felt his throat tighten. 'You know' Max kept his voice low 'sooner or later, you're going to have to start talking to her again. Elliott stared at the carpet. 'She's our Mother.' Elliott didn't reply. 'Okay, whatever about Mum, do me a favour will you?' said Max. Elliott looked up. 'Dad's heading off on his trip to the Arctic soon; if you haven't mended the situation before he goes, will you come with me to see him off?' Elliott stared at the carpet. 'It's a dangerous trip' said Max; 'you'd feel shit if anything happened to him and you hadn't sorted things between you. Just think about it, okay? Don't do it for him; do it for you. Fuck it. Do it for me. Do it to make your big brother happy. Please.'

'I'll think about it' said Elliott. 'You're not to tell him about this though.'

'I won't. Promise. You know Pirate radio is illegal' said Max said as they began walking back down the stairs '*completely* fucking illegal' an indulgent smile.

Elliott felt his cheeks flush. Probably best not to tell Max about the equipment just yet.

'Sometimes I feel I've got to,   Run away, I've got to,   Get away, From the pain that you drive into the heart of me,   The love we share,   Seems to go, nowhere,   And I've lost my light,   For I toss and turn I can't sleep at night,   Once I ran to you,   Now I'll run from you,   This tainted love you've given,   I give you all a boy could give you,   Take my tears and that's not nearly all ... Tainted love ...'

'They're incredible!' Iris shouted as the crowd swelled around them. She was pressed right up against him. The closest they'd ever been. He could smell her perfume, feel the heat of her skin beneath her sweat soaked T-shirt and every now and then a wet, slippery cheek pressed on his face as she shouted something in his ear.

Shaft was a small, sweaty basement club off Parnell Square. Mirrored walls, disco balls, and men. Everywhere you looked. Tall men, small men, tight Vees, cut off Tees, Frankie Say Relax. Hairy chests, string vests, tight shaves, flat tops, high hair, plunging fringes. Bodies sardined together, a heaving, sweating, swelling throng, ebbing, rising, lifting, falling as the West End Boyz played one of the best sets Elliott had heard in a long time. Dry ice, cheap aftershave, cigarette smoke and fresh sweat choked a heavy, heady air. Thick sweet hot breath. The heat, the music, and Iris. In his arms. They'd been like this for nearly an hour but it felt like five minutes. It felt like five minutes yet it felt like forever. He pulled her closer and she smiled at him. He pushed his cheek against the side of her head. *Kiss her. Kiss her.*

'... Don't touch me please - I cannot stand the way you tease ...' people chanting, *'I love you though you hurt me so,   Now I'm gonna pack my things and go ...'* The crowd lifted, swayed, pulling them sideways. Iris laughed.

'Let's go!' she shouted, taking his hand in hers. Cool clean night air as they made their way up the tiny steps to street level. 'Shit' Iris looked up in dismay as fat rain drops fell thick and fast.

'Here' Elliott threw his coat around her, pulling it up and over their heads. Slipping her arm around his waist she leant in against him and they fell into an easy step together as they began walking across the Square and back towards O'Connell Street.

'They're amazing' he heard her say as the rain drummed against the coat. 'We've got to give them a slot. Did you see that crowd?' her words faded back into a happy hum as they turned the corner and began to walk down the long hill towards the taxi rank.

Kiss her. Just stop and kiss her. Side by side, his free arm slung over her shoulder as she circled his waist, the warmth of her body against his, her head tucked in by his chest. A row of terraced houses to their left. A couple entwined in a doorway, oblivious to the rain. *Pull her into a doorway. I can't pull her into a doorway. Just pull her in and kiss her.* There were five doorways left. He could hear her talking but the words were a blur. Two doorways. *Fuck. I can't.* They passed the last doorway. The taxi rank was getting closer. *Ask her back to the flat.* The realization he was going to have to act soon. *That's going to look like I want to sleep with her. You do. Drink … we'll go for a drink* he glanced at his watch. *Shit … too late. Pubs will be closed.* They had arrived at a small queue of people, huddled against the rain. *Get in the taxi. Go back to her house.* He felt her turn to face him underneath the coat.

'Night so' she gently pushed his belly.

Kiss her. She looked up at him. Something soft, shy in her eyes. 'Iris' he swallowed. She smiled. 'Night' he heard himself say. *Shit.* The light in her eyes faded and he saw something else flicker. Disappointment. *What?* She pulled back and the warm space she'd occupied was empty. Cold. 'Iris …'

'Night Elliott' she stepped into the taxi.

'No, wait …' he began.

'See you tomorrow' her goodbye was casual. Too casual. 'Iris …'

'Night Elliott' a polite smile and whatever he'd seen in her eyes was gone. Frozen he watched the taxi loop and head northside. He dropped his coat and let it hang by his side. The rain on his face. Big fat drops of rain collapsing around him.

'Fuck' he whispered. 'Fuck.'

. . . .

Drilling. A high pitched whine interrupting the silence of sleep.

'No' a whispered sigh. Lumpy swallow against a dry throat. 'Not now' she willed it to stop. Warmth. Delicious warmth. Sinking. The bed around her. She swallowed again. Deep breath. Sleep sucking. Bang! Bang! Bang! More drilling. 'Christ' she whispered. Creaking, the sound of splintering wood, another bang and a loud crash. 'Oh for fucks sakes' she murmured, pulling the duvet tight. Silence. Nothing. Deep breath. Sleep sucking, a long spiralling winding tunnel.

'Miaow' Leonard Cohen padding across the duvet woke her some time later.

'Mmm' she cleared her throat. Stretched. Leonard Cohen's paws stepping in and over her legs at the end of the bed. 'Hey Lenny' she popped her head up over the duvet. She glanced at the bedside table. Twelve o'clock. 'Shit' rubbing her eyes she pushed back the covers and swung her legs out. Squatting down by the turntable in her knickers and t-shirt she yawned as she flicked through the albums leaning against the wall. 'What would you like Len?' she said over her shoulder. 'Mmm?' she pulled an album up and studied the cover. 'Okay' she slipped the vinyl from its sleeve 'don't say I didn't ask' she let the needle fall and turned up the volume, her body rocking as the bass began to build.

'Feel it closing in' Ian Curtis echoed around the room 'Feel it closing in' Iris pulled on her jeans 'The fear of whom I call, Every time I call, I feel it closing in, I feel it closing in' she sang along as she pulled open the bedroom door 'Day in, day out, Day in, day out' she stepped onto the landing 'Day in, day out, Day in, day ... Fuck!!' Iris dropped sharply through the air. 'Aaahh!' she screamed, catching the edge of the roughly cut hole just in time, her legs swinging in the emptiness beneath her. 'Mum!' she shouted 'Mu-uum!!'

'Oh my God!' Jackie, somewhere beneath her. 'Arthur! Arthur quick!' A scuttle of feet.

'Oh dear, oh dear me, hold on' she heard her father say 'hold on' the hall door opening, the sound of something being dragged.

'Where are the stairs!' Iris shouted as she gripped the edge of the hole. 'Where are they!' she shouted as her legs flailed.

'They're in the garden!' Jackie shouted up. 'Your father wanted to change the direction ... for the tower ...' Iris felt something brush her feet. She glanced down and saw her father struggling with a ladder.

'Hold on' he called up. 'Hold on.'

'What do you think I'm doing!' Iris shouted. Her foot tapped the top of the ladder.

'Hang on, it's not ...' Arthur began. The ladder fell away and she heard it crash below as her legs swung once more. Gripping the edge of the hole, she air-kicked, pulled, pressed, and caterpillared her body back up and over, dragging herself onto the landing. Rolling away, she lay on her back looking up at the ceiling as she listened to her parents struggle with the ladder in the hall below. 'That's it' she heard her Father say.

'No ... it's too heavy Arthur ... I can't ... hold it.' Another crash.

Day in, day out, Day in, day out' Ian Curtis sang from inside her bedroom, *'Day in, day out, Day in, day out, Day in, day owwwut ...'*

Iris lay on the landing and looked up at the cobwebs clinging to the naked light bulb hanging overhead. She stared up in silence for several minutes.

'Sweetheart?' Jackie's head popped up through the hole in the landing beside her. 'Are you okay?' she gave her a bright smile. Iris rolled her head to the side and looked at her mother. 'The ladder's secure now' said Jackie 'perfectly safe ... look' she raised her arms 'no hands' she smiled.

'Why does he do this?' said Iris. 'Why? And why do you let him?'

'I don't know' said Jackie, her head looking strangely vulnerable floating in the centre of the hole. 'It relaxes him' she said. Iris turned to look at the ceiling again.

'Doesn't relax me' she said.

. . . .

'Studio One, eleven thirty. Time for our restaurant review. Who have we got? Line one, it's Pat. Talk to me Pat.'

'Hi Rachel ...'

'Right Pat, what restaurant did you go to?'

'Well ... I ... I went to Jaspers Rachel.'

'Marks out of ten?'

'Well ... Rachel ... I think .... I think I'd give them six.'

'What happened the other four Pat?'

'Well Rachel, someone beside me was smoking ...'

'Oh smoking, smoking, well we all *hate* smoking! So you complained?'

'Eh ... no, I didn't actually Rachel.'

'I see. You were a coward Pat ...'

'Jays I wouldn't mess with her' said Squirrel. 'Can ya imagine her as yer Ma?'

'Doesn't bear thinking about' Elliott smiled. They'd taken Rachel on for the morning show. Razor sharp, with a biting, cutting wit, within a matter of weeks she had a strong following and regular callers to her show.

'What's the story with *your* Ma?' said Squirrel.

'How do you mean?' Elliott knew exactly what he meant.

'Have ya seen her?' said Squirrel 'since, ya know' he looked around the studio 'since all ah this.' Elliott shook his head. Silence. 'How long is it since ya've seen her?' said Squirrel.

'Dunno' Elliott shrugged.

'Yes ya do' said Squirrel.

'Three years' Elliott stared at Rachel behind the glass.

'Jays' said Squirrel 'couldn't imagine not speakin ta my Ma for three days never mind three years.' Elliott blinked. 'You need ta sort that out' said Squirrel. Silence. Elliott blinked. Behind the glass Rachel's figure blurred. 'None ah my business I suppose' Squirrel picked up his helmet. 'Catch ya later, yeah?'

'Yeah ... sure' Elliott's eyes flicked 'catch you later.'

'You're in trouble' said Katie the next day.

'Why?' said Squirrel.

'Ma's after findin' out you're workin' with Eamo. Throwin' a wobbler so she is. Took the head off me this mornin'.'

'Shyte. How'd she find out?'

'Da.'

'How'd Da know?'

'Tommy.'

'Shyte' Squirrel sat down on the sofa. 'Don't know what her problem with Eamo is anyway' he leant his elbows on his knees 'he's alright, ya know? Not like we're not doin anything illegal.' Katie eyed him. 'Alright' said Squirrel 'but it's not like we're drug runnin. Just playin' a bit ah music an' gettin' paid for it. Right' he pushed himself onto his feet 'better sort this out. What'd she say ta you?'

'Told me ta stop' Katie shrugged. 'Told her I'm gettin paid; it's a job.'

'Exactly' Squirrel picked up his helmet. 'Enough people outta work. Right. Catch ya later.'

Belinda was in the garden hanging clothes when Squirrel got home. He stood at the back door watching her for a minute or two. She glanced at him, then returned to the washing, throwing it up and over the line with a force he knew was directed at him. Pushing pegs, pinning down, battoning shirts and sheets.

'Alright Ma?' he said from the doorstep. Belinda didn't reply. Squirrel walked out of the shade of the house and into the sunlight. He sat down on an old metal basin turned upside down in the grass. 'Katie said ya wanted ta talk ta me.' Belinda didn't answer. Push, push, push went the pegs. 'Look Ma …' the silence was starting to get to Squirrel.

'No' Belinda turned around and picked up the washing basket with the same force she'd used to get the clothes on the line 'you look' she stabbed the air with her finger. 'What did I tell you?'

'Told me lots ah things' Squirrel laughed 'lots ah things.'

'I told you' Belinda's voice shook 'that man is trouble. The one thing' her voice rose 'the one thing I asked ya ta do …'

'Ah Ma.'

'Stay away from him' said Belinda 'that's all I asked. What did I tell you?' she didn't wait for a response 'I told you not ta bring trouble ta my door.'

'I'm not *bringin'* trouble ta the door' Squirrel's voice rose.

'That man *is* trouble' Belinda's voice trembled. 'He' she pointed at the house 'is the worst kinda trouble. The one thing I asked' anger congested her voice, cutting her short.

'Ah Ma.'

'Who am I?' Belinda said in a strange voice. Squirrel stared at her confused.

'Who am I?' she was scaring him.

'You're me Ma.'

'That's right' said Belinda. 'I'm your Ma. I'm the one that loves ya. I'm the one that looks out for ya. I'm the one …' her voice broke.

'Jaysus Ma, what the …' Squirrel went to comfort her.

'Don't' she choked, pushing him away 'he's trouble' her voice was strangled. 'Ya don't understand' she wouldn't look at him 'he's trouble' a sob caught in her throat as she pressed the heels of her hands against blotched red cheeks. She took out a handkerchief and blew her nose. Squirrel stared in dismay.

'I'm sorry Ma' he whispered. Belinda said nothing. She stared down the garden, small, pale, defeated. 'I don't understand …' Squirrel began.

'I know ya don't' her face twisting as she began re-arranging the washing on the line. 'I can't stop ya' she stared at the shirt in her hands 'I can't, but I …'

'Alright' Darren was walking towards them. 'What's goin' on?' he looked at Belinda. Belinda didn't reply. Darren put his arm around her. 'Y'alright?' his voice was soft. Belinda nodded.

'Look if it's gonna cause this much hassle …' Squirrel began.

'It's not causin' any hassle' said Darren. 'Your Ma's just upset.'

'Yeah, but …'

'It's alright' Darren put a hand out to silence him 'do your station. We're proud ah ya. Go on' his eyes were solid, steady.

'Yeah, but what's the …'

'It's nothin' Darren was firm 'nothin, d'ya hear me? Now go on about your business.' Squirrel stared at him for a minute or two.

'I'm sorry Ma' he said to Belinda. Belinda nodded but didn't say anything.

'Look, if ya want me ta stop I will' said Squirrel. 'D'ya want me ta stop? I will. I'll call a halt to it now if it's gonna cause this much hassle.'

'I said it was alright' Darren sounded annoyed. 'I said ya have our blessin.'

'I have yours' Squirrel looked at his father.

'Ya have ours' Darren tightened his grip around Belinda's shoulder. 'Doesn't he?'

'Course ya do' Belinda stepped forward and gave Squirrel a hug. 'I just don't want ya gettin hurt' she choked, pressing her face into his chest.

'Eamo's not goin ta hurt me' Squirrel laughed. 'How the fuck could Eamo hurt me?'

. . . .

'... Studio One, the Godfather with ya this Sunday and every Sunday. I have a dream Dublin, a dream where the airwaves are free, where freedom reigns, freedom for any man, any woman, any station, ta broadcast from wherever, or whenever they so choose. From the backstreets ah Dublin, ta the green fields ah Connemara, let freedom reign ... right ... now... eh ... this is a special request for Sadie an' Angela listenin' out in Artane ...'

'What d'you ever do on my Ma?' said Squirrel to Eamo the following day. He'd swung by the showroom with a package and they were sitting in Eamo's office.

'Dunno' Eamo shrugged. 'Guess she just took a dislikin' ta me' he picked up his cigarettes.

'Puttin' it mildly' said Squirrel.

'That's women for ya' said Eamo. 'They get notions' his eyes flicked.

'Me Ma's not that kinda woman' said Squirrel. 'She's sound. Whatcha do on her? Ya musta done somethin.'

'Your Ma's just lookin out for ya' Eamo extracted, then lit a cigarette 'same way yer Da would, only different. Forget about it' he threw the lighter on the desk. Squirrel looked at him. 'You're on ta somethin' good with this station' said Eamo 'ya know ya are. An' your Ma knows that too. You're a good kid' he looked at Squirrel. 'You're a great kid' his voice became gruff 'great young fella' he cleared his throat. 'G'wan. Get outta here. Don't worry about yer Ma. It'll blow over. I'll see ya later' he turned back to his desk.

'Alright' Squirrel picked up his helmet. 'I'll catch ya later' he walked out the door. Eamo watched him go through the showroom, out the doorway and out onto the street. Squirrel straddled the bike, stuck the key in the ignition and just as he was about to push down the helmet he looked up and caught Eamo's eye through the window. A wide blue eyed grin as he waved. 'I'll see ya Eamo!' he shouted.

'See ya!' Eamo saluted him. He watched Squirrel kick start the bike and pull away from the path, then he stared at the space the bike had been in. 'I'll see ya Squirr' he said.

'*... Well we know where we're goin, But we don't know where we've been, And we know what we're knowin, But we can't say what we've seen, And we're not little children, And we know what we want, And the future is certain, Give us time to work it out ...* Studio One, Talking Heads from the new album Little Creatures, this is Road To Nowhere ...'

Elliott pulled back the fade and let the track play out. Two weeks since he hadn't kissed Iris. Two weeks and a handful of aborted attempts to talk to her about it. *Shit. Shit. Shit.* He stared at the empty studio. *I should have kissed her. I should have just fucking kissed her. She gave you a signal. She gave you a very clear signal. And you fucked it up. Squirrel's right. I'm never going to move forward. She likes me. I know she likes me. I saw it in her eyes. I'll talk to her tomorrow. Maybe I should wait for another signal. No!*

She already gave you a signal. The signal was the signal. How many fucking signals do you want?

. . . .

'Captain's log, stardate October 85 ... Captain, we're picking up a signal from Dublin'

'What kind of signal Spock?'

'A radio signal Captain, on an FM frequency.'

'Well tune it in Spock.'

'Phzzz ... sssss ... fzzzz ... LIVE from *Studio One*!! It's the Waaaayne Conroy Show ... and here's your host Waaaynnnne Conroy !!! ... *Flash!! A-ah, Saviour of the Universe , Flash!! A-ah, He saves everyone of us ...*'

Wayne smiled at Elliott and gave him a thumbs up through the glass as the track played out. His hair had been freshly permed and streaked blonde and he was wearing a pair of bright red baggy trousers with a matching red and white Hawaiian shirt.

'He really fancies himself' said Iris. She'd dropped in for coffee while she was on her break from work. It was just the two of them in studio.

Talk to her. Talk to her now. 'Iris ... listen ... about the other night ...'

'Have you seen the photos he's had done?' she said.

'Photos?' said Elliott.

'Wayne' Iris nodded at the glass. 'He's had photos of himself printed with his autograph on them.'

'Are you serious?' Elliott laughed.

'He talks too much' said Iris. 'Look at him; he's talking all over that song. And what's with the time checks? How many time checks has he done in the last hour? He's like a talking clock' she took out her cigarettes 'and by the way, if he says *Wayne Conroy, The Wayne Conroy Show* one more time I'll kill him.' Wayne looked up and gave the two of them a thumbs up from behind the glass, winking as he pulled down the fade and leant into the mic:

'... **Wayne Conroy, The Wayne Conroy Show, nine**

thirty am, Rachel and Christian up at ten, Carly with you til three, then it's Mad Donna followed by Candy with the charts ...'

Iris gave Elliott a dry look. 'Three time checks, and that's the fifth time in the last hour he's read the station schedule' she cupped her hands around the lighter. 'Fucking fader wanker' she muttered 'wanking up and down the fade' she puffed, pulled 'just so he can hear the sound of his own voice' she blew a neat line of smoke at the glass. 'You're a fader wanker' she said to Wayne, who smiled and gave her a thumbs up from behind the glass. 'You are' she waved back at him 'you're a fader wanker.'

'Iris, listen' Elliott began 'about the other night.'

'What night?' was it his imagination or did she look uncomfortable?

'At the club, with Gary and Barry ...'

'They're great' the slightest edge in her voice.

'They are' Elliott took a deep breath 'but that's not what I ...'

'Brilliant reaction to their first show' she interrupted him.

'Good. Look, Iris ...' Elliott was determined to have the conversation.

'Did I tell you Mick asked me about live broadcasts?'

'Live broadcasts?' she'd thrown him.

'From Berlin. He wants me to do The Sound of Music live from the Club.'

'Are you serious?' said Elliott. 'Shit, that'd be amazing.'

'I know' Iris sat back in her chair. 'He wants to talk to Tommy about the technical side, but he'll test it with me, and if that works he'll do it with The West End Boyz and maybe Benny's Show. Be good wouldn't it?'

'Good?' said Elliott. 'It'd be incredible.' *Shit. A live broadcast.* His mind veered, then straightened as he remembered what he'd been trying to talk to her about. 'Iris' he started again 'I really want to ...'

'We are the Champions' the Studio door pushed open and Squirrel swaggered in, arms swaying over his head 'and we'll keep on fighting 'til the end' he sang. Hovering behind him, Christian, the journalism student they'd taken on to produce and present their news held up a copy of the Irish Times. 'We are the champions' Squirrel swayed his arms '*WE* are the champions' he sang louder.

'Have you seen this?' said Christian, intelligent eyes blinking slowly.

'No time for losers' Squirrel chanted.

'What are you *talking* about?' said Iris.

'Read it' Christian handed Elliott the Times.

'Read it an' weep' Squirrel shouted. 'Number One' he stopped singing and tapped an article about half way down the page. 'Right there. Number One. Number fuckin' One.'

. . . .

STUDIO ONE HEADING FOR NUMBER ONE IN THE RATINGS

Interim research reports suggest that the Pirate Radio station Studio One could be heading for the Number One slot in the ratings. The station which was launched shortly after market leaders BBR and Rocket were taken off air, has come tops in an independent poll with over eighty percent of the valuable 15-24 year old market tuning in daily and fifty four percent of 24-35s listing it as their preferred station of choice. The station's music heavy format is cited as the main reason behind securing such an overwhelming proportion of the youth audience and the poll points to their Breakfast and Morning Chat Shows as having made significant inroads into the 35+ market. Despite several attempts to return to the airwaves, Rocket and BBR remain off air. RTE were unavailable for comment on either matter.

. . . .

'Christ …' Roger muttered as he read the newspaper clipping Breda had left on his desk. 'Christ all fucking …' his voice tightened and the colour on his face deepened as he re-read it. A knock at the door and Bobby entered, followed by Tom.

'Who, the fuck?' Roger weighted each word with the full

force of his anger 'are Studio One, and why am I only hearing about them now?'

'They're a Pirate Roger' there was an impatient edge to Bobby's voice 'you know they are.'

'I know now' Roger fumed 'I know now that they've eaten into a significant part of our market, I know now that it's in this report' he shouted. 'What I'd really like to know, is why neither of you saw fit to bring them to my attention up until this.'

'It's not up to us to monitor the Pirates Roger' Bobby wasn't backing down.

'Were you aware of this station?' Roger turned on Tom.

'Yes' said Tom quietly. 'Of course.'

'Of course?' said Roger. 'Oh *of course*' his voice rose 'did it not *of course* cross your, tiny fucking mind, that perhaps I should be made aware of them? That maybe, just maybe, the livelihood of the station depended on it?'

'Well the last time we spoke Roger' Tom's face flushed 'you were very clear that I should focus on managing the station and nothing else.' Roger reached for the packet of Dunhill on his desk, extracted a cigarette and lit it quickly, in one sharp, irritated motion.

'I see' he exhaled 'so you decided to take that personally and fuck with the station's future?'

'No' said Tom 'not at all …'

'Have you listened to them Bobby?' Roger cut Tom off. Bobby nodded.

'And?'

'They're good' said Bobby. 'It's a great sound. It's as good as ours. I hate to say it but it is.' A small smile escaped, curling around one side of his face.

'What's so funny?' said Roger.

'They steal our news' Bobby grinned.

'What do you mean they steal our news?' said Roger.

'They point a mic at it' said Bobby 'broadcast it over their frequency. It's an old trick. BBR did it when they were getting started. They've all done it at one stage or another.'

'I don't believe this' Roger's face was practically purple 'I don't *believe* you people!' he stood up. 'Why, *why*?' he began to pace the office 'did none of you think to tell me about this?'

'Because you wouldn't listen' Tom muttered.

'Sorry, what did you say?' Roger turned on him.

'Nothing' said Tom.

'I'm not paid to listen Tom' said Roger. 'I'm paid to act. Your job' he pointed at him 'your job is to listen.'

'You said my job was to manage' said Tom. 'You were very clear about that a few months ago.'

'Did I?' Roger snapped. 'Well let me be even clearer about this Tom; you're fired. How's that? Clear enough for you?' Tom's face paled.

'He can't do that' said Bobby to Tom. 'The Union won't stand for it.'

'The Union will do what they're told' said Roger.

'The Union won't do what they're told' said Bobby 'hang on, where are you going?' Tom was standing up. 'You're not fired; he can't do that to you; he's no right.'

'It's okay' said Tom in a quiet voice. 'No, honestly' he said as Bobby started to protest again 'I don't actually want to work for him anymore Bobby. I really don't' he turned and walked out the door.

'There you go' Roger gave Bobby a tight smile 'you heard the man; he quit. Union can't take issue with that, now can they?' Bobby stared at him in silent shock. 'Maybe you'd like to join him?' Roger was unnervingly calm as he leant forward and pushed his cigarette out in a glass ashtray. 'Because you can' Roger quickly lit another cigarette. 'I don't give a fuck' he pulled, exhaled 'about the Union, because if we don't close the Pirates, there won't be a Union; there won't be anything. We'll be gone. Wiped out.' Turning his back to Bobby he stared out the window at the giant aerial masts in the grounds. Silence. Outside the window, trees bent and swayed in the wind, leaves whispering, flashes of green. Roger pulled on his cigarette and exhaled slowly. He stared at the masts. Behind him Bobby shifted on his feet. Cleared his throat.

'So what do you want me to ...'

'Kill them' said Roger. 'I want them off-air by midnight.'

. . . .

'Ohh ... yeah ... alright ... We're jammin, I wanna jam it wid you ... We're jammin, jammin ... and I hope you like jammin too ... 'Studio One, dis is jah manne Declanne .... Fffffzzzzz ...... zzzzzzzzzsssssssssss .... Hiss ... ssssss ...'

It happened on Declan's show. A low silent hiss that began in the middle of a track. A never ending fizzing, hissing white noise, and somewhere, faint in the background, if you strained your ears, the distant sound of Declan introducing the next track.

'Fuck!' Elliott jumped up and made for the small transistor they kept in the outer room, where he'd been sitting while Declan broadcast. 'Fuck, fuck ...' he started working up and down the dial, tuning in and out of other stations, but he knew what this was. He'd known the moment he'd heard it. 'Come on, please, please ...'

'Oh my God!' Barry and Gary burst through the door, 'we just had the most amazing thing happen to us. We were recognized!!'

'These girls asked us for our autographs' Gary shrieked 'they came up to us and ... what's that noise?' he looked around the Studio for the source of the hissing.

'We've been jammed' Elliott's voice was flat.

'Ahhh!' Barry screamed. 'Are we going to be arrested?'

'We're going to jail!' Gary shouted. 'Oh my God, we're going to jail!!'

'No-one's going to jail' Elliott snapped. 'Just shut up' he stared at the hissing radio. His mind was numb. A blank white wall. 'Fuck' he put his head in his hands. *There's nothing I can do.* He couldn't collect his thoughts. 'Go home' he heard himself say to Barry and Gary 'go home. We'll sort this in the morning' but his heart was hollow. *We won't sort it. We can't. They'll just jam us again. And they'll keep jamming us. It's over. Studio One is over.*

. . . .

'Where does he live?' the four of them were in Eamo's office.

'He won't talk to you' said Elliott 'and if he does it'll just be to tell you to fuck off.'

'Where does he live?' said Eamo.

'He *won't* talk to you' said Elliott. Eamo reached for the phone book.

'I'll find him whether ya tell me or not' he began thumbing through the pages. 'Can't be too many Ingrams' he ran a finger slowly down a page.

'Sutton' said Elliott 'he lives in Sutton, but he's not going to ...'

'Twenty-two Offington Avista?' Eamo looked up.

'Eamo, he's not going to ...' Elliott began.

'Is that him?' Eamo tapped the phone book. Elliott swallowed.

'Yeah' he said reluctantly 'that's him.'

'Right' Eamo reached for the phone. 'G'wan.'

'What do you mean?' said Elliott.

'I mean' Eamo started dialling 'go on about your day. In fact, you' he pointed at Elliott 'take the day off. Ya'd a late night last night an' they're grand in there' he thumbed in the direction of the showroom. Elliott swallowed.

'What are you going to do?' his voice suddenly high, childish, 'what are ...'

'Come on' Squirrel stood up, jerking his head in the direction of the door.

'No!' said Elliott. 'Eamo? What are you going to do?'

'Less you know the better' said Eamo.

'Shit Eamo' Elliott's heart hammered 'I can't be part of ... what are you ...'

'Get him outta here' said Eamo to Iris and Squirrel. 'I don't want ta see any of yis 'til the mornin.'

'C'mon' Squirrel took Elliott's arm.

'No!' Elliott shouted. 'What are you going to do? Eamo! Don't hurt him.'

'I'm not gonna kill him if that's what you're worried about' Eamo finished dialling. 'Think I'd do time for a prick like him?' he sat back in the chair.

'What *are* you going to do then?' said Elliott.

'I'm gonna scare him' said Eamo as the phone began to ring. 'I'm gonna scare the almighty fuck out of him. Godfather style.'

'Oh Christ' said Elliott as they stepped outside. 'I don't like this. I don't like this at all.'

'Chill out will ya' said Squirrel. 'Eamo's not gonna … *He's trouble* Belinda's voice cut into his head. 'Eamo's not stupid' Squirrel pushed the thought away. 'Let's just go about our day. See what happens.'

'I don't *have* a day' said Elliott. 'There's no station. Eamo doesn't need me the showroom …'

'Come and help me in the shop' said Iris. 'Sandra's on a half day and I have to do a stock take.'

Two hours later Elliott was counting cock rings when the door to the shop opened.

'Good afternoon Irith' it was the small man they'd seen that day Squirrel tried the mask on.

'Thuperman' Elliott mouthed as the man made his way to the changing room. Iris nodded, winking as she pulled a selection of rubber suits off the rail. She went into the changing room for a minute or two then came back out.

'He'll knock on the door when he wants me to go back in' she whispered. She leant on the counter close beside him. 'Are you sorry you did it?' brown eyes, searching, seeking.

'Did what?' his face tingled.

'The station.'

'No' his voice was hoarse 'no, I'm not.' *Kiss her.* A sharp knock on the changing room door. Iris pushed back from the counter, brown eyes holding his as she reversed to the changing room. She opened the door and stuck her head in. Low voices murmuring. Elliott put a cock ring in his mouth, oh-ing his lips around it. *Tell her. Tell her how you feel.*

'Doesn't like the mask' Iris returned to the counter. Elliott took the ring out of his mouth. 'Wants a different style' she rooted through a box beside him.

'Iris …'

'How about this?' she held up a small black hood with no face, no eyes, no nose, just a single silver zip running down the back.

'Will that fit?' Elliott frowned. 'It's kind of tiny.'

'Well, he's got a kind of tiny head' Iris turned and went back to the changing room. Elliott looked at his watch. The shop would be closing soon.

Go for a drink. Back to the flat. Play some music.

'What are you thinking about?' she was back beside him. A smile curled around Elliott's face. He couldn't help it.

'What?' she grinned.

'Nothing' he smiled 'look, why don't we …'

'Arrggh!! Arrgggh!!' muffled cries and a loud thumping on the changing room door. Iris looked at Elliott then ran to the door. 'Arrrgggg!!! Arrrrggg!!' the small, now semi naked man fell from the changing room his hands scrabbling frantically at the black mask zipped tight on his head.

'Okay … hold on … wait …' Iris tried to get at the mask but the man was flailing wildly as he crashed around the shop, tugging and pulling at the mask. 'Elliott, help me!!' she shouted.

'Okay … don't panic … sir … if you'll just let me …' Elliott tried to catch hold of the man as he ran and crashed into a stand.

'Arrrrgggg' a gurgling sound as the man frantically scrabbled at the mask on his face. 'He can't breathe!' Elliott had managed to get a hold of him.

'Shit! The zip's jammed!' Iris yanked the back of the mask.

'Get a scissors; get a scissors, quick!' said Elliott as the gurgling turned to a series of chokes and groans. Iris bolted for the back room. 'Just hang on sir, try not to panic' said Elliott. The body went limp in his arms, the weight of it pulling them both to the floor. 'Iris, quick!!' Elliott shouted as she came running from the back room.

'Here' she handed him a Stanley knife. Elliott looked at her in horror.

'It's all we have!' she shouted.

'Fuck!' Elliott stared at the blade.

'Oh Elliott, get him out of there' the panic in her voice pushed him into action.

'Shit' Elliott held the leather taut, drew the blade against it and began to saw. 'Come on' he sawed harder 'come, on …' fibre giving way, a small pink chin appearing.

'Hurry!' said Iris 'hurry!'

'Christ' Elliott slipped his fingers beneath the end of the mask pulling it up and over the man's nose as he continued to saw the leather back. He stopped and stared at the small wet face.

'He's not breathing' said Iris. 'Elliott, he's not breathing!'

'Shit' Elliott tilted the half masked head back and gave him the kiss of life. 'Come on' he thumped his chest 'come on!' Nothing.

'Oh God' he heard Iris say, then slowly, rattling from somewhere far away, a long deep wheeze. Another. Wheeze followed wheeze as Thuperman slowly came back to life. Elliott grabbed the Stanley knife and cut away the rest of the mask.

'Get some water' he said to Iris. Pulling off the remains of the mask, Elliott reached for his jacket and propped it under Thuperman's head. A low soft moan.

'It's okay' Iris knelt down beside him 'you're alright' she dipped a cloth into the water and patted the small pale face.

'Where am I?' Thuperman moaned. 'Where am I?' eyes flickering.

'You're in Slave' said Iris. Thuperman's eyes opened properly and he looked at her. 'Your mask jammed' she said. 'Elliott saved you' Iris nodded in Elliott's direction. 'Elliott saved your life.'

'Sit him up' said Elliott and they helped him into a sitting position against the wall. 'Here, drink this' said Iris. Thuperman sipped the water for a minute or two, then he took a deep breath.

'Thank you' he said to Elliott' the breathless high pitched girlish tone returning. 'Thank you.'

'You're okay' Elliott felt his face redden.

'You thaved me' said Thuperman. 'You thaved my life.'

'You thaved him' Iris whispered, when Thuperman was back in

207

the changing rooms getting dressed. 'You thaved Thuperman. You're a Thuper Hero' she laughed.

'Yeah, well' Elliott grinned 'let's just hope Eamo can *thave* Studio One.'

. . . .

'The air attack warning sounds like ... this is the sound ... when you hear the air attack warning you and your family must take cover ... ow-ow-ow ... ow-ow ... let's go ... oh-ohh ... when two tribes go to war, a point is all you can score, when two tribes go to war ...'

Roger pushed in a tape, cutting off the radio. He had specifically requested that song not be given air-time. However, nothing, not even the slow traffic across the East Link could upset him today as he cruised home, Howth's peninsula stretching out to his right, Beethoven's fifth now turned up high. Privately congratulating himself on the handling of yesterday's events he turned into his driveway, noticing with some irritation a dirty red Hiace parked outside number twenty-four. Sheila was right. Sutton was slipping. As he put his key in the door manic barking began on the other side. Swearing to himself, he edged the door open.

'Careful now Princess Grace ....'

Sheila Ingram kept two things on a tight lead. Princess Grace, her King Charles spaniel, and Roger, her husband. Grace because she was a pedigree and Roger because he was a man. Far too many stray bitches running loose. Sutton had been such a lovely area when they moved in, but lately, well; strange goings on. She'd heard rumours in the Yacht Club, which cross checked and correlated with those she'd heard in the Golf Club, about a swingers club five doors up from them. Disgusting. She couldn't wait for Roger to be made Director General so they could move further up the hill. Away from that sort of thing.

'Roger, time for Grace's walk' she said after dinner, a light fish supper with steamed vegetables; she had to watch Roger's weight because he certainly wasn't. At the word 'walk' Princess Grace, dressed in a little pink dog jacket shot through the living room barking loudly as she made her way through the kitchen and back into the living room, before starting this small warm up circle all over again. Roger sighed. 'Don't sigh' said Sheila. 'You know she needs her walk, and besides, you need the exercise' she eyed his belly. Roger pushed himself out of the armchair. He pulled on his overcoat as Sheila attached a pink lead to Princess Grace's collar. 'I won't be here when you get back' she said. 'I'm going to bridge.'

'Right' Roger replied, as he headed out the door. Turning out of the driveway he noticed the red Hiace was still parked at number twenty-four. He'd really have to have words. Maybe get Sheila to call into them tomorrow. Princess Grace screeched to a sudden stop at a freshly deposited dog turd on the pavement. 'Come *on* Grace' he tugged the lead but she jammed her legs down stubbornly to get one final sniff. 'Come on' Roger snapped, yanking hard, lifting Grace up in the air, landing in a scrabble of paws before finding her feet. 'Christ' he muttered to himself, as Princess Grace picked up the pace behind him, falling in line with his step.

His head turned once more to the day's events and so immersed was he in his thoughts he didn't hear the Hiace start quietly up a few hundred yards behind him.

Nor did he notice a balaclavad man spring quietly from the back of it and softly sprint up the road behind him, across the front lawns of the houses, easily clearing the low walls that divided each property. He didn't notice as the van drew near, but he became aware of it as it pulled up beside him.

'S'cuze me' a low rough voice 'you live around here?'

'I do' Roger noticed that the side door of the Hiace was open. He couldn't see the person leaning out the front window properly; he had a baseball cap pulled down over his face.

'You're not Roger Ingram by any chance are ya?'

'Yes' said Roger 'I am. Why?' then suddenly everything went black as a rough sack was thrown over his head and two arms locked around his upper body.

'What the hell?' Roger shouted. Struggling hard, he muffled

a series of 'helps' from beneath the sack, but it was too late. Someone had his legs, the ground was gone from beneath him and he was thrown into the back of the van. He heard Princess Grace barking, the door sliding shut and the van took off. He could feel the ridges in the road bumping underneath them, his head knocking gently against the floor of the van as they went over them, then through the darkness of the sack, a soft voice began to sing

'Who are the people in yer neighbourhood? In your neighbourhood? In yer Neigh... Ber ...Hood?'

'Help!' Roger shouted 'help!!' A hand clamped around his throat.

'I'd shut the fuck up if I were you' said the voice. 'I'd be very quiet.' Roger swallowed. 'Now Rodge' said the voice 'we're goin' for a nice drive around Howth. Just you an' me.' A match flared. The smell of sulphur and the glow of a cigarette tip through the sack. 'One ah me favourite places Howth' the voice was saying. 'Love those moors an' mountains. Stole a horse once and hid it up those mountains. Stallion it was. Big fucker. Me very own Shergar. Kept it there for weeks.' The van was twisting now, sharp turns then suddenly it began to go over rough terrain, and the floor rattled, bumped and thudded underneath him, steady bumping, interspersed with dips and hollows, down in a pot hole, the van lurched left, right; then he felt it begin to climb.

'Not much further now Rodge' the voice said. 'Just want to have a little chat witcha, and thought we'd do it on your own turf so ta speak. The van came to a sudden halt and Roger's head bashed hard against the floor.

'Ahh!' he shouted.

'Sorry about that Rodge. Come on. Out ya get.' His hands were bound behind his back, the sack still on his head. Someone behind him, pushed him to walk on. They were going up what felt like a small hill. The ground beneath his feet was stony. He stumbled a few times and each time the person behind pushed him on. They stopped. His hands were undone briefly and he felt himself being put into a harness of some sort. What was this? His hands were bound again, tighter this time.

He felt a metal hook being pushed through the harness at the back. Jesus, what were they going to do to him? Who were these people? From the van Princess Grace barked.

'D'ya know where we are Rodge?' the voice soft but dangerous in his ear. Roger shook his head. 'Well let's have a look then' the sack was whipped off his head. Roger blinked. He couldn't see anything. It was pitch dark. The outline of four heads in black balaclavas formed roughly in front of him, and there in the distance, far far away were the lights twinkling around Dublin Bay. They were up on the mountain, but he wasn't sure where. 'Now da ya know Rodge?' the voice said, pulling on the end of the cigarette as he did so, before stamping it out.

'I … no … the mountain?'

'The mountain Rodge' the voice confirmed. 'And d'ya know where on the mountain?' Roger shook his head. 'Well look behind ya.' Roger turned around, his eyes adjusting. Perfectly polished trellised silver metal poles gleamed in the moonlight stretching off to his right and his left, and as he looked up, there, looming over him, was the giant RTE aerial that sat right on the top of the West Mountain. He often passed this aerial in the distance from the far side of the mountain on Sunday walks, but now he was standing directly beneath it. It was bigger up close, a giant climbing frame towering up into the darkness. The wind blew hard and cold as he tipped his head back to look up, the top of the mast barely visible, just the echoing sound of the wind whistling and through the darkness, far up in the distance, a tiny red flashing light.

'Big, isn't it?' said the voice. 'How high would ya say it is Rodge?'

'Eh … fifty feet?' said Roger.

'Sixty' said the voice. 'Would of expected the boss man ah RTE ta be a bit more accurate when it comes ta aerials.' Roger suddenly felt very uncomfortable. How did they know he headed up RTE? Christ. He'd been kidnapped.

'I don't have any money' he rambled. 'I've no money … I …'

'Shut up' said the voice. 'I don't give a fuck about your money. What I do care about Rodge, is this' he grabbed Roger by the collar and dragged him, stumbling back down the small slope to the van where a driver, also in a balaclava, sat behind the wheel. 'Turn it up' the voice instructed and the balaclava behind the wheel leant over and turned up the radio. A high pitched hissing sound, a song barely audible in the background. 'D'ya hear that?' the voice asked him. Roger swallowed. Nodded. 'Now whaddaya reckon that is?' the voice asked him.

'I … I don't know' Roger lied.

'No? Ya sure about that?'

'Really … I don't know' Roger tried to steady his voice.

'Well now' the balaclava turned him around and began walking him back up the small hill 'that surprises me, you bein' a big boss man in RTE an all that, but I tell ya what Rodge, I'm a generous man; I don't mind sharin' the information with ya. That Rodge' he pointed down at the van 'is the sound of a radio station in distress.'

'I see' said Roger.

'An' d'ya know what's distressin' for me?' said the dark roughly shaved, shadowed mouth from behind the balaclava.

'What?'

'It's my station' said the mouth. Oh dear God. Roger quietly pissed himself. 'Like a child to me that station' the voice continued 'an ya'll never guess what happened last night Rodge, or will ya? D'ya think ya can tell me what happened ta shift my usually sunny nature into an altogether darker place? What happened ta make *my* station make *that* noise? Can ya guess Rodge? Can ya!' the voice raged. A sudden sniff and the mouth turned down. 'Oh dear Rodge. Oh dear me. I think one has pissed oneself.' The other balaclavas laughed. 'One has indeed' said the voice. 'Which would lead me to believe Rodge that my suspicions are correct and you know exactly what happened last night, dontcha?'

'No! I don't, I really don't' Roger cried. 'Please let me go. I've no idea what you're talking about.

'That's a pity, isn't it boys?' the balaclava turned around to the other three. 'Tell ya what Rodge. Maybe ya've just had a long day an' ya need some fresh air ta clear yer head. But before ya go …' the balaclava turned away, here's somethin that might jog yer memory. Hope ya like this Rodge' he bent down, picked something up and opened it. 'Bought it meself.'

'No!!' Roger screamed as the hand came towards him, and the two men behind him held him firmly as he struggled. No! Please!! No!!'

'Don't worry Rodge. Just a nice bit ah …' something sticky being smeared across his face. What was that smell? Apricots? It smelt like apricots. 'Jam' the voice finished 'nice bit ah jam. Now, up ya go for a bit an' see if ya can remember.' A sharp ripping sound then a large piece of masking tape was affixed to his mouth. The two men holding him moved away and began pulling ropes beside him. Roger felt the metal hook at his back tighten and press into him, the ground went from beneath him, and he was hoisted in the air, travelling up along the side of the aerial.

'Arrhggg … mmmph … arrrhh!!' his terror silenced beneath the tape.

'Long way up Rodge' the voice laughed from down below 'hope that rope'll hold ya.' Up he went. Up and up, thumping and bumping against the cold steel frame of the aerial. Christ, he couldn't be going all the way to the top? Oh God.

Don't look down. The wind grew stronger. Cooler. Whipping around him. The sound of a pulley creaking as the rope tugged him up. The soft red light flashing overhead as he reached the top, then he felt arms either side grab him and lash him to the aerial, tying him tight. He groaned, ready to tell them he had remembered, but they wouldn't listen and then they were climbing down the frame below him as the red light flashed above. His heart slamming wildly against the front of his chest. He could be electrocuted. What if he was electrocuted? Somewhere way below he heard the Hiace doors open and close, then it started up and drove off, back down the little track, down the rocky road, the sound of stones under tyres, until it was just a distant hum and the only sounds he could hear were the wind whistling around the aerial, the rusty pulley squeaking above him, and the clanking of the harness against the metal rails. He blinked, the apricot jam sticking at his eyelashes, Dublin Bay an orange twinkling blur. The red light shone overhead, lighting up the apricot jam on his cheeks. He closed his eyes and prayed to God.

Time passed. The pulley creaked and squeaked above him, the wind teased, calm one minute, then whoosh, a giant blow and the whole top of the frame would rattle, bringing him with it. After what felt like an age he heard an engine in the distance, drawing closer now, then closer again. Nothing for a while, then the sound of the doors sliding back, and after a while, from way below, the soft sound of shoes hitting poles as they made their way up. Closer, closer, then they were behind him, untying him from the main frame of the aerial and his body swung out in the breeze causing him to moan again in fear. One of the men shouted down and pulled on the rope attached to the pulley overhead. The pulley jerked roughly and he shot suddenly down, sky-diving deep in the darkness, screaming in terror beneath the tape on his face. A series of shouts and curses and the rope came to a sudden halt, yanking him the way he'd yanked Princess Grace earlier. He swayed in the breeze for a few moments, whimpering, then the rope jerked again and he began moving down at a steadier pace. The rope yanked to a halt again about ten feet off the ground.

'Right Rodge' the voice shouted up. 'Did ya have a nice think up there? Are ya ready ta tell me the truth?'

'Mmm!! Mmm!!' Roger tried to say 'yes' beneath the tape.

'Because I'm not in the mood for lies' the voice said. 'I've had a few pints an' I'm ready ta go home. So no fuckin' around. We're gonna have a man ta man conversation and it's gonna be a quick one, alright?'

'Mmm' Roger whimpered. The rope went slack and he plunged down towards the ground. 'Mmmm!' he screamed, 'mmmm!' The rope pulled up about two feet before the ground, pinching him one last time, and then he was let gently down. His legs collapsed when they touched the ground. Hands in the darkness held him up.

'Now Rodge' the balaclava came closer, and ripped off the tape on his face. 'Did you jam Studio One's signal last night?' Roger nodded.

'Yes' he whispered.

'Grand' said the voice. 'Now here's what we're gonna do Rodge. We're gonna go home an' we're all gonna have a nice kip. Then tomorrow Rodge, bright n'early, you're gonna to go inta RTE, an' fix what ya did. You're not gonna to tell anyone why, you're not gonna to call the police, you're just gonna do it.'

'Yes' Roger whispered 'yes.'

'Good man' the voice patted his face, then 'Jaysus' disgust at the apricot jam. Wiping his hand on Roger's jacket the voice said 'that wasn't too hard was it? Nothin' like a bit ah fresh air ta clear the mind.'

The sack was thrown over his head and he was pushed into the back of the van again where he bashed and bumped off the floor as they went back down the rocky road. More twists and turns, then he could feel the smooth main road underneath them, another turn, then the familiar ridges from earlier as they drove through what he guessed must be Offington. The van came to a halt.

'Now Rodge, safe an' sound' the voice said again. 'Just a small matter ah security before ya go. I do trust ya Rodge. I don't think yer stupid, but just ta be on the safe side I'm gonna hang on ta this fella here' Roger heard Princess Grace whine. Christ. He'd sooner go back up that aerial than return home without Princess Grace. 'Just as a matter ah security' the voice continued. 'You lift the jam tomorrow mornin, and this little fella'll be home by lunchtime.'

'It's my wife's dog' Roger cried 'please … she'll go mad. Please! I promise you …'

'An' I promise you Rodge, no harm'll come ta yer dog. Just

lift the jam and we'll all be happy. Now get out. Yer smellin' up me van.' The door shot open, the sack was pulled off his head, his hands untied, and he was thrown out onto safe clean Sutton streets. 'Remember Rodge' the voice said from the belly of the Hiace. No police. No tricks. Just lift the jam.' Princess Grace barked, the door slid shut and the van pulled off.

He was a mess. Freezing, soaked in cold sweat, piss and apricot jam. Shaking, trembling he began to walk towards the house, then stopped. What would he tell Sheila? What time was it? He checked his watch. Twelve o'clock. Bridge finished at ten-thirty. He stopped, thought for a few minutes, then turned into the driveway. He put the key in the hall door, but she was there before him.

'Where the *hell* were you?' she shouted. 'I was just about to call the police. Jesus Christ!! What's happened? What's that on your face? Oh my God! You're having an affair! I knew it!! I *knew* this would happen. Who is she? Where's Grace? Where's my dog?'

'She ran off' said Roger, angry now. Christ, he'd just had the worst few hours of his life and she thought he was out having sex. He wished he had been having sex. Sex was something he hadn't had in a long time. 'The lead Sheila' he said curtly, attack being the only plausible defence 'wasn't on properly. She ran off, and I've spent the last few hours trying to catch her.'

'Grace would never run off' Sheila screeched. 'She's a pedigree!! You're having an affair' she began to cry 'you are, and you forgot all about my baby while you were with some wom … wom-wom … woh-man!!! Wahhhh!!! Waahhh!!! Haw-haw-haw-haw!!! Wah!! Haw-haw …. ahhhhhh ….' she sobbed and cried, grabbing a Kleenex from the console in the hallway, then walking into the living room where she really let rip.

'Sheila' Roger repeated above the howls 'there *is* no woman!'

'No? Then what's that smell?' she sobbed. 'I smell sweet perfume. Jesus, look at you' she stood back, her eyes travelling up and down. 'Your trousers … oh God' she recoiled in disgust. 'And what's that on your face?' she snapped. 'Is that jam?' She

stuck her finger on his face, swiped and tasted. 'It's apricot jam!!
Oh dear God' she moaned 'you've been having some sort of sex
game. Oh ...' she put her hand to her mouth 'you're involved
with the Keoghs ... that swing club' her voice snapped, yo-yo'ing
up and down 'Oh my *God*, this is worse than I *thought,* if this gets
out – your *job* – the *neighbour*s –the Yacht Club, oh! oh!' she
hyperventilated, muttering in quick succession 'the yacht club,
the golf club, the yacht club, the ...'

'Sheila!!' Roger shouted 'I am not ... if you *must know*' he
drew himself to an indignant height 'I was kidnapped by Pirates'
he said in a deep, hurt voice.

'Whaaat!!' Sheila screamed. 'Pirates!! What sort of a *fool* do you
think I am? Just how many lies do you think I'm capable of
swallowing' she shrieked. 'I suppose the Pirates put the jam on your
face' she grabbed a crystal bowl from the sideboard 'I suppose the
Pirates *stained* your trousers!! What sort of a fool' she flung it at
him, then grabbed a vase 'what sort of a *fool* ...' she panted. A soft
buzz as the vase winged his right ear. 'You go out there' she snarled,
Roger ducking left, then right as she began firing photo-frames
from the sideboard in quick succession 'you go out and find my
dog. I don't want her anywhere near those sick people. Oh God'
she moaned, the strength draining from her body as she sat down
on the sofa 'why do they want her?' her face crumpled as she started
to cry again. 'Oh for the love of God Roger, indulge in your own
sick fantasies, but don't involve a harmless, innocent creature. She's
a pedigree!' she howled.

· · · ·

' ... *Hissss ... fzzzzzzz ... hisss ... fzzzzz ... zzzzzzzzzz ...
hissssssssssssss ...*'

'Where'd ya get the dog?' said Squirrel.

'Pet shop' said Eamo.

'What happened?' said Elliott.

'Ask me no questions an I'll tell ya no lies' said Eamo. 'Your
Daddy better fix this' he said to Princess Grace who was sitting
on his lap, still in her little pink coat.

'Is that ... did you ... is that Roger Ingram's dog?' said Elliott.

'Like I said' Eamo stared across at the radio hissing in the corner 'ask me no questions an' I'll ...'

'... *fzzzzzz ... sssss ... 'Risin' up, back on the street, did my time took my chances, went the distance now I'm back on my feet, just a man and his will to survive ... It's the eye of the tiger, it's the thrill of the fight, risin' up to the challenge of our rival ...'* the transistor on the filing cabinet burst back into life with the mix tape Elliott had looped on their frequency.

'Yah-hooo!!' Eamo jumped up, releasing Princess Grace, who saw her moment and made for the door. She was after all, a pedigree.

'Yesss!' Squirrel grabbed Iris and spun her around. 'We're back!! Eamo!' delight on his face. 'Ya did it!!'

'Yeah, well' Eamo glanced around 'sometimes ya just ...' his head twisted; 'shyte! The dog, where's the fuckin' dog?' he sprinted through the showroom and onto the street. 'Oh gee!!' he groaned staring up and down a dogless Capel street. 'Bollox, fuck and *gee* on it anyway!' he stormed back into his office.

'So it is his dog?' said Squirrel. 'Yer man who runs RTE?'

'Yeah' Eamo's face blackened 'an' he's such a baldy fuck I wouldn't put it past him ta jam us again if I don't get it back. Shy-yyte! What am I gonna do? I need a dog. I said I'd give him back his fuckin' dog.'

'Eamo' said Squirrel 'if ya need a dog let's just go down ta the kennels an' get one.' Eamo stopped and stared at him.

'Ya know what it is?' he said.

'Ya alright there Eamo?' Squirrel grinned. 'Not goin' soft on me are ya?'

'No' Eamo straightened himself up. 'Never. Where's yer bike?'

'Outside' Squirrel jerked his head towards the street.

'Right. C'mon' said Eamo.

The kennels had three St. Charles Spaniels.

'Which one?' said Squirrel.

'Sssh, I'm thinkin' Eamo studied three sets of brown eyes,

pink tongues and wagging tails. They all looked the same. 'That one' he pointed at the dog in the middle who looked the friendliest. Fucked if he knew. 'Any ah them little coat yokes?' he asked the kennel lady as he handed her a tenner.

'Sorry' she smiled.

'Not ta worry' Eamo looked at Squirrel. 'We'll just say it got too hot.'

At 12.30pm a courier walked into the main reception building in RTE.

'Delivery for Roger Ingram' he put the St. Charles Spaniel down in front of the surprised receptionist. 'Call him' he said. 'He's expectin' it.'

'Darling' Roger sang as he came through the front door. 'I'm home!! And guess who I've got with me? Her coat's gone, she must have pulled it off, but here she is, safe and sound' he strode into the living room, holding Grace up like a trophy. And then his face dropped. Because there, sitting on the couch was Sheila. And on her lap, still in her pink coat, was Princess Grace.

'Oh really Roger' Sheila's tone was arctic. 'Well that's *funny*, because Joyce Hunter called me from a telephone box in Henry Street, to say she'd spotted Grace at a Moore Street market stall, that she recognized the coat, checked the collar, and would I like her to bring her home. So while that thing in your arms might bear a passing resemblance, clearly it's not Grace. Did you honestly think I wouldn't know my own dog? You might have been lying to me for God knows how long about your sordid association with those perverts up the road, and I might have been naive and trusting enough not to spot it, but did you think, did you actually *think*, I wouldn't recognise my own dog? You disgust me' she stood up and pushed past him. 'I'm going to give Grace a bath. You can do what you want with that' she nodded at the dog in his arms. 'Take *that* to your orgies' she stomped up the stairs.

. . . .

'You are an obsession, You're my obsession, Who do you want me to be, to make you sleep with me, I will have you, Yes I will have you, I will find a way and I will have you, Like a butterfly, a wild butterfly, I will collect you and capture you ...'

'He's a moron' Elliott muttered as they watched Neal dancing and pointing at Iris from the other side of the glass.

'He's an operator' said Squirrel.

'She hates Synth' Elliott tried to ignore the fact that Iris was smiling as Neal mouthed *'I will have you'* at her through the glass.

'Shit like that goes out the window' said Squirrel as they watched Neal pull down the fade, eyes fixed on Iris as he leant into the mic:

'... **Studio One, Neal O'Neill, that was Animotion, a gig they did in London last week, Julie Andrews is here, she's lining up The Sound Of Music, you have no idea how gorgeous this girl is ...**' toothpaste smile through the glass, that gun, that gun, that fucking gun, '... **I'm telling you, I could sit here and look at her all night; coming up to eight-thirty-eight, The Cure are on the way, but first, Kraftwerk ... The Model ...**' Neal slipped off the phones and ran his hands through his hair. 'Hey guys!!' he spotted Elliott and Squirrel on the sofa. You like this track?' he called over the mic, then before they could answer 'Iris' he called 'don't sit out there. Come in' he beckoned.

'Nah, we're okay ...' Elliott started, but Iris had pushed the studio door open and was making her way inside. Through the glass he saw Neal stand up and hug her, watched her smile widen as they stood and talked, then turning her back to the glass she perched on the edge of the sound desk. Elliott stood up and walked to the desk, pretending to study the albums Iris had been lining up. Sneaking his eyes upwards, he watched the curve of her cheek through the glass as she smiled at something Neal was saying. Watched her laugh, accept a cigarette, lean in for a light. Watched Neal rest his hand on her leg. 'Great show' Elliott cut in over the mic.

'Cheers' said Neal through the glass. 'You think the live stuff is going down well?' he twisted and teased his fringe.

'Yeah' Elliott reluctantly had to acknowledge that it was. 'I think it's going down really well.' *I just wish you'd fuck off, that's all.*

'All set for the Human League?' said Neal.

'Can't wait' Elliott cocked a fake gun in Neal's direction.

'Hey man!' Neal fired a gun back at him through the glass.

Hey man … prick. Elliott watched Neal whisper something in Iris' ear, his lips pressed close to her face, watched her gasp, throw back her head and laugh. *What did he say? What the fuck did he say?* anger stinging, surging. From the sofa Squirrel caught his eye.

'Tellin' ya' he said. 'On a mission.'

. . . .

'Ahh …' Eamo gasped, 'shyte …' he panted 'shyte … come on ya bastard' eyes squeezed in pain he leant one hand against the urinal. 'Holy Mother ah fuck' his face tightened as he watched a slow painful trickle hit the bowl, wincing with each dry sharp stabbing pain that accompanied it. 'Shyte' he zipped himself 'Holy Mother ah God' he winced again.

. . . .

'You have enormous testicles' said a nurse two hours later. 'Incredible' she murmured. 'I've *never* seen anything like them' cool fingertips gently lifting and turning his balls as she examined him.

'Yeah, well' a smile of pride slipped across Eamo's face as he stared at the chart on the wall in front of him 'you're not the first ta say that' he grinned, then 'Ow! Jaysus!' as she squeezed and pressed.

'Mmm' the nurse pressed again.

'Ow! Ow! Fuck! Eamo shouted.

'I'll get Doctor Feehy' said the nurse.

. . . .

'What are ya doin!' Eamo's face fell back in horror. 'Where's that goin?' he backed away.

'We need to take a rectal tissue sample' said the doctor. 'It won't take a minute. If you'll just bend over.'

'Bend over? Will in me fuck bend over' Eamo yanked up his trousers. 'That's not goin' inta me' he pointed at the long silver nozzle in the doctor's gloved hand.

'Mister Rourke' a clink of metal as the doctor put the instrument down on the tray beside him 'you're displaying all the symptoms of prostate cancer.'

'Cancer?' said Eamo.

'Prostate' the doctor nodded. 'A very common, curable cancer if it's caught early enough, but left untreated, well ...' he trailed off. Flies still undone, Eamo swallowed.

'Cancer?' he sat down on the chair. 'I'm only forty-four.'

'Yes, and you could live to be eighty-four if it's treated' said the doctor 'but we can't do anything until we test you.'

'An' what happens then?' said Eamo.

'If the tests establish that it is prostate' said the doctor 'the treatment will depend on how advanced it is. We'll need to do a biopsy to determine what stage it's at. We might be able to treat it with radiation, or we may have to consider surgery.'

'Surgery? Is this gonna kill me?'

'If we treat it now ...'

'You're not answerin' my question.'

'With early detection, the percentages of recovery ...'

'Is it gonna kill me?'

'A bus could kill you' said the doctor. Eamo stood up.

'Bus isn't growin' inside me' he unzipped his trousers 'bus isn't drivin' around me bollox knockin' the fuck out of it' he muttered. 'Right' he bent over the examination table 'get this over with. Mother ah fuck' elbows on the table, head in his hands, he closed his eyes.

. . . .

'*...You're gonna die, die die ... die, die ... you're gonna die, die die ...*' Elliott reached across the counter and turned the tape off.

'Sorry' he said to the Heavy Metal head standing at the counter 'it's not what we're looking for.'

'You're making a mistake' said the long blonde haired guy in the faded denim jacket. 'Studio One needs a Metal show. You're the biggest station and you don't have a Metal show? Big mistake' he shouted as he walked out of the shop 'big fuckin' mistake!' he knocked against Eamo coming through the door.

'Watch! Where yer *goin!*' Eamo roared, slamming a hand out, bouncing the Metal fan against the door frame. Firing a dark look in Elliott's direction, Eamo turned, then jerked to a stop. 'Who's in my office?' he pointed at the figures behind the blinds.

'Squirrel and Mick' said Elliott. 'They want to talk to us about something.'

'I'm not in the humour ah talkin' ta anyone' Eamo growled. 'Get rid ah them.'

'They've been waiting for an hour' Elliott reasoned 'for you *and* Iris. She's off at five; she'll be here any …'

'Hey' Iris walked through the door. 'What's up?'

'I don't know' Elliott glanced at Eamo 'Squirrel's very excited whatever it is but he won't talk until we're all here.' Eamo muttered something under his breath.

'Better be quick' he turned towards the office.

'What's wrong with him?' said Iris.

'Don't know' said Elliott. 'He walked in like that.'

Mick was small, nocturnal, with eyeballs that had a tendency to slide left to right as he talked.

'Hiya' eyeballs left. 'Nice ta meet ya' they slid to the right.

'Yeah' Eamo glanced around 'you an' all. What's this about?'

'Tell them' Squirrel's eyes were shining with excitement. 'Go on' he pushed Mick, 'tell them.' Mick leant forward and lowered his voice.

'I'm openin' a new club' the eyeballs slid left. 'Have a premises; warehouse down on the Docks. I've had it a while, but I haven't been able ta settle on what kinda club it should be. I wanna do somethin' that'll blow everything else outta the water. Somethin's never been done before.'

'What's that got ta do with us?' said Eamo. 'Is he lookin' for free ads?' he said to Squirrel.

'No' a flash of annoyance on Squirrel's face. 'Listen ta what he has ta say Eamo.'

'Been thinkin' said Mick, 'ya know the way we've been doin' the live broadcasts in Berlin?'

'Yeah?' said Eamo.

'Well, what if we were ta make that a more permanent situation?' the eyeballs slid left, right, then left again.

'How do you mean?' said Iris.

'What if we called the new club Studio One …' Mick began.

'That's our name' said Eamo.

'I know that' said Mick.

'Yeah, well ya can't take *our* name for *your* club …'

'Eamo, will ya fuckin' listen to him!' said Squirrel. 'G'wan' he nodded at Mick.

'I'm talkin' about live radio' said Mick 'live in every sense ah the word. Studio One would be a club, it'd be a venue, but three or four nights a week, it'd also be a radio station, a station ya could visit, watch the broadcastin' live; the listeners are part ah the experience, d'ya get me?'

'Go on' Eamo scratched the stubble on his chin.

'We'll make it like Studio 54 in New York' said Mick 'wrap the place in tinfoil, lots ah art, make it the place to be, fill it with celebrities …'

'Yeah? Howaya gonna do that then?' said Eamo.

'Johnny Fontanni's a partner' said Mick.

'Who's Johnny Fontanni when he's at home?' said Eamo.

'Concert promoter' said Squirrel 'does all the big gigs.'

'Right' Eamo lit a cigarette. 'What's our cut?'

'No cut' said Mick. 'Benefit ta you is yer the only station with yer own niteclub, an' this'll be the biggest club in Dublin. Makes you number one in the public's eyes, which'll help keep ya at the top if competition comes back in. I'm givin' ya first shout; if you don't jump at it someone else will.'

'Oh my God!' Iris couldn't contain herself 'our own club, our own niteclub!'

'Whaddaya reckon Eamo?' said Squirrel. Eamo didn't answer. He was staring out his office window. 'Eamo?' said Squirrel.

'What?' Eamo looked around, then stared back out the window again. 'Alright, yeah. Go ahead. You sort it' he said to Squirrel. 'I'll see ya later' he turned and left the office.

'The fuck's wrong with him?' said Squirrel. 'Biggest thing we're gonna do' an' all he can say is *yeah*! Fucks sakes' a confused disappointment on his face as he stared at the empty showroom door. 'Live radio' he turned to Elliott 'our own club, an' by the way, Mick's right an' all; if other stations do set up this is what's gonna separate the men from the boys.'

'Is that a yes then?' said Mick. Elliott grinned.

'I think it's a definite yes.'

'Number one' said Squirrel. 'Number fuckin' one.'

'Let's go for a pint' said Elliott when Mick had gone 'we need to celebrate' immense happiness bubbling up inside him.

'I can't' said Iris. 'I'm meeting someone.' The bubbles hissed, fizzed and the excitement flattened.

Who? Who's she meeting?

'Me either' Squirrel picked up his helmet. 'Up ta me bollox.'

'Sure' Elliott tried to suppress the suspicion stinging at him. *Stop. Stop. He wouldn't. Would he?*

'We'll celebrate tomorrow' said Squirrel 'at the gig.'

'Sure' said Elliott. He looked at Iris. 'Have a good night.'

'Thanks' she wouldn't look at him. 'You too.'

Back in the flat Elliott lay on his bed and threw darts at the wall. *It's your own fault. You've had a million opportunities. Who's she meeting? It's not Squirrel. He wouldn't do that to you. I'll ask her out tomorrow. I'll just go straight up to her. Yeah? What are you going to say? I don't know. I'll figure it out.* His mind flickered, and from nowhere the situation with his mother pierced his thoughts.

Sooner or later you're going to have to start talking to her again Max's voice.

How long is it since ya've seen yer Ma? Squirrel in the studio. *I couldn't imagine not speakin' ta my Ma for three days never mind three years.*

You're pathetic a cold hard voice.

He stared up at the ceiling for several minutes then rolled his head to the side. His eyes fell on the staplegun Iris had used to put up the posters that first day he moved in and the T-shirt she'd stuck to the wall. He looked at the bags of clean laundry lying in the corner. Pushing himself off the bed he squatted down by the nearest bag and pulled out a T-shirt. Standing up he held it against the wall, positioned the staple gun against it, pressed down and felt a staple fire through. He stretched the T-shirt across and gunned the other side. He stared at it for a minute, then reached in and grabbed another, positioned it just above the first and gunned it to the wall. A third went up. A fourth. Half an hour later he sat back on the bed and looked at the wall, covered in his clothes. Silence. He walked over to the window. Pressed his head against the glass. 'What the fuck is wrong with me?' he looked out at the street 'why can't I just tell her how I feel … such a simple thing … what is my *fucking* problem?'

. . . .

'When you're in love, You know you're in love, No matter what you try to do, You might as well resign yourself, To what you're going through …'

Can't believe I'm at a Human League concert … Elliott made his way through the crowd. *What the fuck am I doing here? You know what you're doing. You're going to find Iris, get her to sit down somewhere quiet and you're going to tell her …'*

'Elliott!! Over here' it was Neal. 'You want a drink?' he shouted.

'Nah, you're alright' Elliott shouted back. Last thing he needed was Neal hanging around while he was trying to talk to Iris.'

'Come on! Have a drink!' Neal shouted, then 'Iris! Hey Iris!!' he called and Elliott turned in the direction Neal was waving towards. His heart flipped. She was in a dress. A short black dress, silver studded belts circling her hips, thick black tights, endless legs flowing into suede buckled Clash boots. Something softer about her tonight.

'Hey' she smiled at the two of them.

'Babe!' Neal shouted.

Babe? What do you mean babe? Elliott glared at him.

'Hey Babe' Neal wrapped his arm around Iris and kissed the top of her head.

What the … Elliott couldn't quite believe what he was seeing. He watched Neal shout something into Iris's ear, watched her look up and smile. Then Neal leant in and kissed her. Just like that. Right in front of him. A soft slow kiss. He cupped her cheek and kissed her. Somewhere, from nowhere, a hand reached down inside Elliott, travelled to the pit of his stomach, pulled the plug and he felt hope drain out.

'*… I love your love action, Lust's just a distraction, No talking, just looking, Watching your love action …*' the crowd sang along.

Pain. Black pain. He turned away. *I don't believe this. She must … they must … you don't just …*

'Alright!' it was Squirrel, a girl on each arm. 'What's the story?' he shouted. Elliott inclined his head in the general direction where Iris and Neal were still entwined. Squirrel's face dropped, then re-arranged. 'That's alright' he shouted 'don't worry about that.'

'What are you *talking* about?' Elliott shouted.

'I'm not worried about that' Squirrel was dismissive 'that won't last. C'mon, let's get a drink.'

'I don't want a drink' Elliott shouted. 'What do you mean don't *worry* about it? How the can you … he's … she's … I'm going home. I'll see you tomorrow.'

'Don't be a fuckin' eejit' Squirrel shouted 'have a drink; come on. Elliott!! Elliott …' his voice faded back.

I don't believe this Elliott pushed his way through the crowd, *I don't believe …*

'*… I believe, I believe what the old man said, I believe in truth though I lie a lot, I feel the pain from the push and shove, No matter*

what you put me through, I'll still believe in love ...' the crowd
chanted as the exit doors swung behind him.

They became a collective. 'Where's Iris? She's with Neal. Iris and
Neal are up in Studio. Has anyone seen Iris and Neal?' Had
anyone not seen them? Neal with his arm circling her waist,
draped on her shoulder; casual, careless, carefree. Laughing.
Always laughing. What the fuck was so funny all the time?
Smiling at each other. Engrossed in each other. Oblivious to the
rest of them. Oblivious to him.

Only one way to deal with it. He worked the shows. He sat
with Wayne every day, pulled him in check each time he
reached for the fader. He got Declan in studio and recorded
different impersonations, took off the station IDs for a while and
dropped Declan's other characters into the schedule to shake it
up and keep it fresh. He recorded promos with Gary, Barry and
Benny, snippits from their shows and dropped them in across
the day to try to pull more nitetime listeners in. He scoured the
clubs and took on a new jock called David Boner; a Disco, Soul,
Funk set, high energy mixing injecting new life into the
weekend schedule. He met with Squirrel and Mick and figured
out how the new Studio One niteclub would work. They
briefed artists, designers, and watched Ireland's first custom built,
live radio club, emerge from the shell of a warehouse on the
docks.

'Figures are through the roof' said Squirrel just after Christmas.
  'Yeah?' Elliott watched a woman try to pull her child's legs back
out from the end of a carpet roll in the centre of the showroom.
  'Banked ten grand last week.'
  'Ten grand?'
  'Ssshhht!! We're up ta forty eight' Squirrel glanced at the
woman 'an' if we keep goin' the way we are, we'll hit the
hundred in the next four or five months.'
  'Are you serious?' said Elliott.
  'Ad agencies are ringin' *me*' said Squirrel. 'Used ta be me

chasin' them, now they're ringin' me. Priority bookins, fixed spots, invitin' me ta all sorts ah shit.'

'Like what?' said Elliott.

'Golf' Squirrel made a face. 'No interest in golf' he stared down the showroom. 'Nice young ones' he winked 'workin' in those ad agencies. Take a swing at them alright.'

'Yeah?' Elliott smiled.

'Yeah. C'mere, d'ya wanna come ta the pictures tonight? Amanda said she'd bring her sister.'

'No, you're alright thanks' Elliott bent down behind the counter and lifted up a wide heavy carpet sample book. Squirrel watched him place it on the counter and disappear down to pick up another.

'You need ta get over her.'

'I don't want to get over her' Elliott came up from behind the counter with a second sample book. 'Besides, you were right' he bent down to pick up a third. 'It won't last.'

'How d'ya know?' said Squirrel.

'Because' Elliott began to stack the books 'there's only so much Synth you can listen to.'

. . . .

'Roger?' the secretary's voice was soft amidst the thickly carpeted, high ceilinged Georgian office. 'You can come through now.'

'Thank you' Roger stood up and followed her into Minister Horn's office.

'Roger' the Minister beckoned from his desk at the top of the enormous room, bright shafts of light flooding through the high windows behind him. 'Have a seat' he indicated towards a chair in front of his desk, then as Roger sat down, the Minister stood up. 'We've made a decision' he said. 'We're going to lift the jam.'

'What! Why? You can't *do* that' Roger exploded. 'What are you saying? You're going to let them all back on-air? Are you mad? They'll take the market, they'll take the *entire* market; we'll be left with nothing!!'

'Roger' the Minister's voice had a decidedly irritated tone.

'The PR on this situation has been a disaster from start to finish. I got hauled upstairs last night for the bollocking of all bollockings. Our Taoiseach kicked my arse up and down the corridor.'

'Oh fuck the Taoiseach' Roger muttered. 'He's not the one having to deal with this on a day to day basis.' The Minister spun around.

'Sorry? Did you just say *fuck the Taoiseach*? Did I hear that correctly? Did you actually just say *fuck the Taoiseach* while you're sitting here in Government buildings?' Roger's face reddened.

'I didn't actually mean fuck the Taoiseach.'

'Oh really? Well what did you mean? Fuck the Prime Minister of Bulgaria? You know what; doesn't matter, I'll pretend I didn't hear it. The publicity Roger, as I was staying before you decided to assassinate our Taoiseach ...'

'I never said I wanted to assassinate the Taoiseach.'

'... The publicity' the Minister raised his voice 'is killing us. Negative, negative, negative. We're like the Kodak factory. And what's about to come marching around the corner? What's on its way right when we need it most?'

'Eh ...' Roger's mind had gone blank.

'The election Roger. An election, a recession, and a *very* unhappy public. There they are, struggling to pay the bills, to feed their children, and here *we* are, the big bad Government turning off the one bit of happiness and comfort they have in these spectacularly difficult times, their only friend in the world, the one thing that doesn't cost them any money, their fucking radio stations!! I tell you what, well done Roger, *well done*. Jamming the Pirates really was one of your all time great ideas.'

'Oh it's *my* fault now?' Roger shouted. 'You're the one who rode into my office on your *kill the noise* horse.'

'Kill the noise, not sink the Department. There's a distinct difference, and I thought you would have known that, but you know what? I should have known better. If you want something killed, kill it yourself. There's a press release going out on Monday.'

'A press release?' Roger laughed. 'You're going to kill it with a press release? Well let me just run home and grab my stapler.

Because I'd really like to back you up on this. I'd really like to be standing there by your side as you send out your *press release*. Tell me, what's it's going to say? What's going to be in this *press release* that's going to sort out a situation nobody, specifically this Government, have been able to deal with since the Sixties?' The Minister stopped pacing.

'We're going to regulate the market.'

'You're …'

'The press release, Roger, will announce the tendering of two new local radio station licences for Dublin. A national tender. Anyone can apply, except those currently operating an illegal broadcast. So, in order to apply, existing Pirates will have to go off-air. Voluntarily.'

'Voluntarily? You actually believe the Pirates will voluntarily go off-air?'

'They will when we dangle the licence carrot in front of them. When they see how much money they could make.' He paused. 'They will when they see the new laws we're bringing in.'

'Oh the new laws' said Roger. 'Christ *they're* finally happening. They've only taken, what, ten years?'

'The new legislation' the Minister ignored him 'which comes into effect by the end of this year will mean that anyone operating an illegal broadcast will face a twenty thousand pound fine, imprisonment, or both. Show's over.'

'The Pirates won't take any notice of …'

'Show's over.'

'They'll never …'

'Show's over Roger. The new laws are here. And they will be enforced. A twenty thousand pound fine, imprisonment, or both. Show's, over.'

Roger was silent for a moment or two.

'And where does that leave us?' he said.

'It leaves you' said the Minister 'with a short time frame in which to get your act together. You need to re-launch the station.'

'Re-launch? Why would we …'

'Because you need to' said the Minister. 'The Pirates have shown that there's room for competition. They've proven that people want choice and that the radio market has the potential to expand. This is the future Roger. Legalised local radio. We'll test in Dublin. If it works we'll roll out Cork, Limerick, Galway; by 1990 we'll have local stations in every major city. Two new stations won't detract; they'll open the market up; what's critical here is our position. We need to ensure that the National Broadcaster is poised to be a central, relevant player. The one thing the Pirates have proven is that if you get the format right, a radio licence is to all intents and purposes a licence to print money. And like it or not the Pirate format is working. They're taking share and making money. A lot of money.' He paused for a moment. 'I want you to study the Pirates Roger. Study their format, and adapt it to fit the framework of the National Broadcaster. And while you're at it, you can do a bit of pirating of your own.'

'How do you mean?'

'I want you to cherry pick the best DJs from the leading Pirates and recruit them for your new station. That way, when the old stations disappear, the DJs the public love so much, the people they think of as their friends, are still here.' He smiled. 'Only now they're with us.'

. . . .

'... *Darkness falls across the land, The midnight hour is close at hand, Creatures crawl in search of blood, To terrorize y'awls neighborhood, And whosoever shall be found, without the soul for getting down, Must stand and face the hounds of hell, and rot inside a corpse's shell* ... Studio One, it's Thriller! We are live, live in every sense of the word ... celebrating with you tonight, the number one station in Dublin. Studio One, officially your number one ... '

'Haaay guys' Carly shouted as they stood on the balcony of the new Studio One Niteclub watching the crowds on the dance floor below. 'How incredible is this?' she yelled. 'You remember that freakin' kebab restaurant? Look at us now! Number One baby!' she shouted at Squirrel. 'Number One!'

The JNLRs had come in. Studio One was officially the Number One station in Dublin. The jocks went nuts. The showroom was over-run with listeners. Elliott ran promos celebrating their success, the news had made the papers and tonight they had thrown a massive party in the Studio One Niteclub for the jocks, station staff, the advertising agencies and as many listeners as the club could fit.

'We did it!' Squirrel punched the air. 'What did I tell ya?' he shouted at Elliott over the music. 'A hundred grand reality!! C'mere you' he grabbed Iris and pulled her in between himself and Elliott. Cheekbones high, like Squirrel she hadn't stop smiling all night. 'You're amazin' Squirrel shouted 'both ah ya' leather arms squeezing the two of them. '*You* did this.'

'We' Elliott shouted. 'We did this. All of us.'

'Yeah, well' Squirrel reached for his pint 'here's ta ... hang on, where's Eamo? Eamo!' he shouted. A short distance away Eamo leaning over the balcony, whisky glass dangling from one hand, a cigarette in the other, glanced across, smiled, and toasted them from where he was standing. 'Eamo' Squirrel shouted 'come over!' Eamo pushed himself back from the rail and made his way across. 'Number One!!' Squirrel shouted. Eamo shrugged. 'Eamo' Squirrel pointed down at the dance floor 'we're standin' in our own niteclub an' we're the Number One station!'

'It's Mick's club' Eamo pulled on his cigarette.

'Ah for fucks sakes Eamo!' said Squirrel 'what's wrong with ya? Are ya not buzzin'?' Eamo smiled a half smile and Squirrel noticed lines on his face he hadn't seen before.

'Course I am' Eamo looked weary. 'Listen, it's great. Ya've done a great job.'

'*We've* done a great job' Squirrel shouted 'all of us' he stopped as he caught sight of the expression on his Uncle's face. 'Y'alright Eamo?'

'Grand' Eamo's eyes shifted. 'You're a great young fella Squirr'' he cleared his throat. 'I'm glad' neon lights reflecting out. 'Glad we got the chance ta work together' his eyes were fixed on the dance floor. 'Ta know each other.'

'Me an' all Eamo' Squirrel shouted. 'Tell ya Eamo' he leant on the rail 'I don't care what me Ma says. I think you're sound. I do.' Silence. Disco music pulsing pounding.

'You an' all Squirr' Eamo stared at the dance floor 'you an' all' he knocked back the rest of his whisky. 'I'll catch ya later' patting Squirrel's arm he turned away.

'Where are ya goin?' Squirrel shouted. 'It's only early!!'

'Gettin' too old for all ah this' Eamo called over his shoulder. 'I'll catch ya later.'

'The fuck is wrong with him?' Squirrel watched his retreating figure.

PIRATES BACK ON-AIR BUT NOT FOR LONG

Ahoy there! Heave Ho! Pirate Radio set to go!! That's the message from Minister for Communications Richard Horn in a statement released today. BBR, Rocket and other stations jammed by RTE are being given a brief reprise to go back on-air as RTE lifts their jam, but ALL stations will close by the end of the year in accordance with tough new legislation, which is intended to stamp out Pirate Radio and provide the framework for legal Commercial Radio. The new Act will see those who try to continue to broadcast after December this year face a fine of up to £20,000 and/or up to two years in prison.

The Minister's statement was released in conjunction with a separate announcement that two new local radio station licences are to be put out to tender for the Dublin region, and that subject to how these new stations perform, similar licences may be tendered for Cork, Galway, Limerick, Kerry and Waterford. The Minister confirmed that anyone can apply for a licence and said he 'expected the majority of the 25 Pirate stations currently operating in Dublin will apply, but in order to do so they must cease broadcasting. Applicants operating an illegal broadcast will not be considered.'

'Fuck that' Squirrel shook the Evening Press back into shape. 'Fuck that for a game ah soldiers' he threw it on the desk. 'Whaddaya reckon?' The three of them were in Eamo's office; Squirrel in Eamo's chair, feet up on the desk, Elliott on the couch, Iris perched on the grey filing cabinet, legs softly kicking the drawer behind her.

'Do you think we should apply?' she said.

'Course we should' said Squirrel. 'Number One station. Hafta give us a licence. They can't *not* give the Number One station a licence.'

'Why do they want us all off-air?' Elliott had picked up the paper and was re-reading the article 'that's the bit I don't understand. What difference does it make if they're going to hand two of us licences anyway?'

'We're not going off-air' said Iris.

'Well, according to this we can't apply unless we do' said Elliott.

'So don't apply.'

'We have to apply' said Elliott 'we can't *not* apply. It's a once in lifetime opportunity. If we got a licence ...'

'Which we would' said Squirrel.

'We *can't* go off-air' Iris persisted. 'We'd lose our listeners, lose jocks; it would be the end of us.'

'How long'd we be off?' said Squirrel.

'Doesn't matter' Iris was angry 'you're missing the point; it doesn't matter if it's a day, a week, a month; once we're gone, we're gone. We'd be starting from scratch again. I can't believe you're even *thinking* about this' she turned to Elliott, 'look at all the work we've put into getting the station to this point; do you really want to just pull the plug on it?'

'Of course not' said Elliott 'but do you really want to sit back and watch someone with half our talent take the one thing we've always wanted?'

'Who says it's the one thing we've always wanted?' Iris retorted. 'When did we *ever* have a conversation about wanting a licence?'

'Don't be stupid Iris' said Squirrel. 'Course we want a licence.'

'Fuck you' Iris pushed herself off the filing cabinet 'don't call me stupid' anger flashing. 'Prick' she muttered, heading for the door.

'Ahh come on Iris' Squirrel began.

'Shove your licence up your hole' she banged the door hard behind her, rattling the venetian blinds. Elliott and Squirrel stared at each other in shock, then Squirrel started to laugh.

'What the ... what the fuck was that? What did I say? What did I fuckin' say? Jaysus! Women! What did I *say?*'

'I don't know' Elliott laughed 'I'm just glad I didn't say it.'

'Fuckin' head on her' said Squirrel. 'Right, well we know where she stands.

'What about you? What do you wanna do?'

'Why don't we get an application form and see what we're up against' said Elliott. 'See how long we'd have to be off-air for. Take it from there.'

'Fair enough. C'mere where's Eamo? Have ya talked ta him?'

'No' Elliott shook his head. 'He hasn't been in a lot lately.'

'Somethin' goin' on with him' said Squirrel. 'D'ya reckon he's got a bird stashed somewhere?'

'Dunno' Elliott shrugged.

'Somethin' definitely goin'' said Squirrel. 'Duckin' an' divin' all over the shop. Where is he now? Where is he *right now?'* he tapped the desk. 'Wednesday afternoon, showroom are flyin', station's facin' a crisis; where the fuck is Eamo?

. . . .

Eamo sat in the waiting room. Tap-tap-tap went his foot. Jig-jig-jig jerked his knee. A man and his son sat opposite him. The boy looked about three. He was holding a small yellow truck.

'Daddy go doctor?' he ran the truck along his father's thigh.

'That's right, Daddy's going to see the doctor' the man watched the truck drive up his chest and down his arm.

'Daddy sick?' the boy leant on his Father's leg and looked up at him.

'Daddy caught *your* cold' the man ruffled his son's hair 'but the doctor is going to give me some medicine like he gave you and that's going to make it better.' The boy knelt by the coffee table and began driving the truck across it. He looked up and caught Eamo's eye.

'That's my Daddy' he pointed back at his father behind him. Eamo nodded.

'Daddy sick' said the boy to no-one in particular, as he stood up to drive the truck down the length of the table. '*My* Daddy' little eyebrows locked in concentration as the truck negotiated a magazine pile.

'Eamon Rourke?' the nurse popped her head around the corner. Eamo stood up.

. . . .

Doctor Feehy gave him a warm, if somewhat forced smile as he sat down.

'How are you?' he said.

'Grand' said Eamo. 'Ya can cut the small talk. What's the verdict?' The doctor's eyes shifted.

'The radiation hasn't worked. We're going to have to operate. It's a standard procedure; you'll be in and out in a matter of a day or two.'

'Right' Eamo's face remained still.

'The success rate on this is very high' said the doctor 'and I *am* confident we've caught it early enough.' Eamo nodded.

'When?' he said.

'I see no reason to delay' said the doctor. 'I'd like to send you in tomorrow.' Eamo nodded. Silence. 'I really can't stress enough …' the doctor began.

'Save it' Eamo stood up. 'Let's just get it over with.'

'We need to do some paperwork' said the doctor. 'If you'll have a seat, it won't take a minute.'

'Sure' Eamo sat down again.

'Now' the doctor studied the form in front of him 'name … address' he ran his finger down the page 'we have all that … next of kin?'

237

'Me brother' said Eamo, and gave him the address.

'Dependents?' said the doctor.

'How d'ya mean?' said Eamo.

'Children' said the doctor. 'Have you any children?'

'No.'

'No children' the doctor ticked the 'No' box. 'VHI?' he looked up.

'What difference would it make?'

'Well, VHI will significantly reduce the cost.'

'No' said Eamo. 'What difference would it make if I had kids?' The doctor studied him for a moment, then he put down his pen.

'Prostate cancer is genetic. Men with a father who has prostate cancer are twice as likely to develop it, so if you have a son, it would be important to have him tested.' Eamo's eyes flicked, then fixed on the medical chart behind the doctor's desk. The sound of the clock ticking.

'My Daddy's sick' the child's voice echoed through from the waiting room outside. 'That's my Daddy.' *That's my Daddy.* Eamo stared at the chart.

'If you have a son' he heard the doctor say 'if you have a son Mister O'Rourke, you have an absolute responsibility to tell him.'

. . . .

'Come on!! Hurry! We'll miss them. Stop dragging your heels' Max had persuaded Elliott to come and see Anthony off on his sailing trip to the Arctic, but as they approached the Yacht Club Elliott felt his legs grow heavy.

'This is a mistake.'

'It's not a mistake' Max was punching in the security code for the gate at the side of the Club.

'What am I going to say to him? We've nothing to say to each other' Elliott called as Max pushed the gate and headed across the tarmac to the gangplank that bridged the mainland to the marina. Elliott followed slowly. In the distance, at the end of the fourth row of floating jetties, he could see Anthony's boat, moored in the same berth it always was, stick like figures scrambling around it as they readied for the off.

'Come *on* Elliott!' Max shouted.

'What am I going to *say?*' Elliott made his way reluctantly down the gangplank.

'Look, all you're doing is wishing him well' said Max. 'Just stand there and say *hey Dad, hope you have a good trip*; that's all you have to say' the jetty rocked softly beneath their feet. 'You'll be glad you did this' said Max. 'I promise you will. Whatever happens you'll be glad you came.'

'Yeah, right.'

'Elliott' Max grabbed his arms. 'He is who he is. Remember he left us in the Zoo? When we were kids. Remember he was so wrapped up in that case he was working on, when he suddenly figured out a loophole, and he was halfway home in the car before he realised we were still in the chimpanzee house?'

'Yeah' Elliott grinned. 'I remember that.'

'Well he hasn't changed' said Max. 'And he won't. It's always going to be whatever's going on in his head that counts. But he's still our Father. And we just have to work around that.' Elliott stared at the ground.

'He still sponsors the Zoo you know.'

Does he?' Max looked surprised.

'Yeah' said Elliott, remembering the conversation in his bedroom the night he'd tried on the suit; 'he got a letter about it just before we had the blow up. Funny isn't it? I presumed he'd stopped once we'd grown up.'

'We need to get down there' Max wasn't listening. 'Boat's ready' he assessed the activity at the top end of the jetty. 'They'll go any minute. Come on' he tugged at Elliott's jacket. Elliott hesitated. 'Come on Elliott!!' Max pulled his jacket again.

'Okay, okay' Elliott jerked his arm free and picked up his step, trying hard to ignore the nerve endings tripping inside his stomach.

'Hi Dad' Max called out, as they reached the boat. Anthony,

standing on the deck, dressed head to toe in red oilskins turned around.

'Max' a curt nod as he stepped off the boat. He looked at Elliott. 'Come to your senses have you?'

'I … I just came to wish you well on your trip' Elliott repeated the line Max had given him.

'I see' Anthony's face was impassive. 'That it?'

'Pretty much' Elliott swallowed. Anthony turned to Max.

'Was this your idea? Because if it was, it wasn't one of your better ones.'

'Oh come on Dad …' Max began.

'Pathetic' Anthony cut him off 'both of you; pathetic' he shook his head as he began uncoiling a long rope.

'See?' Elliott smiled at Max 'what did I tell you?' he turned and began to walk back down the jetty.

'Shit Dad' Max watched Elliott's retreating figure 'how could you … I can't believe you said that. Do you know what it took to get him here? He came to wish you well. Christ Dad, you're an *asshole*! You're a *fucking asshole!!*'

'Cast off!' Tiny shouted and the crew began untying the rest of the ropes.

'I'm getting on board' lifting one leg up onto the deck Anthony grabbed the rails and pulled his bulk up and over. 'Throw the ropes' he barked. Max leant down. He picked up a rope, threw it on deck, then reached for the other. Frankie was motoring back now, the boat a few feet from the pier. Max watched the boat. In the distance he saw Elliott making his way back up the gangplank onto the mainland. He looked at Anthony, sitting on the deck. The boat drifted further back.

'He came to wish you well' Max shouted. 'You're an asshole Dad, you're a fucking asshole!!'

. . . .

'… Studio One, officially the Number One station in Dublin; that's one small step for Pirate Radio, one giant leap for Dublin listeners. Sunday afternoon, this is The Godfather signin' off, we'll see ya back here next week, same time, same place, until then, Frank Sinatra *It Was a Good Year* ... certainly was for Studio One ... Number One Dublin an' it's thanks ta you ...' Eamo pushed off his headphones and stood up as the studio door opened.

'Haaay darlin' Carly breezed through, a stack of records under her arm.

'All yours' Eamo lit a cigarette as he made his way into the outer room where Squirrel, Elliott and Iris sat waiting on the sofas. They were re-convening for a second debate on whether or not they should go off-air and tender for one of the two Government licences.

'Bit stiff there Eamo' said Squirrel as boney knees bent and Eamo lowered himself carefully onto the sofa.

'Stiff in all the wrong places' said Eamo. 'What are we doin' about this?'

'I say we go for it' said Squirrel. He sneaked a look across at Iris. 'Are we friends again?' he winked. Iris lit a cigarette.

'Maybe' a small smile curling. 'I'm not going off-air though.'

'Me neither' said Eamo. 'Be the end of us. An' what about the listeners? How d'ya think they'll feel if we just fuck off for three months?'

'Maybe we should ask them' said Squirrel.

'How d'ya mean?' said Eamo.

'Listeners put us here' Squirrel shrugged 'made us the Number One station. Only fair we ask them what they think about the Government makin' us go off-air. See if we can get a bit ah support outta them. See if we can get them ta help us change the Government's mind.'

'Lobby the listeners?' said Elliott.

'Exactly' said Squirrel. 'We have ta tender for a licence; we're the Number One station; listeners'll be disappointed if we *don't* tender, but they'll be pissed off at the same time if we hafta go off-air. Get them involved.'

'So stay on-air?' said Iris.

'Long as we can' said Squirrel. 'Get the application in; get the listeners talkin; see if we can get them ta help us change the Government's mind about goin' off-air.'

'We're not going to change the Government's mind' said Iris.

'How long have we got?' said Elliott. 'How long from the time we send in the application and the date the Government want us off-air?'

'If we get the application in now' Squirrel scanned the application form, 'we've just over a month to the off-air date; then the tender interviews are the week after that.'

'Right' said Elliott. 'Let's get our application in, let's make as much noise as we can and let's give the Government, and the listeners, a month they won't forget.'

. . . .

'Base to Lady Margaret ... what's your position?'

'Lady Margaret to base ... Seventy four north ... heading for Cape Flora outdoor temperature down to six, small patches of snow appearing on the mountains as we cruise up the coast of Norway ...'

The boat made its way slowly north. Sunshine initially, then as the days rolled by, the skies turned grey, the sea grew heavy, thick rolling waves, the nose of the boat riding high, crashing low, up and over, sea sprays splattering the portholes. Schools of dolphins swimming alongside, and later, in the distance, bellies of whales, slick black hills rolling up, sinking under, great blows of water.

Anthony was silent for several days. The scene with Max on the Marina had made for an awkward start and he retreated to his bunk, emerging only to helm, take his watch or eat with the crew.

'Look what *I've* got!' Richard, the youngest member of the crew sang as he stepped out of his bunk with a square shaped bevelled glass bottle. From his position at the breakfast table Anthony glanced up but said nothing. Beside him, Nick and Frankie cheered.

'Tequila' Peter laughed.

'Mescal' Richard raised the bottle to the light, so they could see it more clearly. 'El gusano' he shook the bottle, and they watched something dark rise up from the bottom, hover for a second or two, then float slowly black down.

'Oh fuck. The worm' said Nick.

'Fifty quid a man' Richard placed the bottle down in the centre of the table. 'We take turns drinking it by the neck. Last shot drinks the worm, pockets the cash.'

'Are you out of your mind?' Anthony snapped. 'Do you want to kill us all? This is a serious trip; we're charting rough waters, dangerous ice and you want us all to get shit-faced and drink hallucinogenic worms? What sort of a fucking amateur are you?'

'Lighten up Anthony' said Nick. 'No-one's suggesting we do anything stupid while we're sailing. It's for a port or if we get stuck somewhere.'

'I'm not having …' Anthony began,

'No!' Nick cut him off '*I'm* not having' he pointed at Anthony '*you,* make this an unpleasant trip for the rest of us. Don't think we didn't notice what went on with your kids on the Marina. You might be able to talk to them like that but you won't be treating Richard or anyone else on this boat like that. If that's your attitude you can get out at Cape Flora. I mean it Anthony. It might be your boat, but you appointed me skipper and I won't do this trip with tension in the crew. If Richard wants to have a bit of fun with the tequila when we're in the safety of a port, we'll all be joining in, so shape up or fuck off.'

. . . .

' *…The air attack warning sounds like …this is the sound … when you hear the air attack warning you and your family must take cover … ow-ow-ow … ow-ow … let's go … oh-ohh …* Studio One is tendering for one of the two Dublin licenses the Government are making available but, in order to tender, the Government want us off the air for nearly three months. We have one month to change the Government's minds; one month to convince them there's no reason for Dublin's Number One station to stop broadcasting during the tender process. We need your help. You put us here, now keep us here. Call your local politicians, write to the papers, drop in and sign our petition, do whatever you think will help us stay on-air.'

The promos went out. On the hour, every hour, right before the news, in and out of all the ad breaks. Out they went, and on they came. In their hundreds. Listeners calling the station, talking on-air, voicing their support. The papers picked up on it and features began to appear. An independent on-street survey confirmed they were the number one station of choice.

'We're gonna get a licence, I'm tellin' ya' said Squirrel. 'They can't not give us one.'

'They still want us off-air' said Iris. 'They haven't backed down.'

'They will' said Squirrel. 'They will.'

'We need ta turn it up a gear' said Eamo. 'What else can we do?'

'Candy said she'll get Dessie to spread the word with all the taxi drivers' said Elliott. 'Mick's putting flyers in the clubs, the jocks are going to talk about it on their shows, and Rachel's doing a phone-in every day until the end of the month.'

'Hey guys' the studio door pushed open and Neal appeared around it. 'Hey babe' a toothpaste smile in Iris's direction.

'Hey' her voice was flat as Neal sat down and stretched his arm behind her on the sofa. 'How come you're here?' a distinct tension in the question.

'Came to take *you* for a drink' Neal cocked a finger gun in her direction.

'Well' Iris didn't look at him 'we're just having a meeting.'

'You're alright' said Squirrel 'we're done here; you're grand.'
Silence. Iris stared at the carpet.

'Okay' she pushed herself up off the couch. Eyes dull, her face was blank, devoid of expression' 'See you tomorrow' she didn't look at them as she pulled the studio door open, Neal following closely behind her. Soft brushing, carpet on carpet as the door closed then sealed. Squirrel let out a long low whistle.

'What was that?'

'Don't know' Elliott stared at the door.

'Reckon the old Synth might be startin' ta wear a bit thin?' said Squirrel.

'Maybe' said Elliott.

'Get in there' said Squirrel. 'Don't hang around.' Elliott was silent. 'You're never gonna do it' Squirrel shook his head. 'You're just gonna sit there.'

'I'm not going to just sit there' Elliott frowned.

'An' even if ya do, ya'll fuck it up.'

'I won't' Elliott's face darkened.

'Ya will. Ya'll fuck it up.'

'I *won't* fuck it up. Do you really think the Synth's wearing thin?'

'Only one way ta find out' Squirrel flashed him a bold smile. 'Get in there for fucks sakes. Life's too short' he made for the door. 'Not a rehearsal' he pulled it open 'not a fuckin' rehearsal' carpet on carpet, then he was gone, the door sucking softly shut behind him.

. . . .

'Good news' the doctor smiled at Eamo. 'You have officially been given a clean bill of health.' Eamo nodded.

'Good.'

'You'll need to have regular checks' the doctor looked at him from across the desk 'but I'm pleased with these results, and you should be too.'

'Thanks' Eamo stood up. 'Thanks for ... well ... ya know ... everything.'

'Mister Rourke?'

'Yeah?' Eamo glanced over his shoulder as he reached for the door handle.

'You will bear in mind what I said?'

'What's that?' cold metal pressing into Eamo's hand.

'That it's genetic' came the doctor's voice. Eamo nodded but did not turn around. 'You have a responsibility ...' the doctor began.

'I know' said Eamo. 'Thanks doctor' he pulled the handle and slipped out the door.

. . . .

Bang! Bang! Bang! Iris looked out her bedroom window. Arthur was kneeling over two long planks of wood set up on a stand in the back garden. She watched him put down the hammer, then take up a saw and begin working his way through the end piece of wood, his body bent in position, elbow rising, falling, rising again as he worked the saw up, down, through the plank.

'Miaow' Ian Curtis stretched on the bed. Iris sat down beside him, dangling her hand just out of his reach as he rolled on his back.

'Fat ... cat' she teased him with her hand, holding it high; four paws scrabbling, grabbing, reaching up. 'You keep away from Alexi' she nodded at the hamster cage on the dresser.

'Miaow' Ian Curtis rolled back and stretched again. From the garden, the sound of a drill being tested; a series of short sharp high pitched revs. Ian Curtis sat up and froze, glassy eyes fixing on the window.

'Hello darling' Jackie glanced up as Iris walked into the kitchen. 'Aren't you working today?'

'Flexi-time' Iris slowed to a stop and stared at the kitchen wall.

'That's handy' Jackie murmured. 'I didn't think insurance companies did that kind of thing' she turned back to the book she was reading.

'Mum' Iris stared at wall 'where's the sink?

'Hmm?' Jackie didn't look up.

'The sink' Iris pointed to the bare grey wall 'the sink ... the washing machine, the cupboards ... where's everything gone from that wall?' through the window she could see the top of Arthur's head as he dragged something heavy across the patio.

'The sink' Jackie's head was deep in the book 'your Father had to clear that wall for the ... the em ...'

'For the what?' said Iris.

'For the ... ' Jackie circled her hand in the direction of the wall. 'Might be a bit of upheaval in here for a while' the sound of a page turning as she hunched closer to the text.

'What kind of upheaval?' Iris stared at the two copper pipes rising up from where the washing machine had been, wet cotton rags wrapped around the top of each one. Behind them, rough pencil marks outlined shapes of spaces the cupboards had previously occupied, a large X scratched into the centre of each square.

'Your Father ...' Jackie's voice faded back as loud heavy drilling began on the outside of the kitchen wall.

'What's he doing?' Iris felt the kitchen floorboards begin to vibrate up through her feet. 'What's he *doing* to that wall?' she raised her voice over the noise of the drill.

'He's knocking it down' Jackie shouted.

'Why?' Iris shouted as she the drilling grew louder.

'He's building ...' Jackie's voice disappeared as metal dug deeper, grinding its way through thick cement.

'Building *what??*' Iris yelled.

'A conservatory' Jackie shouted.

'Why' Iris shouted. 'We don't *need* a conservatory.'

'What?'

'We don't need ...' Iris yelled '... tell him to stop... he's scaring Michael Stipe!' she pointed at the budgie cage where the small bird fluttered and squawked.

'What?' Jackie shouted.

'He's scaring ...' Iris shouted 'oh forget it' lifting the budgie cage she turned and walked across to the music room. 'We don't need a conservatory' she kicked the door open 'we don't ...' her face dropped 'oh for *fucks sakes!!* ...' anger flashing, '*Mum!!*' she shouted over the drilling, '*Mum!!*' but Jackie's head was back in her book. Iris stood in the doorway to the music room, holding the budgie cage, and stared at the long stainless steel double sink leaning up against her record shelves, the kitchen presses filling the centre of the room and the washing machine and dishwasher to the left of her stereo. 'We don't need a conservatory' her words drowned by the drilling 'we don't ...' the drilling cut off abruptly; the loud shrill of the front doorbell piercing the temporary silence.

'That's her!' Jackie jumped up from her chair.

'Who?' Iris scowled.

'Janet Temple' Jackie's hands fluttered as she looked down to check her appearance.

'Who's Janet Temple?' Iris put Michael Stipe's cage down on top of the washing machine.

'She's a Medium' Jackie's voice dropped 'from America. She wrote this' Jackie pushed the book she'd been reading across the table as she ran for the door. Iris looked at the cover of the book. '*Finding The Third Eye*, by Janet Temple, *The Path To Higher Ground*' she could hear Jackie's voice in the hall, high, excited. 'I'll just get the tea' she called as she came back into kitchen.

'What's she here for?' said Iris.

'She's going to help me open my third eye' Jackie began setting up a tray with cups, saucers and a milk jug.

'What does your third eye do?'

'Connects you' Jackie filled the teapot and put on the lid.

'To what?'

'Everything' said Jackie. 'Every*thing*, every*one* ...'

'Like who?' said Iris. Silence. Jackie reached for the biscuit tin.

'Well ...' her voice was careful.

'Frank' said Iris.

'Maybe' Jackie shook some biscuits out on a plate. 'I mean it *is* possible; you never know' fragile, haunted eyes from across the room.

'Sure' through the window Iris watched Arthur raise a sledge hammer high over his shoulder. 'You never know' she said as he swung it hard at the outside wall.

. . . .

'Lady Margaret ... what is your position, come in Lady Margaret ...'

'Lady Margaret over, seventy-seven, forty-nine, should hit our first band of ice shortly, pretty bumpy, doing a good six and a half knots. Refused permission to land in Franz Joseph Land. Ice charts showing seventh tenths ice just off

Cape Flora, so we'll head there, and depending on how thick the ice is, see how far we get...'

Grey seas for several days, then the temperature dropped, ice appeared in the rigging and in the distance, snow peaked mountains as they sailed past glaciers and motored down into fjords. Crystal waters, mirroring blue skies, mud brown and purple mountains tipped with snow. Silence. Arctic silence.

The mood lifted. Richard flew a kite off the back of the boat, Nick and Peter swam, plunging into icy water, swimming quickly back for shots of whisky. Tiny snored his way from Tromsø to Honningsvåg. The radio hissed and spat, latitude and longitude positions were relayed, and every day the fax machine whirred and chugged as Anthony's office sent them the front page of the Irish Times.

'Why are you bothering to get the Times?' Richard passed the fax to Anthony. 'Headlines' Anthony began to study the fax. 'Important to stay in touch. It's what you do when you have your own business; you live, sleep, and breathe it.'

'Like Elliott?' said Richard.

'Hardly' Anthony's face tightened. 'Elliott's a salesman. In a carpet shop.'

'The carpet shop's a front' Richard laughed. 'Everyone knows that. It's a front for the radio station he owns.'

'Elliott doesn't own a radio station' Anthony zipped up his oilskins. 'You should check your facts' grabbing each side of the small wooden stairs he climbed up on deck.

'Those are the facts' Richard popped his head up through the hatch. 'Tell you what' he grinned 'if I can get Elliott's station on the long wave, will you drink the tequila with us?'

'No. I will not' Anthony glared at the horizon. 'I wouldn't touch that muck. And frankly, I don't want to hear my son's voice on some piece of shit station you locate on the long wave. I don't need to be reminded what a colossal cock-up he's making of his life. And if Elliott's achievements are the extent of your own ambitions, you needn't expect to amount to much either.'

'Okay, that's enough' Nick pulled Richard back down into the galley.

'He's a prick' Anthony heard Richard say to Nick.

'He's the prick who owns this boat!' Anthony shouted down the hatch. 'You might like to think about that.'

'Yeah?' Richard shouted. 'Well you might like to think about the fact that your son thinks you're an asshole' he pulled himself back up through the hatch 'and you know what? He's right! You *are* an asshole. You're a fucking asshole!!'

'That's *enough!!*' Nick pulled Richard back down into the galley. 'Anthony' Nick shouted up through the hatch 'you're the grown-up. Back off. Give it a rest. Christ, I'll be drinking that tequila myself if this continues. What time is it?'

'Twelve o'clock' Richard bristled.

'Stick that on' Nick nodded at the radio 'see if you can get the News.'

. . . .

'... Studio One, it's twelve o'clock, the news with Christian Montgomery. The number of independent stations throughout the country diminishes hourly, so in a time of worsening unemployment, as hundreds more people are being forced to join the dole queues the Government is still insisting stations close unnecessarily in order to bid for one of the two licences open for tender ...'

The Minister leant across and turned the radio down.

'They're mounting a clever campaign' he said to Roger.

'They are' said Roger 'and they're getting a lot of support.'

'How are the new station plans progressing?' said the Minister.

'We've poached a cross section of jocks from the top five Pirates' said Roger 'mixed them in with the best of what we have and re-packaged as agreed. New name, new identity; it's a very different look and feel to what's currently in place.'

'Excellent' said the Minister. 'What's your launch date?'

'We're on target to go live the week the Pirates come off' said Roger.

'Good' said the Minister. 'Keep it as quiet as you can. There'll be a certain amount of flak but hopefully the fact that there's a few familiar faces will distract. And then of course there'll be the new licence announcements.' Roger eyed the pile of folders on the Minister's desk.

'How many?' he said.

'Eighteen' the Minister pulled the pile towards him. 'Which is more or less what we anticipated.

'And we're going to interview them all?' said Roger.

'Absolutely' the Minister replied. 'This process will be played by the book from a public perspective. We need to be squeaky clean. If someone decides to challenge or audit at any stage, we have to be seen to have played this straight down the line.'

'What's the timing?' said Roger.

'The list of applicants will be released to the press tomorrow' said the Minister 'and the accompanying release will reiterate that they must go off-air if their tender is to be processed. Now. I want you to have a look at these' he passed across two applications. 'I think you might find them interesting' he sat back in his chair as Roger began to read the first one.

'Hegarty?' Roger frowned. '*John* Hegarty?' he looked confused. 'As in Hudson Holdings? Hegarty's a developer … is this an application?' A small smile curled around the Minister's lips.

'It is' he looked pleased.

'Hegarty?' said Roger 'why would Hegarty …'

'Be interested in a radio licence?'

'Exactly' said Roger. 'Radio's not what he does.'

'It's precisely what he does' said the Minister. 'Hegarty makes money Roger. He makes money.' Roger stared at him, confused.

'He's no radio experience.'

'He doesn't need it' said the Minister. 'Experience Roger, can be bought. The same way you've poached disc jockeys, so can he. There's a wealth of talent out there; it just needs to be harnessed, channelled. Hegarty's smart, sharp; a good operator. He knows how to make money. More importantly, he speaks our language.'

'So you're going to give him a licence?' said Roger. 'He's no radio experience and you're just going to hand him a licence?' The Minister took a long deep breath.

'The licence tender process will be handled fairly' he said in an even, measured tone. 'Everyone who applies will receive a hearing. After that …'

'After that Hegarty will get a licence' said Roger.

'After that' the Minister smiled 'two successful candidates will each be awarded a licence.'

'Who's the second?' Roger flipped the other application form open.

'The second is a consortium' said the Minister. 'You may recognise a name or two.'

'Well I certainly recognise that one' Roger's face darkened as he scanned the front page of the application.

'The important thing with the consortium' said the Minister 'is that like Hegarty, the front runners are people who speak our language.'

'So these are the new stations' Roger held up the two application forms, 'Hegarty and this' he shook the second form 'consortium?'

'Everyone will be given a fair hearing' the Minister smiled. 'Now. I want to talk to you about how we handle the tender. I'm blocking off a week; it'll be a tough week, but it'll be clean. We'll give each station one hour. The panel will include myself, yourself, a second representative from this office and possibly one or two people from the entertainment industry who can be viewed as independent and objective.' Roger didn't reply. He was studying the two application forms.

'There'll be uproar' he said. 'There will be a very public outcry if these people get licences.

'Possibly' said the Minister 'but the public are fickle; their attention is short, and time is a healer. Getting the Pirates off-air for the tender process will play a significant role. Take them off-air for even a week and the public's relationship with them will start to fade. Take them off for a month and they'll be more than ready to listen to anything we have to offer. Fill the new stations with the disc jockeys from Pirates they loved, give them the music they want to hear' pale grey eyes met Roger's across the desk 'I think you'll find they'll move on very quickly.'

. . . .

' ... *Hang the DJ, Hang the DJ ...*'

'I hate Morissey' Iris muttered, a cigarette dangling from her lips. The three of them were sitting on the leather couches, Iris flicking through albums, lining up her set, Squirrel and Elliott on the sofa across from her.

'I think he's alright' Squirrel was rocking along in time to the music.

'He's a pain in the hole' Iris pulled on her cigarette before resting it, ash out, on the corner of the coffee table. Kneeling on the floor she spread a selection of albums out on the carpet and frowned at them. 'Can't *stand* him' she stared at the albums. 'Only one thing worse than Morrissey' she flipped a cover and studied the track listing.

'What's that?' said Squirrel.

'Morrissey fans.'

'Hey babe' Neal's voice came over the speaker. 'You like this track?' he called from behind the glass. Iris looked up.

'No. I hate it.'

'Aw babe' Neal turned his hands to heaven. 'Morrissey is amazing. You gotta get into Morrissey. Man' Neal shook his head 'gotta get into Morrissey' he went back to the decks.

'Sooner get into a coffin' Iris muttered, collecting up the albums.

'Evening all' Wayne pushed the studio door open. 'Whaddaya reckon?' he gestured at the white suit he was wearing. The sleeves of the jacket were rolled and pushed firmly past his elbows. A pair of black ray bans rested on freshly permed, now plum coloured hair. The gold sovereign ring flashed as he smoothed his moustache several times. It was his first night playing at the Studio One Niteclub.

'Lookin' good Wayne' said Squirrel. 'Lookin' very' he eyed the pale pink T-shirt, the wine coloured loafers 'co-ordinated.'

'Gotta make a good impression' Wayne pushed the sleeves higher and smoothed down the jacket. Elliott looked at him. Something different about Wayne tonight. The suit? No. Something else; he couldn't put his finger on it.

'What are ya doin' here?' Squirrel glanced at his watch. 'Cuttin' it fine aren't ya?'

'I was hopin' ta get the three ah yis together' Wayne shifted on his feet, the tightly permed plum curls glossy beneath the studio lights. 'Thing is …'

'Wayne' Iris squinted up at him 'is your moustache purple?' she peered in at his face underneath the light. Wayne grinned. He smoothed his moustache, the sovereign ring flashing as he ran his thumb and index finger over it several times in quick succession. 'It is' Iris leant in for a closer look. 'Wayne, your moustache is purple.'

'Plum' Wayne corrected her. 'Ta match the hair' he pointed at his curls.'

'How …' Iris stared at Wayne's upper lip 'how did you get it like that?'

'Peter Mark' Wayne smoothed the moustache again. 'They mix the colour for your hair an' then they get a little brush an' put the same colour on your moustache. Makes sense' he shrugged. 'Last thing ya want is ta look stupid. Plum hair an' a brown moustache.'

'Yeah' Iris stared at the purple fur on Wayne's upper lip 'yeah, I guess the last thing you want to look is stupid.'

'Anyways listen' Wayne suddenly looked uncomfortable 'been meanin' ta talk ta ya' his cheeks reddened. 'Was kinda hopin' I'd get yis all before now.'

'Is everything okay?' asked Elliott.

'Thing is' Wayne looked down at the carpet. 'I'm leavin.'

'What?' said Iris.

'Why?' said Elliott.

'Is it money?' said Squirrel. 'Is this about money?'

'It's not about money' Wayne looked down at the carpet again. 'I'm after been offered another job.'

'Another job?' said Iris. 'Where?'

'You're on the Number One station' said Squirrel. 'Rocket an' BBR can't touch us.'

'I'm not goin' ta Rocket or BBR' Wayne's eyes were glued to the carpet.

'Where *are* you going?' said Iris.

'RTE' Wayne muttered.

'RTE?' said Squirrel. 'Why the fuck would ya go ta RTE?'

'They're launchin' a new station' said Wayne.

'What kinda new station?' Squirrel's voice grew sharp.

'A youth station' said Wayne.

'A *youth* station?' said Iris. 'What the fuck is a youth station?'

'They're modellin' it on the Pirates format …' Wayne started.

'They're *what??*' Squirrel's voice took on a dangerous edge.

'How?' said Elliott. Wayne shifted.

'Not meant ta say.'

'Yeah. Well ya'd better say' said Squirrel 'cause if ya don't, that moustache won't be the only purple thing on yer face. I'll give ya two eyes ta match. *How*, are they modellin' this new station on the Pirates format?'

'Just … the music. An' they're takin' a few jocks from different stations. Takin' me 'cause I'm the Number One Breakfast Show' Wayne mumbled.

'Yeah! An' ya know why ya are?' anger flashed on Squirrel's face. 'Cause *he* sat with ya through all the shyte' Squirrel pointed at Elliott 'held yer fuckin' hand. You're a *prick* Wayne' disgust in his voice. 'Can't believe you're doin' this.'

'They're takin' jocks offa Rocket an' BBR as well' Wayne glanced at Elliott. 'Sorry' he said.

'When are they launching?' Elliott was trying to collect his thoughts.

'Dry run is next week' said Wayne 'on-air the week after.'

'Next week!' said Iris 'next *week!!*'

'Yeah' Wayne hesitated 'so … tomorrow'll be my last show.'

'Fuck ya Wayne' Squirrel stood up. 'We give ya a break an' this is how ya thank us? You're a prick. RTE? You won't last pissin' time in there. An' by the way' he called as Wayne pulled the Studio door open 'this is yer last night at that club. Ya'll never play Studio One again!!'

. . . .

'That's what this is about' said Eamo. The four of them were sitting in his office. 'That's why those fuckers want us off air. Clear the airwaves for their new station. No way we're goin' off air now. Not after this.'

'And what happens when the new laws come in?' said Elliott.

'Ah they've been makin' those threats for years' Eamo dismissed the suggestion with an impatient wave. Number one station, got our own Jaysus niteclub for fucks sakes. What difference is a licence gonna make?'

'We'd make more money' said Elliott.

'How?'

'Because the Government are serious this time' said Elliott. 'You're right; they've made threats over the years but they never put licences out for tender before. The Pirates *will* close Eamo and when they do, *all* the advertising money that was being spread across them will go straight into whoever the two new stations are.'

'D'ya reckon?' from the corner Squirrel broke his silence.

'Absolutely' said Elliott 'and see what's happened with Wayne? The minute those two new stations get their licences you can bet your bottom dollar every decent jock we have will be approached. And they'll go. One by one they will walk out the door.' Leather creaking as Squirrel unfolded himself in the chair.

'He's right. We hafta tender. We'd be mad not ta.'

'I'm not going off-air' said Iris.

'Look, if we can get the listeners …' Elliott began.

'Oh fuck the listeners' Iris snapped 'that's not working. They've been protesting for weeks; it's having no effect. The only way the Government would take *any* notice of us at this stage is if we took all our listeners, marched up to Leinster House and banged on the door, and even then …' she picked up the Benson & Hedges box on Eamo's desk. 'Can I have one of these?'

'Yeah, work away' said Eamo. 'Here' he held out an arm, shook, then flicked his lighter. 'Ya know that's not a bad idea' he said as Iris bent in for a light.

'What?' said Elliott.

'Protest march.'

'We'd need to make a lot of noise' Iris pulled on her cigarette.

'How?' said Squirrel.

'Don't know' she shrugged. 'Airhorns? Megaphones? Car horns?'

'Car horns'd be good' said Squirrel. 'We could get Dessie ta get all his drivers ta drive with us blowin' their horns. That's thirty-six cars. Thirty-six cars all blowin' their horns at the same time; that's a fair bit ah noise.'

'Why not get everyone to blow their horns?' said Iris.

'How d'ya mean?' said Squirrel.

'Everyone in the city, wherever they are, whatever they're doing, to blow their horn at the same time. If everyone in the city blew their horn at the same time. Think of the noise.' Silence. Traffic on the street outside, the sound of the showroom next door. On the street a car horn sounded, and somewhere in the distance, another.

'Blow yer horn' a slow smile curled on Eamo's face.

'Blow yer horn for *Minister* Horn!' Squirrel laughed.

'Squirr!!' Eamo threw out his hands. 'That's it! That's our slogan!!'

'That is *not* our slogan' said Iris. 'That's a shit slogan.'

'What's wrong with it?' said Squirrel. Iris didn't respond. She walked over to the window, stood with her back to them and muttered something.

'Can't hear ya' Squirrel glared at her.

'Studio One back on-air' the words thrown over her shoulder.

'Whatcha mean?' said Squirrel.

'That's our slogan' she turned around. 'Studio One back on-air, *that's* the message we want the Government to hear.'

'I like blow yer horn' Squirrel sat back in his chair.

'So do I' said Eamo. 'Blow yer horn. We're runnin' with that.' Iris raised her eyebrows, took two short pulls on her cigarette, then leant forward to push it out in the ashtray on Eamo's desk.

'Your funeral' she said.

'Whatcha mean my funeral?' said Eamo, 'You know you're an intelligent young one, but ya …'

'Thanks' cheekbones high, Iris grinned.

'There's merit in both' said Elliott. 'Blow Your Horn is the message we need to get out in the build up to the protest, so people know what do to, but when we're out there on the street, all we should be saying is 'Studio One Back On-air.' We'll run a 'Blow your Horn' promo for the next two weeks, then the minute we hit the streets it's 'Studio One Back on-air' okay?'

'Okay' Iris suppressed a smile.

'What are ya laughin' at?' said Eamo.

'You. Blow your horn. Sounds like a slogan for something we'd sell in the shop. She picked up her jacket. 'Speaking of which, I'd better get back.'

'I'll walk with you' said Elliott. 'See you later' he said to Squirrel.

'Catch ya later' said Squirrel. 'Blow yer horn!' he shouted after Elliott as Iris and himself made their way out the showroom. 'Blow yer horn!' he yelled as they walked past the window. Through the glass Iris grinned and gave him the finger.

Sitting back down on the chair in front of Eamo's desk, Squirrel kicked long leather legs out in front of him, smiling as he stuck a cigarette in his mouth. 'Blow yer horn' a toothy grin 'blow yer fuckin horn' the cigarette danced up and down between his lips as he spoke. Leaning across his desk Eamo stretched out his arm, lighter in hand. 'Ta' Squirrel leant in, pulled, exhaled, pulled again.

'How are the figures?' Eamo sat back in his chair.

'Through the roof' said Squirrel. 'We're gonna hit the hundred Eamo. Elliott's right an' all. If we get a licence an' the other stations close we'd double our figures. Sky's the limit on this Eamo; could be millionaires outta all this.'

Outside on the street, two drunks struck up a fight. 'State ah them' Squirrel laughed, leather arms folding as he stretched his legs out 'fuckin' eejits' relaxed blue eyes as he watched through the window. The drunks were in full flight now, red faced, hurling insults at each other outside the office window.

'The *state* ah them' Squirrel laughed.

'Tell us …' Eamo cleared his throat. 'How's eh … how's yer health?'

'Me health?'

'Yeah. How … howeya feelin?'

'How am I *feelin?*' Squirrel shifted in the chair.

'Healthwise.'

'Grand' Squirrel shrugged.

'Everything alright in the … eh …' Eamo nodded down at Squirrel's leathers, 'in the jacks department?'

'The jacks department?' Squirrel stared at him. 'Whaddaya mean?' a nervous confusion in his eyes. 'Whaddaya mean the jacks department?' Silence. Two sets of blue eyes, frozen like deer in headlights. 'You're losin' it Eamo' Squirrel stood up. 'You are fuckin' losin' it. Is everything alright in the *jacks department?* What the fuck does that mean?'

'Nothin' Eamo scowled. 'G'wan. Get outta here. I'll catch ya later.'

'Yeah' Squirrel stared at him 'catch ya later' reaching for his helmet, he stood up, gave Eamo a final look, before walking out of the office.

Eamo watched Squirrel make his way through the showroom, straddle the bike on the path outside, jump up, down, push on his helmet as the engine revved. Leather leaning forward, the bike rolled off the path and growled away. Eamo looked out the window at the drunks on the street.

'Shyte' he said. 'Shyte on it anyway.'

. . . .

'Mikey, Mikey, Tango, Charlie, Foxtrot Romeo, Lady Margaret, at seventy eight-ten degrees north, just fifty-five east, into bear country now, over four thousand polar bears; this is where they hunt, but don't worry, we have the guns ...'

The first band of ice looked harmless enough.

'Don't let it fool you' said Nick. 'See those' he nodded at the small white islands bobbing and floating around them 'very quickly, they're going to get bigger and closer together, and that's when the trouble starts. Two of those tighten around us the wrong way; they'll squeeze the boat 'til she snaps. Eyes open, poles at the ready. The further in we go, the tighter the ice will get, the less frequent the gaps, and if we don't stay on the ball, we'll get stuck.'

'Hey! Look over there!!' Richard shouted, and they saw them. Three polar bears, hulking, skulking across a small island of ice. White on white, soot black trace-lines framing their shape with noses and paws. More appeared, white furriness rising up through the icy water, surfacing from nowhere, padding softly on frozen ground.

'Look at that fellow' Nick, pointed at a large boney male eyeing the boat.

'Will I get the gun?' said Richard.

'No need' Nick's voice was soft. 'There's plenty of seals in the water. A juicy seal would be far tastier than any of us. Once they're fed, they've no interest. Right! All hands on deck' he shouted 'heavy ice ahead. Tiny! Up that mast. Frankie, you're on the bow, Anthony the helm, Richard, upfront with Frankie. Poles at the ready!' The boat pushed forward, mountains of white ice rising around them, the landscape slowly reversing as grey sea gave way to white ice. Silence. Ice cold Arctic silence.

. . . .

'... Travelling in a fried out crombie, on a hippie trail, head full of zombie, I met a strange lady, she made me nervous, she took me in and gave me breakfast, and she said do you come from a land down under, where women blow and men plunder, can't you hear, can't you hear the thunder ....'

Elliott sat with his head in his hands, slumped over the mix desk, trying, failing, to bring himself to life. The inside of his eyelids felt like sandpaper. Four days of early starts on the back of late night shifts with Declan, Gary and Barry. *How does Wayne do it? How can anybody be upbeat at this time in the morning?* Leaning forward he pulled hard on his cigarette, swallowed a mouthful of scalding coffee, opened the mic and injected false energy into his voice, pushing up, projecting out **'...Studio One, the Breakfast Show, with you all the way til ten o'clock, reminding you that on Friday the 12th at 5pm, wherever you are, we want you to blow your horn for Minister Horn and if you're in the area at lunchtime, join us as we march to Government buildings. You put us here, help keep us here, wherever you are on Friday the 12th, don't forget to blow that horn; stay with us for sport after these ...'** he pushed in the advertising cart, and picked up the request slips Katie had left on the desk, sifting through them, trying to work out what he had time to cover. He picked up the coffee in front of him and took another hot swallow. 'Come on Elliott, come on' he whispered, rubbing his face.

'Elliott' Katie's voice cut in from the other side of the glass 'phones are hoppin'' she gestured at the switchboard. 'They're all askin' where Wayne is. I can't keep puttin' them off. What am I gonna tell them?'

'Shit' Elliott sighed. 'Tell them ...' he struggled. Behind Katie the Studio Door pushed open and Wayne appeared around it. Denim baggies, a tight white T-shirt beneath a green bomber jacket, flashes of gold about his hands and neck, the plum perm flapping as he crossed the room. 'Tell them he's right behind you' Elliott blinked. Katie spun around on her chair. 'What are you doing here?' said Elliott through the glass. Wayne didn't answer. He pulled the studio door open, and only when the second door had sealed behind him and he was alone with Elliott did he speak.

'They fired me' embarrassed, angry eyes, circling the studio.

'What?' said Elliott. 'Why?'

'Didn't like my enunciation, whatever the fuck that is' anger stinging at Wayne's face. 'Fuckin' eejits the lotta them.'

'Your enunciation?' Elliott stared at him 'how, I mean … what …'

'I said 'eighteen after eight' Wayne scowled 'did a time check; said it was 'eighteen after eight, an' yer man Ingram came inta the studio this mornin an' said I hadta say 'eighteen minutes past eight o'clock' if I wanted ta keep my job. Said I hadta learn how ta tell the time properly.' Silence. 'Fuckin' humiliated me' Wayne's voice was bitter 'front ah everyone' he fumed. Silence. 'An' he was very insultin' about my moustache' colour seeped into his face. 'Prick' anger stinging around Wayne's face.

'So what did you tell him?' said Elliott. 'About the enunciation?'

'Told him ta shove his enunciation up his hole' Wayne scowled. 'Yer ads are over' he nodded at the desk. Elliott leant forward and pushed in the pre-record sports cart Robbie had done up for him, then sat back in the chair as it played. Silence. Head bent, Wayne ran his hand back and forth along the console.

'How's it all goin' here then?'

'Not bad' Elliott shrugged. He picked up a single and placed it down on the turntable.

'So you're doin' the Breakfast Show now?' Wayne glanced around the studio.

'Mmm-hmm' Elliott leant across, ejected the sports cart and brought up the track he'd lined up.

'Must be knackered are ya?'

'Mmm' Elliott shrugged 'it's not that bad.'

'Look, I know I was outta order' said Wayne 'but ya need a Breakfast Show; ya can't go for this licence without a Breakfast Show.'

'We have a Breakfast Show' Elliott pulled the fade back on the track in front of him and flipped on another. 'This is the Breakfast Show' he said as the new track came up 'just a different presenter.'

'Look I know I was outta order' Wayne was genuinely upset 'I know I was' pleading eyes 'but this is what I do. I can't not do this, I can't …'

'Go on' Elliott pulled off the phones. 'Here' he held them out.

'Serious?' Wayne looked like he might cry. 'Ahh cheers Elliott' he grabbed him 'fair play ta ya' hugging Elliott hard, he jumped into the chair 'you're a star so ya are. I won't let ya down' he shouted as Elliott pulled the door open.

'Better not' from the outer room Elliott flicked the switch on Katie's desk 'and I'd keep out of Squirrel's way for a while if I were you' he said through the glass, but Wayne already had the phones on:

'**Studio One**' a neatly trimmed purple moustache pressed up to the mic, '**Wayne Conroy, the Wayne Conroy Show, Number One Breakfast Show in Dublin, wake up motherfuckers! It's Monday!!**'

'Wayne!!' Elliott shouted. Wayne winked at him through the glass, a wide grin on his face as he leant into the mic again:

'**Wayne Conroy, Studio One, the Number One Breakfast Show, waking you up today and every day, time now eight thirty-eight and this, is Prince …** *Dig if you will the picture, of you and I engaged in a kiss, the sweat of your body covers me, can you my darling, can you picture this …*' fingers clicking, plum perm shaking in time to the track, Wayne pulled back the fade.

'Enunciation *me hole!*' he shouted through the glass. 'Cheers Elliott' he reached for the albums on the sound desk in front of him. 'I won't let ya down' he began flicking through them.

'Better not' said Elliott. 'You alright?' he looked at Katie.

'Grand' she nodded at the lights flashing up on the switchboard.

'Good' said Elliott 'fill him in on the protest; make sure he runs the promos in and out of every ad break and get him talking about it on-air.'

'No problem' Katie reached for her headset. 'Studio One' she started working up and down the switchboard 'Studio One, can you hold please … Studio One, yes Wayne Conroy is back, can you hold … Studio One, can you hold please …'

Elliott arched his back, yawned and stretched his arms open wide. Fuck. He squeezed his eyes tight, yawning again, as tiredness refused to wring itself out. Grabbing his jacket he made for the door. If the shop wasn't busy he might get a few hours kip before he came back in for the nightshift.

· · · ·

Loud drilling as Iris opened the front door. She'd come home to get albums for her show.

'Jesus Christ' she coughed. A cloud of thick white cement dust hung in the hallway. 'What the …' waving her arm like a windscreen wiper, she made her way towards the kitchen. Bang! Bang! Bang! A sledgehammer bearing down. Bang! Bang! Metal pounding concrete. The taste of cement filling her mouth. She felt her throat squeeze, constrict. Coughing hard, she pulled her jumper over her face, grit in her eyes as she crossed the kitchen and pushed the door to the record room open.

'Hello sweetheart' Jackie was curled up in an armchair reading her Third Eye book.

'Mum' Iris coughed 'you can't *breathe* in there' she kicked the door shut. Jackie, head deep in her book, didn't reply. Iris looked at the stainless steel double sink, standing tall in exactly the same spot it had been the week before, leaning up against her music shelves, the kitchen presses stacked around it.

'How long is this going to take?' she climbed up on a press and began pinching her nails along the row of albums she was eye level with.

'How long is what going to take?' Jackie didn't look up.

'The conservatory' Iris located the album she was looking for. Pulling it out, she craned her neck to peer in at the music on the shelf blocked by the sink.

'Not sure' Jackie murmured 'some sort of problem with the tower.'

'What's wrong with the tower?' Iris strained her arm in behind the sink.

'There's a crack in it' Jackie frowned at the page. Iris gave up trying to reach the album. Jumping down from the kitchen press she was standing on, she took hold of the sink's stainless steel frame. Placing a hand each side she angled it left, then right, waltzing it slowly across the room. 'Mind that on the glass' said Jackie as Iris leant the sink up against the sliding door windows. Iris looked down at the top of her Mother's head.

'There's a crack in the tower?'

'Apparently' Jackie continued reading.

'Do you not think he should fix the crack in the tower before he knocks down half the kitchen?' Jackie, deep in the book, didn't reply. Iris looked at the large eye on the front cover. 'What was she like?'

'Who?'

'The Third Eye woman. The one who came here.'

'Disappointing' Jackie didn't look up.

'Why?' said Iris.

'She just wasn't very encouraging' Jackie shrugged. 'And she said the strangest thing.'

'What?'

'Well' Jackie closed the book. 'We talked for a while. She asked me about your Father, then she asked me about you; she didn't seem to want to know anything about *me*. Or Frank. Anyway, I said I wanted her to help me open my third eye ...' a puzzled expression crossed her face.

'And?' said Iris.

'She said I needed to learn how to see through the two I had before I could hope to open the third' Jackie's face scrunched. 'What does *that* mean?' The door to the record room opened and Arthur walked in, a cloud of cement dust drifting behind him. Dressed in old clothes he had a plastic bag tied on his head, thick goggles strapped across his eyes, and a dust mask covering his nose and mouth. 'I mean I can *see*' said Jackie '*anyone* can see …'

'The dishwasher' Arthur's voice was distorted by the mask 'is in the garage' small eyes blinking behind the goggles 'and the washing machine is in the bathroom.'

'Shut the door!' Iris pointed at the cement cloud trailing Arthur. 'That's dangerous Dad; you can't *breathe* with that.' Nodding behind the goggles Arthur began to back out the door.

'They're both plumbed in' his voice muffled behind the mask as he reversed back into the kitchen, closing the door behind him.

'Now this is good' Jackie held up the Third Eye book 'this is fantastic but *she* was off the wall. *I need to see with the two I have*' she opened the book again. 'Do it myself. I will' Jackie's voice was determined, defiant. 'I am going to open this eye.'

'Right' Iris moved back to the shelf that had previously been blocked by the sink 'and in the meantime we have to wash dishes in the garage and clothes in the bathroo…' her head jerked abruptly to where the washing machine had been standing the last time she saw it. 'Where's Michael Stipe?' From the kitchen, the drilling started up again. 'Mum' Iris tried to ignore the panic rising 'where's Michael Stipe?' Jackie didn't reply. 'I left him there' Iris pointed at the space the washing machine had been in 'Mum, I left his cage on top of the machine.' Jackie didn't look up. 'Dad? Iris shouted, moving to the door 'Dad!'

'Arthur' Jackie called vaguely as she continued to read.

'Dad!' thick cement dust enveloped Iris' face as she opened the door. Coughing, choking, she pulled her jumper up over her nose. 'Dad!' her voice muffled as the sound of the drill reverberating through the kitchen. Loud drilling, machine gun rattling, metal blasting thick concrete. 'Dad' Iris coughed, the kitchen barely visible as she moved through clouds of cement. Coughing, choking, she was about to turn back when she saw it. Sitting on the counter. Thin metal bars, the air too thick to see down inside. Grit scratching at her eyes, she picked up the cage, turned and quickly crossed the kitchen. Pushing the door to the record room open, she stepped inside and kicked it shut.

'Did you find him?' Jackie didn't look up from the book. Iris bit her lip.

'Where was he?' Jackie turned a page. Iris stared at the small form lying on the bottom of the cage.

'Kitchen' her eyes hung on the tiny bird, covered in a thick layer of white cement dust. 'He was in the kitchen.'

'Is he alright?' Jackie looked up. Iris didn't reply. 'Sweetheart?' Jackie pushed herself up out of the chair. 'Oh' her eyes fell on the cage. 'Oh sweetheart' she pressed her hand against Iris's arm. Iris stared down at the tiny bird. 'Sweetheart I'm sorry ...' Jackie began.

'Doesn't matter' Iris jerked away. Reaching for her record bag, she grabbed the albums and began stuffing them down inside.

'But you loved him' said Jackie 'I know how much you ...'

'It's just a budgie' Iris pulled the straps on the bag tight.

'Sweetheart ...' Jackie reached out.

'It's just a fucking budgie. I'll see you later' Iris swung the bag over her shoulder, pulled the door open and disappeared out through a cloud of cement dust.

. . . .

' ... *Aha, Aha, Aha, what you do and what you don't, Aha, what you will and what you won't, Aha, what you can and what you can't, Aha, this is what you got to know, loved you though it didn't show, ich lieb dich nicht, du liebst mich nicht, ich lieb dich nicht, du liebst mich nicht, Da, da, da ...*'

Elliott and Squirrel were watching Neal do his show.

'This time next week' said Squirrel.

'I know' Elliott stared ahead.

'Reckon we'll get a call?' said Squirrel. Elliott shook his head.

'No. Iris is right. The Government are hoping we'll just go away. They're not going to back down.' Squirrel shifted on the sofa.

'What about the protest? 'Think we should stay on-air if it doesn't work?'

'Don't know' Elliott rubbed his face. 'I don't know.'

'... *Da, da, da, Da, da, da, Da, da, da, ich lieb dich nicht, du liebst mich nicht, ich lieb dich nicht, du liebst mich nicht ... Da, da, da ...*'

'What is that shyte?' Squirrel nodded at Neal, rocking out behind the glass, flipping an album as he lined up the next track.

'Trio' said Elliott.

'Reckon you're right' said Squirrel.

'About what?'

'Synth' said Squirrel. 'Only so much ya can take' the soft sound of carpet brushing carpet, as the door pushed open and Iris walked in, record bag slung over her shoulder.

'Hey babe' Neal called from behind the glass. Iris didn't answer. Face fixed, eyes blank, she walked across to the desk, pulled out the chair and sat down.

'Not sayin' hello?' Squirrel made a face at Elliott as Iris sat down with her back to them and began pulling albums out from her bag.

'Babe' Neal was facing her from the other side of the glass 'what do you think about Visage?' against the black of Neal's trousers Elliott could make out Iris's reflection in the glass. Her face, distorted by the studio light, looked strange, the shine on the reflection twisting it. Neal leant in and opened the mic: **'Studio One, Neal O'Neal with you for the next twenty minutes, Julie Andrews just walked in, she's lining up her set, but right now, it's a Studio One exclusive, live from a gig they did in Birmingham last week, it's Depeche Mode and I just can't get enough'** fringe plunging Neal jumped and bounced behind the glass as the track came up. 'Babe' he shouted 'what do you think? I just can't get enough! I just can't get enough!' he sang through the glass.

Elliott stared at the back of Iris's jacket. Something was wrong. As Neal jumped and spun behind the glass, Elliott caught her reflection again. Eyes swollen, squeezed tight, tears rolling down her face.

'Iris?' he stood up. Behind the glass Neal jerked to a halt.

'Babe!' his face fell. Pulling off the phones he made for the door.

268

'Iris?' Elliott put a hand on her shoulder 'what's wrong?'

'Babe!' Neal was out of the Studio. 'Babe!' he grabbed the chair she was sitting on and spun it around to face him 'what is it?' anxious concern as he bent his head in underneath her, trying to get a proper look at her face, but she curled down tight, head in, spikes out, as she rocked back and forth on the chair. 'Babe' Neal took her hands in his, pressing them softly 'what's wrong?'

'My ... my' Iris choked 'my ...'

'Your what babe?' Neal pushed her head up 'your what?'

'Michael' she choked, then her voice dissolved. 'Michael Stipe' she broke off, crying hard.

'Babe?' Neal looked frightened 'what's happened to Michael Stipe?'

'He's dead ... he's dead ...' she cried.

'Oh my God' Neal's face paled. 'Oh my fucking God!!'

'He couldn't bree ... bree' Iris sobbed and choked 'he couldn't breathe ...' pressing her hands into her face her shoulders shook as her voice broke down.

'Michael Stipe?' Neal began pacing the studio 'Michael Stipe, I can't *believe* this!! Babe' he knelt down in front of her again 'are you *sure* he's dead?' Head bent, shoulders shaking, Iris nodded. Neal pressed a hand to his face. 'How?' he said to Iris 'babe *how* did he die?'

'I don't know' muffled cries from between Iris's hands 'I don't know' hot tears spilling through blotched, swollen eyes. 'I think it was a heart attack, I think ... he just ... ohh ... shit' catching her breath she dragged her hand beneath her nose. 'Sorry' she whispered 'sorry, sorry... thanks' she took the handkerchief Elliott was holding out. 'Shit' she blew her nose. 'Fuck' shaky breath as the tears began to subside. Neal stood up.

'We have to do something' he said to Elliott. Turning sharply he pulled the studio door open and went back inside. Red eyed, from behind the handkerchief, Iris blew her nose again.

'Sorry' tears drying as she blew hard again. 'Sorry, it's stupid.'

'It's not' Elliott squatted down beside her and took her hand.

'It is' she gave him a half smile through watery brown eyes. Behind the glass, Neal flipped out an album, sat in at the sound desk, opened the mic, and when he spoke, his voice was heavy, sombre:

'Studio One, Neal O'Neill on a *very sad day* for music. Michael Stipe has died. The singer passed away of a heart attack earlier this afternoon. That's all the information we have at the moment, we'll update you as soon as we hear more, but for now, let's take time to remember one of the greatest musicians of our time ...' sliding the fade, he brought up 'Free Radio Europe.'

'What the ...'

'Neal! What are you doing?' Iris shouted at the glass.

'Babe, it's a tribute ...' Neal began.

'Neal' said Elliott 'Michael Stipe is Iris' budgie. It's a budgie that died, not Michael ... *Stipe!*'

'What!!' Neal looked horrified 'what?' He pulled off the phones. 'Oh man!' he threw them down on the mix desk. 'Why didn't you *tell* me!' he shouted at Iris through the glass.

'I thought you knew' her face looked small.

'Oh fuck' Neal stared at the sound desk in shock. 'I've just told everyone Michael Stipe is dead' dismay on his face. 'I've just ...' he broke off.

'Look at the switchboard' Squirrel pointed as one by one the lines lit up, flashing in silence.

'What am I going to do?' said Neal.

'You'd better go back on-air and tell them you made a mistake' said Elliott 'tell them it was another Michael Stipe.'

'I can't!' Neal looked embarrassed as he sat back down behind the desk. 'I don't believe ... you should have *told* me!' he snapped at Iris through the glass.

'I thought you knew' she said.

'A budgie, a fucking budgie!' Neal's face had turned a deep shade of red 'for *fucks sakes*' he pulled the phones back on and waited for the track to finish. 'A fucking budgie!!' he roared, anger burning through the glass as he glared at Iris. White-faced she stared back at him in silence. Behind the glass Neal put his head between his hands.

'Okay' Elliott broke the silence. 'Come on' he pulled Iris to her feet 'you're not doing your show tonight.'

'I have to.'

'No, you don't' Elliott gathered up her albums. 'I've a million mix tapes in there will cover it. You need a drink. We're going across the road.'

'I can't.'

'I'm not letting you go on-air' Elliott swung her record bag over his shoulder. 'You're not up to it.'

'Do what you're told' said Squirrel. Iris looked at Neal behind the glass. Head now resting on his left hand he was staring down at the desk in blank dismay as R.E.M played out. 'Go on' Squirrel gestured towards the door. 'I'll sort this.'

They were half way down the stairs when Elliott remembered something.

'Shit. Hang on' he said to Iris 'I never showed Squirrel where the tapes are' he sprinted back up the stairs. Squirrel was in studio with Neal as Elliott pushed the door open. Catching sight of Elliott, Squirrel said something to Neal, patted him on the shoulder, then pulled the door open and came out to meet Elliott.

'What's wrong?'

'I never showed you where the tapes are.' Squirrel smiled, a wide grin stretching as he reached into his back pocket and pulled out one of Elliott's mix tapes.

'D'ya think I came up the Liffey in a saucer? I watch what ya do; now go on' he nodded at the door 'get in there.'

'This isn't about me getting in there.'

'I know' Squirrel grinned. Elliott turned, and made for the door.

'Elliott?'

'What?'

'Don't fuck it up.'

'It's not about that' Elliott grabbed the door handle.

'Elliott?'

'It's not *about* that' Elliott stepped out the door.

'Elliott, seriously, c'mere. Wanna tell ya somethin.'

'What?' Elliott stuck his head back around the door.

'Just wanta tell ya' Squirrel made his way across.

'What?'

'C'mere, c'mere' Squirrel jerked his head back. 'Serious. C'mere; somethin' ta tell ya.'

'Squirrel' Elliott grinned as Squirrel leant in close again.

'Just wanta tell ya' Squirrel pressed his mouth to Elliott's ear 'don't *fuck it up!!*' he shouted. Elliott laughed, pushing him away, sound bouncing, reverberating in his ear drum as he rubbed the side of his head and made his way back down the stairs to Iris.

'How did your brother die?' the question came from nowhere. They were sitting in the pub, four drinks down; a fresh round in front of them. Pint for him, Beck's for her. The drink had done its job; done it and done it well. Taken the sting from the afternoon's events, offered comfort, allowed them to smile, laugh eventually, at what had happened with Neal. The warmth of the pub, the two of them, relaxed, comfortable; a soft easy silence as they sat at the table by the fire. Then the question. From nowhere. Why had he said that? What *made* him say that? Budgie was one thing; her brother was another. Silence stretching as he reached for his pint.

'Meningitis' Iris answered the question just as he was about to apologise and retract it. She cleared her throat. 'He …' she picked up the bottle of Beck's sitting on the table in front of her, nails curling, flicking, scratching at the label 'he had it for a while. Apparently' she tore off a strip. 'My parents …' she ripped a second strip away 'they didn't know; there weren't any signs. No *visible* signs' she turned the bottle around and began scratching at the label on the back. Elliott watched her profile; soft Mohican stubble, four small looped ear-rings running in line down to a final hoop. Boney knuckles bending, sharp nails scratching. A ripping as the second label came away, three small white strips left behind. She raised the bottle and pressed it to her lips. Elliott watched her tilt back her head, the silver spiked dog collar loose at the base of her neck, a soft throat rising, falling as she drank.

She put the bottle back on the table. Stared at it, turning it slowly, fingers and thumbs circling it round. She tilted it back and ran her thumb nail up the length of the silver foil on the neck of the bottle. 'He fell' she said. Silence. Elliott watched her push her thumb in under the silver foil and peel it off in one whole piece, the neck of the bottle wet, sticky with traces of the glue that had held it there. 'My Dad' she reached for her cigarettes 'my Dad was playing football with him in the garden.' She picked up her lighter. Flick. Flick. 'Frank was in goal' she puffed, pulled. 'My Dad kicked the ball' her voice, matter of fact as she blew a thin line of smoke in front of her. 'Anyway' she shrugged. Silence. Elliott picked up his pint and took a sip. Ice cold bitter bubbles surging at his tongue, lips, the roof of his mouth. 'He fell' Iris picked up the bottle and knocked back the remainder of its contents. 'He dived for the ball and hit his head off the post' she placed the empty bottle back down on the table. 'Not a good time to hit your head' she pulled on her cigarette again. 'When you have meningitis' she exhaled. 'Doctors said he just hit the wrong part of his head at the wrong time. Anyway' she reached for the second bottle. 'I didn't know him' nails curling as she began flicking, scratching at the second bottle's label 'I didn't ...' she cut off abruptly. 'Doesn't matter' she shrugged. 'Doesn't matter' tilting the bottle she took a fresh sip. Behind the bar the bell for last drinks rang. Brown eyes turned; met his own. Soft. Open.

'Last drinks now *pleeze!!*' the barman shouted.

'I'll get these' he wanted to kiss her.

'Get a take-away' she reached inside her jacket.

'A take-away?' Elliott started, then his eyes followed her hand to what she had extracted and was holding just inside her jacket.

'Let me guess' he eyed the loosely rolled, generously filled joint, pinched between her finger and thumb. 'Declan' he said.

'Declan' she smiled. 'Skunk. Come on. We'll smoke it on the bus.'

Forty minutes later throat burning, mind expanding, he floated off the 31B.

'Shit' he swallowed 'what was in that?' dizziness followed by a wave of nausea. Iris grinned. Cheekbones high, an amused smile on her face as they crossed the road and began the walk down towards her house.

'How?' everything had started to move very slowly.

'How what?' she glanced at him.

'How?' he started to laugh. 'How?' giggles bubbling up inside him.

'How what?' cheekbones high, she was laughing with him.

'How ...' he stopped and held onto a lamp post, bent over, laughing uncontrollably. 'How?' he couldn't get past the word. Every time he said it. 'How.'

He couldn't stop. Everything. So funny. He looked up, still clutching the lamp post for support. Iris had slid down against a garden wall and was sitting on the ground laughing hard. 'How' he fell on the ground and rolled around, reaching for breath in between laughs.

'How *what?*' she laughed from her position on the path.

'How?' he broke off, laughing hard.

'What?' she laughed 'what?'

'How did you ...' he broke off, catching his breath 'how ... Neal, how did you ... why Neal Iris? Why, Neal?' the words fell out of his mouth just as the question about her brother had earlier. *Shit*. Queasiness. A slipping, sliding stomach.

Don't fuck it up. His stomach lurched. *Don't fuck it up*. Swallowing the nausea he pushed himself to his feet, and held onto a leafy hedge he suddenly found himself in front of.

'Shit' his head was starting to swim. 'Iris' he swallowed.

'What?' he heard her say beside him.

'I just' he swayed. A hollow throat, then his stomach

ballooned. 'Fuck' he coughed. Spat. 'Sorry' he said in an upside down voice as he hung over the hedge.

'It's okay' he heard her say. A flutter by his face. It was the handkerchief he'd given her earlier.

'Thanks' an embarrassed acceptance. He blew his nose. 'Fuck' straightening up, he blew it again. 'Sorry' he couldn't look at her. 'Sorry Iris.'

'Don't worry about it' he heard her say. 'Maybe you shouldn't smoke Elliott. I'm not sure it agrees with you. Come on' she turned and began walking down towards her house again. He suddenly felt angry. Trailing a few steps behind her, like a child with a parent.

'Didn't answer my question' he mumbled. She glanced back at him. 'My question' he stopped on the path. She turned and appraised him slowly. 'Didn't answer my question' he felt like a five year old but he couldn't help it.

'What question?' direct eyes through the darkness.

'I said' he raised his voice 'why Neal?'

'Why not?' she said. Silence. 'Go on. Tell me Elliott. Tell me why not.'

'Well' he began, but something in his brain had jammed. 'Neal' he tried to focus but his thoughts were cloudy 'the thing is ...' he struggled, then suddenly the clouds parted and it came to him in a blinding flash of clarity. 'He's Helsinki' his face felt frozen, like he'd been at the dentist.

'Helsinki?' Iris stared at him.

'Yes' Elliott felt something scratch at his neck and he realised his left hand side had somehow sunk into the hedge beside him 'he ... you're Asia' another blinding flash of clarity as he struggled to push himself out of the hedge.

'I'm Asia?' she sounded irked. 'What are you *talking* about?'

'What I'm saying' Elliott splayed his arms 'is that you're bigger.'

'So?'

'So' Elliott struggled. 'He's Poparama. And you' the cloud parted again 'you're the Tube. More. More! You're Channel

Four. You're.Channel.Four' he tapped each word out on her chest with his finger.

'Elliott, what are you *talking* about?' she pushed his hand away.

'Neal' why couldn't she see what he was trying to say. 'He's Poparama. Iris. In Helsinki. And you're the Tube' the clouds closed and he was lost, confused, stumbling in a thick fog. 'You're the Tube on Channel Four' his voice was melting. Sliding down. 'Finland' his head felt heavy. 'You ...' the weight of his head pulled his eyes to the path. 'You're in Finland. And you need to get back to Channel Four' he stared at the path.

'Elliott' he heard her say 'Elliott?' He lifted his head.

'You're not to smoke again' she said. He stared at her. 'Do you hear me?' her face was floating. 'You can't handle it. Are you okay to get home?'

'No' he replied, then 'yes. No. Yes' a lever in his head controlling his voice.

'Okay' her face had stopped floating and now it just looked tired. 'Go home Elliott' she pushed the key in the door. 'I'll see you tomorrow' she said over her shoulder. 'Get some rest, yeah?' she was dismissing him. Giving up on him.

'No! Wait!' he struggled. 'You don't understand what I'm trying to say.'

'I don't think *you* understand what you're trying to say' Iris snapped. 'Rambling on about Neal and Helsinki and the Tube; what are you trying to *say*? Tell me Elliott. Just tell me what the fuck you're trying to say!'

'I'm trying to tell you I love you!!' he shouted. 'I *love* you' thrown suddenly to the cold night air, the words felt small, weak, the sentiment unformed. 'I love you' he whispered. She had a funny look on her face. 'You're the Tube' somewhere in the back of his head a voice. *Stop calling her the Tube*. 'I love you' he said.

'Because I'm The Tube?'

'Yes' he said 'well no. You're a lot more ...'

'Go home Elliott' she sounded tired. 'The Tube?' a dry, disappointed laugh. *'The Tube?'* brown eyes cutting into him. You're not in love with me Elliott. You're in love with the *idea* of me' she turned the key in the door, stepped inside and closed it. Elliott stood for a minute staring at the door.

'No!' he shouted. 'Wait! What do you mean the idea of you?' he pushed the flap of the letterbox open. 'What does that mean?' he shouted through the empty flap.

'What does that mean?' his voice echoed down the empty hallway.

. . . .

'Ya fucked it up' said Squirrel as soon as he saw his face the next day.

'I fucked it up' Elliott dumped his record bag on the showroom counter. 'I fucked it up about as much as you could possibly fuck something up.'

'What did ya say?' said Squirrel. Elliott put his head in his hands and leant on the counter.

'We smoked some skunk that Declan gave her and I told her Neal was Poparama in Helsinki and she was the Tube on Channel 4.'

'Ya what?'

'I know' Elliott lifted his head 'I know.'

'Why didn't ya just tell her you're inta her?' said Squirrel.

'I did' Elliott picked up his cigarettes. 'I just came out with all that other shit first' he cupped the lighter. Flick. Flick. 'And I threw up' he pulled, puffed.

'Ya threw up!' said Squirrel. Elliott nodded, exhaling a long thin line of smoke. 'Over a hedge' he pulled on the cigarette again.

'Jaysus' Squirrel stared at him. 'You're a fuckin' disaster.'

'What's a disaster?' Eamo breezed past them as he made his way in behind the counter.

'Tryin' ta teach Elliott here a few facts ah life' Squirrel winked at Elliott as Eamo began flicking through delivery dockets for the day.

'Yeah?' Eamo stared down at the docket in his hand. 'Like what?' he reached for the phone on the counter and punched in a number.

'Like how ta get his end away.'

'Reggie!' Eamo shouted into the phone 'who did the dockets this mornin? Yeah? Well tell him he made a bollox ah them. What's he sendin' sixteen rolls ta Lucan for? Wouldn't use six, never mind sixteen. An' why's he givin' Cabinteely more underlay? More Jaysus underlay out there than they have carpet. Tell him I want the lot re-done, an' tell him I'll be all over him like a rash if he doesn't get it right. Fuckin eejit' he slammed the phone down. 'An' you shoulda spotted that an' all' the barrels of two fingers squeezing a loaded cigarette in Elliott's direction. 'Here long enough' fingers swiftly to mouth. Eamo sucking hard. Elbows on counter. Eyes back on dockets. 'Fuck's sakes' he picked up a pen. Black brows pinching as he put a line through the page.

'Morning!!' Rachel sang, as she appeared through the door of the showroom. 'Excellent' she smiled at the three of them 'the very men I wanted to see.'

'Yeah?' said Squirrel.

'We're doing a piece on men's health next week' Rachel pulled a leaflet out of her handbag. 'Ironic' she stared at it 'the Government want us off-air but the Department of Health have no problem asking us to run programmes helping them get their messages across.' Squirrel pulled the leaflet from her hands and studied the photograph of a smiling man in a knitted jumper.

'He looks like a right ponce.'

'Well he's a healthy ponce' Rachel snapped the leaflet back off him. 'Now' scarlet nails disappeared down inside her handbag 'I need to pick your brains. Little pre-production survey' her hand emerged holding a small white note-pad.

'Yeah?' said Squirrel. 'What kinda survey?'

'Very simple; can I borrow that?' Rachel pointed at the pen in Eamo's hand 'one question and that's it. Do you ...' she broke off as she wrote each their names at the top of the notepad 'do you check yourself for lumps?'

'How d'ya mean?' said Squirrel.

'Your testicles. Do you check your testicles for lumps?'

'Testicles are lumps' said Squirrel. 'Why would ya check lumps for lumps?'

'Because the lumps might be cancerous?' said Rachel. 'Because they might kill you if you don't catch them early enough?'

'Yeah, well' Squirrel adjusted his position against the counter 'I'm only twenty-four. I don't think I need ta worry about that kinda thing for a while.' Behind the counter Eamo stood very still.

'No harm checkin' he said in a low even voice.

'Exactly' said Rachel. Squirrel laughed.

'I'm twenty-four Eamo. People don't get cancer at twenty-four.'

'What are you *talking* about!' said Rachel. 'Children get cancer, teenagers get it, people of *all ages* …'

'Yeah-yeah' Squirrel waved her away 'but most ah them are on their way out anyway. Aul ones an' aul fellas.'

'Really?' Rachel made a note on the pad. 'Well I certainly know what category to put you in. Gobshites. What about you?' she turned to Elliott.

'Well' Elliott felt his cheeks redden 'yeah, I guess …'

'You'd know?' Rachel pushed 'you'd know if there was a lump?'

'Yeah' said Elliott 'I would.'

'Eamo?' Rachel's eyes flicked in Eamo's direction. Silence.

'I think it's very important' said Eamo. He looked at Squirrel. 'You should listen ta what she's sayin' he nodded at Rachel.

'I'm not *not* listenin' Squirrel laughed; 'just tellin' ya I think I'm a long way from dyin' ah cancer.'.

'It's eh … hereditary isn't it?' Eamo glanced at Rachel 'testicular, prostate; all that kinda thing's hereditary, isnit?'

'Well, it *can* be …' Rachel began.

'I'm alright so' Squirrel's face stretched into a wide toothy grin 'cause me Da's never had it!' he looked triumphant.

'Yes but that's not a guarantee you won't get it' said Rachel.

Listen' Squirrel zipped up his jacket 'If me Da doesn't have it, chances are I won't. An' even if me Da does get it, he's gonna get it a long time before I do, so I'll have plenty ah warnin' won't I? Gotta go' he picked up his helmet. 'I'll catcha later' he shouted as he lopped out the showroom doors.

'See that?' Rachel pointed at the window as they watched

Squirrel swing a long leather leg over the saddle of the bike outside. 'That is exactly the type of person the Department is concerned about. The people who think it'll never happen to them, the people who don't even bother to check. And the pity of it is that if they did stay on top of it, if there *was* something wrong ...' she stopped. 'Oh don't look so worried Eamo' she laughed, 'if there's no history of it in his family I'm sure he'll be fine. Right' she snapped the note-pad shut 'let's see what Reggie and the boys have to say. Three days to protest!!' she sang as she made her way down the showroom.

Through the open door, across the street, Elliott caught sight of Iris heading for work.

'Iris' he shouted 'Iris!' he sprinted out the showroom doors. Mohican tall, shoulders back, she hadn't heard him. 'Iris' he ran to catch up with her. 'Iris, wait!!' She glanced back, then kept walking. 'Iris' he caught up with her. 'I'm sorry' he caught his breath 'I'm sorry about last night' he fell into step alongside her.

'Don't worry about it' eyes ahead, she kept walking.

'No ... look, wait, please! Just wait a minute!' Elliott caught hold of her arm and turned her to face him. 'I'm sorry' he began, 'I shouldn't have ...'

'It doesn't matter' she looked away.

'It does' said Elliott. 'I was out of line. Neal's your boyfriend. I shouldn't have ...'

'He's not' Iris stared at something far down the end of the street.

'What do you mean?' said Elliott.

'I mean he's not my boyfriend. We split up this morning.'

'Oh' Elliott wasn't sure what to say. 'Look, Iris ...'

'I don't want to talk about it.'

'I know, but ... Elliott started.

'You know what Elliott?' brown eyes flashed briefly in his direction, then away again 'the next few days are going to be full on. Why don't we just focus on what we have to do; get the protest done, tender for the licence; let's just focus on the station.'

'Sure' Elliott heard himself say. 'Of course.'

'I have to go' she turned away.

'Okay' he nodded.

'I'll see you later' she called over her shoulder.

'See you' Elliott watched her walk away.

Eamo sat in his office. Outside the sound of the showroom, cars on the street, soft sunlight filtering through the venetian blinds in long flat slates. Eamo looked at the phone on his desk. Tap-tap-tap went his foot. Jig-jig-jig jerked his knee. He reached for the phone.

'Eamo' Lorraine appeared around the door with a bunch of pink and yellow slips in her hand 'Reggie says will ya come an' check these; he thinks they're missin' a roll.'

'Be there in a minute.'

'Reggie says yer man's goin' mad …'

'I said I'll be there in a minute' Eamo snapped. Silence. He looked at the phone. 'Fuck' he jigged his leg beneath the table. 'Shyte' he leant his face on his hand again, then he pulled the phone towards him. Tap-tap-tap. Jig-jig-jig. He stared at the phone for a minute or two, then he picked up the receiver and quickly dialled a number. Glassy eyes, fixed and staring.

'Hello?' a voice said at the other end. Eamo swallowed. 'Hello?' said the voice. Eamo put down the phone.

'Eamo' Lorraine's head appeared around the door again. 'Eamo, yer man's throwin' a wobbler out there …'

'Right' Eamo stood up 'on me way.'

Over in Donaghmede Belinda frowned at the receiver in her hand.

'Who's that?' Darren called from behind the paper.

'No-one' Belinda shook her head. 'Kids messin'' she replaced the phone onto the handset and went back into the kitchen.

. . . .

'Mikey, Mikey, Tango, Charlie, Foxtrot Romeo, Lady Margaret, at seventy eight ten degrees north, fifty-five fifteen

east. Sailing cautiously at the moment. Surrounded by ice not actually shown on the chart, which is a concern, but we'll follow the leads we have and hopefully find clear water sooner rather than later...'

Slowly, silently, the sea slipped away until all that was left was a series of small channels for the boat to push through. A sea of ice, interspersed only with more ice; deceptively flat on the surface with huge shelves lying directly beneath.

'I'll tell you what' Nick was standing on deck 'you can get heartily sick of ice' he was using a long spiked pole to push the boat back from the edge.

'This is incredibly slow going' said Anthony, poling from the port side.

'Well unfortunately' Nick lunged at a piece of ice jutting dangerously close to the boat 'we don't know what we're dealing with, because whatever this is, it's not on the chart, so there's going to have to be a lot of patient navigation for the next twenty four hours. Frankie' he shouted 'any sign of open water?' From the bow Frankie shook his head.

'Same channel we've just come up. We're going around in a circle, and the ice is closing in.'

'Wonderful' the colour on Anthony's face began to rise. 'That's just fucking bloody marvellous. I thought you knew what you were doing' he glared at Nick. 'The whole reason I appointed you skipper ...' he felt the spike of an ice-pole press against his oilskins.

'Tell you what Anthony' Nick's voice was dangerously soft 'why don't you go downstairs, make contact with the Norwegian Met Office, give them our bearings, and ask them to fax us an up to date chart for these waters with a suggested course. Alternatively, you could just step overboard onto the nearest piece of ice, and frankly I'm not pushed at this point which of those two options you choose. But I suggest you decide fast.' Silence. The crew looking at him. Frankie on the bow, Tiny on the wheel, Nick and Richard standing side by side. Anthony pushed the pole away from his chest and made for the galley.

'Right!' he heard Nick shout behind him 'Tiny! Shove her round. Shove the bow round. Hard! Come on! Over! Over!! One last push!!'

Reversing down into the galley Anthony pulled off his gloves, picked up the radio and made contact with the Norwegian Met Office, who promised to fax through a new series of charts as quickly as they could. From the deck above, the sound of the crew shouting as they shifted the boat around. Anthony looked at the fax machine. Nothing. Something caught the corner of his eye. Richard's tequila bottle. Square cut, bevelled glass, dark amber contents. He reached across and picked it up. The skin on his eyelids folding down, creasing up as he turned it over and read the back.

'Alter our fucking course' the sound of a metal seal breaking. Navy eyes narrowing, the clink of glass as he poured a generous tumbler. He glanced at his watch as he took his first sip. Dublin would be awake now.

. . . .

'Wayne Conroy, the Wayne Conroy Show. This is it folks, last chance ta get the Government ta change their minds and let us stay on air while our licence application goes in. Don't forget, 5pm this evening, wherever you are, Blow your horn for Minister Horn, an' if you're in the City Centre, we're staging a peaceful protest from Studio One in Capel Street, up ta Government buildings, we'd love you to join us if you're in the vicinity, but if you're not, please remember to blow that horn ...'

The morning of the protest started quiet enough. No cars, the early morning sun warming sleepy red bricked shops, the sound of traders on Moore Street in the distance. Elliott lit a cigarette and stood smoking it in front of the showroom, enjoying the feel of the sun on his face. Eamo stepped outside.

'D-day, whah?' he squinted at Elliott. 'Reckon we'll get a big crowd?'

'No idea' said Elliott. 'Your guess is as good as mine.'

'We'll know soon enough, won't we?' Eamo stared down the empty street.

'And are you coming to the protest Geraldine?'

'Am I what Rachel? Just try and keep me away! We're all coming. Everyone in the office. We're coming straight up after work.'

'Fantastic Geraldine, we'll look forward to seeing you, line four, it's Pat.'

'Rachel, I just want to say what disgrace I think it is they're takin' you off air. Why are they doin' this? What is the point?'

'Well Pat I hope you're going to blow your horn.'

'Rachel darlin, you're gonna feel my horn all the way from Shankhill.'

'Ohh *Pat!!* Well, I'll look forward to that. Line three, who's on three? Jenny! Jenny, what have you got for us ...'

The morning passed quickly, the switchboard jammed with calls.

'I want the music up' Elliott instructed the jocks 'big songs, fire it up, belt it out, make people realise how much they're going to miss this if we go. Open house when we get to twelve. Everyone in studio, jumping in and out, whatever feels right, pull listeners in off the street, call Rocket and BBR and see if someone wants to come down and comment.'

'Rocket an' BBR?' said Eamo. 'They're the competition.'

'Doesn't matter' said Squirrel 'we're all in the same boat. Family, that's what we are on a day like this Eamo, we're ...' he stopped. What the fuck. 'Are you alright Eamo? Are ya feelin' okay?'

'Grand' Eamo looked away 'grand. Right. Whatever ya want' he pulled the studio door open. 'I'll catch ya later.'

' ... Studio One, it's Carly. Gotta tell ya, the excitement is building here, lots of people buzzing around in studio. With me right now, two guys I never get to see, because they're always on at 2am; it's the Westend Boyz, Gary, Barry, what are you guys wearing? I love this look you've got going on.'

'Hey Carly, these are Blow Your Horn T-shirts a friend of ours made; we've got lots of them in different colours for people to wear on the protest this afternoon so if you're listening out there, make sure you get in here early enough to collect your T-shirt; they'll be collectors items after today ...'

Shortly after one o'clock small groups of people began arriving, trickling in off the street in threes and fives. The showroom filled by 2pm, so Eamo brought them through to the warehouse. More arrived. More.

'Leave the door open' Eamo instructed Lorraine, pointing to the small door at the end of the showroom. 'Soon as they arrive, send them through; Reggie'll look after them.'

'Studio One, Maaad-Donna!! Last-day-ah school-whaddaya-gonna-do-this-afternoon-I'll-tell-ya-what-yer-gonna-do-yer-gonna-blow-yer-horn-for-Studio-One. See-this-Charlene?'

'I do Donna.'

'What's-this-in-my-hand-Charlene?'

'It's an air-horn Donna.'

'It-is-Charlene-it's-an-airhorn-an-guess-what- I've-got-FIFTY-ah-these-horns-fifty-horns-now-all-I-need-is-fifty-listeners-ta-get-up-here-an-blow-them-with-me ...'

By 3pm the studio was jammed with jocks, traders, photographers and reporters.

'Are you the owner?' an Irish Times reporter had cornered Elliott. 'When did you set up the station? What age are you? Had you any previous radio experience? When did the station reach the Number One slot?' questions firing in quick succession; Elliott, struggling to answer as he scanned the studio. The room, buzzing with energy. The jocks, their friends, and a bunch of people he'd never seen before.

'Elliott' Squirrel's face, excited as he pushed his head around the door. 'Television's here' blue eyes wide, shining, as a cameraman appeared behind him, followed by a man holding a long furry sound boom. 'RTE' Squirrel whispered, jerking his head to indicate a presenter making his way in the door.

'RTE?' Elliott looked at the news reporter 'but we're a Pirate.'

'Doesn't matter' the newsman cut him off. 'It's objective reporting on a national matter. How many people would you say are down in that warehouse?'

'Emm …' Elliott hadn't stuck his head outside studio all morning.

'I'd say it's about five hundred' the newsman glanced at the activity around the room and in the studio beyond. 'Let's set up there' he instructed the sound guy 'we'll do a piece to camera with the studio in the background and then I want us in-studio for the close-down; can you clear that room?' he said to Elliott, nodding at the crowd of people behind the glass as Mad Donna continued to broadcast. 'Not all of them; just enough for us to get the camera in and film your last broadcast.'

Elliott looked at the newsman and it hit him. *Enough for us to get the camera in and film your last broadcast.* He stared at the newsman. 'Is that okay?' said the newsman 'can we do that? Bernard' he called to one of the crew 'I need to get mic'd up here. Is that okay?' he said to Elliott. *Your last broadcast.* Elliott stared at him. 'And you know what else I need?' the newsman straightened his collar, tightened his tie 'I need you to round up a few jocks for interview, then we'll do a piece with you. We've got a couple of sound bites with the listeners in the warehouse … are you okay?' he looked at Elliott. Elliott blinked.

'Yeah' he said, 'yeah, sure. That's … that's fine.'

'… Well I think the real pity of it is that there are sixteen people in permanent employment with this station; that's sixteen jobs that could be on the line here for no reason. That's the shame of it. We're a commercially viable, professionally run station. We're providing a service; there's a genuine demand for what we offer, we pay our music rights, not all Pirates do, but we do, and there is simply no reason why we should have to go off-air. No reason and no logic behind it …'

'He's good' Squirrel and Elliott were watching Christian being interviewed.

'Perfect spokesperson' said Elliott.

'Probably hopin' he'll get a job with RTE if this all falls through' said Squirrel.

'Probably' Elliott smiled. 'Are there really five hundred people down in the warehouse?'

'An' the rest' said Squirrel. 'Reggie says they're spillin' onta the street.'

'Wow' Elliott's skin began to tingle.

'Better than a kick in the hole' Squirrel glanced at his watch. 'Still a while yet. Might get a few more.' Across the room Elliott spotted Iris, perched on Katie's desk, chatting to Carly, Candy and a few of the jocks from BBR. Behind her in-studio, Neal, Benny and Declan had taken the mic. He watched her for a minute or two. Head down, spikes out, rolling a Rizzla. That was new.

'Cheaper' she'd said when he'd commented on it.

What are we going to do if this ends? I don't want this to end. He took in the crowded room; the jocks in studio, Donna and the girls laughing, jostling, fixing their hair as they got ready to talk to the TV newsman, Rachel and Christian talking to reporters. Iris, rolling, licking, lighting. Brown eyes glancing up; catching his. Cheekbones pushing back. Smiling. Standing up. Making her way across.

'Alright?' a gentle tug on his T-shirt.

'Yeah' he nodded 'grand.' A pause. The room, filled with noise behind and around them. Smokey air, the jocks in studio, music playing, the rising hum of people talking. 'Actually, no' Elliott ran a hand through his hair 'I'm not. How weird is this? The news guy just talked about filming our last broadcast.'

'It's not our last broadcast' said Iris. Elliott looked at her.

'I hope you're right. I really hope you're right.'

'I'm always right' she grinned. 'I'm the Tube, remember?' an amused smile curling. Mischief in her eyes. Boldness pushing through. Elliott felt himself smile.

'I really fucked it up, didn't I?' he stared over her head at the jocks behind the glass. 'You know …' he began.

'We're gonna hafta make a move' Squirrel had arrived back up from the warehouse below. 'Warehouse is jammers. Street's full outside an' all. Eamo reckons if we don't go in the next twenty minutes the Gards'll break it up. Who's doin' the closin?'

'Elliott' said Iris. Elliott looked at her. 'I think you should' she said. 'Come on' she slipped her hand in his 'I'll sit in with you. It's ten to five' she nodded at the clock above Katie's desk. 'We'll do it at five.'

'Grand' said Squirrel. Elliott pushed the door to the studio open. Declan, Benny and Neal were stationed around the desk.

'Okay' said Elliott 'ten minutes and counting. You ready?'

'Ready as we'll ever be' said Benny. 'Here' he pulled out the chair 'all yours.'

'Ffff-ffff-fuck the seat; have a drink' Declan placed a large bottle of vodka down on the mix desk.

'Where did that come from?' Elliott realised everyone had a drink in their hand.

'Ssss-ssss-ssss …' Declan began.

'Squirrel?' said Elliott.

'Nnnn-nnn no' said Declan 'sss-sss one ah two bottles a listener dropped in. The gu-gu girls have the other one outside.' Through the window Elliott watched Donna, Charlene and Mandy pouring drinks for the RTE newsmen.

'Great. That's all we need. Here' he picked up the vodka bottle 'why don't we leave this until the protest is out of the way' he placed it up on top of the cart machine. 'We can get drunk when it's over.' Through the glass he watched the outer door open and saw Squirrel pushing his way across the room. Eyes bright with excitement as he came into studio.

'They're goin' fuckin' mental down there!! Warehouse is jammers, an' they're all singin' an' chantin. Eamo's up on top ah the carpet stack with a megaphone, revvin' them up. Are ya ready? Are ya ready ta go?' Elliott looked up at the clock. Three minutes to five.

'Ready as we'll ever be' he smiled at Benny, then sitting down at the desk, he pulled on the headphones, leant in and opened the mic:

'Good evening Dublin, with just under one minute to five o'clock, this is Studio One, broadcasting, not we hope for the last time, on one hundred kilohertz in the medium wave band and on eighty six FM in stereo. We want to thank you, the listeners, for getting us where we are today, and for turning out to support us in such huge numbers this evening. The time now is five o'clock, so wherever you are, we want you to blow your horn. Blow your horn for Minister Horn, blow it loud, blow it long, and let's make as much noise as we possibly can as we take this all the way to Leinster House ...'

He pulled back the fade, and the studio fell silent. Nothing for a moment, then somewhere in the distance the sound began. Singular at first, then it began to build. Far away, then growing closer. Air horns, car horns, high pitched, fast beeps, slow whines. From the quays in the distance. From the street outside and the warehouse below. Up the street, down the Quays, around the city. Filling the warehouse, swelling the Studio. Ten thousand horns blowing together in one loud, glorious, out of key symphony. Silence in studio as they listened, then swallowing hard, Elliott leant forward and opened the mic the sound of horns loud in the background as he spoke:

'Well there you have it. That's the voice of Dublin. The voice of Dublin telling the people who *should* be listening ... what Dubliners want to listen to ...' pushing the fade up, he let the sound of the horns outside play on for another minute or two, then he glanced up at the clock. 'Right' he pulled back the fade, closed the mic and stood up from the desk. 'That's it. We're off-air. Studio One is off the air.' He looked at Squirrel. 'Come on. Let's get this show on the road.'

A giant roar from the crowd in the warehouse as they pushed the studio door open and the jocks and reporters began filing down the stairs to warehouse below.

'Over here' Eamo shouted, beckoning to them from the top of the carpet stack. Ya'll never get through that' he yelled, pointing down at the tightly packed crowd. Swinging a leg over the stair rail, Squirrel stepped out onto the carpet stack.

'Come on' he shouted, holding his hand out to help Iris across. Elliott followed and one by one they made their way to the front of the carpet stack, where Eamo stood in the centre, megaphone in his hand.

'Young people of Ireland!!' Eamo roared from the megaphone and a huge cheer went up 'Studio One loves you!!' another huge cheer. 'Thank you for comin' out today' Eamo barked through the megaphone 'ta support us, for showin' your solidarity. Thank you for makin' noise, for makin' the right kinda noise, at a time when we need it the most. Now let's take this ta the man who needs ta hear it the most. Let's take our message ta Minister Horn. Studio One back on-air! Studio One back on-air!' boney knees bending, bouncing, as he took up the chant. 'Studio One back on air! Studio One back on air!' the crowd shouting as they began making their way down:

STUDIO ONE BACK ON-AIR
STUDIO ONE BACK ON-AIR
STUDIO ONE BACK ON-AIR

The crowd cheering. Chanting. Hands reaching out, helping them down, lifting them up and over until they found themselves at the door to the warehouse.

STUDIO ONE BACK ON-AIR
STUDIO ONE BACK ON-AIR
STUDIO ONE BACK ON-AIR

Banners, placards, teddies, balloons. Eamo, leading the way. Iris, Elliott, Squirrel and the jocks, stretching out across the street.

STUDIO ONE BACK ON-AIR
STUDIO ONE BACK ON-AIR
STUDIO ONE BACK ON-AIR

Up they went, past the traders, past Arnotts, up Henry Street, the crowd of five hundred swelling behind them, a giant rolling wave of people, pushing them on.

'Fucking Hell!!' Elliott shouted, raw energy surging, coursing, pumping through him.

'Fuck!!' Squirrel shouted at him, 'Fuck!! Fuck!!' he roared over the noise. But Henry Street was nothing. Henry Street was just a drop in the ocean, because as they reached the top, a stadium sized roar rose up from O'Connell Street. A sea of faces. People with placards stretching far and wide. 'Up Studio One' and 'Down Minister Horn' banners and placards. Big signs, smalls signs, hand painted, professionally done. Teddies, balloons, flags and signs waving in the air. Car horns, air horns, 'Blow your horn' T-shirts. Banners on buildings, posters on telegraph poles. People hanging out of office windows. Dessie's taxis; a long line of them stretching up the side of the street, all of them sounding their horns. The Gardaí watching from various points and and outside the GPO, Elliott spotted a Red Cross ambulance.

STUDIO ONE BACK ON-AIR
STUDIO ONE BACK ON-AIR
STUDIO ONE BACK ON-AIR

Horns sounding. High pitched, slow whines, fast beeps, honkety-honk-honks. A long loud, magnificent, glorious, out of key symphony. Above them, around them, the crowd, fast and thick, chanting:

STUDIO ONE BACK ON-AIR
STUDIO ONE BACK ON-AIR
STUDIO ONE BACK ON-AIR

'Elliott!!' Squirrel shouting in his ear. 'Dessie has a float for us' he roared, pointing at an open backed truck in front of the GPO. 'Come on!' he shouted. 'We need ta get the jocks on!! Come on!!'

O'Connell Street full, bursting at the seams. Scrambling up on the truck, hands lifting, helping, pulling them on. Declan, Carly, Rachel, Christian. Reaching out. Helping each other on. Neal, Candy, Gary, Barry; one by one, until everyone was on board.

'I feel like a Jaysus rock star' roared Eamo over the noise, holding on tight as the truck revved, jerked and pulled slowly forward. Climbing up on the wooden frame just behind the cab, positioning himself as high as he could, Eamo pressed the megaphone to his lips and picked up the chant:

STUDIO ONE BACK ON-AIR
STUDIO ONE BACK ON-AIR
STUDIO ONE BACK ON-AIR

Up they went, up O'Connell, onto Westmoreland, the crowd spread wide around and far behind them. Car horns, air-horns, people hanging out of office buildings. A photographer trying to climb up on the truck. Falling, scrambling, reaching up. Elliott leant over the side and helped him on.

'Irish Times' the photographer shouted. 'Are you one of the owners?'

'Yes' Elliott shouted.

'Great! Stay there!!' the photographer climbed up on top of the cab. To Elliott's left, Eamo, bouncing up and down as he pumped the chant through the megaphone. To his right, Squirrel, hanging over the side of the truck talking to someone. Elliott looked around for Iris. Where was she? 'Up here' the photographer shouted 'look up!!' Elliott turned and looked up.

Christ, he's going to fall he thought as he stared at the photographer, squatting down on the top of the cab. *He's going to fall* he watched him shoot a roll of film, then jump down.

'Thanks' he shouted to Elliott 'I got everything; GPO, the crowd, everything; what's your name?'

'Elliott.'

'Elliott what?' the photographer shouted.

'Barrington!!' Elliott yelled.

'Great' the photographer shouted. 'I need to get off.'

'What? You only just got on!!'

'They're holding the page' the photographer shouted, 'you'll be front page tomorrow, but I need to get off!!' his voice was raw.

'Okay, hold on. Eamo!!' Elliott shouted, 'Eamo!! Give me a hand!'

STUDIO ONE BACK ON-AIR
STUDIO ONE BACK ON-AIR
STUDIO ONE BACK ON-AIR

From behind the curtain in his office Minister Horn looked out at the crowd, chanting and cheering outside the gates. On the television, the clip of Christian being interviewed was playing. The phone on his desk rang.

'Richard Horn' he said, as he picked it up. 'Yes, yes I have. Of course I can see them. They're outside my window. No, no comment. Yes' his voice was weary 'I'm watching the news. I'm watching it now' he eyed the television which had cut to a shot of the crowds outside his office. He listened to the voice on the other end for a minute or two, then said

'Alright. From a PR perspective I don't think we've any choice. No. No, I'll handle it. What? Don't worry, I'll get a photo. I'll get exactly what we need.'

STUDIO ONE BACK ON-AIR
STUDIO ONE BACK ON-AIR
STUDIO ONE BACK ON-AIR

They'd been outside Government Buildings for nearly an hour. Elliott's throat was hoarse from shouting. Behind the black iron gates, in the distance, three suited figures were making their way across the lawn.

'It's the Minister' someone shouted. 'The Minister, the Minister' a ripple ran through the crowd as TV and Radio newsmen surged forward, anxious to get the best position. From the truck, as they watched the figures get closer, the crowd picked up the chant once again

STUDIO ONE BACK ON-AIR
STUDIO ONE BACK ON-AIR
STUDIO ONE BACK ON-AIR

The chant grew louder, stronger, as the Minister, his Private Secretary, and Press Officer grew closer, then the crowd erupted into a mighty roar as they emerged through the black iron gates. A forest of furry grey microphones thrust forward, but the cheering continued, and for several minutes, despite making repeated efforts to speak, the Minister's voice was drowned out.

'Well well' he laughed eventually. This is quite a crowd, quite a crowd.' Jeers, boos and "Blow Your Horn" taunts drowned him out again for a moment or two before he continued.

'The local radio station licences represent a bright new future in Irish Broadcasting' he raised his voice above a series of boos. 'Industry growth' he shouted 'mass employment, and *real choice* for the listeners. The Government very much hope that Studio One will be part of this future. We recognise their success, their popularity ... I ... I listen to them myself.'

'Whaddaya takin' them off-air for then?' someone from the crowd shouted, which drew a further series of jeers and taunts.

'Our intention' the Minister shouted 'in asking not just Studio One, but all illegal broadcasts to come off-air in the run up to the tender process was simply to level the playing pitch and make it a fair process for everyone concerned.'

'Takin' jobs when ya should be makin' jobs' shouted someone from the crowd, which drew a loud series of boos and the atmosphere began to take on a dangerous edge. The Minister looked at his Press Officer, who nodded his head.

'Where are the Studio One station owners?' the Minister shouted. 'Could the station owners step forward please?' From the truck, Eamo, Iris, Elliott and Squirrel climbed down, and the crowd parted as they made their way through. The Minister, spotting Eamo, reached forward, grabbed his hand and pulled him in close beside him. Facing Eamo to the cameras, and firmly shaking his hand, the Minister shouted

'Studio One can go back on-air !! They can go back on-air, and we look forward to receiving their tender for a licence at the hearing next week.' A mighty roar as flash bulbs popped and ten thousand hands shot in the air, the crowd shouting and cheering.

'Studio One and *any other* station' the Minister strained to be heard. The licence tender is a fair process; everyone will be given a fair chance. The new radio licences represent employment and choice. The listener is the winner here. The listener is the winner ...' but the crowd weren't listening. Cheering, shouting, jumping up and down, they were celebrating. Someone grabbed Eamo, then a group of men lifted him up on their shoulders, as he barked through the megaphone:

STUDIO ONE BACK ON-AIR
STUDIO ONE BACK ON-AIR
STUDIO ONE BACK ON-AIR

TRIUMPHANT RETURN FOR STUDIO ONE AS STREET PROTEST BRINGS DUBLIN CITY TO A STANDSTILL

Studio One, the station hotly tipped as the Number One favourite in the race for one of the two local radio station licences, brought Dublin City to a standstill yesterday as over ten thousand listeners turned out to protest against the station going off-air. The station, which is based in Capel Street, secured the Number One position in the JNLR results released in April. Leading yesterday's protest were station owners Eamon Rourke and Elliott Barrington (pictured). The march, which passed peacefully, without incident, commenced in Henry Street before making its way to Government buildings. While no official statements have been released, Studio One was back on-air last night and it is understood they will be permitted to proceed with their tender tomorrow morning. Speaking to the press, station owner Elliott Barrington said they were 'overwhelmed by the response' and that 'it was a clear indication how the public feel about the station.' At twenty years of age, Mr Barrington is the youngest station owner tendering for a licence. Mr Barrington set up his first station aged sixteen in his bedroom at home and broadcast from there for two years, before establishing Studio One with three business partners. A total of eighteen applications have been received for the licences, sixteen of which are from existing Pirate stations, with separate applications received by an independent consortium and businessman John Hegarty of Hudson Holdings.

'Size ah yer mush' Squirrel was studying Elliott's face staring out from the front of the Times. 'Size ah at that crowd an' all. Like an Ireland–England match. Outside the GPO. That's history that is.' Elliott looked at the photograph again, the GPO columns in the background, Eamo on his left, megaphone in hand, shouting at the crowd, Iris and the jocks in the background.

'What were you doing?' Elliott pointed to Squirrel's leather jacket, in shot to the right of the picture, blonde spikes hanging over the side of the trailer.

'Chattin' up a young one walkin' alongside the truck' said Squirrel. 'Aerobics teacher' he winked. 'Has all the gear.' Elliott smiled.

'Did you get the figures done?'

'Did them this mornin' Squirrel reached into his jacket. 'Here' he handed Elliott an envelope.

'Great' Elliott picked up the folder he'd been slowly filling over the last month.

'What else have ya got?' Squirrel nodded at it.

'Mix of everything really' said Elliott 'station schedule, list of the jocks, press clippings, letters of endorsement from the ad agencies, the petition from the listeners, what we'd do if we got the licence; how we'd run the station in line with Government guidelines; it's all there' he slipped Squirrel's envelope with the figures inside.

'Should bring that an' all' Squirrel pointed to the cover of the Irish Times. 'Can't get a better endorsement than that.'

'You're right' Elliott picked up the Times. 'Kind of says it all really' he stared at the photo.

. . . .

'Foxtrot Tango to Mikey Lima, do you read me? Over. Foxtrot Tango. Come in Mikey Lima, have you received the Norwegian charts …'

Anthony picked up the radio mic. Pressed the receiver and held it to his mouth.

'Mikey Lima to Foxtrot Tango. We've had one ice chart come through, but the fax keeps jamming; actually … it's starting again now' he put the receiver down as the fax jerked and began to whirr and grind beside him.

'About time' he muttered, then 'what the …' angling his head sideways he stared at the photograph inching its way through the fax. It was Elliott. Elliott in the middle of some sort of crowd. *Triumphant return for Studio One* Elliott's face staring out. The sound of metal slicing. The fax releasing. Anthony held it up. It was Elliott. On the front of the Irish Times. Eyebrows frowning in, fax in hand, Anthony slid in at the table, reached for the tequila and poured himself a second glass.

· · · ·

'Studio One, back on-air, Rachel with you until twelve pm, thank you ALL, so much, for the incredible support we got at the protest, thank you for voting with your voice, with your feet, a huge thank you to everyone who marched; Studio One is back on-air and it's down to you. Now, the Department of Health have asked us to cover something of a taboo subject. Testicular cancer! While we girls are very good at checking ourselves for lumps and bumps, it appears the men in our life are not ...'

'You should be listenin' ta that' Eamo nodded at the small transistor beside his desk.

'Yeah, right' Squirrel flicked the blinds, and glanced down the street. They were waiting for Elliott and Iris to go and make their official tender for a licence.

'Simple check' said Eamo 'stead ah riskin' yer health.'

'Riskin' me health me arse' Squirrel was starting to get irritated. 'Nothin' wrong with me' he glanced at his watch. 'Gonna be late if they don't get here soon.'

'Ya don't know there's nothin' wrong with ya' Eamo persisted 'that's what that programme's all about; makin' sure ya don't have a problem.'

'Get off me case' Squirrel snapped. 'Yer not me Da. Stop shytin' on about it. Pain in me hole witcha' dark angry eyes flashing, as he turned to the window. 'Where the fuck are they?' he scowled.

'All I'm sayin ...' Eamo started.

'Eamo' Squirrel's cheeks flamed 'shut-up for fucks sakes will ya? Yer doin' me head in. I don't have cancer, alright? I don't have it, me Da doesn't have it, none of us have fuckin' cancer, but I tell what we do have Eamo; the biggest meetin' of our lives in less than two hours time, an' that's we need ta be concentratin' on. Where the *fuck* are they?' he shouted, striding out of the office and onto the street outside.

Eamo leant back in the chair. Rubbed his hand against his face. The sound of the street; voices calling, catching, passing by. The showroom next door; phones ringing, Studio One playing in the background. Squirrel on the path outside, six foot of leather, smoking, pacing. Spikey blonde hair. Hand circling. Agitated. Waiting. Eamo looked at the phone on his desk. Blue eyes searching, seeking. Shifting left, right, light catching in flints of stone. He sat still for several minutes, then he reached for the phone and rang up to Studio.

'Yer Da around?'

'Me Da?' said Katie. 'Whatcha want me Da for?'

'None ah yer business. Is he around?'

'Nah' said Katie. 'Gone up North ta get parts. Left early this mornin. Ma said he'll be home around six.'

'Grand' Eamo put down the phone.

'Eamo' Squirrel whistled from the street outside. Eamo looked up to see Elliott and Iris standing on the path, Elliott dressed in his Louis Copeland suit with a shirt and tie, Iris in a fitted black jacket, and skin tight black jeans, Mohican sharp and shining.

'Right' Eamo shouted. He stood up, tightened his tie, smoothed his hair and made his way out of the office.

The sun hot on their backs they walked up Westmoreland Street. 'Could you not ah worn a suit?' Eamo glanced at Squirrel in his leathers. 'Made a bit of a fuckin' effort' he nodded at Elliott in the Louis Copeland.

'Don't annoy me Eamo' Squirrel scowled. 'Money. That's all they're gonna be interested in' he pointed at the folder tucked underneath Elliott's arm.

'Might help if ya looked the part.'

'Might help if you shut the fuck up' said Squirrel. Silence. On they walked, past the Central Bank, around Trinity's black railings, along Nassau Street. Turning right on Kildare Street.

'Studio One' the receptionist ticked their name off a list. 'The tenders are taking place in the Connaught Suite' she indicated a set of double doors just across from the reception desk. 'The committee are still with the last group. If you take a seat over there, the clerk will call you' she indicated a row of polished dark wooden benches behind a row of marble columns.

'Thanks' Elliott turned and they made their way across the lobby, through the columns, where they sat on one of the benches.

'I need a cigarette' said Iris after a minute or two.

'Yeah, well ya can't have one' said Squirrel. 'None of us are goin' anywhere 'till this is done.' Beside him Eamo, staring ahead at the navy carpet on the stairs, jigged his left leg furiously. 'Jaysus Eamo, give it a rest will ya?' said Squirrel. Eamo stopped jigging.

'I need the jacks' he said.

'No-one's goin' anywhere' said Squirrel. Five minutes passed. Ten. 'Fucks sakes' Squirrel ran a hand through his hair 'what's keepin' them?'

'I *need* a cigarette' Iris stood up.

'No!' said Squirrel.

'I'll only be a minute. 'I'll just be there' she pointed at the steps. 'You can call me if they …' she broke off as the doors to the Connaught Suite opened. Shiny shoes clicking on hard tiles as the BBR team made their way across the lobby.

'Six ah them' Eamo counted.

'Six fuckin' eejits' said Squirrel.

'There's yer man Horn' said Eamo as they watched the Minister speak briefly to the receptionist, who nodded, stepped out from behind her desk and made her way across the lobby.

'They're going to take a ten minute recess' she said. 'I'll call you when they're ready.'

'Right, I'm definitely going for a smoke' Iris stood up.

'Where are *you* goin?' Squirrel called after Eamo who was making his way across the lobby.

'Jacks' Eamo called over his shoulder, as he headed in the direction of the Gents toilets just across from the Connaught Suite. Squirrel leant back against the bench, leather creaking as he stretched his legs out in front of him.

'Ya nervous?' he said to Elliott.

'Not really' said Elliott. Squirrel looked at him.

'I'm confident about what we have to offer' said Elliott. 'Great jocks, strong schedule, healthy figures. We're the number one station. I don't see how they could justify not giving us a licence.' Squirrel's face broke into a toothy grin.

'What?' said Elliott.

'You' Squirrel's grin got wider. 'Yer a long way from the napkin.' Across the lobby the door to the Connaught Suite opened and Squirrel watched the Minister and someone else, someone vaguely familiar, walk with him to the Gents toilets. 'Recess me arse' he whispered to Elliott 'goin' ta the jacks, that's what they're doing.'

'Where?' Elliott leant around him.

'Ya missed them' said Squirrel. 'Here' he shifted over on the bench so Elliott could get a clearer view. 'Can't wait ta get this over. Nerves are killin' me so they are' he jigged his left leg furiously.

'You just gave out to Eamo for doing that' said Elliott.

'Yeah, well' Squirrel continued to jig. 'Gettin' onta me about not wearin' a suit.'

'He's nervous' said Elliott.

'We're all nervous' said Squirrel. 'Eamo needs ta relax so he does.'

Eamo dropped his trousers, lowered himself down onto the toilet seat, took a deep breath and felt his bowels relax. Closing his eyes he rested his head in his hands for a minute or two.

You're not me Da. Pain in me hole witcha.

'Shyte' Eamo whispered. 'Shyte.'

The Gents door creaking. Two sets of shoes clicking across the black and white tiles.

'I think that went pretty well' the Minister's familiar clipped dialect. The sound of flies unzipping.

'Well you certainly gave a good impression of being interested in what they had to say' Eamo's eyes narrowed as he recognised the sound of Roger Ingram's voice from the night of the kidnapping. A series of trickles. Two streams of piss hitting urinal bowls.

'Hugely important' the Minister's voice echoing louder now as a waterfall of piss thundered down. 'I don't want to give any of them any room to think it wasn't a fair race' his voice dropping as the waterfall trickled off. Change jingling. Flies zipping. 'I want every one of the stations we meet this week to walk out of here convinced they have it in the bag' the Minister again. 'I want them to believe, to one hundred percent believe, that we were impressed by their ideas and they're going to be successful in their tender.' Shoes clicking their way across to the wash hand basins. 'That way' the Minister's voice echoing 'when they don't get the licence, the only thing they can possibly think is what a tough decision it must have been for us.' Taps running. Sound muffling. From inside the cubicle Eamo leant in the direction of the sinks, straining to hear. 'You need to be more enthusiastic' the Minister's voice again' as taps turned off.

'Enthusiastic!' Ingram, irritated now. The sound of the towel barrel being pulled. 'How do you expect me to be enthusi ...'

'Roger' the Minister, impatient. 'There's a lot riding on this. For both of us. You know there is. Putting the people we want in place is one thing; having to deal with a public enquiry challenging the integrity of our decision is another.' Shoes clicking past the cubicle. 'We need to make every station we meet this week believe, really believe, they were in with a chance. I'm not taking any risks ...' the door to the Gents squeaking again. Voices fading down the corridor.

'Here they come' Squirrel sat up straight, elbowing Elliott.' Elliott looked across the lobby and froze. 'Who's yer man with the Minister?' said Squirrel. The floor of Elliott's stomach reached the back of his throat.

'It's Roger Ingram. Shit' he stepped behind the large marble column directly in front of them. 'Fuck' his heart started to pound. Squirrel stared across the lobby at the Minister and Roger. He watched them talking, then they turned, went inside the Connaught Suite and shut the door behind them. Squirrel moved to where Elliott was standing behind the column.

'What's he doin' here? Licences have nothin' got ta do with RTE.'

'Why are we hiding?' Iris, returned from her cigarette, had an amused grin on her face.

'Yer man Ingram's here' Squirrel muttered. 'From RTE.'

'So?'

'So he's gonna recognise Elliott isn't he?'

'Who cares?' said Iris. 'Elliott's a free man; he's entitled to set up a station.'

'He'll know we took the equipment' said Elliott. 'He'll put it together.'

'No he won't' said Iris. 'That was ages ago. He won't remember.'

'He might' said Squirrel. 'Might recognise me an' all; he gave me fifty quid ta shift the gear.'

'He won't recognise you' said Iris. 'Whatever about Elliott, he's hardly going to recognise you from one brief meeting.'

'Fuck' Squirrel's face flamed. 'What he *doin'* here? RTE's nothin' got ta do with this.

'I can't go in' said Elliott. 'He'll put it together.' Behind the column, across the lobby, the sound of the doors to the Connaught Suite opening.

'Studio One' a clerk's voice echoing out. Silence. The three of them looked at each other. 'Studio One' the clerk called again.

. . . .

'Foxtrot Tango to Mikey Lima, do you read me? Over. Foxtrot Tango. Come in Mikey Lima, have you received the Norwegian Ice Charts ...'

'Hard! Hard!' Nick's voice from up on deck as Anthony sat

reading the Irish Times article down below. 'Over! Over!' a series of shouts. The sound of ice tightening in against the boat. Cups rattling as the galley shook. More shouts. Two legs dropped down through the hatch. A thump as the rest of Nick landed.

'Well that's it' he pulled off his gloves 'we are officially stuck.' He picked up the radio receiver. 'Mikey Lima, Mikey Lima, the Lady Margaret is frozen in. Norwegian ice charts are coming through' he glanced at the fax machine busy beside him 'we'll take a look and radio back. Over.' Putting down the receiver he picked up two ice charts sitting in the tray. 'I'd better have a look at that as well' he gestured to the fax Anthony was reading at the table, the tequila bottle half empty beside him.

'It's not a chart' Anthony didn't look up.

'What is it?'

'The Irish Times.'

'The Times?' said Nick. 'Marvellous Anthony. The boat's frozen in, the crew are out there working their backsides off, and you're in here drinking Tequila and reading the Irish Times. You know Richard was right' clutching the ice charts in one hand, Nick began pulling himself back up the stairs 'you are an asshole' he shouted as he stepped out on deck 'you're a fucking asshole!!'

. . . .

'Studio One' the clerk's voice echoing from the top of the lobby.

'I can't go in' said Elliott.

'Studio One' clicking shoes, the clerk's voice crossing the lobby.

'We can't do this without you' said Iris. 'You *are* the station.'

'I'm not the station' said Elliott. 'We all are.'

'But you run it' said Iris. 'You're the Station Manager; this is *your* programming' she tapped the folder. Footsteps getting closer.

'She's right' said Squirrel. 'We can't do this without ya.' A blustered clerk's face appeared around the column.

'Are you Studio One?' he stared at the three of them.

'Eh, yeah …' Squirrel looked at Elliott.

'Well? What? Are you deaf?' the clerk snapped. 'They don't

have all day you know. Follow me please' he turned his back and marched towards the double doors.

'Shit' Elliott felt his stomach shrink.

'Come on' said Squirrel. 'He won't put it together' he said as they followed the clerk towards the double doors of the Connaught Suite.

'He will' Elliott swallowed.

'Hang on' Squirrel glanced around 'where's Eamo? Where's he after ...' the door to the Gents toilet creaked open and Eamo stepped out. 'Eamo' Squirrel called.

'Wait here please' the clerk said as he stepped forward to the door.

'C'mere' Squirrel whispered to Eamo 'yer man Ingram from RTE's in there.'

'I know' said Eamo. The clerk knocked the door. A loud sharp knock.

'Ya know? How d'ya know?'

'Come!' a voice shouted from the belly of the room.

'Studio One!!' the clerk announced, his voice echoing up as he pushed open the doors to the Connaught Suite, then stepped back as one by one they began to file inside.

'How d'ya know?' Squirrel whispered. Eamo didn't answer, his face dark, hard, staring ahead. 'Eamo?' said Squirrel 'Eamo?'

High Georgian ceilings, a wide spacious room, the Tender Committee seated in a row across the top. Minister Horn, his Private Secretary, a woman and a man Elliott didn't recognise, and Roger. Head down, he was studying their application.

'Good Morning' Minister Horn gave them a warm, pleasant, smile. 'Please' he indicated chairs on the opposite side of the long wide table 'take a seat. So, Studio One!! That was quite a crowd turned out to support you the other day. Very impressive. My colleagues and I have been looking forward to this presentation immensely.' Beside the Minister Roger glanced up, looked down, then his head jerked and shot back up again. Eyes wide, he stared at Elliott. Heart hammering, Elliott forced a smile. A relaxed, confident, everything is normal smile. A we did not steal your equipment smile. Roger looked at him for several minutes then Elliott watched him check the names on the front of their application form.

'Now' said the Minister 'let me introduce the panel. To my left, we have Saibh Ni Ghonaill, Head of the Music Rights Association in Ireland, Larry McGuirk, Chairman of the Record Industry. On my right Private Secretary for the Department of Communications Michael McDonough, and beside him …'

'Just a second Minister' Roger interrupted 'I think I should make the Committee aware that I know this gentleman' he gestured towards Elliott.

'You know *this* gentleman?' the Minister pointed at Elliott.

'Yes' said Roger. 'He completed a work experience programme in RTE about a year and a half ago. It's probably important to note, given the circumstances.'

'Quite' the Minister looked unsure as to how to proceed. 'Well, it's irregular' he glanced at Michael McDonough 'but once there's no conflict; perhaps we should ascertain for the record; do you have any interest in this station Roger? Are you a shareholder or a partner, are you in any way personally connected to the station; would you be *biased* in any manner either towards or against them?'

'No' said Roger 'there's no bias either way.'

'And today is the first time you've become aware of Mister Barrington's association with the station?' asked the Minister.

'Yes' Roger stared at Elliott 'yes it is.'

'Well, note it for the record' the Minister nodded at Michael McDonough 'but other than that, as there appear to be no conflicting issues, I don't see any reason why we shouldn't proceed.'

The presentation lasted just over an hour. Elliott led the way, walking them through the station schedule, their programming format, outlining how they'd work if they were awarded a licence.

'You were a Law student' Roger interrupted suddenly.

'Yes' Elliott swallowed 'that's … that's correct.'

'What happened to that?'

'I left to pursue this.'

'I see' said Roger. 'Very commendable. You left Law to break it. How does your father feel about this?'

'He …' Elliott's throat was dry 'he doesn't actually know.'

'Really?' Roger laughed. 'Well, I should imagine he'd be very interested …'

'I don't see what any ah this has got ta do with the licence' Eamo's anger sliced through the conversation, cutting it short. Squirrel, Elliott and Iris turned in surprise.

'Nor do I' the Minister's eyes silenced Roger. 'Take us through your financials please, breaking down overhead, operating costs and revenue projection for the next three years.' Squirrel was half way through when Roger cut in again.

'Who gave you the backing for the station?' he said to Elliott.

'I did' Eamo's voice, menacing, dangerous. 'It's my station' his eyes bore into Roger. *It's my station.* Roger's blood ran cold. *It's my station.* The sound of that voice clenched in his ear just before he was hoisted up the mast on the West Mountain. The rest of the presentation continued without interruption.

. . . .

'**Foxtrot Tango to Mikey Lima, do you read me? Over. Foxtrot Tango. Come in Mikey Lima, please update your position …**'

Anthony picked up the glass, opened his mouth wide and let the last mouthful of tequila slide down his throat. Then he coughed. Sat forward.

'What the …' something had caught in his throat, 'what …' he felt a softness slide down his gullet. Richard's legs dropped down through the hatch.

'Anthony, Nick is really pissed off' he sounded older than his years. 'We're in serious trouble out there; the boat's frozen in.' His eyes fell on the empty tequila bottle. 'Anthony' he picked it up 'did you drink this?' Anthony didn't reply. His face felt hot. 'Anthony'

Richard's face split into a grin 'you drank the whole bottle!! Hey' he held the bottle up to the light 'did you? You did … Anthony, you *ate* the worm!!'

Anthony swallowed. His head felt strange. Adrift from its moorings. Richard's voice. Slow. Distorted. His face. Peering in. A strange intensity. Up through the hatch, framed like a picture, the sky began to glow.

'Hmmph' the weight of his head pulled his face to the table. Spotting the fax sticking out beneath Anthony's arms, Richard reached over, tugged it out and stared at the photograph of Elliott. Nick's legs dropped down through the hatch.

'Hey Nick' Richard scanned the article 'Elliott's in the Irish Times.'

'We'll all be in The Times' said Nick. 'We'll be in the fucking obituary section if we don't break through this ice. Christ' he caught sight of Anthony slumped over the table 'Anthony!' he shouted 'Anthony!'

'Anthony! Anthony!!' Nick's voice, distorted, distant.

'Hmmmph'Anthony's head lifted, hovered, then dropped back on the table.

'He ate the worm' said Richard.

'I don't give a fuck what he ate' said Nick. 'He's a disgrace. You're a disgrace!!' he shouted at Anthony. 'Come on' he said to Richard. 'According to the Norwegian charts, there's a break less than a mile away. If we can hack through the section at the front of the bow, we'll get into a slipstream that'll bring us across. Richard looked at Anthony's sleeping figure, slumped across the galley table.

'Why won't he wake up Nick? He ate the worm, he ate …'

'He *drank* Richard' Nick's voice angry, impatient. 'He drank an entire bottle of tequila. Trust me when I say the worm has very little to do with this. He's shitfaced. Now come on' he turned Richard towards the stairs 'I need you back up on deck, if we're to stand half a chance of getting out of this fix.'

. . . .

'It's a fix' said Eamo as the fresh air hit them.

'Whatcha mean?' Squirrel handed each of them a cigarette.

'I mean it's a fix, that's what I mean' Eamo's face darkened as lit his cigarette. 'Heard them in the jacks' he inclined his head in the direction of the revolving doors; 'the Minister an' yer man Ingram.' The three of them stared at him. 'Shoulda fuckin' known' Eamo took a long hard pull on his cigarette.

'How's it a fix?' said Squirrel.

'They know who they want' cynical blue eyes stared at the building they'd just left. 'They've picked the stations. They already know who they're givin' the licences to.'

'Who?' said Iris.

'Don't know' Eamo pulled hard on his cigarette again 'don't know, don't care; all I know is, it's not us. Or any ah the other poor fucks been in there this week. C'mon' he turned and began walking.

'Eamo! Wait!' Elliott hurried along beside him. 'Are you sure? What did they say? Maybe you made a mistake' he broke off as hard eyes stared him down.

'Listen ta me' said Eamo. 'Are ya listenin?' Elliott nodded. 'Ya know a lot about radio; the two ah yis do' he gestured at Iris. 'But ya know fuck all about life. An' the pricks ya meet along the way. It's a fix' his eyes lifted and landed on the revolving doors. 'I know what I heard. We won't be gettin' a licence. Rocket an' BBR won't be gettin' a licence. None ah the stations goin' through those doors this week'll be gettin' one.'

'But I don't understand' said Elliott 'if it's not one of us, who ...'

'I don't know' Eamo cut him off. 'I don't know, an' I don't care. What I do care about is protectin' what we have. C'mon' he jerked his head in the direction of the gates 'back ta the station. Figure out what we're gonna do.'

. . . .

'**Foxtrot Tango to Mikey Lima, do you read me? Over. Foxtrot Tango. Come in Mikey Lima ...**'

'Mmmmph ...' a navy eye squinting, blinking against the harshness of the light. Head heavy. Rising. Blood surging.

'Mmmph.' Hands. Pushing down. Bulk. Pulling up. Squeezing out from behind the galley table. Steppedy-step, stagger, crash. Pots and pans clattering off the stove. The Midnight Sun through the open hatch. 'Fresh air' he mumbled 'fresh air' he grabbed the stairs. Blinding light. Head twisting in search of the crew. A small group, up at the front of the boat. Out on the ice, kneeling down, ice picks rising, falling, as they hacked hard.

'Hello?' Anthony called in their direction. No answer. Ice-picks rising, falling. 'Hello?' Anthony tripped on a rope and stumbled. 'Nick!' he swayed 'Nick!!' Rubbery rails. Over the side. Onto the hard. 'Nick!' he rolled and thrashed. Cold ice. Hands and knees. 'Nick' he staggered towards the crew at the front of the boat. 'Whas ... whassa-situation?' he squatted down beside Nick who was on his knees, shoulder pressed in against the side of the boat as he worked the ice. Silence. Nick hadn't answered him. 'Nick' he jugged at his jacket 'whassa-situation?'

'The situation, Anthony' said Nick, hacking hard at the ice 'is that you're shit-faced. Now why don't you walk it off while we try to sort this out.' Anthony glanced around at the rest of the crew. His eyes fell on a small silver hip flask lying on the ice. 'Seriously Anthony' said Nick 'just fuck off for a while. Walk it off, sleep it off, whatever it takes, just get very far away from me for the moment. I'm furious with you.'

'Alright, alright' Anthony held up his hands in mock surrender 'walk it off' bending down, he swept up the silver hip flask, stuffed it inside his oilskin jacket. Step-step stagger, then he zigzagged determinedly away from the boat, making his way across the hard ice, shielding his eyes against the blinding sun.

Behind him, from nowhere, as the crew continued to work, a furry whiteness rose up through a hole in the ice. White on white, soft black trace-lines outlining the polar bear's mouth and eyes. He stood for a moment, sniffing the air as he assessed the small crew working at the front of the boat, ice picks rising, falling. The bear's head turned in Anthony's direction. He studied the red oilskinned zig-zagging figure for a moment or two, then he began to move. Thick white legs, solid round paws, padding silently across the ice.

The padding became faster. Faster. Soft white paws, trotting fast on the hard ice, breaking now into a rolling gambolling loll, cantering silently behind Anthony as he zigzagged forward across the ice.

. . . .

Roger was back in his office. The Minister was due any minute to record a news interview about the opportunities the new licences would create. Something was niggling at him, something; he couldn't quite put his finger on it. *It's my station*. He'd been thrown by coming face to face with his own kidnapper. *It's my station*. How did Barrington's son go from Law into Pirate Radio? How did he get involved? Something wasn't adding up. *It's my station* the voice in his head again. Thoughts clouding. *Studio One*. He studied their application form. Something not sitting well with him at all. A thought hammering at the door but he couldn't unlock it. *Studio One … Studio One …* the intercom on his desk buzzed.

'The Minister's in reception' said Brid.

'Send him down to Studio Wuh …' a series of images flashed through Roger's mind. Elliott in the corridor the day they were gutting Studio One, standing outside the station with the courier, the *courier* was at the presentation today, the same courier he'd paid …

'What studio did you say Roger?' Brid's voice cut through his thoughts.

'Studio Wuh …' Roger's mind was racing.

'Studio One?' said Brid 'will I send them to Studio One?'

It's a great sound. It's as good as ours. Bobby's voice.

Where on earth did they come up with such a stupid name for a station? the familiar feeling he'd had when he'd first heard the name. 'Studio One' he felt the anger began to rise inside him

It's a great sound. It's as good as ours.

'That's because it is ours!!' he roared. 'That's our fucking equipment!!'

Sirens wailing in the distance. Long low slung whines, interspersed with high speed electronic heartbeats. Eamo lifted an eye.

'Three cars' he said 'that's a bank job.' The four of them were sitting in his office. Squirrel flicked up a blind and looked out on the street.

'Gettin' closer. Where's the nearest bank?'

'What are we going to do?' said Elliott.

'Keep goin' said Eamo 'just keep broadcastin.'

'I agree' said Iris. 'BBR and Rocket will come straight back on air if they don't get a licence …' she broke off as the sirens came wailing down Capel Street.

'Think you're right Squirr' Eamo stood up and flicked the blinds 'that's definitely somewhere close by' three squad cars came to a screeching halt outside the shop. 'Shyte' said Eamo. The sound of six car doors opening, closing; the rush of feet, a blur of blue as Gardaí uniform flooded the showroom. 'Alright. Take it easy' said Eamo 'stay calm. Sit down. All ah yis. Sit!' Iris and Elliott sat back on the couch. Squirrel leant against the filing cabinet. 'Let me do the talkin' Eamo moved back to his chair. They watched the Gardaí speak briefly to Lorraine then make their way towards the office. Elliott's stomach flipped as he caught sight of Roger taking up the rear.

Shit. His heart began to hammer.

'Eamon O'Rourke?' the Chief Inspector said.

'That's me' said Eamo.

'Eamon O'Rourke I have a warrant to search these premises' the Inspector put a piece of paper on Eamo's desk. 'We have reason to believe you are in possession of stolen equipment.

'That's him' Roger pointed at Elliott.

'Are you Elliott Barrington?' said the Inspector.

'Yes' Elliott swallowed. 'Yes I am.'

'Did you remove various pieces of radio equipment from the RTE premises on the 5th of April 1985?' the Inspector studied the list 'a sound desk, mixer, cart machines and' he looked up at Elliott 'soft furnishings including two sofas and a chair?'

'I …' Elliott began.

'The brother got the equipment for us' said Eamo. 'Has an electronics shop.'

'He's lying' Roger growled.

'Well there's a very easy way to solve this' said the Inspector. 'The equipment is registered to RTE. We need to examine the serial codes.'

'No problem' Eamo didn't miss a beat. 'C'mon' he pushed himself out of his chair 'we've nothin' ta hide.'

Carly was on-air as they entered the studio. Wide eyes from behind the glass.

'They're our sofas' Roger shouted. 'Those' he pointed at the leather couches 'are RTE sofas.'

'If you'll just take us to the equipment' the inspector said to Eamo. Eamo nodded and led them through to the studio.

'You'd better hope your Father can dig you out of this' said Roger to Elliott 'because you're in deep. Well?' he shouted as the Inspector emerged from the studio.

'It's your equipment' said the Inspector. He turned to Elliott. 'Elliott Barrington' he said 'I am arresting you ...'

Elliott Barrington, I am arresting you.

'... for theft. You do not have to say anything, but anything you say ...'

'Now hold on' Eamo shouting 'that proves nothin! The brother bought that equipment ...'

Elliott Barrington, I am arresting you.

'But anything you do say ...'

'How was he ta know it was stolen?' Eamo shouting.

Elliott Barrington, I am arresting you.

'My brother bought that equipment in good faith. This proves nothin!'

'You have the right to remain silent.'

The right to remain silent.

'Say nothin!!' Eamo shouted.

'Anything you do say may be taken down and used in evidence. Is there anyone you'd like to phone?' said the Inspector to Elliott.

Elliott Barrington I am arresting you.

'Max' Elliott heard himself say. 'I … I'd like to call my brother.'

. . . .

'You *stole* equipment?' Max shouted. 'From RTE!! Christ Elliott!! What were you *thinking!*' The two of them were sitting in an interview room in Store Street Garda Station.

'I know' Elliott felt sick. 'I know it looks bad.'

'Bad?' Max shouted. 'For fucks sakes Elliott, bad doesn't come close. Ingram's suing. He's suing for' Max studied the charge sheet 'larceny, loss of earnings, damages, assault, kidnapping … *kidnapping* … well clearly they've got that wrong. Obviously you didn't …' he broke off as he saw the expression on Elliott's face. 'Elliott' his skin paled. 'Elliott, who the fuck did you kidnap?'

'Roger Ingram' Elliott muttered.

'What? Elliott … why … *why* would you …'

'I didn't personally kidnap him' Elliott couldn't look Max in the eye. 'It was Eamo, when he shut the station down, when he jammed us.'

'Oh Christ' Max sat down. 'I don't *believe* this' bewilderment, lost eyes searching 'I'm going to have to call Dad.'

'No!' Elliott's head shot up. 'I don't want him involved.'

'Elliott, you could do time for this. This is serious' Max shook the charge sheet. 'I'm in over my head. You need Dad. You *need* him.' His face dropped. 'Fuck. He's in the Arctic. What date …' he studied the charge sheet again. 'The court hearing's set for the tenth. Dad's not due back until the fourteenth. He won't be back. I'll see if I can get it put out' he stood up. 'I can't believe you actually kidnapped … you know what; it doesn't matter. Stay here, I'll see if I can get bail' he pulled the interview room door shut behind him.

'What's the story with the rest ah them?' Eamo stared at the form that had been placed on the desk in front of him. They'd each been put in separate rooms for questioning.

'Elliott Barrington has made a full confession' the Inspector replied. Eamo's face remained still, impassive as he felt the

Inspector watch him for a reaction. 'They're going to charge him' said the Inspector 'but your son and the girl should be released shortly. It is your son isn't it?' the Inspector reached for the form and turned it around. 'They haven't filled this in properly' irritated, he ran his finger along a blank section. 'Who did this paperwork?' he looked up at the Garda standing by the door, then not waiting for an answer 'this should have been filled in.' He pulled a pen from inside his jacket. 'Your son is it?' his voice was matter of fact. 'Same surname' he tapped the form.

'Nephew' said Eamo. 'He's me nephew.'

'Nephew' Eamo watched the Inspector's fingers slice and pince the pen across the blank section. Slide, pince, slide and pince. The word 'nephew' appeared beside Squirrel's name. The Inspector's hand moved up the form. Slide, pince, slide and pince. The word 'Uncle' appeared beside Eamo's. 'Right, sign there and there' the Inspector X'd two sections before turning the form back around to face Eamo. 'Your nephew'll be another minute or two' he said. Eamo glanced at his watch. Quarter past five.

Ma said he'll be home at six.

'You can wait in reception if you like' said the Inspector.

Your son and the girl.

Stop shytin' on about it. You're not me Da.

'Mister Rourke?' the Inspector was waiting. Eamo looked at him. 'Would you like to wait for him? For your nephew?' Eamo looked at his watch again.

Twenty past five. 'You can wait in reception if you like' said the Inspector.

'Nah' Eamo stood up. 'Somewhere I hafta be.'

. . . .

'Foxtrot Tango to Mikey Lima, do you read me? Over. Foxtrot Tango. Come in Mikey Lima, what is your position ...'

The radio barking to the empty galley, the crew hacking, cracking, breaking ice, as off in the distance, red oilskins staggered, stumbled, zigzagged away, oblivious to the silent white furriness fast closing the distance between them.

You're an asshole Max on the Marina. Anthony stopped and squinted up at The Midnight Sun. Bright blue, brilliant sky.

I just came to wish you well.

The carpet shop's a front. Everyone knows that.

Elliott's face, staring out from the cover of the Times.

Your son was right. You are an asshole. You're a fucking asshole.

'Arrrr' a low growl behind him. Anthony turned, jerked, then staggered backwards, catching his heel. A hollow thump as his arse hit the ice. Squinting up, he shielded his eyes against the sun. The polar bear, an enormous male, towered high above him, standing tall on thick hind legs. Flashes of sunlight as huge paws clawed the empty air above his head, a low echoing growl as the shadow of the bear blocked his sun. *At twenty years of age, Mr Barrington is the youngest station owner tendering for a licence.* Dark eyes. Serrated black gums. Hot polar breath against cold Arctic air. The wide flat underside of two huge heavy black paws, cutting the still air with swift, soft sounds. *Mr Barrington set up his first station aged sixteen in his bedroom at home and broadcast from there for two years.* A low growl, a long echoing bray, filling the hollow arctic air then the sun hit his face as the shadow of the bear began to sink. *I just came to wish you well.* Shielding his eyes Anthony watched hind legs hinge, a white tower descending as thick fur collapsed, folding in on itself. Two big paws hit the ice, planting down as a wet snout leant in. Dark eyes level, meeting his own. *You're an asshole. You're a fucking asshole.*

Anthony reached for the silver hipflask stowed in his jacket and extracted it. 'I suppose' he said, unscrewing the cap with small careful turnings 'I suppose you think I'm an arse-hole as well?' Silence. 'Well' Anthony pressed the metal against his lips 'I am. I'm a fucking arse-hole' tilting his head he knocked back a shot.

The bear's head turned, his gaze shifting out towards the vast white cold surround. 'All this ice' Anthony gestured at the horizon. 'How do you live here?' he pressed the hipflask to his lips again. 'I

315

couldn't live here. I'll tell you what; you're a better man than I am.' To their right, the sound of water breaking, falling back; a white furriness rising, as a second smaller bear appeared a few feet away and began padding around on the ice. 'Ah-hah' Anthony pointed the hipflask 'a lady bear. That's why you hang around this God forsaken place.' They watched the female for a minute or two, soft whiteness rolling on the ice. 'I had a ladybear' said Anthony. 'I did you know. She was magnificent.' Tilting back his head he emptied the remainder of the whisky down his throat. 'She was something else' he gasped, wiping his mouth. Silence. The wind whipping. 'You want my advice?' Anthony twisted his head around to look up at the bear. Dark eyes staring down a long white nose. 'I'm going to give you a piece of advice' Anthony propped himself up on his elbow. 'I'm going to tell you something, and you should listen by the way, you really should, because people pay for my advice; they queue around the fucking block for it. Are you ready? This is good advice' he swayed, then steadied himself. 'Here it comes. This, is my advice, to you. Don't' he pointed at the female 'don't fuck with your ladybear. If you get one thing right in your life, just one thing, don't mess it up. Do you understand me?' he stared up at the big white face. 'What I'm telling you, and you need to be very clear about this. What I'm saying is, pay attention. Pay attention or you will lose her' his eyes began to flicker. 'You will lose her, and then you will be stuck' his voice grew faint 'in this shithole' he gestured at the ice 'and you will be on your own' his eyelids grew heavy. 'You will be alone' he slumped to the side 'and I'll tell you what' he lay down on the ice 'it's a cold place' he murmured 'it's a very cold place to be.' Somewhere in the distance, Nick's voice and the sound of gunfire. 'It's colder than here' he whispered, just before he passed out.

. . . .

Iris hung up the black payphone on the wall and walked back over to the wooden bench Squirrel was sitting on.

'My Dad's going to give us a lift.'

'What'd he say?' said Squirrel.

'Nothing' Iris took out her cigarettes. Squirrel frowned.

'What d'ya tell him?'

'Nothing' she stuck one in her mouth.

'Did he not ask?' said Squirrel. Iris shook her head, flicked the lighter, pulled, puffed. Squirrel stared at her.

'Does he not want ta know why you're in a cop shop?'

'No' staring ahead she blew out a thin line of smoke.

'Jaysus' said Squirrel 'my aul fella'd go through me for a short-cut. An' as for me Ma ...' he broke off. Silence.

'What are we going to do about Elliott?' said Iris.

'His brother said ta sit tight' said Squirrel. 'He's tryin' ta sort bail.'

'Fuck' said Iris 'I don't feel good about leaving him here. Where's Eamo?'

'Dunno' said Squirrel. 'Fella at the desk said he's gone about twenty minutes.'

Half an hour later the station door pushed open and Arthur, small and slight appeared around it, dressed in a navy mac, blinking behind his glasses under the fluorescent light of the station reception.

'Hey' Iris stood up and walked towards him, followed by Squirrel.

'Hiya Mister Henley' Squirrel kept his tone upbeat.

'Hello Squirrel. How are you?' Arthur shook Squirrel's proffered hand.'

'Not bad' said Squirrel as they followed him to the car.

'Elliott not with you this evening?

'No ... he's eh ... he's been detained' said Squirrel.

'Ah, well' Arthur opened the car door. Iris got in the front and Squirrel slid his long frame into the back seat. Arthur started the car and drove slowly out of the station yard.

'Nice jammer Mister Henley' Squirrel broke the silence.

'Yes. It is' Arthur flicked the gas converter to the left of the steering wheel.

'What's that yoke?' Squirrel straddled the centre of the back seat and hung forward between Iris and Arthur.

'It's a converter' Arthur explained, just as he had to Elliott the day they'd done the interviews in the Big Kebabby. 'There's a gas tank in the boot. See here?' he pointed at the switch 'flick left' he turned it 'we're on gas. Turn it right' he tapped the switch 'and we're onto petrol.'

'Where d'ya get that done?' Squirrel was fascinated.

'I did it myself.'

'Serious?' said Squirrel. 'I didn't know ya were a mechanic Mister Henley.'

'I'm not' Arthur replied. 'I just read a book' he turned the car left off Fairview and headed towards Donaghmede.

'Ya read a book?' said Squirrel. 'Ya read a book an' installed a gas tank in yer car? Fair play ta ya Mister Henley. I'd say ya save a bit ah cash on the ole juice?'

'You do' said Arthur. 'You save a lot of money.'

'Is it safe?'

'Well, I've been driving it like this for about a year' said Arthur 'and I've had no problems, though it has been acting up this week; there's smoke coming through when I switch to petrol; see …' he flicked the switch centre for a minute or two then turned it to the right. Almost immediately a smokey air filtered through.

'Jays, ya wanna be careful with that' Squirrel coughed. Arthur flicked the switch back to gas.

'It's probably something very simple' he said.

'Yeah' Squirrel glanced around the back seat. The smell of smoke was still quite strong. 'I don't think I'd drive it until ya get that sorted; could be dangerous Mr. Henley.'

'Probably a filter' said Arthur as they turned into Squirrel's estate.

'Yeah' Squirrel frowned, glancing around the back seat for clues. 'C'mere I've a load ah mates are mechanics' he said as Arthur pulled up outside his house. 'I'll get one over ta ya tomorrow.'

'Not at all' Arthur waved him away. 'I'll fix it. You're very good to offer.'

'I'd be worried about that smell' Squirrel began but Arthur was pulling away.

'I'll call you later' Iris called through the window as the car turned around.

'Yeah. Gimme a shout' Squirrel called after her. 'Let me know if ya hear from Elliott' he watched the Cortina cruise out the end of his road. Frowning, he turned to go into the house. That smell wasn't right. Not right at all. Reaching down for the handle on the gate he stopped as something caught his eye. Eamo's van was parked on the path. What was Eamo doin' here? Musta called in ta talk about what they were gonna do. Shyte. Belinda'd go mental if she knew he'd spent the last three hours in Store Street. Fuck. He hoped Eamo hadn't said anything.

The sound of shouting as he turned the key in the door. His Mother's voice, raised, angry. Shyte. Squirrel stood still and listened for a minute. Eamo shouting.

'I hafta tell him, I hafta.'

'You don't hafta do anything' Belinda's voice 'now get out. I want you outta this house ...' the voices broke off as Squirrel opened the living room door. Silence. His Mother, wild eyed, frightened. Eamo's eyes flicked briefly in his direction, then away again as he walked over to the fireplace.

'What's goin' on?' said Squirrel.

'Nothin'' Belinda ran a hand through her hair. 'Eamo was just leavin.' Eamo took out his cigarettes and lit one.

'Your Ma has somethin' ta tell ya.'

'Ignore him' said Belinda. 'Full ah shyte; always has been. Get out Eamo. Get outta my house.'

'If you don't tell him, I will.'

'Tell me what?' said Squirrel.

'No!' Belinda's voice shook. 'Get out Eamo. Get out now!'

'Tell him' said Eamo.

'Tell me what?' said Squirrel. Silence. 'Tell me what' he pushed.

'I'm yer Da' said Eamo.

'What?' said Squirrel.

'I'm yer Da.'

'No you're not' Squirrel gave a half laugh 'what are ya talkin' about? Me Da's me Da.' Silence. Eamo looked at him.

'I'm yer Da' he said it again.

'You're not' Squirrel felt control slip 'yer not, an' stop sayin' that, right?'

'Ask yer Ma' said Eamo. Squirrel looked at Belinda.

'Ma' said Squirrel 'Ma?' Silence. A small sob escaped from Belinda's throat and as she pressed her hand to her mouth, her face crumpled behind it and tears spilled over. 'Ma?' said Squirrel 'tell him Ma; tell him.' Silence. 'Ma?' Squirrel's throat was hurting him. 'Ma?' he swallowed. 'Tell him. Tell him will ya?' he stared at Belinda. Small, pale, defeated, she'd looked the way she had in the garden.

He's trouble Squirr. He's trouble. Something squeezing his heart; his chest tightening. 'Ma?' he said. 'Tell him for fucks sakes. Please Ma. Tell him.'

. . . .

Belinda. 1962. Her hen night. In town with the girls, and somewhere else in city, Darren with the boys. 'One for the ditch' Bernie dragged them to Leeson Street around 3am. Eamo at the bar. With a purple and orange carpet swatch and a niteclub owner who was having none of it.

'Where's Darren?' she'd shouted.

'Left him with the stripper' he grinned.

'Yeah, ya did alright' she'd laughed. 'What's that?' she pointed at the carpet swatch.

'A bad decision' said Eamo. 'Whaddayis havin?' He bought herself and the girls a bottle of champagne. Then he bought another one. 'Darren's a lucky man' he said five bottles in. Done very well for himself. Considerin' he's not the smart one in the family.' Belinda laughed.

'Jaysus Eamo. D'ya come outta yer Ma's fanny with that kinda

320

shyte? Probably did. Probably winked at the nurse an said *howeya gorgeous, cut that cord for me will ya? An' wash me willy; it's covered in goo.*' Eamo laughed when she said that. They'd all laughed. Herself, the girls and Eamo. They were still laughing two hours later when the girls called it a night.

'Don't worry' Eamo said to them 'I'll get her home.' She didn't remember leaving the club, she didn't remember the drive, she barely remembered the back of the van but she did remember the shame. Shame the next day, shame on her wedding day, shame, deep shame two months later when she told Darren she was expecting.

'Ma?' Squirrel's voice raw beside her. 'Tell him Ma. Please. Fucks sakes Ma will ya tell him?'

. . . .

The smoke started filtering out from underneath the bonnet as they turned off the Stiles road and began the journey down towards Finchbury Park.

'Dad' Iris frowned, sitting forward in her seat 'the car ...'

'Don't worry' Arthur rounded the corner 'it did this last week, it'll be gone in a minute or two.' The smoke grew thicker. Thick black smoke pouring from either side of the front of the bonnet as they drove down the road towards number twenty-six. Iris coughed.

'Dad, are you sure ...'

'Don't worry, it'll clear' Arthur coughed. The smoke began to filter inside the car, black clouds rising up from the floor beneath them. 'It did this last week' Arthur coughed again 'and it cleared after five minutes.' Bright orange flames burst up in front of the windscreen.

'Dad' Iris shouted. 'The car's on fire!'

'Oh my, oh dear ...' Arthur turned the flaming, smoking car into their driveway and pulled up handbrake.

'Get out!' Iris shouted. 'Dad! Get out of the car!'

'Oh dear ... oh my ...' Arthur unbuckled his safety belt and pushed the door open. Staggering back he stood staring in shock as thick black smoke enveloped the two of them. 'The tank ... ' Arthur was staring at the boot '... the gas tank' his voice wooden 'we can't let the flames ... the gas ...'

'What! *What!!*' Iris shouted, then realising there was nothing she could do, 'Dad! Get inside!' she shouted 'get inside Dad! Quick! Come on!' she pushed, pulled him 'come on!' dragging Arthur through the smoke they reached the front door. 'Call a fire-brigade! Mum!' she called up the stairs as Arthur ran to the phone in the kitchen 'have we got a fire extinguisher? Mum!!' she shouted. 'Mu-uuum!!'

The force of the explosion blew her down the hall. A high pitched sound as the living room window shattered, then the hallway lit up as shadows from the flames outside licked the walls. Iris lay dazed in the hall for several minutes. People shouting. An alarm going off. Buzzing in her ears. She looked down. Tiny fragments of glass in her lap, on her legs, all around her. Pushing herself up. The sound of neighbours, doors opening, shouts for a fire-brigade, her mother's voice somewhere in the distance.

'You're lucky to be alive' the ambulance man said an hour later as firemen hosed the flames under control. The three of them were standing on the road outside the house, wrapped in blankets as the Gardaí took statements from the neighbours. 'Two minutes longer in that car and you'd have been toast' the ambulance man unwrapped the blood pressure pad from Arthur's arm. 'If it wasn't for your daughter' he broke off as beneath him the ground shook and tremored. 'What ...' he stared at the ground which continued to shake. 'What the ...' he began as a long crack in the driveway opened up and ran towards the garage.

'The tower' Jackie whispered, pointing, and the three of them watched as the tower shuddered, shook, then slowly collapsed into itself, filling the night air with thick white cement clouds. Shouts as neighbours ran in panic and firemen stared at the rubble. 'Oh Arthur' Jackie's face filled with sympathy 'it must have been the explosion. It must have shaken the foundations. Oh Arthur, your tower, your lovely tower' she put her arms around him. Slipping off the blanket the ambulance man had wrapped around her, Iris turned and began walking up the road, smoke thick in her nostrils as she brushed cement talcum powder off her jacket. Reaching into the inside of her jacket she pulled out a flattened pack of twenty Major, extracted a cigarette, rounded it with her fingers, lit it, then continued walking up the road.

. . . .

A house door slamming. Black leathers kick-kick kicking. An engine revving. The door opening. Shouts and cries drowned by the engine. The sound of a bike weaving its way in, out, growling through the small series of roads; then as it turned onto the motorway the engine opened up and the growl became a roar. Loud. Louder. Wide. Chewing up the road, distance occurred, the roar swarmed, the sound narrowed, faded, and was gone.

. . . .

Elliott turned on the radio as soon as they got into the car and tuned it to Studio One. Nothing. Dead air.

'Where do you want to go?' said Max.

'Home' said Elliott.

'Howth?' said Max. Elliott shook his head.

'Capel Street. I want to see the station.'

'Elliott, I don't think you're going to have a station after this.'

'I know. I just want to go back Max. I need to see it.'

'Okay' Max started the car 'I'll drive you.'

. . . .

'Fare please' the bus conductor eyed the bloody cut on Iris's head, the black smoke mark on her cheek, the jacket covered in white cement dust.

'Seventy-five' she handed him the change. The conductor pushed up the seven, then the five. Winding the handle he tore off her ticket and handed it to her. Brown eyes staring ahead as the bus rattled towards O'Connell Street.

Elliott climbed the stairs, the station floating above him like an exotic fish tank. *Where are they? They could have waited for me. I'm the one taking the rap. I'm the one that could end up in jail here.* Something died inside him as he pushed the studio door open. Gone. Everything was gone. The studio lay bare before him, the outer room an empty shell. Sofas, coffee table, they'd taken it all. Elliott crossed the room, pushed the studio door open and stared in silence. Not one piece of equipment left, just wires and sockets hanging limp from the walls, patches of plaster falling from sections where the sound desk used to be. Only the bottle of vodka he'd placed on the cart machine the day of the protest remained, clear liquid in a clear glass, lying flat on its side on the purple orange carpet swirls. *It's over.* Elliott leant against the wall and slid to the floor. *It's over.*

Silence. Time passed, he wasn't sure how long, then from somewhere below, the sound of footsteps on the metal stairs. Up they came. Up. Up. Carpet brushing as the outer door pushed open and through the glass he watched Squirrel walk in. White-faced, he stood in the outer room for a minute, then he came into the studio, and stood in silence as he took in the empty room. Walking across the carpet, he leant his back against the wall, then slid down to sit on the floor. Neither of them spoke. *They've taken the equipment.* Elliott stared at the room. *They've taken the equipment.*

The outer door pushed again and Elliott watched Iris cross the room. Her jacket and one side of her face had a coating of light white dust and there was a cut on her forehead. She stared at the empty space, then she sat down on the carpet beside the vodka bottle. Silence for several minutes, then one by one they spoke.

'He blew up the car.'

'They've taken the equipment.'

'Me Uncle's me Da.'

'What?' Elliott and Iris.

'Your Uncle?' said Iris 'what *Uncle?*' she stared at him. Squirrel rolled his head to look at her. Hot, hurt eyes; hollow sunken sockets. 'Eamo?' said Iris *'Eamo?'* Squirrel looked away. 'Eamo's your *father*!' she said.

'How do you know?' said Elliott 'how do you ...'

'He told me' Squirrel stared ahead.

'Are you sure?' Elliott struggled. 'What about your Mum?'

'She told me' Squirrel's voice was raw. 'She told me an' all.' Silence. Elliott and Iris exchanged glances. Silence stretching on.

'Are you sure ...' Iris began.

'Course I'm fuckin' sure' anger vibrated as Squirrel's face hardened. 'I need a drink' he pushed himself up off the ground. The door to the studio pushed open and Eamo appeared around it.

'Squirr ...' he began. Squirrel didn't look at him. He pushed a hand through his hair, circling it in an agitated fashion.

'C'mon' he said to Elliott and Iris.

'Squirr ... son ... please ...' Eamo stepped forward. A blur of black leather, the splintering crunch of bone as Squirrel's fist connected with Eamo's nose. A toppling of grey fleck as Eamo hit the ground.

'That's for me Da' Squirrel's voice clenched as he pulled Eamo up by his jacket. 'An' I don't mean you' he shook him hard then threw him back on the floor.

'C'mon' he said over his shoulder as he headed for the door.

. . . .

Pint. Short. Pint. Short. Another short. A double. Two pints. Two doubles. Back passengers in a speeding car, they watched him. The pub closed.

'Berlin' Squirrel pointed at the door, and the three of them left.

. . . .

'... Pulling on the boots and threading up the laces, Shaving our heads and strapping on the braces, There you have a skinhead looking for a fight, Skinhead skinhead running through the night, making lots of trouble, starting lots of fights ...'

White skulls. Hard white shaved heads. A sea of white skulls hammering in short, tight, angry jerking motions.

'What's his problem?' said Mick as Squirrel pushed past him on the door without saying hello.

'Bad day' Iris eyed the 'Oi!' posters either side of the door. Mick's eyeballs slid left, then right.

'He'll have a worse night if he starts anything in there. Tommo' he shouted at a bouncer lurking by the ticket desk. 'Watch him' he stabbed a finger in the direction of Squirrel's retreating figure, the sea of skulls parting then closing, swallowing the black leather jacket, blonde spike tips bobbing on the surface as they pushed their way towards the bar.

Anger building. Like a vast sea pulling and stretching back, as the jaws of a tidal wave opened wide.

'Let's go' Iris shouted. 'I don't want to stay here' she glanced at the scrum on the dance floor.

'Well fuck off home then' Squirrel shouted. He reached for his pint, raised then sank it in a mouthful of swallows; a bang of the empty glass on the counter as he signalled to the barman for another.

'Why don't we go back to the station?' Elliott tried another tack.

'Station's closed' Squirrel shouted 'we don't *have* a station' he pushed Elliott. 'There *is* no station!' he pushed him harder and Elliott felt himself slam against something solid.

'What's your problem?' metal eyes in a bullet shaped head as a hand slammed him like a tennis ball back against Squirrel.

'What's *your* fuckin' problem?' Squirrel shouted at the skinhead, then the two of them lunged.

'Elliott' Iris screamed. 'Stop them' she shouted as Squirrel disappeared. Elbows, fists, shouts from the dance floor, running, jumping, flying kicks. Elliott was pulled, punched, then thrown against a wall opposite the fighting. The music stopped and the house lights came up. Bouncers swarming, glasses, bottles, blood. The Gardaí arrived. Elliott couldn't see Squirrel. He'd disappeared.

They found him outside. Sitting on the ground, his back to the wall of the club, long leather legs stretched out in front of him. His lip was bleeding, and his right eye was swollen. A bouncer stood over him. Squirrel staring ahead. Glassy eyes. Pressing his tongue against his bloody lip.

'Are you alright?' Iris squatted down beside him. Squirrel didn't answer.

'Come on' she tugged on his sleeve 'let's go.'

'There's that cunt' bullet head shouting from the door of the Club. 'There's that fuckin' cunt ...' his voice fading as a Garda and a bouncer restrained him. Mick walked over.

'Get him outta here' he said to Elliott and Iris. 'I'll hold onta this lot, but get him outta here.'

'There's a bottle of vodka in the Station' it was the only way Elliott could think of getting Squirrel to move. Silence.

'Squirrel?' said Iris softly. Squirrel stood up, turned, and without a word began walking up the road.

'Where are you going?' Elliott called after him. Squirrel didn't answer. They followed him. Left off the Quays, onto Capel Street, up past the showroom, around the corner and in the back of the warehouse. 'Hey Reggie' they watched Squirrel climb the stairs to the station. 'C'mon' said Elliott 'we'd better stick with him.'

'Where is he?' Iris frowned as they surveyed the empty studio a few minutes later. Elliott scanned the carpet.

'Well he's got the vodka with him wherever he's gone' he said. Somewhere overhead a door banged. Iris looked up.

'He's on the roof' her face paled. 'He's on the roof.'

Squirrel was hunched over the wall a few feet away from the aerial when they climbed out onto the roof.

'Squirrel?' said Iris as they walked across to him. Squirrel didn't answer.

'Are you okay?' said Elliott. Squirrel didn't answer. Iris and Elliott looked at each other. 'Squirrel' Elliott stopped, not sure what to say.

'What?' Squirrel turned around to face them. 'What!' he challenged, then when they didn't reply 'look at ya' his face was hard, cold 'always *at* me' he shouted 'where's Squirrel, get Squirrel, Squirrel'll fix it; well I can't fix this' he raged. They stared at him. 'Ya don't know what ta say, do ya?' he laughed. 'Look at yis; standin' there waitin' for the answer. Waitin for me' he laughed 'waitin' for *me*, ta give *you* the answer ta *my* problem. My problem' the laugh became manic 'my problem, an' yis are standin' there' he threw back his head and laughed, a raw, rasping sound, 'standin' there' he laughed 'waitin' for the answer' the laughter died. 'Well there is no answer' his face collapsed in white exhaustion. Turning his back to them he leant over the wall. 'There's no answer ta this' he stared out at the city.

Elliott and Iris looked at each other.

'Look, Squirrel …' Elliott began.

'Ah fuck off will ya!!' Squirrel raged 'just fuck off!! Get away from me. I don't want ya, I don't need ya, just fuck off!!' his face flamed.

'We just want to make sure you're okay …' Iris began.

'Okay? Fuck you' Squirrel put the vodka bottle down on the ground, turned and began walking towards the aerial. 'Fuck you' he said.

'Squirrel' Iris shouted 'where are you going?'

'Far away from you as possible' Squirrel shouted over his shoulder. 'Top ah the world Ma' the raw laugh again 'top ah the fuckin' world' he threw out his arms as he reached the base of the aerial.

'Elliott!!' Iris screamed as they watched Squirrel take a drunken jump at the first rung of the aerial 'stop him' she shouted as they watched Squirrel fall back, then get up and take a second running jump. 'Don't let him go up there' she shouted. 'He'll kill himself.' Elliott picked up the vodka bottle and walked across to Squirrel.

'Let's just go back downstairs and have a drink okay?' he said as Squirrel swung wildly at the bottom rung of the aerial. 'Let's just go back down to the station and ...'

'There is no station' Squirrel jumped again and this time his hands locked onto the bottom pole. 'There's no fuckin ...' he began to pull himself up.

'Elliott!!' Iris shouted. 'Stop him! Don't let him go up there!!' Elliott dropped the vodka bottle and jumped up, wrapping his arms around Squirrel's leather legs.

'Let go ah me!!' Squirrel shouted as the two of them swung in the breeze 'let go ya prick!' They swung, struggled, swung some more, then Elliott felt Squirrel's grasp release and his weight fall down on top of him as the two of them hit the ground. 'Fuck ya' Squirrel rolled and punched and kicked 'fuck ya! fuck ya!' he stood up, then shoved Elliott hard, knocking him back on the ground before he could get up. 'Don't make me hit ya, don't make me *fuckin'* hit ya' savage anger as he turned and made for the aerial once again. Elliott scrambled to his feet.

'Don't go up there' he shouted 'don't ...' a loud smack as Squirrel turned and punched him hard, knocking him back down again.

'Ow!' Elliott whispered 'ow, fuck' he rubbed his jaw as he staggered to his feet. His eyes fell on the bottle of vodka lying on the ground. Holding his jaw with one hand, he picked up the bottle and he walked across to where Squirrel was swinging wildly again at the bottom run of the aerial. He hesitated for a split second, then just as Squirrel's hands latched onto the bottom rung, Elliott jumped up, raised the bottle high, brought it down hard and sharp on the back of Squirrel's head and watched it shatter and spray. Nothing for a minute. Silence. Elliott looked at the broken top of the bottle in his hand and Squirrel's long leather frame creaking as it swung off the bottom rung of the aerial. 'Squirrel?' he said 'Squirrel?' Then he watched the tight white knuckles relax, release, and six feet of leather and bones fell back on top of him for the second time.

The starry night sky. A dead weight across his chest. Winded. *Can't breathe, can't breathe.* The smell of leather. Cold leather. Squirrel's hair in his eyes. Blonde spikes prickling at his nose.

'Elliott' Iris's face hovering above the two of them. Something sticky, wet, warm on his face.

'Iris, he's bleeding. He's ...' Elliott rolled Squirrel's frame over, and pulled himself out from underneath. 'Squirrel' he shook him 'Squirrel' cold fear as he looked at Squirrel's pale white face. 'Get an ambulance' he heard himself say. 'Iris, get an ambulance. Get Reggie. Get Reggie quick!'

Sirens for the second time in twenty-four hours. Different this time. High. Loud. Fast. Urgent. The ambulance sped towards Beaumont. Inside, Elliott sat frozen. Iris talking to the ambulance men. Silence. Numbness. Nothing. *Squirrel. Christ. Squirrel.* Elliott stared at the white face on the trolley beside him. Corridors. Shiny hospital corridors.

I don't believe in God.

I do.

Double doors falling back. Double door one. Push. Double door two.

He takes the best ones first. Ambulance men. Iris. Nurses. A doctor.

When I die. The trolley disappearing. Blonde spikes, black leather, a trolley wheeled away. *When I die, I want heaven ta look like this an' I want God ta be a black bird.*

Death lurks in hospitals. It hangs in the shiny clean corridors, where patients shuffle in dressing gowns and slippers; where families sit and wait for hours, where cleaners use chemicals to soften its scent. But Death pushes through, blending with the bleach, waiting patiently in line. Which is fair enough. Death, like the doctors, the nurses, has a job to do. Death is on call.

Death does its rounds, checking up; taking notes, taking lives. But only when the time is right.

They sat either side of him, just as they had the day they met. No machines this time. Just the three of them in a small room, Squirrel on the trolley.

'He'll be alright' said Iris. 'He will. He has to' she looked at the sleeping figure between them. 'He has to' she said.

Different things make you grow up. Nobody expects the young to die, especially the young. Death to youth is continents, worlds, light years away. But blink and it's there, blink and they're gone. The death of a friend. *The death of a friend*. Different things make you grow up.

. . . .

' ... Beaumont Hospital Radio, Dave K with you all the way to 6am. Funny old week for radio; eighteen stations closing as the Pirates all go forward to compete for a licence. Very quiet out there tonight. Dedicating this to the Pirates, from anyone who ever stuck an aerial onto a garden shed, to the stations who brought music into our homes, our cars, offices, shops, factories, hospitals; for being with us through good times and bad, for the music, the laughter, the chat, for Pirates everywhere out there tonight, this is for you, this is Queen, Radio Ga Ga ...'

'Your friend is fine' a nurse walked into the room with a large manilla envelope in her hand 'well as fine as someone with that amount of alcohol in their system can be' she looked at Squirrel asleep on the trolley.

'Why won't he wake up?' said Iris.

'An elephant wouldn't wake up if you pumped that much drink into their system' said the nurse.

'But the bottle; I smashed the bottle...' Elliott began.

'There's no swelling on the brain' the nurse pulled an X-ray from the envelope 'his scans are clear; and by the way, if there was swelling, it'd be down to the alcohol, not the bottle being smashed over his head. You would have had to hit a completely different part of his head for him to suffer any kind of serious damage.'

Elliott swallowed. Blood draining. Something falling back. He put his head in his hands. 'You did him a favour' he heard the the nurse say 'he would have killed himself if he'd gone up that aerial.' When Elliott didn't reply she knelt in front of him. 'He's fine' she said 'he is absolutely fine.' From the trolley, Squirrel began to snore.

'See?' the nurse smiled as the snoring got louder 'not a bother on him. We'll keep him here tonight' she said 'just in case. You can pick him up in the morning.'

'Can we wait?' said Elliott.

'We don't want to leave him' said Iris.

'Well' the nurse looked around the small bare room 'there's no beds.'

'Doesn't matter' said Iris.

'We'll just sit here' said Elliott 'we'll just sit with him.

. . . .

'Foxtrot Tango to Mikey Lima, do you read me? Over. Foxtrot Tango. Come in Mikey Lima, what is your position ...'

When he came to, Anthony was being slapped, harder he felt than was entirely necessary, about the face. Whack! Whack! Whack!

'Anthony! Anthony!' Nick's voice shouting, blurred foggy figures floating in front of him, a long arm with a hard hand rhythmically slapping his face left to right. 'Anthony!' Nick shouted.

'Yes–yes, I'm Anthony! Stop hitting me!!' Anthony pushed Nick's hand away. 'Christ. My *head!*' he felt the heat rise in his cheeks as the blood in his brain seemed to fall somewhere behind his ears.

'Okay, take it easy' Nick stopped him from trying to sit up 'deep breaths, here we go' Anthony felt a glass of water pressed into his hands. 'That's it. Sip slowly' Nick instructed. 'Richard. Get him a cup of hot coffee, *no whisky*, just the coffee; make a pot.'

'What the fuck' Anthony put his hand to his head.

'I'll tell you what the fuck' said Nick. 'You, out there on that ice' he pointed at the porthole 'rat-arsed Anthony, fast asleep beside a ginormous polar bear.'

'Christ' Anthony rested his head in his hands. 'Christ' a searing pain slicing through.

'Here' Frankie pushed a small tin mug with hot black coffee into his hands.

'You're lucky to be alive' Nick was still annoyed 'seriously Anthony, what were you thinking?'

'Sorry to interrupt' Tiny pushed his way into the cabin, 'this just came in' he held out a piece of paper, 'I think you'd better have a look at it' he said to Anthony.

FAX

To:	Anthony Barrington
From:	Max Barrington
Date:	19th August 1986
Subject:	Elliott

Dad

Elliott stole radio transmission equipment from RTE to set up a radio station in partnership with three other people. RTE have discovered this and have taken an action. Larceny, loss of earnings, illegal broadcast, misrepresentation. Justice Thompson presiding. Extremely concerned. Delay application refused. If you get this please contact me.

Max

PS – There is also a kidnapping charge – I will explain when we speak.

Anthony stared at the fax in silence, his face set as he read, then re-read it.

. . . .

'Where is he?' Katie was standing in front of the showroom counter.

'He's in the flat' said Elliott. 'I'm going back up to him on my lunch-break.'

'Me Mam's up the walls' said Katie. 'Second night he hasn't been home.'

'I know' said Elliott 'but I don't know what to do. He's not talking. He's just sitting there. He hasn't said a word.'

They'd brought him home from the hospital the day before.

'I'm not goin' to me gaff' was all Squirrel had said as they got into the taxi.

'Okay' Elliott glanced at Iris 'well why don't you stay with me? Crash in the flat for a while; see how you feel later on.' Squirrel nodded, leant his head against the window and stared out. He didn't speak for the rest of the journey, he didn't speak when they got to the flat, and twenty-four hours later he still hadn't said a word.

'He's pretty upset' said Elliott to Katie.

'Yeah, well he's not the only one' Katie looked annoyed. 'Me Mam's in bits. I'm gonna hafta tell them where he is.'

'Fair enough' Elliott nodded. 'Here' he handed Katie a key 'that's the spare to the flat; if your Mum or Dad want to drop in. I should be there, but just in case.'

'Thanks' Katie took the key.

Squirrel was in the same position Elliott had left him when he pushed the flat door open just after lunch. Back to the wall, sitting on the floor. Staring ahead. Flat, vacant, empty eyes.

'Katie called in' said Elliott. Squirrel didn't reply. 'Look, Squirrel ...'

'I don't want ta talk.'

'Okay' Elliott sat down on the bed 'okay, fair enough, I can understand that' he looked at his clothes which were still staple-gunned to the wall. 'Tell you what. You don't have to talk. You don't have to say a word, but maybe you'll just listen to me for a minute. Not for long. I'll keep it short, but there's something I want to say, and then I'll leave it at that.' Silence. Flat blue eyes staring down at the carpet. 'Do you remember that day in studio?' said Elliott. 'When we were watching Rachel?' Silence. 'You asked me about my Mum. You asked me how long it was since I'd seen her, and you said you couldn't imagine not speaking to your Mother for three days never mind three years.' Squirrel didn't reply. 'Well, it's day two' said Elliott. Silence. 'You just started day two' he watched the bent leather figure, the broken face, the empty eyes.

'Don't let this take you over' Elliott heard himself say. 'Because it will. Trust me. It will consume you. It will define you. It will become who you are. And what you are, is lost. You will flounder, and you will go nowhere. You, the person who lectured me about not moving forward. You will grind to a halt and you will go nowhere until you sort it out. And three days will turn into three years very quickly. Believe me, when I tell you that the time will pass very quickly.' Silence. The sound of a key scratching at the the door below. A lock turning. Footsteps making their way up the staircase. A movement by the door, then Darren appeared around it. Elliott stood up. 'I'll see you later' he said to Squirrel.

Darren watched Elliott shut the door. He glanced at Squirrel on the ground, then pressing a hand to his face he sighed, the air making a soft hissing sound as he blew through his fingers. He walked to the window and stared at the street outside.

'Your Ma's very upset' he said. Squirrel didn't reply. Darren walked over to where Squirrel was sitting and squatted down in front of him. 'Listen ta me' he said. 'Are ya listenin?' Squirrel stared ahead. 'I knew about this' said Darren. Squirrel's head came up. 'I've always known' Darren was matter of fact. 'Your mother and I squared this off a long time ago. About six months after ya were born.' Squirrel stared at him. 'We sorted it out' said Darren 'an' we put it behind us.'

'Ya put it *behind ya?*' Squirrel's voice was hoarse.

'I'm not *sayin,* it was easy' Darren's voice tightened 'I'm not *sayin* it didn't take time, but we sorted it. We sorted it because we love each other. 'Sides' he looked away 'your Mother wasn't the only one outta order that night.' Silence. 'I woke up with a stripper the next morning.' Squirrel stared at him. 'Hadn't a clue where I was, hadn't a clue who she was; no idea what we'd done. Coulda been me got someone pregnant. Shit meself yer Ma'd find out. Convinced I was gonna lose her. Worried about it for weeks. So when she told me …' he broke off. 'Oh when she told me' his voice filled. 'I'm not sayin' it was easy' raw eyes looked out at Squirrel 'I'm not, but we sorted it. We sorted it because we love each other.' Silence. 'Me own brother' Darren's face tightened. 'Tommy had ta drag me off him. Didn't speak to him for nearly five years.'

'Why did ya?' Squirrel felt the anger return.

'Because family's family' said Darren 'because one ah me mates lost a brother, an' that was a wake-up call, but mostly because one day I looked at you sittin' on me lap, an' I realised he'd never have what I had with ya. I'm yer Da' solid blue eyes, *'I'm,* yer Da' a firm, steady voice. 'I don't give a fuck about blood or genetics or any ah that shyte. You're *my* son, an' I'm *your* Da. I've been yer Da since the day we took ya home from that hospital an' *nothin'* is ever gonna change that. Look at me' he said. 'Look at me. I *watched you* come inta this world. I held ya in my arms. D'ya understand me? Do ya?' blue eyes fixed and holding. Squirrel swallowed, nodded.

The room fell silent again. Faint noises from the showroom below, telephones ringing, the low murmur of voices, the sounds of the street outside. Darren stood up and walked to the window.

'Your Ma's very upset' he said. Workmen drilling on the road, the steady thud–thud–thud of a jack hammer, interspersed with woodpecker drilling. 'She's in an awful state' said Darren. Whistles and shouts as a delivery truck was directed into a parking spot. Silence. Leathers creaking.

'I'll eh …' Squirrel pushed himself up off the ground 'I'll go on over an' see her.'

'Good man' Darren's voice was gruff. 'Good man. I'll catch ya later.'

'Catch ya later Da' said Squirrel.

'Good afternoon, it's RTE, the time now is one o'clock, the headlines with Paul McCabe. Government awards two new local radio station licences, and reasserts the drive to close all Pirates. Businessman John Hegarty promises to change the face of Irish radio and the consortium awarded the second licence confirm they will recruit disc jockeys from existing Pirate stations …'

'Twelve ninety-five' Iris wrapped the vibrator in three layers of tissue paper, before tearing a black and gold paisley plastic bag off the roll beside her. 'Thanks' taking the twenty she put the package in the bag, and handed the customer their change. The door to the shop pushed open.

'Hey' said Elliott.

'Hey. How is he?'

'Okay I think' Elliott shut the door behind him. 'I left him with his Dad. Are you on a break soon?'

'Ten minutes.'

'D'you want to have a drink?' Elliott jerked his head in the direction of the pub.

'Sure' she said 'that'd be …' the changing room door opened and Thuperman stepped out, a black rubber suit gently bouncing over his arm, a hollow headless, footless body. Making for the counter, he stopped as he caught sight of Elliott.

'Hello' Elliott felt embarrassed as he remembered the small wet lips beneath his own, the cold clammy face, the panicked, frantic feeling and the huge relief that had flooded through when the limp body had begun to breathe again. 'How are you?' he smiled. Silence. Nothing. Not even a flicker of recognition as Thuperman stared right through him.

'I'll take thith pleathe' he turned to Iris and handed her the suit.

'Sure' Iris darted an apologetic glance in Elliott's direction, as she began to fold and wrap. Elliott watched Thuperman reach inside his jacket pocket and extract a slim, well worn leather wallet. Clean, manicured hands pulling out crisp ten pound notes. Small, circular metal rimmed glasses, neatly trimmed white hair, pink skin, sharp eyes counting, then folding the cash. As Iris pushed the package down into a bag, the small head lifted, silver hair turned and Elliott felt the eyes rest upon him. Silence. Nothing. Just a small, cold, hard stare.

'I'll em … I'll see you over there' Elliott said to Iris, nodding his head in the direction of the pub.

'Sure' Iris nodded.

'Bye' said Elliott to Thuperman. The small pink face stared at him for a moment or two, then silver hair turned back to Iris.

'What a prick' Elliott said as Iris sat down opposite him of him ten minutes later. 'He didn't even have the courtesy to say hello.'

'He's embarrassed' Iris shrugged off her jacket and sat back against the seat.

'He's rude' said Elliott. 'Either that or he's forgotten who I am.'

'No' Iris shook her head 'he knows exactly who you are; you saved his life, remember? He just wants to forget the whole thing happened. He's private Elliott' she arched her back and stretched 'he barely talks to me and when he does it's only about what he's going to buy.' Elliott studied her for a minute. Her hair was starting to grow out. She'd stopped shaving the sides. Stubble had grown, stretching out into a soft, short down.

'What?' she was looking at him.

'You're growing your hair.'

'Yeah, well. Things change' she shrugged, reaching inside her jacket and extracting a tobacco pouch. Elliott looked at her.

'They do' she said. 'Things. People. The station. Inevitable really' she'd pulled out an orange Rizzla packet, and was busy sticking two thin white cigarette papers together.

'What is?'

'Change' she separated a small clutch of yellow and brown tangled tobacco strands. 'Nothing's forever' she teased and pulled them along the white Rizzla base she'd laid out on the table.

'Nothing?' he said.

'Nothing' she tidied the ends.

'Not even us?' he watched her face for this was the real reason he'd asked her to come for a drink. Not to talk about Thuperman, her hair, the station, Squirrel, not to talk about any of it. He wanted one last shot. One last sober, cards on the table, nothing to lose, shot. He watched her face. Skin pausing. Hands hovering, hesitant as she held up the small white tobacco filled package just below her chin.

'There is no us' she said to the Rizzla.

'Doesn't mean there can't be' his voice, soft.

'Doesn't mean there can' fingertips starting to press and roll.

'Says who?'

'Says me' but she didn't sound convinced. 'You have this fantasy Ellliot, this idea of us … of me' she stopped. 'You have this …'

'What do you want to drink?' the stool scraping as he rose abruptly.

'Beck's' her voice flat, disappointed. 'Thanks' she added.

He stood at the bar and ordered the drinks. In the mirror behind the optics, he watched her roll, lick, then light the cigarette.

'Two-twenty' the barman pushed a bottle of Beck's and a pint in front of him.

'Thanks' Elliott handed him a fiver. He picked up the pint then he stopped. Put it back down. He picked up the bottle and began a series of small, fast precise movements.

'Two-eighty' the barman's disapproval extending across the counter as he handed him the change.

'Hang onto it' Elliott picked the bottle back up. 'Sorry about the mess' he took his pint and turned away.

Boney knuckles cupping a small lighter. Rizzla paper thin, delicate between her lips as she pulled. Mellow tobacco filtering through. Soft smoke at the back of her throat. She stared at the table. Closed her eyes. Exhaled slowly. The sound of a bottle placing down. She opened her eyes, reached forward. Stopped. Stared at the bottle. The labels had been ripped off, front and back; only one or two small stubborn white strips remained. Her eyes travelled up to the neck, where silver foil had been pushed back, peeled away, rough trails of glue left in its wake. She looked up. Inky eyes.

'It's not the idea of you' he said. She stared up at him. 'It was' he said. 'At the start. I used to sit on the bus and watch you. Watch you, think about you, wonder about you; every time I saw you, you'd float around in my head for weeks, and then, just as I was beginning to forget, you'd appear again. The idea of you, shit Iris, I *lived* for the idea of you.' Silence. 'And then one day' he shrugged 'I woke up in hospital. Faced the reality of you.' She grinned at this point, a small laugh escaping despite herself. She ducked her head. Stared at the floor. 'And guess what?' Elliott reached for then gently tugged, a Mohican spike.

'What?' an upside down voice.

'The reality was a million times better. The reality' he stroked the side of her head. 'I don't care about the station' fingertips circling soft new hair. 'I don't Iris. I care about you. I care about us. If there is an us. I want to know, I *need* to know, that you're not going to just walk out of my life now that this is over.' Spikes shifting. Moving up. 'Because I want you in it. I want you in my life. And not just as a friend.' Brown eyes. 'I mean … I'll take you as a friend if that's all you want, but it's not what I …'

'Shut up' she said. 'Close the mic.'

'Close it *for* me' he said. Brown eyes smiling. Coming closer. Blurring. 'Definitely better than the idea of you …' he began.

'Ssssh' soft lips pressing. Soft, sweet lips.

'Much better …'

'Ssssh' a warm mouth, silencing him. Silence. Hot, soft, sweet silence.

. . . .

The 31B rattled along the coast road. Elliott, sitting upstairs, rested his head against the window and watched the peninsula get nearer. Sun shining through the glass, hot on his hair, warming his skin. Gentle vibrations from the window, buzzing his head as he leant on the glass. Eyes drifting, he watched the mountain as Howth drew closer.

An empty echo as he turned the key and pushed the door. Soft Converse on clean tiles as he walked through the hall and into Anthony's study. The familiar smell of polished wood as he sat down behind the walnut desk. Pulling the phone towards him, his eyes fell on the silver framed photos sitting to the left of the desk. Max and himself on the beach in Nantucket. His parents skiing, a long time ago, white peaked mountains in the background. He looked at the skiing photo for several minutes, then pulling away he reached for the rolodex, slowly flipping through until he came to the card he was looking for. Easing it left, then right, he slipped it off the plastic teeth, stared at it for a minute or two, then picked up the handset. Something surfacing. He punched in the number and the phone began to ring. Rushing, surging, surfacing up. The receiver picked up at the other end.

'Hello?' the compressed sound of a long distance call. Up he came. Up. Up. 'Hello?' said the voice. Surfacing, surging, crashing through.

'Hey Mum …' the air, the sea, sky, fresh, fresh air, 'hey Mum' he said 'it's me.'

. . . .

'I think I might move out' Iris was sitting in the kitchen with Jackie.

'Why?' Jackie's face fell. 'Why would you do that sweetheart?'

'Don't know' Iris shrugged 'just think it might be time, you know …' she trailed off. 'I'm nearly twenty.' She looked at the remains of the kitchen wall and beyond it, the wooden frame Arthur had erected for the new conservatory.

'Twenty' big soulful eyes as Jackie looked at her. 'I remember when you were a little girl; playing out there with Frank' her eyes ghosted back and suddenly she looked small and vulnerable.

'I'll visit' said Iris. 'I'm not going to go too far' she leant across the table and squeezed her mother's hand.

'Where will you go?' said Jackie.

'Town.'

'Is it for work? To be near the insurance company?'

'No' Iris shook her head 'I just think it's time. 'Actually' she hesitated 'I might leave insurance. I think I might try for a job in radio.'

'Radio' Jackie's eyes opened wide. 'Radio, oh you'd be fantastic at radio; look at all your music; now that's *much* more like the kind of job you should have.' Her face fell. 'Do you think it'll be hard to get a job? You don't have any experience sweetheart. I know you like music but you've no experience of working in a radio station.' Iris smiled.

'I'll figure it out.'

'You will' said Jackie 'you've always been very capable; anything you put your mind to, you do it. You're like your Father that way I think.'

'Mmm' Iris looked at the conservatory frame. 'Possibly.'

. . . .

Elliott walked up Talbot, crossed O'Connell and headed down Henry Street. Lighter. Everything seemed lighter, brighter. And different. He felt different. Released. Such a complete release. He ran a hand through his hair, stretched his arms up and over his head, felt the breeze around his waist as his T-shirt lifted. He lit a cigarette as he rounded the corner onto Capel Street.

Half way down the street he spotted them. Two long legs stretched out on the path in front of the door to the apartment. Long, slender legs, red tartan trousers flowing down into tightly laced docks. Mohican spikes bent in concentration as boney knuckles co-ordinated Rizzla'd fingers, poking, coaxing tobacco. A large army bag slumped on the path, strapped and bulging, a stripey jumper hanging out.

'Are you homeless?' he said.

'Depends' she grinned.

'On what?' Elliott watched her roll the Rizzla tight. Cheekbones lifting, smile stretching as a soft pink tongue licked the length of the paper.

'On whether or not you want me to move in with you' the grin widened as she rolled and pressed the cigarette tight. Elliott reached down, took her hand, pulled her to her feet and stared into her eyes.

'What do *you* think?' he cupped her cheek. 'What do you think?' pulling her close. 'What do you think?' he kissed her.

'Disgrace' said an old lady as she walked past the couple in the doorway.

'Carryin' on like that' said her friend beside her.

'Have they no homes to go to?' the voices trailed off down the street.

. . . .

'... And that's the news; sport and weather are next. Well, they think it's all over; it is now. A low point for Eoin Hand as last night's 4-1 Lansdowne Road defeat means Ireland are officially out of the World Cup. Calls for Hand's resignation as rumours that the FAI are already in talks with a U.K. manager continue to circulate. Finally, baton down the hatches. Northerly winds of over one hundred miles an hour expected in the next twenty-four hours ...'

Bodies clambering, scrambling, all hands on deck as down below the galley radio picked up a signal on the long wave. The wind whistling high in the rigging as the gale they'd hoped for whipped up around them. Jib in, full genoa, jib out. Eight and a half knots, four thousand miles, five men, seven weeks. A small boat pushing home.

Capel Street. Early morning sun warming sleepy red brick. Arms, legs, tangled in the sheets. The softness of her. Smooth polished skin, shoulder blades jutting out like small finely carved fins. He ran his hands the length of her back, felt it dip, rise again as he cupped the cheeks of her bottom. Her head pressed in against his chest as she slept. Content, steady breath, her back rising, falling. Deep sleep. The softest of snores. He closed his eyes and smiled.

Donaghmede. The baby, covered in porridge.

'State ah you' Squirrel on the way out the door, a slice of toast in his mouth. Grabbing a cloth. Hot water under the tap. Squeezing it out. 'C'mere' fine blonde hair, a tiny head, struggling left, right, beneath the cloth. Shiny pink cheeks, a small face emerging. Bright blue eyes, white milk teeth, smiling up. 'That's better isnit?' Squirrel threw the cloth on the table. 'In his hair an' everything' he said to Belinda as she came back into the kitchen. 'Right' he grabbed a last bite out of the toast 'I'll see ya later' toast rolling, chewing as he picked up his helmet.

'Sure ya don't want us with ya' Darren, leaning in the kitchen door.

'Nah' Squirrel caught his eye 'be grand. I'll see yis later.' Belinda's face, pale, strained. 'Be grand Ma' said Squirrel. 'Relax, will ya? It's Elliott they're after chargin.' They followed him out.

'Let us know how you get on' Belinda called as he swung a leg over the bike. A black helmet nodding. Leathers jumping up, down, the engine revving. Leaning forward. The bike growling out the gate, off the path, weaving its way down the road.

'We should get out of here' a muffled voice.

'How d'you mean?' Elliott was looking up at the ceiling.

'I mean let's go away' she pressed her cheek against his chest. 'Let's just fuck off somewhere.'

'We're in court in a couple of hours.'

'After this. When it's over.'

'I might be in jail when it's over.'

'You won't' she rolled away from him and onto her stomach, propped herself up on her elbows and lit a cigarette.

'Max thinks I will' Elliott stared up at the ceiling. 'Where'd we go anyway?'

'London.'

'London?'

'Cheaper than America' she said. 'Don't need a visa. Lots of radio stations.' A sharp whistle from the street outside pierced the air. 'Squirrel' she smiled. Elliott pushed back the covers and walked across to the window. A sharp whistle again as he pushed it open. Blonde spiky hair. A hand circling through. Black leathers leaning against a parked car.

'Are you not roasting?' Elliott called down from the window.

'More worried about the roastin' you're gonna get from this judge' Squirrel squinted up. Iris, dressed in a t-shirt, appeared at the window beside Elliott. 'Are yis right or what?' said Squirrel. 'Less than an hour 'til we hafta be in court.'

'Okay' said Elliott 'we'll be down in a sec.'

Squirrel leant back against the car and finished his cigarette. The sun, hot on his head. A gentle breeze pushing through. To the right of the flat, the Persian Prince showroom windows, filled with bright yellow signs. Super Summer Sale. 50% off. A footstep on the path, and when he looked up, Eamo beside him.

'Squirr' said Eamo.

'Eamo' Squirrel fixed his eyes on the door to the flat.

'I … eh …' Eamo stopped. Squirrel glanced up. A deep purple blue stain circled Eamo's right eye. He remembered the crunch of the bone as his fist connected. On the left hand side of Eamo's face, a second similar bruise seeping down. 'Yer Da gev me the other one' Eamo was watching him. Silence. Squirrel looked away. 'Sorry' said Eamo. 'I was outta order.'

'Yeah' said Squirrel. 'Ya were.' The door to the flat opened and Iris stepped out, followed by Elliott. 'Right' said Squirrel. 'Get this over with.' The four of them turned and began walking up Capel Street in the direction of the courts.

Penguins. Black and white penguins gathered outside a grey stone building.

Penguins and humans, huddled in small groups, talking, briefing.

Black cloaked, white wigged barristers, assembled with their clients, dressed for the day in ill-fitting, uncomfortable suits, mismatched with awkward looking shirts and ties. The impersonal smell of a functional space. Cold grey steps, voices echoing high around them, heavy swing oak and glass panelled doors, brass handles giving way to thin, hard-wearing carpet-tiled corridors. Silent authority weighted, ingrained, in each courtroom door. Clerk's voices echoing, calling cases Moriarty, McIntyre, Doherty. Heads, bodies, moving around them. Hushed tones, murmurs rising. A flurry of cloaks. Suddenly, from nowhere, Max.

'This is Rupert' a barrister in his thirties was standing to the left of his brother.

'Rupert's going to try and help us.'

'Yes, but Max, I think we need to be realistic about what we can hope to achieve' Elliott knew immediately that there was no way Rupert was going to be able to help them. 'We might as well be frank' Rupert's mouth moving; clean white teeth rolling out the facts 'theft, illegal broadcast, misrepresentation, *kidnapping*, and we're standing before Thomspon, the worst possible judge. He is *ruthless* where juveniles are …'

'Hardly juveniles' Max interrupted.

'Doesn't matter' Rupert was emphatic 'anyone under twenty-five, Thompson just fires them all into the same bracket. He really is the worst possible judge …'

'Right' a deep matter of fact voice 'you'd better brief me.' It was Anthony, white wig, black robe, dressed for court. Six sets of eyes turned to look at him. 'Well don't just stand there' Anthony barked 'talk to me.'

'Well I was just saying …' Rupert began.

'Not you' Anthony cut him off. 'Very kind; so on and so forth, but I'll take it from here' Elliott felt his Father's hand gently squeeze the back of his arm, then they were turning, moving, as he propelled him through the nearest glass and oak panelled door, up a corridor, to a quiet empty bench. 'Now' Anthony sat down beside him 'just give me the facts. Did you steal this equipment?' Elliott swallowed. Nodded.

'I stole it with him' Squirrel cut in. 'He didn't do it on his own.'

'How did you steal it?' said Anthony.

'They were gutting a Studio in RTE, and they asked us to help move the old equipment out of the way so the new equipment could be installed' said Elliott.

'So they asked you' Anthony rubbed his face 'they asked you.'

'They asked them to transport it to a storage area on the RTE grounds' said Max.

Did they pay you?' said Anthony. 'Did money exchange hands?'

'They gave us fifty quid' said Squirrel.

'Good' said Anthony. 'Who gave you the fifty pounds?'

'Yer man Ingram' said Squirrel. Anthony was reading the charge sheet again.

'Who did you kidnap?' he said to Elliott.

'Roger Ingram' Elliott felt his face redden.

'I kidnapped him' said Eamo. 'Your son had nothin' ta do with it.'

'How long did you hold him?'

'Bout four hours' said Eamo.

'Did you harm him?' Anthony suddenly noticed the purple swelling on Eamo's face. 'What happened your eyes? Did somebody assault you?'

'Nothin' ta do with this' said Eamo.

'Right. Well it doesn't look good' said Anthony. 'You'd better sit behind me when we go inside' his eyes returned to the charge sheet. Elliott watched his father's profile. Bushy eyebrows beetling in. Skin tightening. A look of worry. Genuine concern.

'I'm sorry' Elliott began 'I shouldn't ...'

'We all shouldn't' Anthony continued to study the charge sheet. 'Starting with me.' Elliott stared at the floor. Somehow his father's humanity only served to make him feel worse than he already did. Beside him, Anthony suddenly leant in close, dropping his voice so only Elliott could hear. 'I can't condone stealing, on any level' he said 'but I want you to know ...' his voice seemed to catch 'I want you to know that I am incredibly proud of what you achieved with that station of yours' a thick gruff, sincere whisper. Elliott swallowed. Nodded. 'And whatever happens today' Anthony cleared his throat 'whatever the outcome, I will support you. Right?' it wasn't a question. Silence. Elliott swallowed. Nodded.

'Now' Anthony's voice picked up a beat as he looked up at the rest of them 'we're up before a very strict judge. Manners and court behaviour are a real hot potato; he will not tolerate interruption of any kind, so whatever happens, whatever might be said, I want no outbursts; let me do the talking. Follow my lead, and as I said' he nodded at Eamo 'I think you should sit behind me. 'Right' he stood up. 'Let's get this over with.'

'RTE versus Studio One!!' a clerk calling as they made their way up the corridor, 'RTE versus Studio One!' Elliott felt his legs weaken as they approached the courtroom, Anthony, tall, broad, leading the way, Max and Iris beside him, and taking up the rear, Squirrel and Eamo. The low murmur of talking as they entered. Roger and his defence team at the front of the room, seated to the right. Anthony stood back, as one by one they filed into the front bench on the left.

'Look up' Max nodded up to the balcony behind them.

'Who are all those people?' Iris whispered.

'Press' said Max. 'There's a lot of interest.'

'Great' said Elliott 'all the more reason for this judge to make an example of us.'

'Probably' said Max. Elliott glanced at his Father. Silent, brooding, staring ahead, resting his chin in his hand. Navy eyes narrowed in thought. He stood up abruptly. Elliott watched him cross the aisle and squat down beside Roger Ingram's barrister. Low murmuring. The barrister leaning across to Roger. A short exchange of words. The barrister back to Anthony. Up behind them, in the gallery, a flutter of notepads as journalists leant forward and watched the exchange. Anthony's lips moving. A nodding head, then Anthony stood up and made his way back across to where they were seated. He slid his bulk into the bench beside Elliott and stared ahead. Elliott looked behind at Max, who shook his head.

'What did you say?' Elliott whispered to Anthony.

'Tried to appeal to Roger's sense of decency' Anthony muttered out of the corner of his mouth. 'Turns out he doesn't have one.' Elliott looked up at the clock. A minute to eleven.

'How was your trip?' he said.

'Interesting' Anthony replied. 'I'll tell you about it sometime.'

'All rise!!' a voice called. Elliott felt his stomach shrink as he leant forward, pressing his weight down on his knees. Beside him, Squirrel and Iris standing up. 'All rise for Judge Thompson!!' the clerk's voice echoing through. Fifty chairs scraping back, the sound of a room coming to its feet.

In the far right hand corner, a door handle turned and heavy oak swung back. Footsteps. Around the corner of the witness bench the top of a white wig. A tiny figure making his way up the steps. Beneath the wig a small pink face and tiny round silver rimmed glasses. A fussy pink face making its way to the pulpit, in profile beneath the wig, then it turned. Iris leant forward.

'Is that?' she whispered. 'Elliott …' she strained forward. 'Oh my God' she whispered. 'Elliott' she leant across Squirrel and tugged Elliott's arm, just as a rumble of loud talking broke out across the room.

'Thilenthe!!' an angry pink face as the small judge rapped his hammer. 'Thilenthe!!' he shouted. 'I will not have my court dithrupted in thith manner! Thilenthe! Thilenthe! Thilenthe in court!!'

'It's Thuperman' Iris whispered. 'Elliott, it's Thuperman!'

. . . .

'Unbelievable' Max shook his head.

'Astonishing' said Anthony.

'He didn't …' Max broke off.

'I mean he … he actually' Anthony shook his head, he didn't even …'

'Didn't even *caution* them!' said Max. Beside them Iris grinned at Elliott.

'Caythe dithmithed' she whispered in his ear. He laughed 'Say it again.'

'Caythe dithmithed.'

'Well he dismissed it on the grounds I was intending to argue' said Anthony, 'which is that Ingram paid you' he looked at Squirrel 'to take the equipment away.'

'But he didn't even give you the chance to present that' said Max.

'I know' said Anthony. 'Did the job for me; first question he asked, then he just threw the case out. Completely out of character. Whatever about leniency on the grounds of misunderstanding, but this …'

'Barrington!' a deep voice boomed 'what's this I hear about Thompson?' an excited fat barrister, cloaked and wigged, had appeared beside them.

'Incredible' Anthony shook his head, then turning with the barrister they began walking down the corridor. 'Threw it out' Elliott heard him say '*dismissed* it.'

'You have no idea how lucky you've just been' said Max. Elliott smiled.

'I think I do' he looked at the corner Anthony had disappeared around.

'What'll I do?' he said to Max. 'Will I wait …'

'I'll go after him' Max turned and made his way up the corridor. Squirrel looked at Iris, then Elliott.

'Guess that's it' he said.

'Guess it is' said Elliott. 'What now?'

'Fuck off outta here' said Squirrel.

'That's what she said this morning' Elliott nodded at Iris.

'Yeah?' Squirrel looked at Iris.

'I was thinking about London' she said. Squirrel said nothing. He stared at the floor as he seemed to consider the prospect of London.

'We haven't settled on anything' Elliott began 'we were just …'

'Nah, you're right' said Squirrel. 'I've been thinkin' about Ibiza.'

'For a holiday?' said Iris.

'Mick's openin' a club' Squirrel lit a cigarette. 'Wants me ta go over.'

'To run a niteclub?' said Iris.

'Wouldn't mind gettin' outta here for a while' said Squirrel. 'Clear me head.'

'But your family' said Iris 'what are they …'

'Me Ma an' Da think it's a good idea' Squirrel lit a cigarette. 'Gonna come out with me. Help me find a gaff. Bringin' Katie an' the rest ah them for a holiday.'

'You're going to run a niteclub in Spain?' said Iris. Spain?'

'Ibiza' Squirrel corrected her. 'This'll be big' he pulled on his cigarette. 'Club's gonna be the size of a warehouse.'

'A *warehouse?*' said Iris. 'Squirrel, people go to Spain to get a suntan, not to hang out in a warehouse.' Squirrel eyed her. Strong, confident eyes. 'And you'll be on your own' Iris was upset 'you'll be alone.'

'Beaches are full ah senoritas' Squirrel grinned. 'C'mere, we need ta divvy out this cash.'

'What cash?' said Elliott.

'Cash we earned from the station.'

'Is there much?' said Iris.

'Hafta wait an' see wontcha?' said Squirrel. 'Meet me in Eamo's office. Two o'clock.' He looked at Elliott. 'Let Eamo know, will ya?'

'Sure.'

'Where are you going now?' said Iris.

'Bank' said Squirrel.

'You wouldn't give me a lift to Clontarf would you?' she said. 'I have clothes I need to get. We need a wardrobe' she said to Elliott. 'Staplegun was fun, but I need somewhere to hang my clothes.' Elliott smiled.

'Leave it with me.'

'C'mon' Squirrel shouted, already half way down the corridor.

'Thee you later' Iris leant in and kissed Elliott.

'Thee you later' he watched her run down the corridor to catch up with Squirrel.

'Elliott' said a voice, and he turned. It was Tom, the station manager he'd worked with in RTE.

'Hey' Elliott was thrown. 'How … how are you?' he scanned the corridor, half expecting Roger to appear.

'Great' Tom looked relaxed, happy.

'Are you with Roger?' said Elliott.

'No' Tom smiled. 'I just knew the case was on today so I came down to see how it worked out.'

'Oh' said Elliott. 'Listen Tom, I'm sorry about the equipment. I hope I didn't land you in it with Roger.'

'I don't care about the equipment' Tom cut him off. 'Or Roger. The equipment would have just sat there. You took it and you did something with it. Studio One was a great station. You went to number one. In less than a year.'

'Well' Elliott smiled 'we might have been helped by the fact that Rocket and BBR were pulled off-air just as we were getting started.'

'Undoubtedly' said Tom 'but either way I think you'd have given them a run for their money in the longer term.'

'Roger might not see it that way.'

'Fuck Roger. I don't work for Roger anymore. I left about six months ago. Got involved with a consortium of people and we pitched for one of the radio licences.'

'You pitched for a licence?' Elliott's eyes widened.

'Sure did' Tom smiled. 'And guess what?' the smile grew. Elliott stared at him.

'You didn't.'

'We did.'

'You're in that consortium? Who else?'

'Bobby' said Tom. 'He was here earlier. He was hoping to talk to you. Both of us were. I'll get to the point Elliott. We'd like you to join us. We'd like you to be part of our new station.'

'What?' said Elliott. 'Are you serious?'

'Very' said Tom. 'Bobby and I liked a lot of things about Studio One. There's a couple of shows and people in there apart from yourself that we'd be very interested in working with.' He reached inside his jacket. 'Here's my card. Have a think about it and give me a call.'

'I will' Elliott stared down at the business card. Then he remembered. 'I'm going away for a couple of weeks' he said as Tom began walking down the corridor.'

'Anywhere nice?' said Tom.

'Yeah' Elliott smiled. 'Yeah it is.'

One hour and forty five minutes later he was back in the flat beside a wardrobe freshly liberated from a skip outside Bargaintown, surveying the mess and trying to figure out where everything was going to go, once Iris arrived with the rest of her stuff. From the bottom of the stairs he heard the outer door open.

'That was quick!' he shouted 'did you get a taxi?' Footsteps on the stairs. Slow, heavy steps. 'Squirrel?' he called 'is that you? I thought you were ....' he broke off as Anthony's frame filled the doorway. Silence. The sun streaming in, dust catching rays of light. Anthony stepped into the room and surveyed the small space, taking in the unmade bed, the sofa with the Indian throws, the piles of music, and on the wall beside him, a pair of pink knickers Iris had staple-gunned up to mark her arrival. Anthony considered the knickers for a moment or two, then he turned to Elliott.

'I was wondering if you'd like to come to the Zoo' he said.

. . . .

Eamo's office. The sun streaming through the blinds in long flat slats. Eamo behind his desk, feet up, eyes quiet. Iris and Elliott on the couch. The sound of the showroom outside, the radio in the background, phones ringing. Eamo lit a cigarette and smoked in silence. Picked up his lighter. Tapped it on the table.

A bike growling outside. Through the window, familiar leathers swinging over the saddle, the sound of the kick stand, leather arms pushing a helmet up, blonde spikes emerging. Lorraine's voice greeting Squirrel as he walked through the showroom doors.

'Alright' he said to no-one in particular, as he pulled off his gloves and sat down on the chair across from Eamo's desk.

'Eight-six' he got straight to the point.

'How do you mean?' said Iris.

'I mean we made eighty-six grand' said Squirrel.

'What?' said Iris.

'Eighty six, but by the time we pay what's owed ta the jocks an' the music royalties, we're lookin' at around seventy-eight for ourselves.'

'Seventy-eight' Iris was in shock. 'Hang on, that's …' she began to count.

'Nineteen thousand, five hundred each' said Squirrel.

'Twenty grand!' Iris shouted. 'We could buy a house with that. A studio, we could buy a new studio!!'

'Do what ya want' said Squirrel. 'It's yours. Ya've earned it. We all have' he stared at the filing cabinet and Elliott realised no eye contact had been made with Eamo. 'I set up a bank account for the two ah yous' Squirrel glanced at Iris and Elliott 'an' Eamo' Squirrel's eyes stayed fixed on the cabinet 'if you give Sharon your details, she'll transfer yours in.'

'Ya know what' Eamo's voice, gruff, dismissive 'why don't yis split it three ways; I'm alright here' he gestured to the showroom. 'I don't need …'

'No' Squirrel's voice was firm. 'We had a deal.'

'Grand' Eamo swung his feet down off the desk, leant forward and ground his cigarette out in the ashtray in front of him. 'I'll see yis later' he stood up and walked out into the showroom.' Squirrel stared at the filing cabinet for a moment.

'When are ya headin' off?' he said to Elliott.

'Tomorrow.'

'I'll see ya before ya go.'

'Twenty grand' Iris laughed.

'Better than a kick in the hole' Squirrel picked up his helmet.

'Don't spend it all at once' he called as he walked out through the showroom.

Eamo was standing on the path outside smoking a cigarette in the afternoon sun. Six foot of grey fleck leaning against the lamp post Squirrel's bike was parked beside.

Squirrel glanced at him briefly, then threw his leg over the saddle and stuck the keys in the ignition.

'That it then?' said Eamo.

'Reckon it is' head down, voice detached, Squirrel elbowed the weight of the bike left, right, shifting it beneath him before he flicked the stand and rolled it slowly back off the path.

'I never meant ya any harm.'

'I know ya didn't' Squirrel stared at the ignition.

'Yer Da says yer goin' ta Spain.'

'I'll catch ya later' Squirrel turned the key.

'Squirr!! Wait' Eamo's hands on his jacket. 'Don't go. Not like this ...' he broke off as Squirrel pulled back from his grip.

'Leave it. Just leave it Eamo' he stared at the ignition. Silence. 'Maybe' Squirrel flicked at the keys 'ya know, someday. But not now. Not now Eamo.' Silence. Tall grey fleck. A rough hand pushing its way through slicked back hair. 'I'll catch ya later' Squirrel stood up, jumped down, kicking the bike to life in one fast fluid motion. The visor on the helmet flicked down, then Eamo stood and watched as black gloves revved and the bike growled forward, weaving its way slowly in, out, working its way down through tightly woven Capel Street traffic.

. . . .

'You know I heard your Mother before I saw her.' They were at the Zoo. Anthony, Max and Elliott, the three of them hanging over a long black railing. 'It was in her parents' house' Anthony stared ahead. 'Huge house; far too many rooms. I called to collect your Uncle David for sailing and there was no answer. The door was open so I ventured inside, called out his name' he broke off. Elliott looked at Max.

'The most incredible voice' Anthony stared out past the railings 'floating down through the house ... laughing ... she always had the most wonderful laugh. *I'm not David* she kept laughing; *I'm not David* ... I said *you certainly don't sound like David* and she said *well thank God for that* ...' Anthony stared at the water. 'You know I could sit in a room for hours just listening; I mean she'd talk about *anything* and I'd just ...'

'Mr Barrington?' an apple cheeked man in a brown uniform had appeared.

'Yes?' Anthony jerked back to the present.

'Mr Barrington' the zookeeper extended his hand 'I just wanted to thank you personally for sponsoring the polar bears this year; I can't tell you how much we appreciate your generous contribution; we wouldn't have been able to afford their new saltwater pool without it' he gestured to the water on the other side of the railings.

'Mmm' Anthony rumbled 'pleasure, pleasure' he waved the thanks away. 'We're going to put a brass plaque here' the zookeeper pointed to the railing just in front of them 'acknowledging your sponsorship, and we were hoping you would name our latest arrival' he pointed to a young polar bear swimming across the saltwater pool.

'You want me to name a bear?' said Anthony.

'Yes' said the zookeeper.

'*That* bear?' Anthony pointed at the bear in the centre of the pool, who had started to play with the fountain, pressing his paw down over the valve, playing and spraying the other bears.

'Yes' the zookeeper smiled 'it's a very generous sponsorship and we would be delighted if you, as our sponsor, would name the new bear. The bear's name will appear alongside your own on the plaque.'

'Well ... I don't know ...' Anthony looked uncomfortable. 'Never named a bear before ... hmm ...' hands plunging down into his pockets, he rocked on his feet for a second or two. 'Elliott, why don't you name the bear? My son' he explained to the zookeeper 'works in the radio business.' Elliott suppressed a smile. 'And Max here' Anthony patted Max on the shoulder 'now Max is in the same game as me ...'

Elliott tuned out of the conversation as he watched the young polar bear, bobbing in the dark green water, a white paw covering the water jet, forcing spray up and over himself, before turning it toward the other bears.

'Squirrel' he said.

'What's that you say?' Anthony's head twisted around.

'I think we should call him Squirrel.'

'Squirrel?' said the zookeeper. 'Oh' he laughed 'you can't call him Squirrel. He's a polar bear. You can't call a polar bear Squirrel; it would confuse the visitors.'

'Squirrel' said Anthony. 'I like that. Industrious creatures. Squirrel it is. Excellent' he patted the zookeeper on the shoulder.

'You can't ...' the zookeeper began, but Anthony was already walking away.

'I'll be back next week to inspect the plaque' he called over his shoulder. 'Squirrel ... his voice faded back '... excellent ...' Max looked at Elliott.

'Well at least we're old enough to find our own way home this time' he said. In the distance Anthony turned and stopped.

'What are you standing *there* for?' he shouted. 'Come along! Hurry on!!'

. . . .

'That it then?' Squirrel put his pint down on the table. They were in the pub. The three of them.

'Don't go' said Iris. 'Come to London.'

'Thought London was off the cards' said Squirrel. 'Thought ya were runnin' with this other station?'

'Well ...' Iris began.

'Nothing's decided' said Elliott 'and we're not under any pressure to make a decision. We'll definitely meet them. See what they have to say and if it stacks up, we'll see' he shrugged.

'Make sure they give ya a piece of the action' said Squirrel.

'Absolutely' Elliott met his eyes.

'Taxi' the barman shouted. 'Taxi for Barrington!!'

'Come out an' visit' said Squirrel. 'Whether ya go ta London or not, come out an' see me in Ibiza.' Elliott nodded.

'Will do' he said quietly.

'Taxi for Barrington!!' the barman again. Elliott stood up.

'Right. Come on' he picked up the small suitcase he'd placed beside the table. Out the door. Up the steps. Blinding sunlight. 'Thanks' said Elliott as the driver took his case and put it in the boot.

'Right' a leather arm stretching, reaching. A hand grasped, locked, pulled Elliott into a rough hug. 'Catch ya later' two solid claps on Elliott's back.

'Catch ya later' said Elliott. 'We'll visit.'

'Yeah, we will' Iris smiled.

'Better' said Squirrel. 'Good luck with the other thing. Let me know how ya get on' leather turning, walking, moving away, down the street.

'You won't be able to wear those leathers out there' Iris called after him. Squirrel turned and grinned, a bold smile flashing.

'Told ya' he shouted 'I'll find a nice senorita ta sort me out!!'

Elliott looked at Iris. 'Right' he said.

'Right' she hugged him. 'See you in two weeks.'

'Will you be lonely up there?' he nodded at the window to the flat.

'Nah' she grinned. 'Gonna move a new man in while you're gone.'

'Yeah? Who?'

'Have to wait and see won't you?'

'Ya know there's a meter runnin' here' the taxi driver stuck his head out the window. Elliott stared at her. Boldness flashing. Brown eyes full of mischief.

'Who?' he said. She grinned. 'Iris! Who are you moving in?'

'Still runnin' the taxi driver called out the window.

'Alexi, you fool' she hugged him. 'Get into the taxi.'

'Okay' Elliott slipped his arms around her waist. 'I can handle a hamster' he squeezed her tight. 'God, I don't want to go' he whispered.

'Go' she gave him a gentle push. 'Sooner you go, sooner you're back.'

The taxi door opened and he slipped inside. Little Tree air freshener, stale cigarettes. A blend of strange smells from passengers past and driver present, embedded in badly sprung, randomly stained green and grey upholstered seats. Elliott wound the window down.

'Bye' he stuck his head out the window.

'Bye' brown eyes smiling. Indicator ticking, then the car pulled away from the kerb. Mohican crossing, a slim arm waving, the car turned a corner, and she was gone.

'Where to boss?' said the driver.

'The airport please' Elliott leant his head against the window as the taxi pulled away and Dublin began to flash slowly by.

'Anywhere nice?' the driver leant forward and pressed a button on the car radio.

'France' said Elliott. 'Provence.'

'Goin' with yer mates?' the driver pressed another button on the radio panel.

'No' Elliott paused. 'I'm going to visit my mother. She lives there.'

'Very nice. She been out there long?' the taxi driver's eyes met Elliott's in the rear view mirror.

'A couple of years.'

'Very nice' the driver leant forward to adjust the radio again. 'I'm after gettin' a new radio' he said over his shoulder. 'Ya can pre-programme all the stations so when ya press the button the dial goes straight to the station ya programmed. No more windin' up an' down the dial.' Elliott smiled.

'That's great.'

'Tellin' me it is' the driver leant forward. 'Technology, whah?' he changed station again. 'Only problem now is I can't make up me mind which station I wanta listen ta' he pressed another button 'it's that easy ta hop from one ta the other.' Elliott's thoughts began slipping as he stared out the window. 'Any particular station ya'd like ta listen to yerself boss?' said the driver. Elliott stared out the window, watching fields and trees fly past.

'Is there?' said the driver.

'Sorry. What's that you said?' Elliott sat forward.

'Just askin' said the driver 'is there any station ya'd like ta listen ta? Any particular radio station?' his eyes met Elliott's in the mirror again.

'No' Elliott smiled. 'No, I don't mind. Whatever you want to listen to yourself. You decide.'

. . . .

A NOTE ON THE TYPE

The text of this book is set in Bembo. This type was first used in
1495 by the Venetian printer Aldus Manutius for Cardinal Bembo's
De Aetna, and was cut for Manutius by Francesco Griffo. It was one
of the types used by Claude Garamond (1480-1561) as a model for
his Romain de l'Université, and so it was the forerunner of what
became standard European type for the following two centuries. Its
modern form follows the original types and was designed for
Monotype in 1929.

To RTE and 2FM for teaching me much of what I know and love about radio. To Sunshine, Nova, Big D, ARD, Luxembourg and Atlantic, for the music. For sharing their Pirate Radio memories, I am indebted to Robbie Robinson, Colm Hayes, Martin Block, Tony Fenton, Willie O'Reilly, Phil Cawley, Peter Lennon, Bill O'Donovan, Lucia Proctor, John Clarke, Dave Fanning and Ian Dempsey. To Gerry Ryan (RIP), a dear friend, who also took the time to sit and chat with me about his Pirate Radio days. Bold, brave, bright and brilliant, he embodied the kind of raw talent first heard through the early Pirates. A professional radical, a lovable rogue, a voice we will never forget, he was, is, and always will be, much loved and deeply missed. For providing me with the backbone to my research, the author of 'Radio Radio, The story of Independent, Local, Community and Pirate Radio in Ireland' Mr Peter Mulryan. To Chris Carey (RIP) for Nova. To Tony Allen (RIP) for the closing. To John Gore Grimes who has sailed to the Arctic many times, and enjoyed several enlightening conversations with polar bears, thank you for sharing those experiences with me. To Marianne Gunn O'Connor, thank you for your wise words and steady guiding hand. Your support, especially when the road got stony, has meant everything. To Ali and Bono, I love you mighty and hold you dear. To JOHN MOORE. To James Hickey, Andrew Meehan and The Irish Film Board. To Roddy Doyle and Eoin Colfer. To Gerardine Costigan and Marcell Madden. For early support and constant encouragement Susan Hunter, Tracy Tucker, Carla Delaney, Vivienne Seymour, Susie Smith, Sharon Blankson, Niamh Gogan, Siobhan McKenna and Senta Rich. For cover design Tim Mudie. For photography Julian Seymour. For web design Paddy Gunn. To Alan Clancy and everyone at 37 Dawson Street. To the warm and wonderful Patricia Hope. To my first readers Lara O'Brien, Maire Moriarty, Caroline Gore Grimes, Greg Koster, Conor Cawley, Ruth Lawless, Kathy Keane, Alison Walsh, Karl French, Paddy Costigan, Peter Lloyd, Kathy Gilfillan. Special thanks to Gerard Beshoff, Gavin Friday, Simon Carmody, Catriona Garde, Frances McCahon, Aoife Woodlock, Hannah Strickland, Eimear Clonan, Grainne Flanagan, Ray Lynn, Susan Waine, Steven Hope, Sarah Burke, Andy Mollard, Louise Dobbin, Brid Ni Cuillin, Cormac Kinsella,

Eveleen Coyle, Irene Stevenson, David Cagney, Brendan Murtagh, LHM Casey McGrath, Patsy Murphy, Anita Notaro, Haiyan Wang, Gary Cooke, Declan O'Regan, Wendy Morrison, Marc Fitzgibbon, Roisin Fitzgibbon, Emer Crowley, Geraldine Mahony, Siobhan O'Farrell, Ross Golden-Bannon, Aisling O'Toole, Bronwyn Reilly, Natascha Garrard, Chuck Robinson, Simon Garrard, Kate Bryne, Josh Garrard, David Gogan, Holly Gogan, Poppi Gogan, Seb Gogan, Andrew Weld-Moore, James Mooney and Billy Scurry. To everyone I worked with at the Oar House Restaurant in Howth while I wrote this book – happy, happy memories of our times together. To the Punks, Skas, Skinheads, Mods, Rastas, Bikers and New Romantics who hung out in Howth Riding Stables during the Eighties. To the Stable Girls. To the Fishermen of Howth. To Jerry O'Brien (RIP), King of the East Mountain. To all my friends, and I am blessed with the best. To my teachers in the Burrow National and Sutton Park Schools. To everyone at Fighting Words for the great work they do for young Irish Writers. To my God-Children Lily Garrard, Mabel Rose Scurry, Dinny Day, Florence Weld-Moore and Harry Weld-Moore. To Donagh Tanham, the boy next door. Finally, to my nephew, Nathy Gunn, whose favourite word is tractor and whose bright-eyed determination, kind nature and good humour are a source of endless joy and inspiration. Pure gold as Wicked Granny would say; you are pure gold.

Helen Seymour

Helen Seymour was born in Dublin in 1968. She grew up in
Howth where she continues to live.
Beautiful Noise is her first novel.